This Was Tomorrow

By ELSWYTH THANE

The Williamsburg Novels

DAWN'S EARLY LIGHT

YANKEE STRANGER

EVER AFTER

THE LIGHT HEART

KISSING KIN

THIS WAS TOMORROW

HOMING

Other Novels

RIDERS OF THE WIND

ECHO ANSWERS

CLOTH OF GOLD

HIS ELIZABETH

BOUND TO HAPPEN

QUEEN'S FOLLY

TRYST

REMEMBER TODAY

FROM THIS DAY FORWARD

MELODY

Non-Fiction

THE TUDOR WENCH

YOUNG MR. DISRAELI

ENGLAND WAS AN ISLAND ONCE

THE BIRD WHO MADE GOOD

RELUCTANT FARMER

Plays

THE TUDOR WENCH

YOUNG MR. DISRAELI

Elswyth Thane

This Was Tomorrow

Buccaneer Books
Cutchogue, New York

International Standard Book Number: 1-56849-478-5

For ordering information, contact:

Buccaneer Books, Inc.
P.O. Box 168
Cutchogue, N.Y. 11935

(516) 734-5724, Fax (516) 734-7920

ACKNOWLEDGMENTS

Much of the background material for the 1930's is drawn from my own personal experience in England during those years. Because I could not return to get the answers to questions which naturally arose, my thanks are due to several old friends there who took time and trouble to supply me with reliable details—especially to Derrick de Marney, Percy Marmont, Eric Sleight, Daphne Heard, Mary Clarke, and Dr. Joan Walker. As might be expected, Thomas Cook's obliged (through Mr. Walmisley) with the necessary travel schedules to the Continent in 1938—now a matter of history which is no longer even current.

There is a point to be underlined, outside the framework of the story, regarding the religious movement in which Evadne becomes involved, and which Hermione plays up merely to get her own way. I do not disparage any sincere belief which can comfort or guide any honest disciple. But I do deplore the use, so easily made, of vague emotional dogmas which can be prostituted to a selfish or harmful purpose. They do not seem to be the right answer to Stephen's old-fashioned query: "Have you been to church lately?"

—E. T.

CONTENTS

This Was Tomorrow

I.

Williamsburg

Autumn, 1934

Jeff Day laid a gentle hand on the low white gate with its cannon-ball weight and chain, passed through, and heard it close quietly behind him. For a moment he stood still just inside, on the curving red brick walk which ran up to the white pillared porch between low-cut box borders. No one came to meet him, because Aunt Sue was dead. Otherwise everything about the house looked normal and reassuring. They had buried her while he was still in Europe, and now even the scent of the funeral flowers would be gone from the rooms. The blinds were raised, the windows shone and twinkled in the late afternoon sunlight, the brass knocker on the closed front door was freshly polished. He had asked them to keep the house just as she had left it, till he came. It was his now. She had willed it to him. He was the last of them named Day.

Carrying his small travelling bag, he walked slowly towards the porch—tall, thin, seeming casually hung together, but with a breadth of shoulder and an easy way of holding himself that had often sent Sue's mind back proudly to her brother Dabney, who lost a leg at Richmond in '64, back to her father, whom General Lee had loved, back to stories of Great-grandfather Julian, who married little Tibby Mawes after the British surrender at Yorktown. Jeff was a Day throughout all his lanky inches, and now at twenty-one his likeness to Julian's portrait over the mantelpiece in what had been Great-grandmother Tibby's bedroom was even more marked than even Sue had ever realized.

Diffident, yet sure of movement, with the sobering weight of his inheritance upon him, Jeff mounted the two shallow steps to the porch and the panelled white door opened inward before him. Hagar stood there in her old-fashioned white kerchief and apron, stout and comfortable, with her broad white smile.

"We been expectin' you, Marse Jeff."

He knew that the "we" was habit or euphemism, for Hagar was all the household Aunt Sue had had for years, except for a couple of bright-eyed young nieces who came in extra to oblige when there was company. But somehow the wide-open front door and the soft-voiced black woman with her hand on the knob constituted a little ceremony of arrival, as though the hall was full of curtseying, bowing servants as he crossed the threshold and set down his bag.

Hagar took his hat and asked if he would care for a cup of tea.

"Perhaps a little later," he said kindly. "I'd like to just look round a bit first. It seems a long time since I was here."

"Hopin' to see somepun of you from now on, suh."

"Thanks, Hagar, I expect you will."

She watched him go from her into the drawing-room, and returned with the cheerful philosophy of her race to the pantry to set out the silver tea service, which required no extra polishing on this momentous day.

Jeff paused again inside the drawing-room doorway, and as memories rushed over him his eyelids stung. Everything was just as Sue had left it, yes. But empty. Or was it? He crossed the room to where a sweet grass basket held some soft blue knitting with the needles still in it—the stuff was somehow warm in his fingers.

He picked up the small basket between both his hands and sat down on the sofa which faced the white mantelpiece. The fire was laid ready for lighting, though the day was mild. And as he sat there, the basket in his lap, almost as though he was waiting for something, he met the knowing, greenish eyes of the portrait which faced him from above the mantel shelf.

That was Great-grandmother Tibby, painted when she was in her forties and the mother of three, in the days when Dolly Madison was setting the style for rather buxom beauty. Tibby looked frail and childish in the high-waisted white satin gown which left her arms bare above the elbow and was cut low over her small bust. And Sue could remember her well, as a wise, serene, beloved presence in the upstairs front bedroom where the family had taken all its dilemmas, just as more lately it had run confidingly to Sue herself.

Jeff sat cherishing the basket between his hands, remembering how he had first come to this house as a child. It was the second year after he had been so ill—everything dated from that—when he first saw Williamsburg to recognize it, although he had been born here, in the same room where Tibby had died. He was at school in England when the illness began in 1925, and nobody seemed to know what it was at first, though there was a parade of doctors—he just ached all over and felt very queer. When he got better and stopped aching his heart had begun to beat in a funny way, and in the spring he was brought back to New York to see a doctor there, who was very nice, but a bit gloomy. Jeff spent most of that year in bed, not allowed to study and getting very bored with the light amusements which were all that they permitted him. But the year after that, when he was fourteen, Dinah brought him down here to Aunt Sue in this house where, waited on by Hagar and her youngest niece, whose name was Salomey, he had thoroughly enjoyed himself, except for the process known as feeding him up, which meant that he had to eat practically all the time.

He was given the same room his grandfather Dabney had slept in as a boy, and lying there in the big bed with the morning sunlight streaming in, he absorbed in detail the simple, touching stories Sue loved to tell of the big family the house had sheltered in her youth, and of the Sprague cousins across the way in England Street.

✻ This was the house which Great-grandfather Julian had bought eight years after Yorktown—bought with the proceeds of his flourishing little school eked out with a generous loan from St. John Sprague, his devoted friend. Here he and Tibby had settled in, not long before the birth of their third child. Till then they had lived in a couple of rooms above the school, and Tibby, who had been born in a cabin down by the Landing, must have been very proud of having such a grand house to keep.

It was here in this house, Aunt Sue had told him, that Bracken's mother was courted by the Yankee newspaper correspondent she had fallen in love with before the war began—the War Between the States, that was—and it was a dreadful thing, in those days in the South, to love a Yankee. And it was here to this house that Sue had brought Cousin Sedgwick, wounded in the battle at Fort Magruder—right through the Yankee Army she had brought him, with only a half-grown colored boy to help her with the horses when she went down to the battlefield herself to find him. That story broke off there, in a mysterious way. The childhood devotion between those two had come to nothing, and Sue had never married at all, while Sedgwick married Melicent Murray, and Sylvia was their granddaughter. . . .

The journey which had brought him back to Williamsburg now in this smouldering autumn of 1934 seemed a strange one, in the sanctuary of Sue's drawing-room—back from an apprehensive Europe through a still normal London, where he had paused briefly to attend the wedding of an English cousin, all white satin and orchids, and on a fast boat to oblivious New York and by the first train South. He needed Sue now, again. He needed to know what she would have said to a man—he was twenty-one—who had to live out his life, such as it was, with his handicap. He wanted to tell her what he knew about himself, though no one had told him the whole truth about it, as he was now aware. He wanted to tell her how he had discovered that although he wasn't frightened—he had got through all that, and there was nothing to dying, when you came right down to it—living could be rather a nuisance.

He wanted to ask her if there was some *way* to live, some magic formula, so that no one need ever know what he knew about himself. Because he might live as long as anybody—they said—if he remembered all the Better-nots. Perhaps even if he didn't. But the nuisance was that if he got careless about them, or if he ran into something—unexpected—it might show. His most secret dread was of some kind of public collapse which would give the thing right away to people who had thought till then that he was all right. And was it morbid to hate the times when he couldn't ask a girl to dance, couldn't ride to hounds with the rest of the house-party, couldn't dive into cold water, couldn't suddenly clasp hands and race up hill. . . .

Was it just childishness to want to be like everybody else, or was it some perverted kind of conceit which perhaps really *enjoyed* being a crock? Some people were able to give themselves airs about a disability. Some people, he knew, even invented imaginary ailments to get sympathy and attention. Why was he so unable to endure the sympathy and attention he was unfortunately entitled to? How—if only he could have asked Aunt Sue before it was too late—how could he get himself into some kind of reasonably disciplined state of mind about his Better-nots, instead of having to wear them like a ruddy crown of thorns?

The blue wool in the work-basket between his hands had no answer for him. She was gone. But was she? The house was silent, seemingly empty, but it was not, somehow, deserted. The house itself was alive all round him, the air he breathed was vital and fresh and stirring, the answer was here, he was sure, a part of Aunt Sue's legacy, if only he could find it, if only she had left him some sort of clue—

"Jeff, darling, I came in the back way with some flowers for the house and Hagar said you'd arrived on the afternoon train!"

He turned his head slowly towards the open doorway into the hall, without rising. The most beautiful girl he had ever seen stood there, her arms full of long-stemmed greenhouse flowers. The Sprague greenhouse was famous. He simply sat there, looking at his cousin Sylvia.

2

He had known before he reached New York on his homeward journey that Sylvia would be in Williamsburg now, and yet at the last moment he had deliberately omitted to wire her of his arrival. This afternoon when he left the station on foot, carrying his bag, he had avoided the Sprague house in England Street and come straight to Aunt Sue's alone. Because he knew now, quite definitely, that he and Sylvia were going to have to slow down on this thing somehow. And he would have liked to ask Aunt Sue's help on that too.

The blue wool in the work-basket could have been something she was making for Sylvia, who was fifteen when he had come to Williamsburg that first time in 1927—a leggy girl with straight shoulders and soft brown hair curling on her little neck. The fact that she was a year older was a sore point with him, but she never rubbed it in. She had brought him handfuls of flowers from the greenhouse, and tirelessly played games with him—quiet games like checkers and Authors and cribbage. He had always looked forward to her coming, and always hated to see her go. She was easy and cheerful and didn't seem to pity him. He was grateful to her for that. And she looked so frail and small-boned herself that her obviously adequate health did not intrude itself on his consciousness. It was hard for him not to envy or resent people who were too robust and rather threw it in your teeth. Sylvia was not a strenuous girl, and her tact in a convalescent's presence was flawless. The first walk he had ever taken in Williamsburg was with Sylvia—once down to the College Gate and back, and never mind the house where she lived in England Street until the next time.

When he left Williamsburg the following year he was practically well again, until he tried to do whatever he liked, and then someone was sure to say Better-not-today. That summer was spent in England, renewing acquaintance with his English cousins, whom he had not seen for more than two years. It was a widely scattered family, knit by strong bonds of tradition and articulate devotion, its relationships complicated by the marriage of cousins, its generations mingling without effort in the same households, its perpetual travels punctuated by faithful reunions at holidays and times of crisis, at one or another of its several headquarters abroad and at home. To his own surprise, Jeff found himself thinking of Williamsburg as home, once he had been there. He and Sylvia had promised never to lose touch, and they wrote long letters often. Hers were good, she wrote just as she talked, and not everyone can do that. He himself, already in training as Bracken's assistant and successor on the newspaper, never found writing letters a chore, and he tried to keep her straight on the English branch of the family, which was centered in the Gloucestershire house called Farthingale.

At Christmas time in 1929 everyone available rallied to Williamsburg because of Aunt Sue—Sedgwick had died in the autumn. She was very good about it, but quieter now, and the sparkle had gone out of her. Sedgwick's widow clung to her and wept, and Sue was the brave one, reminding her that nothing could take from them the years they had had him, and the laughter he had given them. She was so glad to see the family again, some of whom had come all the way from England and France to be with her, that her cheeks were often wet with tears which she swore were only happy ones.

Sylvia was seventeen that Christmas, ahead of him as usual, and she was taller than he remembered her, but only came up to his cheek because like all the Day men he was himself unusually tall, and she was thinner than when he had seen her last, and her eyes had got very large and blue, and they looked straight at you, honest and kind. After dinner her brother Stephen and her older sister Rhoda had rolled up the rugs and everybody danced to old tunes played on the piano by her mother, who used to be on the stage. Everybody but Jeff, who wasn't allowed to dance because it was one of the Better-nots.

The family had just received with its usual tolerance the astounding news that Stephen and Rhoda had actually signed contracts to do a specialty dance number in their father's new musical comedy when it opened in New York in the spring. As children, they had always danced at the family gatherings, steps their mother had taught them and that they had invented themselves. When they grew older they had been allowed to study under the best and most thorough instruction to be found in New York. And before long the word went out on the Broadway grapevine—Fitz Sprague's kids had something new—everybody recalled that their mother had been a dancer, though few could really claim to remember Gwen LaSalle's one appearance as a star before her marriage and retirement—agents and snoopers began to haunt the school where Stephen and Rhoda worked —but Fitz was firm—nothing doing—not till they shaped, he said. Their first brief appearance together at a routine school entertainment caused a small riot. And now they were in. There hadn't been anything like it since the Castles, said the grapevine. And so far from having to use his influence to get his offspring a job, Fitz had had to fight to keep them for his own show. Just a couple of hams, he said philosophically, grinning at Gwen, who had never given her career another thought after she fell in love with him.

Sylvia had always performed docilely in their childish theatricals at home, enduring an agony of nerves and stage-fright the other two knew nothing of, but she begged off going to dancing school with them in New York. She had a better singing voice than Rhoda's, but she begged off having it trained. Fitz was puzzled but patient. There didn't seem to be anything in particular that his youngest wanted to do. "Maybe she'll just get married," Gwen suggested hopefully, for it was Gwen's idea of the thing for a woman to do.

That Christmas party had been planned before the Wall Street crash was dreamed of, and the family fortunes weathered the storm under Bracken's unhysterical management. Jeff spent the next four years working with a tutor to catch up on his studies, making a trip abroad every summer to accompany Bracken on his annual tour of his European news bureaus. And what with one thing and another, it was the spring of this very year 1934 before he got back to Williamsburg to see the Rockefeller Restoration buildings they had all heard so much about, and Sylvia wasn't there.

A great deal had happened in the Williamsburg family during that four years. Rhoda, after a sensational debut on Broadway, had just got married, boom, and wouldn't dance any more, like her mother over again. She not only wanted to live in Connecticut and raise a family, she wanted to spend her evenings at home, with no curtain going up at eight-thirty every night. She explained all this in passionate detail to an outraged, stranded Stephen who was not in love himself, and was not getting married, and loved the very smell of a theater—any theater, any curtain going up, any call of *"Overture!"* So what happened then? Sylvia got roped in.

She was prettier than Rhoda ever was, the greatest beauty the family had produced since Aunt Sue's mother Felicity, and she had a lovely light, true singing voice. And she could learn. She had to. Stephen wanted a dancing partner, and the whole thing was good publicity after the near calamity of Rhoda's marriage. Sylvia photographed like a dream from any angle, danced and sang like a trouper, and hid her shyness behind a calculated composure which deceived almost everybody. Jeff got glimpses of what it cost her, through the long letters she wrote him during that four years' separation. The times Jeff was in New York and they might have met, Sylvia was in Chicago or Cleveland or Detroit with Stephen and a show. They moaned at each other down the long-distance telephone, past the three-minute limit, and he would be off to Europe again before her tour ended, and the letters went on, building up an intimacy of allusion and confession and personal exposition that made it seem as though they knew each other a great deal better than was warranted by the amount of time they had actually spent together.

They were cousins, they had been children together, but something more than kinship had lilted and vibrated down that telephone wire to Chicago or Cleveland or Detroit. They were, he had realized a few months ago, the last time his Cunarder had slipped down the New York harbor on the way to Southampton, falling in love with each other's letters. And the old, inevitable, nagging admonition which had dogged his impulses for years presented itself promptly:

Better-not. The nicest things, the things he wanted most, always turned out to be Better-nots. He had come to accept the relentless tabu with a philosophy beyond his years.

So he had tried to let the idea of Sylvia slide as it were through his reluctant fingertips, as a lot of other ideas had gone before it. It was just one thing more that was not for him, and let's see, now, what was there to put in its place? He was committed to the summer in Europe with Bracken, who was getting very gloomy about the Nazis, and it was in Austria that they were caught by the cable saying Aunt Sue had died. Bracken as her executor knew the terms of her will. The money was to be divided between Stephen and Rhoda and Sylvia, and the house was to be Jeff's, because he was the only son of Miles Day, who had married his cousin Phoebe and died before his child was born. And it was much too late to say Better-not to Aunt Sue.

He had supposed ruefully that Sylvia's success as Stephen's partner would entail a lot of proposals from eligible men, Hollywood offers, and all the things well known to go to a girl's head, and he had waited for signs in her letters. But there weren't any signs. Her letters remained quite the same, a little fuller of anecdote and incident, but hiding nothing, holding nothing back. Single-minded, single-hearted, the same Sylvia still. And it wouldn't do. But how was he to make her understand that now, without seeming to take too much for granted of things never spoken in words—without betraying his own secrets too, and laying himself open to her quick intuition, her exaggerated loyalty, her inevitable pity? Aunt Sue might have known the answer, if he had the wit to find it here in the tranquillity she had left behind her. But now, before he was ready at all, while he was still shaken and bemused by the impact of his arrival, here was Sylvia, waiting for him to be glad to see her. It was almost as though Aunt Sue were suggesting—

3

Because of the uncordial silence he had allowed to follow her greeting, without having moved or spoken in reply, Sylvia's smile had died away, and her eyes dropped from his face to the work-basket on his knee.

"Oh, Jeff, I'm sorry, you want to be alone. I'll come back later."

As she stepped backward from the door he rose, setting down the basket.

"No, wait—please come in, I was dreaming, I guess—" He moved quickly towards her and she paused uncertainly, on one foot. "It felt very queer, your just suddenly being *there* like that, as though—" He held out both hands to her and she laid the flowers across them, smiling up at him. "I feel like a bride," he said helplessly, holding them.

"Brides are prettier," said Sylvia. "Welcome home, Jeff."

"Thanks, I—" He laid the bouquet on a table just inside the door, took her firmly by the shoulders, and bent to kiss her cheek—and a quick turn of her head brought their lips together briefly. "How are you?" he said inadequately then, looking down, while she stood radiant, looking up.

"I'm fine. And you?"

"I'm all right, I guess. Just—trying to get used to things."

"Perhaps you'd rather I didn't stay now. We didn't know you were coming today. I just keep flowers in the house because she always had them, and—have you noticed how it feels as though they were all living here still?"

"Yes, I was noticing that, among other things. I wasn't alone."

Their eyes went to the portrait of Tibby above the mantelpiece, and she returned their gaze, alert and listening, like a third person in the room.

"That's what Cousin Sue always said." Sylvia's voice was very low. "That she wasn't alone here. I think towards the end she used to talk to them—I think they came back for her—"

Jeff was moving away from her slowly down the room, and he sat down on the sofa as though he was suddenly very tired. Sylvia came up behind him and laid a hand on his shoulder.

"Don't be sad, Jeff. *We'll* miss her—but all the rest of them were waiting for her—"

"I wish I'd come back sooner, that's all."

"We talked a lot about you, she and I."

"What sort of things?"

"About how different it would have been if your father hadn't died, for one thing. So that you had grown up a Day here in Williamsburg instead of the strange, broken-up life you've had."

"They'll never forgive poor Mother for that, will they?"

"Oh, Cousin Sue *forgave* her, it wasn't that. But she was always afraid that you might lose touch altogether, I think, and not *want* the house as much as she wanted you to have it. In fact, I practically promised her to see that you came and lived in it some of the time—every now and then."

"The house isn't in the pattern for me, Sylvie," he said gently, and raised his hands to hers on his shoulders. "Aunt Sue didn't quite understand. She shouldn't have done this to me, she must have known better. I can't think what she was up to, leaving me the house. She knew I couldn't just come and live in it."

"Why can't you?"

"Because I'm booked up."

"How do you mean?"

"Think, Sylvie, think! Bracken has turned sixty, it's time I began to take hold of things for him. He counts on me, it's my job, I can't leave the newspaper now, before I've even started. Bracken has got to take things easy sooner or later, and that's where I come in, it's what I'm trained for, it's all he thinks of now that there's another war coming—"

"Another—!"

"Yes, I shouldn't have brought that up, I suppose." He rose from under her hands, and moved restlessly round the room, pausing at a window with his back to her. "But we're going to get one. A daisy."

"Us too?"

"What do you mean, Us too? If we don't fight it on the Rhine we'll have to fight it here, on the Atlantic Coast."

"The Germans? *Again?*"

"Again. So you see—" He turned from the window and looked her straight in the eyes. "—I can't lay any plans."

"But you—couldn't—"

"Couldn't get into the army. Don't I know that! But I'm supposed to be a journalist, a foreign correspondent, if necessary a war correspondent when I grow up, remember?"

"Even if—"

"Look, Sylvia, how much do you know about this set-up, anyway? Bracken's got no son, you see. Dinah lost her baby and couldn't ever have another. About the same time my mother had a baby she didn't really want—I was born several months after my father died, and let's face it, she wasn't really in love with him anyhow. She left me with Dinah in New York and went back to Europe, she thought for a few weeks—but one thing led to another, with the war and all, and she went on to Belgium as a nurse and finally married Oliver—they'd been in love for years. At the end of the war Dinah took me to England—I couldn't remember my mother, of course, I was about two when she went away—and somehow I was donated to Bracken to carry on *our* family traditions instead of Oliver's. Oliver has nothing much to leave, and Bracken is rolling. You can't inherit a British Army commission, but you can inherit a newspaper.

Don't think I'm sounding mercenary, I'm putting it to you from their point of view, not mine, I was never consulted. And don't think I'm squawking, either, I think the world of Bracken and I'd go out and die for Dinah any day before breakfast. But it all goes to show why I'm caught the way I am. If Bracken hadn't counted on me, he would have been training someone else to take his place."

Sylvia looked back at him gravely, measuring out her words.

"But with the kind of job I've got and the kind of job you've got, it isn't going to leave us a chance to see much of each other here in Williamsburg."

"I guess that's about it." They stood with the room between them, face to face with the thing that had happened to them against the odds. "Well, it's nothing new, is it," he said at last. "We ought to be getting used to it by now. Please don't look like that, I know it sounds heartless, but—Sylvia, don't let's take each other—too seriously, will we. Because it will never do. You can see that, a big girl like you."

"You mean because we're cousins and mustn't fall in love."

"Oh, that. No, I don't think that has much to do with it. What we really ought to remember is that I've got a rheumatic fever heart, and—that's not a very reliable thing to have."

"But I thought you were all well now." She looked frightened.

"I'm supposed to be. And nobody mentions my heart, you know. So if ever we start to run for a bus, or the going gets tough on a Sunday walk, nobody must say, Be careful—remember Jeff's heart."

"I see." There was a long silence, while she walked carefully round the end of the sofa and sat down facing the unlighted fire. "And—if ever you should want to get married?" she asked steadily.

"That's one of the times somebody—meaning me—says Better not."

"But I thought you—"

"Sure, sure, nobody's warned me about it lately. Only it's *my* heart, after all, and I wanted to know a little more about it than they seemed willing to tell me. More than they wanted me to know, maybe. So I read up on rheumatic fever. And now I know."

"Oh, Jeff, you're *not* all right?"

"Now, don't, for Pete's sake, look sorry for me! I might live to be a hundred, like Grandmother Tibby. But if I loved somebody enough to want to marry her, I'd want to be a lot surer than I am now that she wouldn't have an invalid on her hands for the last seventy-five years of it!"

"I don't think you ought to feel that way, I—"

"Darling, we're slipping," he said quietly. "I know how it is with you, because I've got it too. But it mustn't be like that. If we're going to make each other miserable about it, I mustn't come here at all."

"Cousin Sue would be very disappointed if you didn't," she said unargumentatively. "And so would I."

All the cards were on the table now. So soon. But it would have to be like that, he thought, you couldn't fool Sylvia any more than you could fool yourself. And that was what she had become, against his will—his other self, the one you talked to in the dark when you couldn't sleep, the one who never talked back, except to comfort and uphold. And there she sat, within his reach, waiting, willing, and not afraid. He had only to ask her, and he need never be so alone again. But that was against the rules. Looking at her helplessly from across the room, he perceived that he wasn't the only one. Sylvia wanted the same thing he wanted. It was not just himself that he denied.

"Aunt Sue knew very well that I couldn't stay here," he said gravely. "Not for long. Never anywhere for very long."

"How soon?" she asked quietly. "This war."

"There's a sort of superstition about 1938. Writing on the pyramids, or something. Actually, it will come when Germany is ready to start it."

"But—if your heart still bothers you—"

"Well, that's another drawback to this job I've got." He came and sat down on the other end of the sofa. "You see, comes this war, and little old Jeff sets out into his first air raid to do a big story for the paper, and what happens? I've got a right to be scared, anybody's entitled to that, and the heart is beating fast, but that's not all. The strain goes on a little too long, we'll say, or I have to run for a doorway or throw myself flat in the gutter—and then something slips loose inside my chest and the thing is beating up behind my ears, I can't breathe, I don't see straight, I start to wobble, and the only way to stop it is to lie down flat on my back and breathe carefully till it slips back into the groove again. That's going to be very useful in the middle of this air raid we're talking about. In other words, I won't last five minutes in a war. But Bracken doesn't know this. And I can't bring myself to tell him. Not yet. I just go on, waiting for it to happen."

"But isn't there something you can take—"

"I've taken lots of things. But last summer in Berlin I saw what it was going to be like. We were there during the Purge, you know, when they killed off a lot of people they didn't want in the Party. There was some shooting in the streets —not at me—and wholesale executions, and it was all very nasty. We all reacted to it, of course. Bracken lost pounds in just a few days, and Dinah kept losing her dinner. Anything she ate—right away it came up, like being seasick. There's no way to make anyone who wasn't in Berlin then understand what it did to you. The air was thick with evil and terror, and you were helpless—like the dream where you try to run and try to scream and can't move or make a sound.

I'm only dwelling on it because I learned then what to expect."

"Did you have to lie down flat and breathe carefully?"

"Luckily not when anyone was looking. It almost caught up with me once, but we had got back to the hotel and I sat very still on a sofa and just missed it. They were all feeling so sick themselves they didn't notice. But it showed me how much good I'm going to be when any real excitement starts."

"You'll have to tell them."

"I can't possibly." There was a long silence. "It's only a question of how long I can stand up to it," he said with a sigh. "Sylvie, darling, I'm ashamed of myself. I've never admitted to anyone before that I'd read up on the fever. Everybody thinks I believe just what I've been told, which wasn't more than half of it. Maybe I am all right, maybe I'll never have another attack. But you see—*I* know I can go down again tomorrow, and each time I lose ground. But I have to pretend I don't know that, see?"

"Except to me," said Sylvia.

"Except to you, now."

"It must have been a lonely sort of thing to carry round with you, Jeff. How long have you known?"

"Years. Will you swear on a stack of Bibles never to mention again anything we've said here today?"

"No, I won't swear. Because you've told the truth about yourself, and that's very good for you."

"Like a kind of pill." He nodded wryly.

"You'll find people have to tell the truth in this house, Cousin Sue lived here so long."

"You think she had something to do with this?"

"I think she did."

"I can almost believe it," he said thoughtfully. "I threw myself on her mercy—I asked for some *sign*—and then I saw you standing there—"

"Yes, why did I come, just then? I didn't know you would arrive today."

Their eyes held in a long, probing stare.

"Well, why did you come?" he said, and she answered, "I brought her some flowers. It—just seemed like a good idea to bring her some flowers."

"Sylvie—"

"Yes, Jeff?" She stretched out a hand to him along the sofa, and he closed his fingers on her long cool ones. "I'm here, Jeff. I always have been here. I always will be."

"I can't—" He swallowed. "I can't—"

"Darling, don't worry about it. I'm not so bent on getting married."

With a rueful little sound, half sob, half laughter, he leaned towards her and hid his face against her shoulder. After a moment she moved cautiously to put her arms round him, and held him there, her cheek against his straight dark hair, and neither of them seemed to breathe. Then she said, "Besides, we don't have to talk about being in love, do we? We can have good times just as we are—just as we've always been."

"That's not fair to you," he said, his face still hidden. "Pretty girl like you has to get married."

"Who says?" said Sylvia.

"If only you hadn't grown up to be such a *pretty* girl," he grumbled against her shoulder. "Got a lot of beaux?"

"Depends what you call a lot."

"Bet you could get married tomorrow if you only crooked your finger."

"I'm hard to suit, I reckon."

He sat up slowly, without self-consciousness, and looked down at her, his arm along the back of the sofa.

"That's right," he said. "You go on being hard to suit. That way you'll get something better than anything you've seen yet."

"There's nothing better than this, Jeff. Just you and me, together again, and we can lick anything that comes. Even Germans." Her fingers tightened briefly on his and then withdrew. "I'm going home now and leave you to yourself for a while. Wash your face and brush your hair and change your shirt and come to dinner. Seven o'clock, remember?" She rose, and he remained looking up at her remotely, un-smiling, from the sofa. "Can you find your way alone?"

"Blindfolded."

"I'll run along and tell them to lay another place."

She was gone, lightly, with a wave of her hand from the doorway.

4

Jeff sat still. He was certainly very tired, all of a sudden, which he was used to—and he was at peace in himself, which was a less familiar feeling.

The silence of the house closed in on him again, as it were protectively, until with a little clink and rustle Hagar arrived with the tea tray, remarking that Miss Sylvie had said to bring it in now. He found himself wishing that Sylvia had stayed to drink it with him, and raised the teapot to pour his own.

"I'm to go over there for dinner," he said, as Hagar reached the door.

"Yassuh, she done tol' me dat too," said Hagar cheerfully as she went.

"Oh, and Hagar—I'd like to have the room I always had—Grandfather Dabney's."

"Yassuh, she done tol' me—"

"Told you to get it ready for me, I know!" He took the words out of her mouth with a smile, and waved her away.

When he had drunk two cups of China tea and eaten three of Hagar's fresh cookies, he rose, intending to look round the house before he washed and changed, and mounted the stairs. Turning to the left, he entered the large front bed-room which had been Great-grandmother Tibby's when Sue was a girl—the room where they had first hidden Sedgwick, wounded, under the bed, while Yankee soldiers searched the house for him, and Great-grandmother Tibby, sitting up in the bed above him in a becoming lace jacket, had stoically gone on eating her breakfast from a tray—the bed where, a lifetime later, he himself had been born.

He went in with his quiet, loose step, and stood before the mantelpiece looking up at the portrait of Tibby's Julian, which hung there. The likeness to himself was such that he might have been Julian's own son—the long chin and large, humorous mouth, the wide-open, reflective grey eyes, the thick, brushed-looking dark hair with no wave in it. Guess I'm what they call a throw-back, Jeff concluded after a long scrutiny of the canvas. I wonder who Sylvia goes back to. Aunt Sue always said Aunt Felicity was the beauty in their day—how did she put it? The words came obediently from his memory: *Her eyelashes were so dark and heavy they always seemed to make her lids a little weary—it gave her a sweet, sleepy look,* Sue said. Sylvia had eyelashes out to here, but she looked anything but sleepy. . . . Please, he said confidentially to Sue, without speaking aloud, can't you let me off this thing about Sylvia? Do I *have* to be in love with her till it hurts?

He turned and left Tibby's room and went on to the next one, which was above the garden and which had always been Sue's since she and Bracken's mother had shared it as girls. Glass and silver gleamed on the dressing-table. The white ruffled bed was complete to its counterpane and bolster. He wondered if her dresses still hung in the clothes closet, and knew that he could not bear to look or to ask. Again he had the unreasonable feeling that the room was not empty—was not, that is, bereft. She wasn't gone from it—not forever.

Hagar came quietly out of the room across the passage behind him, and paused in the doorway.

"You want I should put heh things away mo'?" she asked anxiously. "Like the perfume an' such?"

"No—don't disturb it. I like it this way."

"Don' seem like she *could* be gone." Hagar glanced wistfully through the door.

"We won't be so lonesome," he said gently, "if we leave it the way it is."

"Yassuh. I laid you out a clean shirt afteh travellin'. An' I put yo' things in the little bureau by the window."

"That's fine, thanks."

But she lingered in the doorway as he passed her and entered his own room.

"Don' look like you aimed to stay long, suh—or is you got anotheh bag at the station still?"

"Not this time, Hagar. But I'll be back."

"Long time sence you been heah fo' Christmas, suh."

"Well, that kind of depends on the folks in New York," he said kindly. "We'll see."

"Sho' goin' to be kinda quiet round heah at Christmas ef you don' stay." She went away, her head down.

He closed the door on himself, and after a quick, loving look round the room he stripped back the white counterpane, kicked off his shoes, and lay down on the bed, sinking luxuriously into the big pillows, remembering. . . . The top shelf of the bookcase he could see from where he lay was full of the books he had read on his first visit—books about the War Between the States, and maps, so that it was all as real to him as yesterday, realer even now than the more recent war in France where his mother had been a nurse—realer than the idea of another war shaping up across the Atlantic. . . . Even the notebooks in which he had written down what appealed to him most were still there. Sue hadn't moved a thing. She had left it for him to find, as though she had

known that some day he would be here like this without
her, groping. . . .

Tomorrow he would get out the books and look at them
again. He wondered how his childish notes would look to
him now. Once he had even thought of trying to write a book
about what Aunt Sue had told him, for printer's ink was in
his blood and bones. Tomorrow he would look at the note-
books again. Tonight he was having dinner in England
Street, with the Sprague cousins. He wondered if it would
be all right to ask them to show him a portrait of Felicity,
whose eyes had always looked a little sleepy—or would they
suspect that he only wanted to know if Sylvie resembled her
as he did Julian? It wouldn't prove anything, would it, if
she did? Separated by two generations of time, Julian and
Felicity had never fallen in love with each other. . . .

Please, he said again to Sue, though his lips never formed
the words, Please get me out of this. It doesn't matter about
me, but don't let's have Sylvie get hurt, and I'm no good to
her. You knew about the fever. Why did you do this? You
must have known about our letters too. But it almost looks
as though you *meant* us to fall in love. You knew about
Bracken and the paper, though. You knew I couldn't stay here
as though I hadn't got a job to do for Bracken. Besides, you
knew what a thin time Dinah's had so often, because of marrying a newspaper man and the risks they take. You wouldn't
wish that on to Sylvie, would you, with me? Somebody has
loaded these dice, Aunt Sue. It wouldn't be you, would
it? . . .

5

There is something rather special about being one of a
large, congenial family, Jeff was thinking as they all sat down
to dinner that night in the Sprague house—not the self-conscious, artificially odd sort of family that gets into semi-

biographical books and plays, and is exploited in a certain type of memoirs—but a family which is accustomed to behave normally, which accepts its inter-relationships without dramatizing them, which enjoys its reunions and is without jealousies and favoritisms and feuds. The Days and the Spragues were all intelligent members of the human race, thought Jeff—able to get along with each other and themselves with a minimum of fuss and why-was-I-born carryings-on, even in the younger generations. They were too clever to be idle and too busy to sit round searching their souls. And they had before them in their elders an example of good manners and domestic harmony they could only hope with a bit of luck and management to duplicate in their own lives.

Freshly arrived from that sultry summer in Nazi-dominated countries where everyone seemed always looking over his shoulder, and where seeds of suspicion and betrayal were deliberately sown in the schooling of children to spy and eavesdrop in their own homes in the name of the Party, Jeff looked gravely round the candlelit dinner-table in Williamsburg, counting his blessings anew. At one end was his Uncle Fitz, his mother's brother, charming as the tuneful songs he wrote—songs which were being sung all over the world now, for a public suddenly enlarged by the radio. At the other end, slender, doe-eyed Gwen, the dancing-girl from the wrong side of the tracks, who loved Fitz so much still that her days sang with it, and who had so fitted herself into the quiet pattern of the family's ways that no one ever thought now how once they had dreaded her advent in their circle. Across the table was his cousin Stephen, so lean as to be bony, so much a dancer that his every move had a fluid ease as though he was strung on invisible wires reacting to inaudible music—but a specialty dancer, mind, nothing arty or effeminate. Stephen wore clothes when he danced, and shoes, and trained like an athlete, and his standard routines were things for an acrobat to respect. His slight, loosely hung body was deceptive—one New York critic had remarked that Stephen Sprague was made of cat-gut, whalebone, and piano-wire. He never tired or flagged, he never even seemed to be breathing hard, and no matter how many times they called him back for another encore he never faked it. He did things with hats and walking-sticks and balloons that were sheer conjuring, as he danced. And he sang—not very musically, but with a passable off-beat authority—whenever he felt like it. His wide, crinkling grin, which drew deep lines down his long, otherwise solemn face and flashed a set of perfect teeth, was the disarming, unconceited grin of anybody's kid brother.

And the fifth at the dinner table, on Jeff's right hand, was Sylvia.

Stephen had made every preparation to celebrate Jeff's ar-rival, and there happened to be pumpkin pie, which you don't get in Europe. Jeff told them all about Cousin Verity's wedding, which he had attended in London just before he sailed—and they were all more than ever interested in the English bunch now that it was almost certain that Sylvia and Stephen would go to London with the new show after its New York run. And oh, yes, said Jeff, Cousin Virginia at Farthingale was writing her reminiscences, if they could bear it—all about life in England in the good old days before the war, when American girls married English dukes and English girls married German princes, and everybody lived fabulously with the most fantastic amount of money to spend, and servants in droves, and dinners in nine courses with a wine to each course, and costume balls, and Royalty at house-parties, and nothing to worry about, ever, before 1914—or shall we say before 1912, when the Balkans be-gan. . . .

"Jeff says there's going to be trouble again with Germany,"

Sylvia put into the pause which overtook him just then, and they all looked at him questioningly, never doubting his infallible knowledge of such things.

Jeff raised his eyes slowly, and met Stephen's across the table.

"Yep." He nodded. "They're winding up again, over there."

"What's the *matter* with them?" Stephen asked lightly, but his eyes held Jeff's.

"They're just being Germans," said Jeff. "Germans are just that way."

"But we settled it once."

"We didn't settle it, that's the trouble. We let 'em off. We let their army march home with bands and flags as though it had won. We didn't rub their noses in the dirt and stamp on their ribs, which is the way they express their own superiority when they get a chance. Show sportsmanship to a German and he thinks you're really afraid of him. Kick him around and he thinks you're braver than he is."

"Nice people," said Stephen, watching him.

"What they've got over there now," Jeff went on, "makes the Kaiser's Prussians look like milk-sops. These Nazis are the real Frankenstein product. They could teach Bismarck about blood and iron."

"You were there," said Stephen.

"I was there, yes."

Still their eyes held, young men of what would be the same military class, linked by a common destiny, which loomed like a common doom in the quiet room, where a chilly wind seemed now to intrude.

"Well, come on—give," said Stephen with some impatience. "Just because we're stay-at-homes doesn't mean we're not interested. We read your newspapers, you know, and we listen to a lot of hot air on the radio. Or is it hot air?"

"Not all of it, maybe."

"Why isn't Bracken on the radio, to tell us what's what?"

"I've an idea he will be, pretty soon."

"What's this story tonight about Alexander? Have the Nazis got anything to do with that too?"

"What about Alexander?"

"Shot. At Marseilles."

"*Killed?*" The word itself was like a pistol going off. Jeff had not moved, he had merely tautened in every muscle. His immobility was frightening, his concentration on Stephen's reply was like a vise.

"Didn't you hear?" said Stephen. "It was on the radio news."

"*Was he killed?*"

"Yes, and Barthou with him, as they drove away from—"

"*Barthou!*" cried Jeff.

"—as they drove away from the ship at Marseilles. The assassin was a Croat, it said. I'm afraid none of this means much to us here in the backwoods, can you make it a little easier?"

"Where's your radio?" asked Jeff, and at the same moment his eyes fell on the cabinet in the corner and he rose.

"There won't be any more news for a while," Stephen said with a glance at the clock.

They watched while Jeff crossed the room and snapped the button. After a few seconds, while nobody spoke, music swelled out of the instrument. He spun the dial—a girl's voice, singing—the gabble of a comedian, and laughter—more music—he snapped it off, and stood staring at the air in front of him. Then—

"Mind if I ring up Bracken in New York?" he said, and was gone into the hall where the telephone lived.

The connection was quickly made. They could not help but hear Jeff's side of the conversation in the dining-room where they sat.

"—I just heard about it, Steve told me, I missed the radio

news tonight. . . . But *both* of them, where were the police? . . . That must have been pretty, and besides, he might have talked. . . . No, *not* a pretty world, is it. Shall I come back tomorrow? I feel kind of cut off down here, no papers or . . . Oh, yes, I'll listen to the radio from now on, I just —for one night I just relaxed a bit, and now look. . . . I shouldn't wonder if the French could run a whole war without me, but they don't seem to be doing too well at the moment. *What about his bodyguard, didn't they give him one?* . . . Well, when you get it worked out maybe you'll let me know down here. We'll have the Richmond papers tomorrow. Has Richmond heard of Jugoslavia, do you think? . . . Yes, they have now, that's right. . . ."

Jeff came away from the phone still looking dazed, and sat down again in his dislocated chair at the table. His preoccupied gaze travelled slowly to Gwen's anxious face with the family's habitual necessity to cherish its womenfolk.

"I'm sorry, Aunt Gwen, but Steve sort of sprung it on me and I reacted just like a newspaper man. Even Bracken feels a bit shook-up, as it were."

"What's it mean, Jeff? War?"

"Maybe not. Can't tell yet. Remember Kipling's line: *'There'll be trouble in the Balkans in the spring.'* There's *always* trouble in the Balkans in the spring!"

"Who was he? The man they killed."

"He was the King of Jugoslavia, which is a country they made up at Versailles, including Serbia. He was the Crown Prince of Serbia in 1914, and it was the murder of an archduke in Serbia that started the last war. Now the Serbian King has been murdered in France—that's near enough. But Bracken thinks it was Barthou they really wanted, and they got him too."

"But—a Frenchman in his own country?" said Gwen helplessly.

"It wasn't a Frenchman who fired the shot," said Jeff.

"Apparently. Barthou was one of the last senior statesmen. He had ideas. He had an idea that Europe could unite against aggression—aggression is diplomatic for Hitler and his crew. Barthou was not popular in Berlin. But that doesn't explain why the French bodyguard was spaced out the way it was, at Marseilles. This fellow ran in on foot and fired into the car which carried the King and Barthou. He had all the time he needed before anybody got there to stop him."

"And you think a war can start—from that?"

"A war can start now if somebody sneezes," said Jeff. "This may be it."

Gwen's hand went uncertainly to her face in a pathetic gesture of confusion and her eyes caught Fitz's down the length of the table. She managed a little smile for him, at her own foolishness.

"I had a funny feeling," she said, almost apologetically. "It was like that first night I came to Williamsburg as a bride, and Bracken was up from Cuba in his war correspondent's uniform, do you remember, and his father came down from Washington and said that the Spanish Ambassador had asked for his passports. It wasn't a week till you were both on the way to Cuba—"

"Now, Aunt Gwen, wait a minute—" Jeff rose repentantly and went to bend above her chair, at the same instant that Stephen flowed upward from his own place across the table, saying, "Here, here, nobody's on the way anywhere *now*—"

Stephen reached her first, because of the oiled and slippery way he moved, and they stood over her, their hands on her shoulders, rueful and reassuring.

"You ought to know about newspaper men by now," Stephen went on. "They always jump the gun."

"No guns yet," said Jeff, and added conscientiously, "Except at Marseilles, that is."

Gwen looked up at them dubiously, her hands in theirs. "D-does Bracken think—?"

"Bracken's sitting tight. If he thought the balloon was really going up he'd be off for France."

"And you with him?" That was Sylvia, so that Jeff began to feel a bit surrounded.

"I'm not ordered back," he told her over Gwen's head. "So long as he leaves me here, things haven't got out of hand."

"Oh, Jeff, you're too *young!*" cried Gwen, and bit her lip.

"What, to carry a typewriter?" Jeff returned to his chair matter-of-factly.

"Correspondents are worse than soldiers sometimes," said Gwen. "They go everywhere, I ought to know!" And she looked with something like pride at Fitz, who had gone up towards San Juan Hill in Cuba, carrying a gun to which he was not, as a correspondent, entitled. "I wish," said Gwen, still holding to Stephen's hand, "I wish I could understand these things. But I never do. I never rightly understood how the last one began."

"It's like jackstraws," said Jeff. "Nudge a little one at the bottom and the whole thing caves in on you."

"What do the Nazis mean?" said Gwen. "What do they want?"

"That's kind of a long story," he warned her.

"Please, Jeff," said Sylvia. "Please try to explain."

So for nearly an hour Jeff tried to explain, while they listened without interrupting. Once Gwen rose to snuff the burnt-down candles and turn on the electric light. Once Fitz moved to make strong black coffee and set one at each man's place. Once Stephen, still listening, quietly laid a log on the dwindling fire.

They heard about the man called Hitler, who had once been regarded as a harmless sort of clown even by his own countrymen, and about what he had made of Germany and might still accomplish there if nothing stopped him. They heard about Berlin during June of that year, with the sound of the execution squads firing all night and all day at Lichtenfeld prison, and about the July day in Vienna when Nazis disguised as Austrian troopers held the Chancellory for hours while Dolfuss bled to death, unattended, on a sofa. Jeff had been in Europe when these things happened, he had seen and heard and felt with his own nervous system the presence of violent death and treachery and terror. He had been taught to choose his words. He spoke as he had learned to write—dispassionately, concisely, without flourishes or dramatics—to the point. So that horror entered the quiet room on his words, and a realization of fear as they had never dreamed it could be. And even then he spared them, and when he finished he was sorry for what he had said, and he said that too.

"But do people *know* about this?" Gwen asked at last. "*We* didn't. Do they know about it in Washington?"

"People over here don't want to know about it," said Jeff. "You can't blame them, can you. They'd rather not n-o-t-i-c-e what is happening in Germany. As it is, I feel rather like an unwise nanny who has been scaring the children stiff with ghost stories at bedtime. But you did ask me, and everybody has got to realize sooner or later what we're up against. Everybody will, eventually, whether they want to or not." He glanced at his watch, and rose to snap the radio on again.

The dance band finished, and the commercial began. They waited tensely for the eleven o'clock news, which was still devoted to the death of a Balkan king who until today was hardly known by name to half the people in America who were listening. . . .

". . . Cut down by the sabres of the French guard, the assassin continued to fire while rolling on the ground. Some bullets struck policemen and women in the front row of spectators. The crowd surged forward and would have torn him apart, but the police carried him, dying, to a nearby news kiosk. The King never regained consciousness. European diplomats deplore the loss of M. Barthou, which could hardly have come at a worse time. . . ."

They all sat without moving till the voice of the commentator gave way again to irresponsible dance music and Jeff turned the button to bring silence. They watched him while he wandered restlessly about the room, they asked bewildered questions which he tried to answer—but the evening was broken, and he soon said good-night and prepared to return to Aunt Sue's house. Sylvia caught Stephen's eye, and Stephen said they would walk over with him in case he got lost, and Jeff said he had been worrying about that, and the three of them set out together.

One on each side of him, they fell into step as they emerged from the gate and turned towards Gloucester Street. Sylvia's hand was tucked under his left elbow, Stephen drifted with his light, rhythmic footfall which turned his walk into merely an interlude in his dancing, on his right. For a while there was silence among them, and then Stephen said casually, "Don't let's have this war till after Sylvie and I get the new show on in London, hunh?"

"I'll try to arrange that, yeah," Jeff replied, also without stress.

"Give us a couple of years, say."

"1936, that would be."

"Just about."

"Of course you realize," Jeff told him solemnly, "that you will have the Olympic Games to contend with that year."

"What? Where?"

"Berlin."

"Oh-oh," said Stephen. "That I'd like to see."

"Well, I'll try and arrange that too."

"What are you, sort of a trouble-shooter for God?"

They laughed. Their feet were gay and crisp on the bricks beneath, and Sylvia gave a little skip, like a grace note, her

fingers tight and confident on Jeff's arm. It was late enough
so that Gloucester Street was almost deserted, dimly lighted,
with the glimmer of white houses and picket fences under
dense old trees. It might have been a generation ago, or
longer, for all that showed on the face of the little town under the serene Southern night. Great-aunt Felicity would
have felt at home there, in her hooped skirts and tied slippers.
Tibby in her old age had seen it look much the same.

"I've kind of got my heart set on seeing England," said
Sylvia. "What's left of it nowadays."

"England is still there," Jeff promised her. "All there, you
might say. But don't wait too long. Williamsburg will be a
lot more comfortable to live in soon. England is going to
have a front-row-center seat when the bombing starts."

"Oh, dear, can't we talk about anything but war?" Sylvia
asked in a small voice.

"By all means. Who's got a car round here?"

"Stevie has."

"I'd promised myself a look at Yorktown while I'm here."

"Sure, we'll all go down tomorrow," said Stephen. "Jamestown is more fun, though. It'll be warm enough for a picnic
on the riverbank, I should think. Cousin Sue's favorite spot,
remember?"

And the rest of the walk went into plans and reminiscences,
stories about the English cousins, stories about the new show.
It was not until Jeff was alone in Aunt Sue's house again that
he remembered he was a newspaper man and that now they
had lost Barthou. . . .

II.

SYLVIA IN WILLIAMSBURG
TO JEFF IN LONDON

December, 1934

Dear Jeff—

Well, we might have known, mightn't we. The idea of having
a Christmas together *anywhere* was much too good to be true.
I suspect that Prince George's wedding was just an excuse to
go to London, and that Bracken is still expecting that balloon
to go up. All we hear now on this side is the Lindbergh case,
and I'm glad in a way that Bracken thinks there is anything
more important.

We are still hung up for a cast, and don't expect to go
into rehearsal now before February. That means opening
much later than was intended, and with any sort of run *that*
means the coming summer is already lost and gone, we
shall be playing in New York till Thanksgiving. Jeff, it is
the best show Stevie's ever had, and you will try once more
to see us, won't you? It isn't that I want to show off, but it's
all I know how to do and I would like your opinion. Of
course as soon as I think of doing a performance with you in
front my hands get clammy, but it's got to come some time.
Have you *any* idea when you will be coming back? I know
what Christmas at Farthingale means to everybody who has
ever been there then, but—we do rather a nice Christmas
ourselves right here in Williamsburg.

Well, nothing came of the shooting at Marseilles, did it.

And if they are holding the Olympic Games in Germany in 1936 I should think they'd be careful not to spoil that because of all the tourist trade. Except for the English bunch, the 1914 war rather skipped our family, but now it would mean you and Stevie first of all. Is your step-father still at the War Office? What does *he* think?

Please write about the Farthing ie Christmas at great length. If I am to meet them all next year I must get them sorted out in my mind, it will be worse than the London first night! Can't you draw some kind of diagram? . . .

III.

JEFF IN LONDON TO SYLVIA IN WILLIAMSBURG

January, 1935

Dear Sylvie—

I'm sorry you missed it here—on Christmas night I looked round the drawing-room at Farthingale and had a sort of private panic. It was too good to last, I thought, and I couldn't but wonder if there would ever be another like it. The whole thing was a beautiful anachronism, "dated" like an old play revived, or a novel you read years ago and then re-read in the light of later experience. Well, I mustn't be literary, must I, all you want to know is who was there and what we did.

Virginia, of course, is always a little sad at Christmas time because her husband used to run these Christmas shows, read off the gifts and make impromptu toasts and so on—Archie died in the war. His brother Oliver acts as host now in his place, not quite so funny, they tell me, but I've always considered him just about perfect ever since the day I first set eyes on him as my mother's second husband. Needless to say, I never knew her first one. She gets lovelier each year, I think —quite grey now, but with a kind of *glow,* as though she was happy just to be alive day by day as they come—and life for a woman married to Oliver must be very desirable, I should think. Hermione—don't forget to pronounce it Her-*my*-o-ne, will you!—came with them, of course, and I still can't abide that girl. We've loathed each other since we were children

46

and she snootered me unmercifully because she didn't approve of her father's marrying my mother, though from what I've learned about *her* mother, here and there, she was a very nasty little piece of work and Hermione takes after her—jealous, spiteful, ingrowing, unfriendly. She doesn't like me any better than I like her, and our little feud is all against the rules in the family, which expects people to get along with each other. I can, with all the rest of them. Hermione can't get along with anybody, including herself. Charitable ones, like my mother, are able to feel sorry for her. I'm not. Charitable nor able. She's asking for it, and so far as I'm concerned she's got it. And the fact that she is her own worst enemy doesn't seem to me sufficient excuse. For anything.

That, with Dinah and Bracken, who were just as usual and always will be and God bless them, made up my immediate household circle. But there were a lot of other people there, of course. Virginia's four children, the two older girls with children of their own—Irene's daughter and I fell shamelessly in love. She was christened Mavis, but everybody forgets and calls her Mab. She is going on ten, and has greenish eyes. I may as well tell you at once, it's serious. The fact is, we held hands. Please don't deduct from this that I am naturally a goof about children. The jolly bachelor uncle with his pockets full of surprises for the little ones. Not me. There are always rafts of children at these family parties and heretofore I never knew one from another and nobody cared. I must have seen Mab before but I don't remember it, and this time we saw each other. I would like to keep her in my pocket from now on, but as she points out, this won't be feasible because pretty soon she will be too big.

Virginia's youngest is the present Problem Child—we always have one, you know, and they tell me Virginia herself was it once. I've always been afraid of Evadne myself, even when we were kids—it's hard to say why, and I don't mean I dislike her, as I do Hermione. I think it is mostly because she is a born Crusader. The games she used to want to play, the stories she used to like best, were always so Intense. Jeanne d'Arc used to be her favorite heroine, and for all I know still is, and then she passed through a phase of wanting to be a nun. That's over now, but she's got all caught up in a highly informal religious movement of which I—*and* the family— take a very dim view. It's a cult with the strangest theology, part biblical and part utter nonsense. And there's much pressure for group discipline and obedience. It's frightening. They're sort of religious Nazis.

Johnny and Camilla Malone turned up unexpectedly from Berlin, where Johnny has had his news bureau headquarters for years. I think Dinah got Bracken to have them come here because she simply couldn't bear to go to Germany again just yet, and they were only too pleased to get away for a while. Johnny and Bracken had their usual weatherwise confabs on the state of the world, and I was allowed to listen to some of it, and it isn't pretty. Germany is arming again, and she has a not-very-secret and entirely illegal air force, uniforms and all, led by Goering, who was one of Richthofen's aces, if that means anything to you. Johnny attended the Nazi Party Congress at Nuremberg last autumn and describes himself as appalled. That's strong language for him. The whole German nation is playing tin soldiers again, and Hitler is regarded as a god, especially by the women.

Does this bore you? It shouldn't. If Hitler goes on living, and he takes great care to, he is bound to have some effect on all our lives—even yours, my far-away darling—and especially if he joins forces with Mussolini, which is on the cards. Call me Cassandra.

The whole German outlook has always interested the family here because my mother's dearest friend since they were girls together is an Englishwoman who married a Prussian Prince, 'way back before 1914. I forget how much you may know of all this, so forgive me if I repeat myself, but

Rosalind is important, it was because of her that my mother went abroad during the war, and it was our same Johnny Malone who got Rosalind out of Germany by the skin of their teeth, around about 1915. The story, as I first heard it when I was a child, always sounded like something straight out of *The Prisoner of Zenda,* except that it had a happier ending. Rosalind came safely home to England and the man who had loved her always. And although her Charles had inherited one of the oldest titles in England himself, he resigned from the Army and they simply went down into the depths of the country and lived there quietly, together. But that's not all, it doesn't end there. Last June the German ex-husband died mysteriously in the Nazi Purge—we were in Berlin then, you remember. And Rosalind's German son, Victor, who was brought up by his father in the Prussian traditions, is now a Nazi. Our Camilla had met him on the Riviera, in the days when everyone met everyone there, all very romantic, and she *almost* married him instead of Johnny! The Purge cured her of that, pretty fast. We suspected that Victor was involved in the betrayal and death of his father, but it's really best not to know too much about what went on then. Anyway, by being there in the midst of it, we got the story first hand (as we might not otherwise have done). Rosalind at least was free of her ex-husband and of the Nazi horror. Though the twisted ethics of her son could never forgive her for divorcing the very man he betrayed and had murdered. Rosalind was at last happy—remarried to Charles Laverham who had loved her all along. Rosalind and Charles live in the dower house at Cleeve—the big house is closed—and that's only an hour's drive from Farthingale, and they come to all our family parties, having no family of their own.

Let's see, now, what else, besides the Christmas doings. Laval has succeeded Barthou in France, and that's not good, but you wouldn't understand and why should you? In January there will be a plebiscite in the Saar, which is very important, but you won't want to go into that either. And there is a war in the Chaco—(*where?*)—and Trouble in Spain. But I know what you are waiting for me to say—patiently, perhaps, but you won't let me off. Yes, I love you—and I don't forget it day or night, particularly night, and it doesn't do any good not to talk about it, does it, because we both know nothing can stop it now till we die, and maybe not then. . . .

IV.

JEFF IN STRESA TO SYLVIA
IN NEW YORK

April, 1935

Dear Sylvie—
Don't believe anything they tell you, this Pact they are cook-
ing up here is no good. Versailles—Genoa—Locarno—Paris—
Stresa—none of it is any good any more. Scraps of paper. We
won't learn. And if you think I'm being pessimistic, you
ought to hear Bracken! They are building public air-raid
shelters in Berlin. When theirs are finished, and ours are still
not begun, they can afford to risk retaliation.

Meantime the day will soon come when you will hate to
see another letter from me arriving with its cargo of dreary
news. And don't think by these contents that your letters to
me aren't eagerly watched for and read again and again.
Three of them have just caught up with me here, and are
much the nicest things that I have encountered for days. We
sit in the well-known lap of luxury under southern spring
skies—there is a South in Europe too—and watch future
nightmares being born. Speaking of which, Mussolini during his attendance at this conference sleeps in, or at least
occupies, the same bed Napoleon used before Marengo.
Well, I just thought I'd mention it.

I started to say, I sometimes try to imagine where and
when you will read a letter of mine—where and when you
will write your reply—and now that you are not in Williams-

burg any more I must necessarily fail. It's a mixed blessing that the show is such a success, isn't it—because the longer it runs there the longer we must wait for it to bring you to London. And the way things are going, I don't see any hope of America for me in any immediate future. This is Jubilee Summer in England, and there will be a lot of special stuff to do there, beginning next month. After that, Geneva again, if this Abyssinian business develops. And so forth. Unsatisfactory letter-writer that I am, please don't stop writing to me, even though at times it must seem rather like shouting down a well. If I appear to get out of touch, that is the curse of the life I lead, so that the house in Williamsburg and a girl coming in the door with her arms full of flowers are like something in a fairy tale. It is hard to believe that they ever existed or might still be found again only a week's journey from where I now sit.

At this point, Bracken would be feeling for his blue pencil. I love you. That's words of one syllable, anyway. . . .

V.

London

Summer, 1935

Mab was keeping quiet in the schoolroom upstairs because her governess had been to the dentist and was lying down after taking a pain pill. The house itself was very still. Everyone was out till tea time, and besides, nobody was living there yet except herself and Miss Sim the governess, and Granny Virginia and Aunt Evadne. Later, when the Jubilee began, they would all come—her father, who was something in the Home Office, and her mother, now making a visit in Kent; Johnny and Camilla from Berlin; Dinah and Bracken and Jeff, now in Paris on their way home from Stresa. Granny had taken this house in Curzon Street for the Jubilee Season, and everyone said what fun it would be, all together again, with week-ends at Farthingale thrown in.

Jeff had sent her a letter from Paris, and there was no need to read it again, for she knew it by heart. It said that Paris was very beautiful still, in spite of the Russians, who were something of a Blot signing their beastly Pact with the French, and that he had just bought her a Gift, and had she grown any, and he had not forgotten that he had promised to take her to the theater, a grown-up one, *not* a pantomime, and she might choose what it would be, within reason, if only she would not require him to sit through anything like *Romeo and Juliet* because he was not up to it, not just now, after

53

all he had been through at Stresa, and would she please settle for something easier, with all due respect to Shakespeare and Mr. Olivier. Mab at once looked up *Romeo and Juliet,* which was in the Curzon Street library, and found she could take it or leave it, and had already chosen *1066 And All That,* which was a very modern piece of nonsense with music and Mr. Naunton Wayne. If Jeff didn't approve of that either, she was quite willing to see something else.

As if it mattered what they saw together. She sat with her feet under her on the narrow windowseat, her forehead against the cool pane, so that she could watch the street below. In a few more days she would sit like this waiting for a cab to deposit Jeff at the curb. She had an unchildlike lack of curiosity about the Paris gift he had promised—whatever it was, she would cherish it because he had chosen it for her, but it was Jeff's own presence she looked forward to, and she would have been just as glad to have him back if he came empty-handed. She had wondered more than once how she could convey this to him without seeming ungracious about the gift—and of course he would bring gifts for the others too, it was not just singling her out as a baby to be pleased with baubles. People always brought back gifts from Paris. For Granny it was almost sure to be something in a jewel-like bottle which smelled exotic and expensive, for Phoebe it would be gloves, for Evadne—what would he bring Evadne?

Mab sighed, and sagged closer to the window frame, a small, somehow resigned and lonely figure. Evadne was the right age for him, and very pretty. It wasn't fair to *blame* Evadne, it was just the accident of when you were born that made you ten instead of twenty when Evadne was twenty-one. At twenty, one might have stood a chance against her. As it was, even if he didn't marry Evadne, even if it turned out to be someone they had never heard of, it was hardly probable that he would remain a bachelor until one could so much as reach eighteen. . . .

A cab drew up below. Not Jeff, not yet. She waited, her face against the glass. Aunt Evadne, home to tea. And oh, bother, Cousin Hermione was with her again. Ever since Evadne had joined what they called the Cause she had spent a great deal of her time with Hermione and had quite suddenly begun to behave as though she was Hermione's best friend. When Granny commented unfavorably on this, Evadne replied that it was quite plain to her now that they had none of them given Hermione a fair chance, and that she was going to change all that. Oh, dear, said Granny, *must* you? The *things,* said Granny, those Cause people have to answer for!

Evadne happened to look up from the pavement and saw the brooding child's face at the window above her, and waved, and made signs that Mab was to come down to the drawing-room for tea. Evadne was kind—so kind that she rubbed it in just a little, how thoughtful she was being. Like taking up Hermione when no one else could bear her. It was almost like showing off, the way Evadne went out of her way to be good to people, but Granny said that was the way the Cause took you. If ever you had been rude to someone or had unkind thoughts about them, or done them a wrong, even if they didn't know, even if they deserved it at the time, you had to confess to them by writing a letter, and share it with them, and ask God how to make it up to them, and do exactly what the cult leadership recommended as restitution.

Just to contemplate so much publicity always made Mab squirm a little. She could not imagine, for instance, writing a letter to tell Miss Sim everything she had ever thought of her, or even Mummy, on bad days. Apparently if you liked a person, and had had only kind thoughts about them, you were not required to share that in a letter—which seemed to Mab the wrong way round, although with equally embarrassing possibilities. She would not like Jeff to know, as a matter of fact, quite how she felt about him, or how large a place in her innermost thoughts he occupied. And she wondered, along with the rest of the family, about the devastating results if Hermione became infected with the same beliefs which had taken Evadne, and began to tell everybody what she had thought about them, from time to time, because Hermione never seemed to like anyone very much, and always looked as though she were simmering with rude remarks even when she didn't speak them. It was interesting to speculate, too, on the really miraculous transformation which would have to take place inside Hermione for her to begin being kind to people as Evadne now demonstrated kindness.

With some reluctance Mab got off the windowseat and started down stairs. Tea in the drawing-room could be fun. But with only Hermione and Evadne there it didn't promise much. Perhaps Granny would come home in time for it today. Granny took the curse off anything, just by being there, with her pretty clothes and her jokes and her way of treating you as though you were grown up, too, instead of as though you were half-witted.

"Hullo, darling," said Evadne affectionately as Mab entered the drawing-room. "What have you been doing with yourself all day? Granny is expected back at four-thirty, so tea will be coming in any minute, and I thought we'd wait for her and then have it here together, won't that be nice? You haven't said good-afternoon to Hermione."

"Good afternoon," said Mab as soon as she could without interrupting, and Hermione smiled perfunctorily and went on powdering her nose, holding up the mirrored lid of a small compact from her handbag and squinting into it.

Evadne, who like Granny never had to worry about her face anyway, had thrown her hat on a chair and run her fingers through her short chestnut curls. Mab noticed again the unusual luster of Evadne's hair, and the brilliance of her red-brown eyes which she got from Granny who was after

all her own mother, and the generous curves of her crim-
soned mouth. Evadne's radiant, effortless beauty both fascinated and depressed Mab, who tried to see it dispassionately without thinking of how it looked to Jeff, and could
only envy its ripe perfection. It did not occur to her that almost everybody else, including Hermione, was envious too.

People wondered why Evadne had not got married before
now, or even engaged. Few of them could have realized, as
Jeff did, quite how taxing her crusading spirit might become
to a man inclined to approach her on a slightly lower plane.
Not that people hadn't tried, even so, and last autumn she
had almost been engaged to her cousin Mark Campion, six
years a widower at thirty-one, who was floored to receive one
of her share-letters after she was changed, in which she said
that it had Come To Her in her Quiet Time that morning
that her feeling for him was largely carnal and vain, because
of his good looks and the Honorable attached to his name,
and his position as the son—even though a younger son—of
an earl, and that she was afraid she had thought far more of
being kissed by him and of the fun of being presented as his
wife than of fulfilling her sober obligations in his household
as the step-mother of his little boy, and so was not really
worthy of so grave a responsibility etc., etc., etc. "I suppose,"
cried poor Mark, trying to argue her out of the letter over
the telephone from London while she was at Farthingale,
"that if I had a hump and a club-foot and you couldn't bear
to touch me with a barge-pole you'd feel more justified in
marrying me!" Evadne replied patiently that she was only
being Absolutely Honest with him, as God had bade her be,
and that if only he would come and be Guided too he would
understand what a wonderful feeling it was to have everything Out In The Open between them. "I *was* guided,"
shouted Mark, just as the time-pips began for the second
time. "No, no, *don't* cut me off—I *was* guided to fall in love
with you, and everything was working out just as it should

have done, until suddenly you go right off the deep end in this cult and I can't get near you! Please let me—" He was interrupted by laughter from Evadne which could only be called silvery. "Mark, *darling*, if only you would come to our meetings and learn to listen in to God you would see how silly you are to resent it like that. Really, Mark, this is something so big, so revolutionary, it will change the whole world. I'm coming up to London on Wednesday, and perhaps you would like to take me to lunch and hear more about it, in a reasonable frame of mind." "I'll take you to lunch with pleasure, but *not* if you go on talking about God as though he were on the BBC!" said Mark regrettably, and was rewarded by another tinkle of laughter from Evadne, for workers in the Cause were advised to refrain from arguing with a patient who put up resistance barriers, and never to lose their tempers over rudeness or flippancy from people who had not yet Surrendered. "But it's very much the same thing, really," she said indulgently. "We were saying at our last meeting that anyone can pick up divine messages if only he will put his receiving set in order." At this point Mark had made a very tired sound and hung up. The next day he took off for the South of France, leaving his six-year-old son in the competent care of the devoted woman who had had charge of Alan ever since his mother's death when he was born. Mark's family had not seen him and had scarcely heard from him since, and needless to say, Evadne was no longer very popular with that branch of cousins. Even Virginia in this case sided with the Earl against her younger daughter. "Ruining Mark's life with her whim-whams," fumed Lord Enstone. "Getting him all worked up and then behaving like a ruddy nun or something, all because of some new bee in her bonnet! 'Tisn't even as though it was something you'd ever heard of, like Chapel and that—they tell me America is full of these new religions. What's the matter with the ones we've already got?" Virginia, who had long since ceased to defend her own American origin against her tactless Tory brother-in-law, said that Mark had been rather childish, to put it mildly, bunging off to the Continent like Byron or somebody, and not remaining on the spot to assert himself, but she agreed emphatically that Evadne could be maddening when she got a bee in her bonnet.

Virginia was now letting herself into the house in Curzon Street, just in time for tea, without a cloud on her beautiful brow. She checked slightly on the drawing-room threshold at sight of Hermione, with an inward groan of *What, again?* while her face maintained a careful brightness, quite genuine in its response to Mab's affectionate greeting and Evadne's filial kiss.

"Tea," said Virginia, throwing down her hand-bag and gloves. "Somebody ring for tea at once, I walked home through the Park and there was only salad for lunch at Clare's. Everyone is reducing but me, and I *starve,* lunching with them!"

"Well, we can't all be lucky like you," said Hermione in that voice which gave her least remark a faintly sardonic if not catty effect. Hermione's own figure was as slim as Virginia's, but she ate no sweets in order to keep it so, and she liked sweets, which created what Evadne called an inner conflict. Evadne both ate sweets and kept her figure, which wasn't fair of somebody somewhere.

"Mummy, *have* you thought it over?" Evadne was plainly bursting with the question. "Did you talk to Clare? Won't you be an angel, and—"

"*Not* if it's that week-end party you're talking about," said Virginia firmly.

"But, Mummy—"

"For the last time, Evadne, and I don't need Clare to back me up on it, you cannot have Farthingale to entertain those people who talk about God as though He were coming to tea and who use the Bible for their own political purposes."

"But He *does,* in a way, don't you see, God is *everywhere,* one only has to tune in and He—"

"Evadne, *please!*" moaned Virginia, with a glance at the rigid countenance of the ancient butler Bascombe as he arrived with the silver tea-service, which he placed on a low table beside her, while Trevor the parlormaid followed with sandwiches and cakes. *"Pas devant les domestiques!"* she added in quotation marks as the servants left the room, and the first crack showed in Evadne's lacquered self-possession as a childish frown settled on her face.

"Really, Mummy, do you think it's wise or kind to make fun of things in front of people?"

"My dear, sometimes you leave me no choice. Have we heard from Bracken? Does anyone know when they're coming?"

"Thursday," said Mab with a certain pride in her knowledge.

"Well, that's good. Who told you—Jeff?"

Mab nodded.

"He wrote from Paris. They saw Mark there."

A slight pause occurred. Then Virginia said, "How was he?"

"Jeff? All right, I think."

"And Mark?"

"He didn't say. Was anything the matter with Mark?"

"No, I just wondered. Anything about Mark's coming home?"

"For the Jubilee, he thought."

"Now, Mummy, don't *begin.*" Evadne took her cup from Virginia's hand without meeting her mother's eyes.

"I didn't say anything," Virginia pointed out mildly.

"Hermione is coming to our meeting tomorrow night," Evadne announced with a defiant change of subject, and Virginia glanced at Hermione under tilted brows.

"Have you decided to join?" she asked.

"It doesn't commit me to anything, to go to a meeting," Hermione muttered, looking into her cup as she stirred her tea.

"Mummy, you can't 'join' and you can't 'resign.' It's all according to the kind of life you live. You simply surrender, listen, and obey. If you keep open to Guidance the inward peace will come."

"I see," said Virginia rather tightly, and Mab, advancing to the cake-plate, remarked with an instinctive into-the-breach irrelevance that Jeff was bringing her a gift from Paris. "Jeff always brings wonderful gifts, doesn't he," Virginia agreed hastily.

"Like the Greeks," said Hermione with her inevitable, often pointless sarcasm.

"Why don't you like Jeff?" Mab asked directly, more from the tone than from the significance of Hermione's words.

"But she does like him," said Evadne in her clearest, most life-changing voice. "If only you would admit to yourself, Hermione, that you are in love with Jeff, and be *absolutely honest* about it, it would stop hurting and then this foolish necessity to—"

Hermione's spoon clattered into the saucer and she stood up, her small tense face quite white and her hands shaking so that the cup lurched as she set it down on the tray.

"Evadne, sometimes you go too far! It's all very well to talk about Absolute Honesty but that doesn't give you the right to invade everyone's life with a *scalpel!* Besides, I'm older than Jeff and he—I—you—I will *not* go to your horrible meeting and make a fool of myself, you can all let me alone, do you hear, and mind your own business!" And she begun rather fumblingly to collect her gloves and hand-bag, while Evadne rose with leisurely grace and went towards her, speaking in the soothing sort of tone one uses to a nervous horse.

"Now, now, darling, it only Came To Me a few days ago,

that if only I could help you to get it all Out In The Open—
if only you would talk things over with some understanding
fellow human being—"

"Like yourself, I suppose! You think because you decided
to turn Mark down you have a right—" Hermione's voice
was a little shrill, and she started blindly for the door.

"But it's only because I've been through it all, with Guidance, and I know exactly how you must feel, so I—" Evadne's
arm was round Hermione's waist as they reached the door,
but Hermione did not pause.

"You know nothing whatever about Jeff and me!" she
cried furiously. "We've loathed each other for years, and I'll
thank you not to talk like that, especially in front of the
children, you have absolutely *no right*—"

"Darling, don't be angry and put up resistance like this,
I'm only trying to help you—"

There was a large, aghast silence in the drawing-room
where Mab and Virginia were left staring at each other in
mutual dismay.

"*Well!*" said Virginia, as though they were also of an age.
And then, "It's so humorless!" she said unbelievingly. "Surely
no child of Archie's and mine—they seem to think they're
being so gay and helpful, and it's all so—*heavy-handed*—"

"But—*is* she?" said Mab.

"Who? What?"

"*Is* Hermione in love with Jeff?"

"Oh, that," said Virginia. "Well, now that it's come up—
I wonder—"

2

But Hermione did go to the meeting with Evadne, and bore
witness publicly that she had always loved a man, since
they were children, she supposed, though not, she was sure,
in any Impure way—and that because the circumstances

were impossible for love between them, and he had not re-
ciprocated anyhow, she had tried to hate him and do him
harm, for which sin she was now prepared to make restitution. She had not realized, she said, that it was love, or that
it was a sin, till Evadne's loving fellowship and understanding had made her see that. There was quite a lot more, about
how she meant to try not to make spiteful remarks and had
started a Guidance Book that very morning, but nothing
seemed to come through that was worth writing down, doubtless because she was so new at it, and that she meant to try
very hard to get her uncle the Earl of Enstone interested in
the Cause, because he needed Guidance if ever a man did,
though they must please believe that that was not said with
any unkind implications in mind, but she realized that the
addition of a famous name and title like his was always a
welcome thing to the organization, and in the meantime she
would like to make a small contribution of her own to the
Funds, though of course nothing like what Uncle Edward
could do if he Surrendered, but just to show that she didn't
mean to be one of the lukewarm ones, and if only she could
learn, with Guidance, to be as happy and self-confident as the
people she saw all round her that night she would gladly devote the rest of her life to changing other less fortunate fellow
human beings, and to pay her own expenses no matter where
they wanted her to go, or rather, where God wanted her to go,
Africa, even, or Germany, or the East, and that she wanted to
thank them one and all, particularly her cousin Evadne, for
this liberation from sin.

When she sat down, shaking and hot and with tears of
excitement in her eyes, there was a little gentle laughter
and some approving looks at her palpable agony of embarrassment, and when after a hymn and a prayer the meeting
became entirely informal she was surrounded by a jovial
knot of welcoming members who assured her of their under-

standing and fellowship and inquired democratically after
the Earl's health and whereabouts these days. Hermione
stood looking from one to another of their smiling, interested faces, a bright spot of color on each cheek, feeling oddly
elated because she had never been the center of so much
admiring attention before. Evadne, watching her with
proprietary pride, for Hermione was her first convert,
thought, There, she looks better already—all she needed
was a little encouragement.

Returning home that evening, still a little heady with her
sudden social success, Hermione faced the colossal task of
writing her share-letters, in which she would confess even
those sins which were long past and which would now, with
luck, never have come to light at all. Evadne had been quite
clear about that, though. In order to get straight with yourself, you must get straight with everyone else first, even
though they weren't yet aware that things were crooked. Of
course, they might be angry with you when it was brought
to their attention, or they might not answer your letter in
any way, or it might be the beginning for them too of a desire to come clean and ask for Guidance in their own lives.
You could only try, said Evadne, and do what was right to
begin your own life afresh according to God's plan for you.

What was to Hermione the most important and difficult
confession to write struck Jeff amidships when he arrived
from Paris the following week, and sent him in some confusion of mind to Virginia to inquire what Evadne had been
up to now, because Hermione, apparently under influence,
had gone completely batty and written him a letter.

"Yes, I know," said Virginia wearily. "I thought you'd get
one of those. This cult requires 'honesty' in order to get the
goods on everyone."

"Well, what am I supposed to do now?" Jeff wanted to
know. "It was always bad enough, but after this I don't see
how we can look each other in the face."

"It's the oddest sensation, you know," Virginia mused,

"to have Hermione being *pleasant*. She really is changed, Jeff, with a little backsliding now and then. Something has brought her out in a most remarkable way, and Evadne says it's only the result of her having surrendered and stopped feeling greedy about sweets, and things like that."

"Yes, and about me, when actually she hates me, or is it the other way round?" said Jeff.

"You'll notice a difference in her, Jeff, really you will."

"That's fine, I could do with one," he said. "But nothing would have convinced me till now that it could be worse instead of better. Oh, I see what you mean, perfectly. Hermione is all wound up in herself, without any gift for making friends, and with a positive genius for putting people's backs up. Now she has friends for the first time in her silly, misspent life. She's landed among people who believe passionately in being friends, by main force, with everybody they can lay hands on. No wonder it's gone to Hermione's head."

"But don't you think—mind you, I'm only asking—don't you think it might do her a lot of good in the end?" Virginia suggested hopefully. "I'm beginning to wonder if it isn't a real godsend to a lot of harmless misanthropes who wouldn't dream of going into a church even to look at stained glass, but who are slowly dying of loneliness because of their own pure cussedness. I mean, it's not for you and me, but it must do some good that way."

"Sure, sure, for some people it acts as a spiritual cathartic which is very good for their rudimentary little souls," Jeff agreed promptly. "That part's all right, I can go along with that. But it doesn't stop there. People like Hermione get drunk on it and make untold trouble for other people like you and me, confessing mostly imaginary sins and injustices, and raking up embarrassing stuff that's better left where it dropped years ago, mulling over motives that are best dead and buried. Well, excuse my eloquence," said Jeff, "but when somebody like Evadne, with a perfectly good family background and no reason to scrape out the hedges and highways for companionship or affection, goes overboard on it and begins to behave like all twelve apostles at once, and as a result I get stuck with a thing like this letter from Hermione, my immediate impulse is simply to spank. Hard. These politico-religious groups can do great harm."

"Quite," nodded Virginia. "And that's not all, either. Now they've got some crazy idea of going to Germany and working on the Nazis."

"Oh, *no!*" pleaded Jeff, with an involuntary hand to his head. "How you ever came to have such a lunatic child is beyond me. She mustn't go *near* Germany, they'd make mince-meat of her in no time!"

"How can I stop her?"

"Stop her allowance, can't you?"

"Hermione's got enough money in her own right from her mother to do about as she likes. And she regards it as a part of her restitution to finance some sort of travelling team, they call it, to go to Berlin and work a miracle there. I thought perhaps you and Bracken could help me think of something to do."

"You mean they think they can change Hitler?" Jeff suggested, and in spite of himself was shaken with sudden laughter. "I know it's serious," he apologized at once, "but I can't help seeing the funny side."

"There isn't a funny side," said Virginia.

"I agree that Hitler isn't funny any more," he conceded, and again was overtaken by unwilling mirth. "Think of the share-letters he'd have to write!" he said. "All right, I know, I know—now, let's see, Johnny and Camilla arrive tomorrow, don't they? Maybe they'll carry more weight than anything we can say. Johnny hasn't any delusions about the Nazis, anyway."

"Jeff, there's something else I want to ask you." Virginia's heart-shaped face was a little drawn, her eyes were wide and shadowed. "I don't want to go on about it in front of the others, but—Jeff, was there something about air-raid drills while you were in Paris?"

"I'm afraid there was. Even in Paris."

"And something about gas warfare too," she insisted unwillingly.

"In the drills, yes. They used gas-masks, of course. It was a routine sort of thing, with dummies or sometimes co-operative people to simulate casualties, and so on."

"*Routine!*" cried Virginia bitterly. "Shall we have that sort of thing here too?"

"Probably, before long. Most of the big Continental cities have done something of the sort—Naples, and I think Venice too. There's something brewing in Italy, as a matter of fact."

"But—could that affect us here?"

"Yes. Because of the Suez Canal."

"Oh, Jeff—" She reached for him blindly, and he caught and held her hand. "I thought that was all behind us!"

"We're working on it," he said. "Disarmament is dead, of course, but we may still work out something at Geneva."

"What does Bracken *really* think?" It always came down to that now, in the family, as once it had been Bracken's father.

"I don't know," said Jeff truthfully. "Nobody does. Why don't you ask him?"

3

But meanwhile it was Jubilee Summer, and King's weather prevailed. London was floodlighted at night, Covent Garden was ablaze with Grace Moore, Lehmann, and Melchior, the Royal Academy was full of Laverys and Salisburys and Brocks, the theaters were full of Ivor Novello, Dodie Smith, Gertrude Lawrence, Leontovich, Hardwicke, and Gielgud, Wimbledon was full of Perry, Austen, von Cramm, Helen

Jacobs, Mrs. Moody, and Kay Stammers, and England was full of strangers and some old friends returned.

And Mab saw Jeff almost every day.

She wanted to hear what he had been doing, but mostly she wanted the latest news from America. As there was no point anyway in dwelling on the uneasy European situation and its futile pacts and conferences and air-raid exercises and sinister rumblings, when he was with her Jeff allowed his natural nostalgia to come out. There was a joke in the family about Mab's American blood, which came to her from Virginia through Irene with two British sires. Ever since she had heard last Christmas about Jeff's inheriting the house in Williamsburg Mab had gone American in a big way. Now he had sent for pictures of the restored buildings in the town as the Rockefeller project proceeded on its painstaking way, and Sylvia had found some snapshots for her of more personal subjects, even one of Jeff as a boy, down by the College Gate. Mab put them all carefully into a scrap-book, even the cheapest postcards of the rebuilt Capitol and the Raleigh Tavern. She asked for American books, and was inclined to argue with Miss Sim about the finer points of that little spot of bother in 1776. She even read up about Red Indians, though Jeff assured her they were no longer a daily feature of American life.

Virginia, racking her brains, had drawn up a family tree on a large piece of paper, which Mab kept pinned to the wall in the schoolroom like a map, and which she soon knew by heart. A favorite game was to put her finger on a name and ask for its personal history, every detail of which was absorbed into her retentive memory. Jeff's mother Phoebe, who had grown up in Williamsburg, was especially good at this, better than Virginia, who had not been back to America since her marriage. Bracken too was always good for a new yarn when he could be cornered, especially about the war in Cuba, at which he had personally assisted. Mab's piano lessons now included songs from the musical comedies Fitz Sprague had written, and she treasured gramophone records from the later shows in which Stephen and Sylvia had appeared. The prospect of their actually coming to London, these fabulous American cousins who sang and danced on the stage to music their own father had written, filled her with an almost holy delight of anticipation, and she was prepared to worship them both with no reservations even for Sylvia, who was by her pictures even prettier than Evadne and who might, Mab knew, be the one Jeff would fall in love with.

Jeff had promised that he would have Sylvia bring with her from the Williamsburg house his own note-books full of family history, which Mab was to have for herself as he now doubted very much that the next few years would leave him much leisure or freedom of mind to reconstruct the past. What no one realized was that it was less Mab's one quarter American heritage than her secret, unchildlike preoccupation with Jeff himself that made the American background such an obsession with her. Unlike herself, Jeff had been born in Virginia, of Virginian parents. That made him all American, undiluted, and his roots were there, presumably he would return there to live in his house if he ever settled down to marry and have children. An absorbing, hidden idea was forming in Mab's mind. She dreamed of it over her lesson books by day, and stayed awake at night to dwell on it in the private dark. During lunch at Stewart's in Regent Street on the day they went to the *1066* matinee, she determined to ask Jeff about it and take the consequences, whatever they were.

"Jeff, do you think—I mean, only if you want to, of course, but *do* you think if *you* asked them they might let me go to Williamsburg sometime—just for a visit—to see your house and—and the restored buildings too, of course—and Jamestown where the picnics were, and Yorktown where the surrender was, and—do you think I might? Or would it cost an awful lot? Mummy says everything is twice as expensive as it used to be, and we must begin to economize somewhere. I've got one pound nine and threepence in my bank to put towards my boat fare."

Jeff swallowed and thought fast. Her astonishing plunges from almost adult intelligence to the innocent ignorance of childhood, like offering her little fortune to help pay for a ticket to America, often caught him by surprise.

"Well, it's not an impossible idea, I should think," he said cautiously, between fear of letting the family in for an awkward veto and his own natural disinclination to let Mab down. "I could take it up with them, if you like. Of course it would have to be some time when Dinah was going there herself, unless your mother felt she could get away to make the trip—"

"Or I thought—even if I had to take Miss Sim—if it wasn't convenient for Mummy, I mean, because she *hates* to be away from Father—surely it could come under the head of education? And of course I'd much rather it was when *you* were going to be there too—"

"Yes, well, we could think about it, couldn't we. Ways and means, you know. Things work out sometimes," he said with what he felt was unpardonable vagueness, but Mab gazed at him across the filet of sole with uncomplicated love and confidence.

"Oh, Jeff, it's so wonderful to talk to you—you never say Perhaps-when-you're-older, or Don't-be-silly, or Whatever-gave-you-that-idea. You always make everything seem so— *reasonable,* a person isn't afraid to let you know what one is thinking."

"Well, I don't think it's so very unreasonable for you to want to see Williamsburg," he said consideringly. "Maybe we could cook up something with Sylvia while she's here."

"Oh, if only she likes me!" Mab sighed.

"She better," said Jeff. "Eat your fish, we don't want to miss anything, do we."

"Does Sylvia—that is, have you ever mentioned me to her?" she asked with sudden shyness, for if he had, what had he said?

"Lots of times, I should think."

"You *have?*" Joy and consternation mingled. "What did you say?"

Jeff had a sudden illumination that it wouldn't do to repeat to Mab that jest about their falling in love. He didn't stop to work it out, he just knew it was better not to, she was such a strange mixture of child and something more, something to which he had never given a name but which made her companionship precious to him and tricked him into talking to her as though she were not handicapped by lack of years and experience.

"I think she must have gathered by now that you're my favorite cousin over here," he said.

"*Am* I, Jeff? More favorite than Evadne?"

"*Evadne?*" He registered horror. "Excuse me for quoting, but Whatever-gave-you-that-idea?"

Mab giggled.

"She's a lot prettier than me," she suggested.

"Pretty is as pretty does," said Jeff grimly. "Give yourself a little more time, why don't you?"

"Jeff, how do you think I'll look when I'm Evadne's age?"

He contemplated her gravely while the waitress changed the plates.

"Who knows what the styles will be by then," he said. "But you'll always have those beautiful greenish eyes, and very few people can match that, and you've got small bones, which is another great advantage. You'll be all right, my girl, just you wait."

"Some people do improve a great deal, don't they, with age?"

"Yes, take your grandmother, for instance. Virginia is just as fascinating now as she was the first time I ever saw her, when she was a young widow, right after the war. I say young, she must have been well into her thirties then. I've never understood, between you and me, why she never got married again. But there's a legend that our Great-grandmother Tibby was proposed to, and refused him, at the age of sixty, and Virginia's still got a few years to go on that. And she'll be fascinating when she's ninety, if she lives that long, just as Tibby was supposed to be. And then there was—" But before he could embark on the legend of Aunt Sally, who had three husbands, all of them wealthy and all of them dead before she was forty, and who went right on inspiring male devotion when to the family's certain knowledge she just *had* to be seventy, Jeff was struck by an idea like a thunderbolt, and he laid down his knife and fork and leaned back, staring across the table at Mab's intent face. "By gum!" he said inelegantly. "Now I know what it is!"

"What? What's the matter, Jeff?"

"Your eyes," he said. "That portrait over the mantelpiece at home. *You've got Great-grandmother Tibby's eyes!*"

"Oh, *Jeff!*"

"Wait till Sylvia comes, she'll see it too, I know she will! I knew there was something about you, and that's what it is!"

"Jeff, *shall* I see the portrait myself sometime? Please?"

"Yes. That settles it. You'll see the portrait. Maybe not this year, maybe not next year—but we'll think of something. We must get you to Williamsburg for sure."

"Oh, how wonderful!" she sighed. "I've just got a *feeling* that I'll go."

"Wait till Sylvia comes. She'll see to it."

And after that the matinee was almost an anti-climax.

4

Johnny Malone, who had been Bracken's Berlin correspondent in 1914 and was now head of his European Bureau and had married his cousin Camilla from Richmond, was not amused when they told him of Evadne's project to change Nazi Germany, and Camilla was frankly horrified. The Cause was not unknown in Berlin, they said, and some Nazis even professed its beliefs, though Johnny doubted if their zeal for restitution and fellowship extended to non-Aryans. The idea itself was worthy enough, he conceded, and certainly the world stood in need of some kind of spiritual rearmament to go with the air-power race which had now begun, but this slightly goofy brand of sweetness and light could only make matters worse, he said, in that it encouraged the fatal German tendency to believe that the English were mad anyway and would never fight another war if they could talk their way through it.

Johnny and Bracken were discussing half incredulously the Anglo-German Naval Agreement which Ribbentrop had come to London to negotiate with the MacDonald Government. Bracken said England never *would,* and Johnny offered rather grimly to bet him. And then one morning at breakfast in Curzon Street, when everyone was pottering peacefully through their letters, Camilla suddenly made an odd little sound over one of hers and said, "Johnny, it's Victor! He's *here!* What do we do?"

"What does he want?" asked Johnny, going to the point.

"He wants to call—or whatever. He wants to be recognized. He wants to get his foot in the door, in other words."

"Not *my* door!" said Virginia promptly.

"Ribbentrop," said Johnny thoughtfully.

"Yes, of course. He's come with the German Naval delegation. He always trails Ribbentrop, for some reason."

"They both speak good English. It's natural for them to work together. Virginia," said Johnny, and *"No!"* said Virginia. "Not here!"

"Now, wait a minute," said Bracken, and there was a gleam in his eye.

"I know!" said Virginia. "You want to cultivate him, and see what you can pick up. He has the same idea about you. It all has a very familiar sound. More than twenty years ago his father came to England and we invited him to Farthingale, remember?"

"Not Farthingale, for Victor," said Bracken peaceably. "Just luncheon here, that's a good girl."

"No," said Virginia. "He might get at Rosalind and upset her."

"How can he? Rosalind is in the country. She needn't even know he's here."

"Unless he chooses."

"Why should he? His father is dead. Rosalind is no good to Victor now."

"She's his mother, and she got away. They don't like people to get away."

"But what conceivable object could Victor have for bothering Rosalind now?" said Bracken, and noticed that Johnny was silent, and waited, watching him. "Well?" he asked finally, and Johnny turned slowly to meet his eyes.

"That's what I was wondering about," he said.

"Well, he's not going to get near Rosalind, if I can help it!" said Virginia.

"You can't," Johnny pointed out. "He'll get to her if he wants to. He knows where she is—or can find out. It's simple enough to locate the wife of the Marquis of Cleeve."

"That's what it is, I think," said Camilla. "He expects to find his mother queening it in London society, and he wants to cash in on her social prestige and mix with London society himself. Or they've put him up to it, perhaps. Victor has 'connections' here. They always like to make use of connections."

"Well, then, if it's as simple as that, once he learns that Rosalind and Charles have no London house and see almost nobody down there in the country and can do nothing for him, he'll lose interest in them," said Bracken.

"If it's as simple as that," said Johnny with reservations.

"But, darling—" Even Camilla regarded him with some surprise. "What else could he possibly want with Rosalind now?"

"I haven't the faintest idea," said Johnny.

"Well, then. This is England, after all."

"Yes," said Johnny.

"I suppose I'll have to take some notice of this letter," Camilla said, fingering it doubtfully.

"Yes," said Johnny. "Virginia—"

"Oh, all right, luncheon here on Thursday," sighed Virginia. "But that is absolutely *all*."

"Thank you," said Johnny with a sweet smile.

No one but Virginia had noticed that Evadne had said nothing, looking from one to the other with bright, attentive eyes while the discussion went on. Half of her reluctance to entertain Victor was because of Evadne's proposed crusade to Germany, which acquaintance with a Nazi here in London might foster.

"What sort of person is he?" she asked, trying to sound casual now that she was in for it, and she saw Camilla's eyes go to Johnny's in a long look so full of understanding and affection that it set her wondering.

"He's presentable," said Johnny, and Camilla laughed outright with real joy.

"The *mot juste!*" she said, and her eyes lingered in his.

"The fact is," said Johnny to the rest of them, "I had a very narrow escape from Victor." He wagged his head knowingly and sighed as though over unspeakable things. "It aged me," he said. "You must have noticed how I'm old before my time. That was Victor."

"No such thing," said Camilla. "It never occurred to you to want to marry me till we got back to Salzburg after the Purge."

"That's what you think," said Johnny.

"What's going on here?" demanded Virginia. "Camilla, were you and Victor ever—"

"Not really," said Camilla. "I had some idea of saving him from himself, I think. Very young of me. I made him an offer," she told them, her chin up, her eyes very bright, for it was a thing she would remember with very mixed feelings always. "I offered to help him escape to London with his soul while he could, and he said, 'My soul? There's no such thing,' he said. 'I saw them die at Lichtenfeld.' And he said, 'Are you suggeshting—' (He was a little drunk at the time, because of Lichtenfeld.) '—are you suggeshting that I should desert the Leader for you—a *woman?*' And then he said he never wanted to see me again." Her eyes fell to the letter in her hand. "Apparently something has changed his mind about that. But how did he know we were here just now?" she mused.

"It's their business to know things like that," Johnny reminded her.

Evadne spoke for the first time.

"What happened at Lichtenfeld?" she asked, and they looked at her with compassion and envy because she was ignorant and young.

"Mass executions," said Johnny briefly. "In squads. When the men firing the guns got sick or fainted they were replaced. Young officers like Victor were required to witness it as part of the hardening process."

"Are you sure?" said Evadne blankly.

"Sure of what?" Johnny asked. "That hundreds of people died that week-end, or that the officers got hardened?"

"Were you there?" demanded Evadne.

"Inside Lichtenfeld? Luckily, no. But we heard the guns. Even Dinah heard the guns, didn't you, Dinah? And people turned up missing for days afterwards—German people one knew quite well, and never saw again. His own father—"

"No!" cried Evadne. "No, I won't listen!" She stood up, pushing back her chair. "How can you sit there talking about such things in cold blood over a plate of food, and not *do* anything?"

"Such as?" said Johnny gently.

Evadne turned and ran out of the room. Virginia sighed, as the rest of them sat speechless.

"I do wish she'd fall in love," she said.

"Would that cure her, do you think?" Bracken smiled.

"It takes their minds off the state of the world," Virginia explained. "When I think how I grew up—it was such a beautiful life for a girl—we had so much room to be happy, with nothing hanging over us. And I don't think it spoilt us a bit for facing up to the war when it came. But we had had our youth. We had been really gay, and really carefree. No one growing up today knows what that means. They live with doom. I'm terribly sorry for my children and their children. We had the best of it, Bracken." Her eyes brimmed over.

"Maybe," said Bracken unwillingly. "It was pretty good, anyway. And I am not one of those loose-thinking orators who can beat his breast over the alleged folly of mankind which has brought us to the brink of disaster. It is not mankind that is to blame. It is only a small, indigestible, insurgent portion of mankind who refuse to be civilized and grown up. They want it that way. And the only way to stop their aggression is to get ready to be just as tough. You don't teach a bad child not to throw stones through window-panes by brushing the broken glass out of your hair and pretending not to n-o-t-i-c-e. You go after him and show him the error of his ways with the flat of your hand or the back of a hairbrush. Internationally, statesmanship won't work any longer because we are up against a gang of hoodlums who have never felt the back of a hairbrush on their backsides. Religion can only work martyrdom, which proves something, perhaps, but is too slow and painful a way nowadays to demonstrate the power of good over evil, and of law over outlawry." He sighed heavily. "That brings us to the subject of preventive war again, doesn't it, Johnny. And nobody on our side is ready for that. Nobody will be till it's too late. We might settle it now with a *little* war, like a big police action. But by the time enough people realize that, it will take a big war."

"Oh, Bracken, not *again!*" cried Virginia, and he turned to her, smiling and kind.

"I've heard that before," he said. "Forgive me for being a realist at luncheon, my dear. And of course there's still Geneva."

"What's left of it," said Johnny. "The Italians will walk out next, and there will be two empty chairs. That will be about enough. Geneva will go *phut*. In the meantime—" His eyes brightened warily. "—let's have another look at Victor."

5

Virginia glanced down her own luncheon table on Thursday with a strange, somewhat groggy sensation of having lived the present moment twice—of having been there before. But it was a different house and a different German prince, the other time—a different Germany, in fact—and Archie had sat where her brother Bracken sat now as host, and Evadne was not born. Prince Conrad's son had the same rich voice with its faintly rolling *r*'s, the same overly correct good manners, the same aggressively British tailoring, the same (let's

face it) slightly sinister charm. Virginia could understand—
or almost—why Camilla had once concerned herself about
his soul, for he had magnetism and intelligence and was indeed presentable. What was it about him, then, she wondered, that made one's blood run a trifle cold?

She looked at Camilla—slim and elegant and poised, Con-
tinentalized to her fingertips—and dear, blunt Johnny who
adored her, and saw how they tempered their known aver-
sion to this man with social grace; saw Dinah's cool, smiling
indifference to the fact that Nazis affected her the way cats
affect people who have aelurophobia; saw Bracken's alert,
smiling, surgical gaze and Jeff's cagey, easy smile. And then,
like running into the edge of a door, she came to Evadne's
fascinated receptiveness, her wide, brilliant eyes lifted to
Victor's face, her parted, listening lips, her dreadful, vulnerable, frightening friendliness. Evadne was pouring over
him the ready interest and warm response with which she
met each new acquaintance, and Victor was reacting in a
logical and obvious masculine way. She was a very pretty
girl, and she was hanging on his every word, under the
eyes of her own people. To Victor it was plain that English
girls were no less susceptible to virile German manhood than
the girls at home. Even Camilla—his long, arrogant stare ran
over the still desirable, arresting creature across the table
—even Camilla was not impervious once. Women were much
the same, whatever language you spoke to them in. And because of his English mother and his English nurse he had
been bilingual from babyhood.

And Virginia, watching Evadne's open, generous welcoming of this exotic stranger into her sheltered life, thought,
Oh, *no*, not Victor—she's too intelligent for *that*.

Then, as from a great distance, she heard Victor saying,
"It is an absurd situation, is it not, to require an introduc-
tion to one's own mother?"

"But surely—don't you remember her at all?" said Evadne, leaning towards him, all sympathy and interest.

"My dear young lady, you do not realize—" The *r* almost escaped him. "—I was nine years old when she ran away from my father's house, and I have naturally not seen her since then. I very much doubt if I should meet her face to face now if I could recognize her as my mother."

"But—you must have seen pictures—" said Evadne incredulously.

"There are no pictures of her any more at Heidersdorf," he told her harshly. "She brought scandal and disgrace to my family. My father would not permit her name to be mentioned in his hearing."

"Oh, but she's a very lovely woman, you must forget all that and be friends with her now!" cried Evadne.

"I should like very much," said Victor.

"Well, we can arrange that, can't we!" said Evadne, with a bright glance round at her spellbound family, whose worst fears were being realized.

"Rosalind spends all her time down in the country," Virginia said, pulling herself together. "She and her husband see almost no one but a few old friends—"

"Well, you might say that Victor *is* an old friend, mightn't you, Mummy?" Evadne chided her gently.

"She has—forgive me—I understand that she has regularized her connection with this man?" asked Rosalind's son with some hauteur of Virginia.

"She and Charles Laverham were friends for years—before she met your father. They were meant to be husband and wife, and they are very happy together," Virginia replied with some asperity. "You mean you defend them, and her divorce?" said Victor.

"Yes," said Virginia, and their eyes locked defiantly and held, and he recognized in her an opponent with whom to reckon.

"I was very glad to hear," he said smoothly after a moment. "It lends more dignity to her position, which was in the meantime perhaps—humiliating."

"Not in the least," said Virginia. "Everyone knew they were meant for each other. Everyone knew how brutally she was treated in *Germany*. Divorce under such circumstances is accepted."

"They could not, of course, attend the Court," he remarked with satisfaction.

"They did not wish to."

"Naturally," said Victor, and his smile was indulgent. "But now that he has—as you say?—made an honest woman of her—"

"No, please forgive me," Evadne interrupted him gently. "But you aren't sufficiently familiar with English to know— it's only right to tell you—we wouldn't say that about a woman like your mother. It's only for servant girls and— people who have made *mistakes*."

"I see." He studied her earnest, appealing face with appreciation. "You are very kind to help me with my English. And you do not consider, then, that my mother made any mistake."

"The mistake was to marry your father," said Virginia, plunging in. "She and Charles Laverham had always been in love. After the war began, her life in Germany became intolerable."

"That I can understand," Victor agreed politely. "But was it quite necessary, do you think, after she returned to England, to—"

"Yes," said Virginia flatly. "They were both dying of it. And her obligation to your father was at an end."

"I see," said Victor again, and now the glance they exchanged was open war.

"If all you want is to take her to task for leaving your father in the first place, and—"

"But not at all," said Victor softly. "As we have been saying, there is no longer any question. My father no longer exists. Therefore this man Laverham *is* entitled to exist. I have no objection to him."

"I very much doubt if you'll have much opportunity to see her." This was Camilla, to Virginia's aid. "She almost never comes up to Town. They take no part whatever in London's social life."

"No matter," said Victor, with a fatalistic lift of his shoulders. "I can go to her. In Gloucestershire, is it not? A few hours' journey. Your distances in England are so small. I shall write to her first, of course, to name a day, it would be only right."

"Victor, does it occur to you that she might not want to see you?" said Camilla bluntly.

He spread his big, well-kept hands.

"Why not?"

"It's all behind her, Victor. Why not leave it there? You'll only be here for a short time, and—"

"On the contrary," he interrupted smoothly. "I am now attached to the Embassy in London. You may remember I told you I would be."

"So you did," said Camilla, remembering only too well.

"Well, that's wonderful!" beamed Evadne. "Any woman would be thrilled to find she had a grown-up son like Victor, wouldn't she, Mummy! The chances are she wouldn't be able to recognize you, either!" she added with a flattering glance at Victor, who almost visibly preened. "Why couldn't he come to Farthingale for the week-end, Mummy?" she went on, for everyone seemed powerless to stop her. "We could ring up Rosalind from there and drive him over to tea or something."

"Surprise, surprise!" muttered Camilla, with a glance at Johnny, and Victor, who must have heard her perfectly well, pretended not to and said that would be delightful.

Without downright unfounded rudeness Virginia was now lost, and the following week-end but one was named for Victor's visit to Farthingale. Jeff dared not look at her, and Dinah began at once to wonder if she could possibly manage to be elsewhere that week-end. Camilla and Johnny seemed sunk in an apathy of resignation, and Bracken wore a small, wary smile because it was all so above-board and interesting and mysterious. And everyone at the table, except Victor, was longing, not for the first time, to spank Evadne till she howled.

6

Victor arrived at Farthingale at tea time on the Friday, driving a black Mercedes-Benz, wearing correct (although too new) English country tweeds, and bringing a correct gift for his hostess. It was his first experience of an English country-house week-end, of which in general he had heard so much, and while he was aware that Farthingale was not one of the more famous stately homes of England, but merely an old Cotswold manor house, its dignity and comfort created an immediate impression. His welcome was all anyone could ask for, and he was soon seated beside Evadne on a chintz sofa in a panelled room bright with afternoon sunlight, drinking hot tea with a piece of excellent cake alongside. It was still difficult for Victor not to be surprised at the abundance and goodness of English food. It was difficult not to eat too rapidly and with too visible pleasure, just as he had found it before now on his visits to France and Switzerland. It would not do for a German to appear to relish another country's commonplace luxuries. In Germany the luxuries had all gone into guns, which was as it should be, as the other countries would learn to their cost before long. But in the meantime this sojourn in England promised to be very rewarding.

No one said anything about the object of his visit, which was Rosalind, until at last he was forced to refer to it himself, and instantly the atmosphere cooled a little.

"Yes," said Virginia in answer to his query. "She has received your letter, and I have talked to her since then. She will see you tomorrow afternoon. Since you came in your own car, it might be as well if you drove yourself over to Cleeve, unless you would prefer to have one of us go along."

"It will not be necessary to trouble you to do that," he said politely, conscious that that was the way they wished it. "She was pleased?" he asked then, unable to let it alone.

"She didn't say so," Virginia admitted. "Are you still determined to go?"

"But naturally," he answered, as though she were being unreasonable, and Evadne said quickly, "Would you like to go and look at the garden now?" and Victor put down his cup and rose, not as an Englishman would rise, in casual unfolding sections, but abruptly, all in one piece, like a German, and stood at her service.

When they had gone out through the French windows on to the lawn Virginia said irritably, to the others, "There must be some *reason*. I suppose we shall know soon."

Rosalind at Cleeve was also wondering *why*. There was no clue in the formal phrasing of his letter to her. He was in England, and asked her permission to come and see her during a week-end visit at Farthingale, that was all. The self-contained, unaffectionate child in whose German upbringing there had been very little time or place for an English mother even in his early years was a total stranger to her now, and there was no stirring of her blood at the idea of seeing him again, with the additional barrier of his Nazi training. He was always less her son than Conrad's, and he stood for things she thought she had left behind forever, and for other things which were even more repugnant to her.

It was infinitely disturbing to be confronted with him now, especially in view of the ugly uncertainties which surrounded his father's death. She had not loved Conrad, nor ever been in love with him, but she had lived gracefully in Germany as his wife for years, and had borne him a child. And she had acknowledged at times, in spite of everything, his certain masculine magnetism and experienced charm.

If the war had not happened, she supposed she might have lived out her whole life as Conrad's wife—lonely always, frightened often, angry now and then, but trapped and helpless and docile. But the war did come, and with it Conrad's appointment to the Kaiser's staff, changing irretrievably their fundamental attitude towards one another, emphasizing their differences, raising new barriers, creating dreadful, humiliating scenes with his German relatives, and even, in the privacy of their own rooms, with him.

Standing now at the window of her bedroom in the dower house at Cleeve, waiting for Victor to be announced, Rosalind heard a quiet step at the threshold and turned with that slight quickening of the heart which the arrival of Charles after even the briefest absence always brought her. He stood in the doorway, his kind, blunt face a little anxious, his eyes searching her composure. He wore rough country tweeds, well-aged, and carried his cap and gloves.

"I'm just off to the south farm," he said in his low, unhurried voice. "Are you going to be all right here?"

"Yes, of course." She came to him, smiling, slim and straight in her soft dark gown.

"Sure you wouldn't rather I was somewhere about this afternoon?"

"I think it would be better not, my dear. I must see him alone."

"I could keep well out of sight, of course." He lingered.

"Charles, darling, he won't want to kidnap me!"

"Well, how do you know? I would, in his place."

She put both hands on his shoulders, looking up, and his arms went round her lightly.

"Yes, dear, but no German would have me now as a gift," she said.

"Then what *does* he want, do you think?"

"I don't know. I can't imagine. That's one of the reasons I must see him. Perhaps Conrad left some kind of message or—obligation, which he must discharge. It's the only guess I have, and it's probably wrong."

"You're minding it rather a lot, aren't you."

"Yes, I am. More than I expected, really. I'll be glad when it's over."

"Sure you don't want me to see him for you? Tell him you aren't well, or something?"

She shook her head and leaned against him, in his arms, her cheek against his coat.

"This is real," she said. "This moment now. The other was the bad dream. It's over."

"Darling—" he began, and she straightened.

"No, Charles—you go along to the south farm. By the time you come back he will be gone."

"If that's the way you want it—"

"There's nothing to be afraid of," she said, reasoning with herself as well as with him. "This is England. There's no Gestapo here."

"True," he agreed. "But I wish I knew what brought him here."

A maid came to the door with Victor's card on a salver, and Rosalind said that she would come down at once. When they were alone again she turned to Charles and lifted her face for his kiss. And when he had given it, and found her lips cold, he said, "I've changed my mind," and dropped his cap and gloves on a chair. "I'm not going. I shall wait here."

She stood a moment with a rueful smile.

"I'm afraid I wanted you to all along," she said. "I'll tell them to bring you some tea."

This is England, she said again to herself, fiercely, as she descended the staircase. I'm shaking just the way I used to do, and this is my own house, with Charles in it, and my own country, and Conrad is dead. There is nothing to be afraid of, there is nothing they can do now. . . .

She entered the room where Victor waited.

"You will forgive me if I stare at you," he said after a moment. "But you are not—not at all what I thought to see."

"Perhaps I had the advantage of you there," she smiled, and offered her hand. "You are very like your father."

He bent formally and kissed her hand, which was at once withdrawn.

"But you are so young," he said, almost with a stammer. "It leads me to think—perhaps there is some mistake? You are—you were the wife of Prince Conrad zu Polkwitz-Heidersdorf?"

"For thirteen years."

"But you—must have been married very young!"

"Yes. Girls were, in those days." She sat down beside a table already laid with a silver tea-service where an alcohol lamp burned under a steaming kettle, and motioned him to a chair on the other side of it. "We had very little to say about it, and we naturally made some mistakes. Your father was a fine man in some ways, but—we were not suited to each other."

"Please, if you do not mind—we do not discuss today my father."

"As you please," she assented, bewildered anew, for it seemed to remove at once the only possible reason for the interview. "Milk or lemon?"

"Nothing, please—just as it pours." He accepted his cup with a formal little bow. And when he had sat down again he was silent, watching her intently as she prepared her own cup, and she dreaded that he would perceive that her hands were not quite steady. The silence lengthened between them. He neither drank his tea nor took his eyes from her face. She could hear the clock on the mantelpiece ticking.

"If we are not to speak of your father," she said at last, with a composure she did not feel, "why is it that you have come to see me?"

"Now that I see you I begin to understand so many things," he said, which was no real answer.

"How do you mean?" She had to meet his intent, almost defiant stare. "What sort of things?"

"Myself, first. It is your blood in mine that makes me so constantly battle myself. That I did anticipate. But not in the same way it transpires."

"I don't quite understand," said Rosalind faintly, wondering how long this must go on.

"You are *soft*," he said, and the word rasped in his throat. "*You* are my weakness. That I knew, it was only logical. But now it is not the same. You are so different from what I supposed."

"How did you suppose I would be, then?"

"Like other shameless women!" he cried, and Rosalind blinked. "Painted—pretty—self-satisfied—cheap. But no, you are soft and sweet and kind—yes, you are good. It is going to be so much more simple than I had thought."

"More simple?" she echoed, as many times she had heard herself blankly echo Conrad's mental involutions.

"That we should be friends," he explained coolly.

"Am I to take it that your—mission here is to fraternize with the English?" she asked ironically.

"To overcome prejudice," he corrected politely. "To win confidence. For why should our two great nations not be friendly? There is no quarrel between us, if we can but understand each other. And where could I start better to understand the English, and vice versa, but with my own mother?"

"Well, as for my part in your program," she said gently, "we see almost no one here at Cleeve. I'm afraid it will be very little use your coming here again."

His face changed suddenly into a scowl, for he recognized dismissal.

"You mean—"

"My life in Germany is behind me. I would rather leave it there."

"You dislike me—your son?"

"How can I tell, in a few minutes?"

"Well, then—let us get acquainted!"

"Why?" she said. "Because you are here on orders from your government to make use of your English connections?"

"But I did not say—"

"You didn't have to *say*. Victor, I have married again. We live very quietly here, managing the home estate. We have no—influence, anywhere. This is all we want, all we are able or willing to undertake."

"You have then no human feelings?" he reproached her. "You not only abandon your home in Germany, you repudiate your son. And yet you do not appear to be a heartless woman."

"I don't think I am," she replied, determined to hold on to things, marvelling again at the way they could always put you in the wrong. "I don't think it's necessary in the circumstances to go into the reasons for my leaving Germany as I did. It is a long time ago now. You must try to realize it was a very complicated situation, with my husband's country at war with all the things I had grown up accustomed to, and—there was also a very acute personal aspect." (I'm talking the way *they* do, she thought—in rounded periods—it's impossible to be natural with them—impossible to make oneself understood without resorting to banalities like theirs. It is not a mere question of language, it goes deeper than that. It is a state of mind.) "We had very little to say to each other, you and I, even when you were little," she reminded him.

"You were *die Engländerin*," he said. "I was always warned that you did not understand our ways because you were English and so not quite responsible. I used to wonder why, if that were the case, my father had brought you to live with us."

"I used to wonder too," she nodded, and there passed between them an unexpected, rather rueful smile.

"Now that I am a man myself, I can see why," he said. "You have allure. He was bewitched."

"Perhaps that was it," she said, trying to speak lightly, aware of the first faint glimmer of a possible relationship between them, recognizing with amazement a hint of humor and warmth behind his woodenness. Like Conrad, she thought in bewilderment. Like Conrad, over again.

"But you were not happy," he said, as though thinking it out in a new light.

"No, I was not. And the war made it suddenly much worse."

"You were not happy even before the war began."

"No."

"A pity."

They looked at each other across her tea table, and now there was something in the air between them that might have been the blood tie—an absence of defensiveness and hostility, rather than the presence of anything so positive as a liking for each other—a moment's truce in which understanding, even sympathy, might take root.

"But why should you hold that against me, your son?" he asked then, reasonably.

"I don't, Victor, believe me, I don't," she said earnestly, and made a half gesture towards him of apology and appeal. "There is nothing to hold against you—or against him, now. But neither is there anything for us to say to each other, you and I."

"I never thought to care about that," he said.

"Nor I," she answered, her eyes resting, honest and troubled, in his. There had been moments like this with Conrad too, in the beginning—moments when one almost hoped for something more, when a strong, exciting attraction existed, briefly, and then was slain, sometimes it seemed inadvertently, as though by a boot heel.

"I wonder what it is," he said, as though to himself, and he set down his cup and rose and walked away from her down the room, and then turned and came back and stood looking down at her. "Camilla—Evadne—and now you—headstrong, wilful, undisciplined women, very foolish, very beautiful, yes, but very— Why is one so attracted?"

"Evadne?" said Rosalind, and her eyes clouded. "I don't see how she comes into it."

"This Cause she talks about—this belief in absolute love and fellowship, and in a personal, articulate God's will—it is an interesting idea, isn't it? Revolutionary, isn't it? It might lead to—almost anything."

"But, Victor, I don't think you quite understand. It is not representative—that is, it has nothing to do with the Government policy."

"Perhaps better if it had."

"How do you mean that?"

"Only that it might save—a lot of trouble."

"You mean that if it were universal, there would be no more aggression—and so no more wars."

"But if there were no *resistance*," he corrected gently, "there would also be no more wars."

The quiet words, in their flagrant casuistry, lay between them. Perceptibly the atmosphere had changed again. She was on guard, he was the invader, as in the beginning.

"Evadne is young and—very impressionable," said Rosalind carefully. "You mustn't take what she says too seriously."

"But she is serious, surely."

"Oh, yes. But she has no influence. She is only—"

"So pretty a girl as that, with her family position, is bound to have influence." He spread his hands with a small, knowing smile for her comprehension. "Even she influences me," he pointed out, with charm.

"Now, Victor—"

"Evadne said, for instance, that you would be proud to have a son like me."

"Yes, I suppose I—"

"I am very healthy and well educated," he suggested.

"I'm sure you are, but—"

"There is nothing, except perhaps the way I speak English, which could perhaps be improved on, that you would feel necessary to apologize for."

"No, except—"

"Except—?" he prompted, as she did not go on.

"You are German, Victor."

"Yes. And so?" The lift of his chin was arrogant.

"We do not—quite like the way things are going in Germany."

"Well, as for that—it is Germany's business, surely. And this new Naval Agreement shows clearly that your Government is on our side now against the French."

"No, Victor, that is a wrong impression, I assure you—"

"Well, let us not trouble ourselves with that now," he interrupted with a little too much haste. "It is after all no concern, shall we say, of you and Evadne whom I admire so much."

"You *admire* Evadne?"

"I do indeed. So much that I am reminded already of how so nearly I made a fool of myself about Camilla only a few years ago in France. I had not then heard of this new so-called religion."

"Neither had Camilla."

"No, Camilla had not Evadne's sincere wish for a mutual understanding between Germany and England."

The afternoon sunlight had faded from the windows of the room, cut off by the high box hedge which bordered the garden on that side. Steam still came from the silver kettle over the spirit-lamp, though tea was forgotten. Rosalind leaned forward and blew out the flame, and it was as though somewhere a door had closed, a bolt had gone home, a light was out.

"If you have some idea of taking advantage of Evadne's rather childish enthusiasms—" she began, and his voice cut in, cool and hard.

"I wonder why it is that every time this Naval Agreement is mentioned, you British all draw the blinds," he said. "It is entirely honest and open—a just recognition of Germany's rights under the sun. Why are you angry with me now?"

"I'm not angry, Victor, I only—"

"Or is it because of Evadne that you go suddenly to arm's length again? I tell you I am interested in this—so-called Cause. It seems to me to have significance. Perhaps it may not have quite the same results that Evadne so confidently expects. It might even be that her ideas of the most desirable results might undergo a change. Nevertheless its effects might be—extremely useful."

"Useful to whom?"

"Why, to—everyone. In the interests of peace, of course." Under her steady gaze, his eyelids flickered once. "In any case, Evadne is anxious to try how it goes on in Germany, and—"

Rosalind rose and stood behind the tea table looking at him across it.

"You will please let Evadne alone, Victor."

He stared back at her, suddenly furious.

"How can you say that?" he demanded, and added as she did not immediately reply, "You are an unnatural woman. You choose to make an enemy of your son."

"My son was born an enemy."

"This is what I cannot understand about the English!" he cried irritably. "So soft—so meek—so loving-kind—and then no feeling at all! *None,* at all!"

"I think you're making rather a fuss about nothing, Victor. You come here uninvited, and take offence because you are not welcomed with open arms. I have tried to explain to you that for several reasons it will be quite impossible for you to have the freedom of my husband's house, and you choose to be offended and hurt. What is more, I refuse to be a party to any further acquaintance between you and Evadne."

"Why now am I warned away from Evadne? Surely she is old enough, the way you run this country, to choose her own friends? And anyway, surely that is the business of her own family first?"

"Yes, it is. But I know how Virginia feels, and I do not intend to make it easier for you to get round her by coming here. Besides, when you return to Germany we are none of us likely to meet again—"

"I do not return to Germany with the delegation. I am posted to the Embassy here."

There was a silence.

"Oh," said Rosalind faintly.

"I confess to you that when I came here I was determined to hate you, along with the English blood which is my curse. I must be—it is essential that I am wholly German. And what happens? After Evadne, saying we must all trust and confide in each other—and not only saying it but *believing* it—and after Camilla, looking tantalizing and amused, as though she knew some secret—now I find you, the way you are. Had I known what you are like, perhaps I would not have come near you at all. That is—" He hesitated and seemed to recollect. "—I should have preferred not."

"I really don't quite—"

"Ask Camilla!" he said roughly, with a rather one-sided smile. "Camilla knows well the battleground I am! But always the German in me wins, do you hear? There is nothing you can do now, you and Evadne, to change that. Camilla knows!"

"Victor, you must realize that Evadne takes everything very hard, very—seriously. You must not—"

"Toils and snares!" he said curtly. "I have seen women as beautiful before. I have my work to do." He passed a hand theatrically across his eyes like a man coming out of a trance. "You must forgive me if I say all the things wrong," he began on a lower note. "It almost sounds as though I did not any longer wish to be friends, isn't it. That is not true. But it upsets one to find that one has been—misled. You see, I am frank with you. That is not diplomacy." He stood a moment, watching her, and his eyes were puzzled and calculating. "There is that link between us, isn't it. You feel it. I know, because I feel it. Believe me, I am as unwilling as you that it exists. You do not deny."

She looked back at him steadily.

"But I cannot—encourage it."

"Cannot?"

"Will not."

"Did you hate him so much?"

"Hate is not the right word."

"What word, then?"

"I just—didn't love him. He would never let me. It is the same with you. There would be—glimpses of a man I could love. Nothing more. You are the same."

"How do you know that?"

"Because you are his son. Never mine. Because you say yourself the German in you always wins. Because you want it to win." There was a pause. "Don't you," she said, and it was not a question, and his answer was slow to come.

"Yes," he said.

She made a little gesture of helplessness and finality and turned away from him to the window above the lawn.

"I think you had better go now," she suggested quietly.

"You really wish me not to come here again." His tone was thoughtful, with an underlying incredulity.

"I see very little point in it. My husband finds it disturbing, and I—"

"Your—husband owes me a little something, I think," he said with the faintest stress on the word.

"Owes you—"

"It is only recently that he is your husband."

"Yes, but surely you aren't implying that you had anything to do with—" Her eyes widened. "Or are you?" And then, as he stood looking at her enigmatically—"Victor, how did he die?"

"He was found guilty of conspiracy against our Leader. There can be but one answer to that. More than once I warned him, which it was not in my duty to do. Finally I had to act on the too self-evident facts."

"You—betrayed him?" she said slowly. "Because of *you* —he was executed?"

"It was not an execution. He fired the shot himself. But for me, in the circumstances he would not have had the gun."

"You—"

"I gave him mine."

Her hands came up before her face. She stood motionless, turned away from him.

"It was a sentimental risk I felt obliged to take," he explained unemotionally. "I put it down to the English blood in me. No one else but you ever knows whose gun he used."

The clock on the mantel ticked.

"Please go now," she said, muffled.

"You perhaps do not appreciate—" He paused, gazing at her motionless figure. "It is a shock, no doubt," he conceded magnanimously. "But believe me, it was better that way than it might have been. He had privacy, which was what he asked for."

"I do not want to see you again," she said, behind her hands.

"But I thought you would be pleased that I— It was a risk," he repeated, and waited.

She did not move, and the clock ticked a full minute. Standing with her face hidden, she heard his footsteps cross the floor to the door, heard a car drive away.

7

Mab and Jeff were down by the stream which bordered the lawn at Farthingale, when Victor's car swept up the drive and braked sharply in front of the steps. By a mutual impulse they remained silent and made no effort to attract his attention while he jumped out and banged the car door and entered the house.

"Temper," said Mab then, in a half-whisper.

"Mm-hm," said Jeff with visible satisfaction. "Whatever it was, it didn't work."

"Now he'll tell Evadne all about it," said Mab, "and she'll take it to her groupleader. You'd think he'd get *sick* of them."

Jeff looked at her with interest and respect.

"Maybe you've got something there," he said.

"Not but what if there's something I want very much I don't hesitate to ask for it myself," said Mab ruefully. "Like going to Williamsburg."

"Oh, that," said Jeff easily. "That shall be given. I'll see to that myself."

"You're so *comforting*," said Mab impulsively, looking up at him with an almost tearful gratitude. "It's such a *satisfaction* to talk to you, Jeff, you make everything seem so simple, as though even miracles can happen."

"Well, how do we know they can't?" he asked unargumentatively. "Look at radio. You've known about it all your life. I'm not doddering yet, but if anyone had described an ordinary drawing-room radio set to my mother the year I was born it would have sounded to her like a miracle. *Anything* can happen, Mab. Don't you ever forget that. *Anything* can happen."

Anything? Mab thought. Even time for me to grow up? Dare I ask even God for that? Could Jeff *mean* that? He knows so much, does he know that too? Does he mean he'll wait for me to grow up? And Jeff, who had not meant anything of the kind, because of Sylvia, was wondering again at the ageless companionship and devotion between himself and the appealing little creature at his side—like a sister, was it, or a daughter, almost, or even a woman, if she had been older. . . . If she were Sylvia's age, he thought with astonishment, I would say I was falling in love. But that's fantastic. I'm in love with Sylvia. I always have been. Mab is a child. . . .

"There's Hermione," she remarked with a sigh, glancing across the lawn. "Oh, bother, she's seen us."

Hermione strolled towards them, carrying some long sprays of pale blue delphinium which she had just cut from the herbaceous border. She wore a pensive, faraway air, and doubtless hoped that the effect was decorative. But there was no doubt about her bearing down on them. Jeff, who because of the share-letter had contrived pretty well to avoid her since his arrival from Paris, resigned himself to being overtaken at last, and was thankful for Mab's presence at the encounter.

"Virginia said I might gather a few of these for Evadne's room," said Hermione as she came up to them. "The roses in her vases have faded. Aren't they a lovely color?"

"Very nice," Jeff conceded guardedly, and Mab thought, Showing off. Picking flowers for Evadne's room. Thinking Of Others. She's changed, and she wants us to know it. Anybody can pick flowers.

"Victor has come back, I see," Hermione went on, as nobody else contributed to the conversation. "I do hope it went well at Cleeve."

"We thought he looked a bit miffed," Mab suggested hopefully.

"What a pity. It meant so much to him that Rosalind should meet him halfway."

"I don't see why he cares," objected Mab. "He's grown up without her. He can get along now, I should think."

"We must try to sympathize with Victor and understand how he feels," Hermione reminded her patiently. "Evadne hopes that we can get him to go to our meetings."

"A *German?*" Mab grinned. "Getting *changed?* It wouldn't last!"

"Lots of Germans have been changed," Hermione insisted with dignity. "Changed individuals mean changed nations. That will bring peace to the whole world. You didn't answer my letter, Jeff."

"Well—er—no, I—"

"That wasn't very kind of you." She gave him a look which was almost arch, if he could believe his eyes.

"I'm sorry, I—just couldn't think of anything to say. That is—I'm perfectly willing to bury the hatchet if you are. But don't go round trying to convert me, because I'm hopeless." He thought as he spoke that he sounded ungracious and

tried again. "One doesn't have to join the Cause to behave decently, you know," he added, making things no better,
but instead of taking it up with him, Hermione gave her
small, tight smile.

"Of course not," she said sweetly. "But it's nice to know
we have made a step in the right direction and can help each
other from now on instead of wasting all that time and
energy hating each other."

"Oh, come, it wasn't as bad as that, was it?" he said uneasily. "We had some fights, maybe, but they didn't go as
far as hating. That's a big word."

"You know, Jeff, you're not half bad when you try." Again
the look, copied from Evadne's unconscious, fleeting co-
quetry, and badly done.

"Well, thanks, the same to you!" he replied, somewhat
flabbergasted, though Virginia had warned him that something had brought Hermione out.

"I'm glad we've had this talk," she went on with another
smile. "It always helps to get things straight, doesn't it. And
there's something I want you to back me up on. Did Evadne
speak to you about the flat?"

"She did, and I don't think it's at all a good idea."

"Well, really, Jeff, I might have known—" For a moment
the old enmity looked at him again from her eyes. "You're
always against anything I suggest," she said.

"Now, look, Hermione, it's got nothing to do with who
suggested it. As a matter of fact, I thought it was her own
idea. In any case the thought of you and Evadne running a
London flat with no one to look after you makes my hair
curl."

"We'd have a char to look after us, every morning. It's
all very new and modern, sitting-room, two bedrooms, a tiny
kitchen, and a tiled bath, all self-contained. The woman I'm
letting it from, she's an American, has a Mrs. Spindle, isn't
that a lovely name, who comes in and gets breakfast, clears

away, and cleans, and is gone by noon. If I let her know before Thursday, I can get her to stay on with us and—"

"It's not the char I mean."

"Very well, *be* difficult, we don't need your consent! If Evadne can't pay her share I can manage the whole thing myself, and she can stay there whenever she likes, just the same!"

"Have you told Oliver?"

"Not yet. But they won't mind getting rid of me for a while. It's only for six months, Miss Adams has to go back to New York till the first of next year, and I've practically promised to take the place off her hands."

"Where is this flat?"

"In Bayswater. Near Whiteley's."

"It would be."

"There's no need to take that tone. It will be very convenient."

"Well, if it's all settled, why did you bring it up?" The old animosity was at work between them again.

"Because I thought just possibly you might have the decency to put in a word for us with Virginia! I was wrong, of course!"

"What do you want me to say?"

"Simply tell her that you think Evadne is old enough to come and live with me in London."

"She's old enough, but you're bound to get into all kinds of trouble between the two of you, sharing a flat. This Victor business, for one thing. You can't have a Nazi always hanging about the place. Ask Camilla. *He's* not changed."

Hermione appeared to consider this.

"Do you think there's any chance of Evadne's falling in love with him?" she asked.

"God forbid!"

"Well, for once we agree. I don't think it's suitable," said Hermione. "I spent all my Quiet Time on it this morning, and it seems I've been Guided to take the flat because I can keep an eye on things better that way."

"Do you think you can do any better than Virginia can in Curzon Street?"

"Evadne and I are very close. We understand each other. I shall see much more of her than if I am living at home and she is in Curzon Street. Besides, when that lease is up she'll go back to Farthingale and we shall be quite out of touch."

"And you think you can fend Victor off?"

"I do, indeed," said Hermione with confidence.

"Well, maybe," said Jeff. "But I don't think much of it as a scheme, all the same."

"I'm perfectly certain her only interest in Victor so far is that she wants to change him," said Hermione. "He's good-looking, of course, and he's making a dead set at her. On the other hand, he can be very useful if we handle it right. And if we should go to Germany—"

"*No,*" said Jeff. "Not that. You'll go to Germany over my dead body."

"The Olympics start this winter," Hermione went on, unmoved. "At Garmisch-Partenkirchen. We thought that would be a good time to begin. And meanwhile we mean to brush up our German. Victor says he will help with that. But you can depend on it—" Her small white teeth showed. "—I shall keep him in his place. I don't intend to lose Evadne now to the first man who proposes to her."

"Mm-hm," said Jeff thoughtfully. "And of course Mark might have something to say to that too."

"Mark is no exception," said Hermione. "She doesn't want to marry Mark, and she isn't going to."

"Oh," said Jeff, and gave her a long, speculative look.

"I suppose you will do just as you like about putting in a word for us in the matter of the flat, but I would thank you not to interfere, at least. For some reason your opinion always seems to have a good deal of weight with the family. Shall we go in now, and hear what happened at Cleeve?"

They moved slowly towards the house, Mab lagging behind, feeling forgotten, her precious time with Jeff quite spoilt. She and Jeff had hardly begun to talk, when Hermione came up to them. Sylvia had sent some more books and pictures, and there was a map of the streets of Williamsburg, like a bird's-eye view, with trees and houses showing— the old houses and the ones the Rockefeller people had restored with loving care. Mab had half-hypnotized herself with it, poring over each separate legend and number, and she wanted to discuss with Jeff the strange, creepy feeling, which anyone else might laugh at, a feeling that she could *remember* things as though she had been there—that things had been left out of the map which might have been included, that she already knew inside herself like a memory how the Palace Green lay in the sun between two rows of trees with the wrought-iron gates beyond, and how a little lane, not drawn on the map, must have led away to the left of the Capitol Building to—what? Why did it seem that if you walked the length of the Duke of Gloucester Street to where it ended at the Capitol—did it end? Why did you want to go on? What lay *behind,* and to the left? A river—deep, tall trees—damp ground—a railing—steps going down to water—as though she had dreamed it. There was something *beyond.* And back of the Raleigh Tavern, rebuilt on its original site, the book said—was there a green lawn?—was it a garden?—what did you see if you went out the side door of the Tavern?—if you went where the map was blank. . . . She had perpetually a groping past the edges of the map. There was *more.* And the longing to go there and see it for herself was growing. She wanted it more than she had ever wanted anything in her life. Jeff understood about that, somehow. Jeff would always listen, and try to answer questions. Sometimes he asked her why she asked this or that, and she never knew. Sometimes he looked at her rather a long time before he spoke. Sometimes it was rather as though he was—sorry for her. Why? And now this chance to talk to him was gone, because of Hermione.

And Jeff, pacing beside Hermione with the blue delphiniums brushing his sleeve, was turning over a new worry in his mind. Wouldn't it be very bad for Evadne, overstrung and emotional already, to share a flat with anyone as moody and domineering and possessive as Hermione, however Changed Hermione was supposed to be? Virginia said there were lapses, as he himself had seen. He would have to speak to Virginia. But Evadne was twenty-one, and Hermione had her own money. There was no way to stop them. There was no way, either, to prevent them from going to Garmisch for the Winter Games. Of course, he could probably manage to turn up there himself and keep an eye on them. Hermione's hateful phrase. And it was not an inviting prospect, to chaperon two headstrong, girl cousins in Nazi Germany.

VI.

*JEFF IN LONDON TO SYLVIA
IN NEW YORK*

October, 1935

Dear Sylvie—
Tomorrow I am joining Bracken in Geneva, to learn about
sanctions in this Abyssinian war. So much for Stresa and all
the other pacts. Even now a little firmness and forcefulness
on our part might put on the brakes, might make them think
twice. But when Italy walked out of the League it left Aloisi's
empty chair beside the empty chair which was Germany's.
The line has been drawn, with Mussolini on the other side
of it. We expect to be back in London for the General Elec-
tion in November. It will be Baldwin, of course, MacDonald is through. Baldwin is a bit of a granny, but Eden may
stiffen him up.

So it is just a year ago that I was in Williamsburg, when
we got the news about Alexander and Barthou. Maybe you
think I have forgotten the rest of the things that happened in
Williamsburg during those few days I spent there. Well,
you're wrong. I suppose you will spend this Christmas
in New York, doubtless playing a matinee. Dear Sylvie, I
ramble on like this, saying futile, impersonal, cold-blooded
things on paper, but don't you believe a word of it. I can still
see you standing there in the doorway of Aunt Sue's parlor
—you laid fresh flowers across my hands and you said brides
were prettier than me—a very bitter truth—and you kissed

me. Your hands are cool and firm, and you are not easily dismayed. I would rather be with you this minute, wherever you are—let's see, it must be about the end of the first act—than in heaven. And if the time ever comes when I can find my way to you freely, without crossing an ocean or a continent, whenever I feel the way I do tonight, they can have heaven, I won't need it.

You ask about little Mab. They talk of sending her to a girls' school in Sussex, and she dreads it. I took my foot in my hand and spoke to her mother, who was polite and pretty impervious. She says all girls hate the idea of school and then like it once they get there, but I am unconvinced. Mab will go right on hating it, and Virginia agrees with me and is going to do what she can to keep Miss Sim on the job a little longer. A perfectly competent woman, I am told, for all her mousiness and that perpetual sniff. I'm always having to speak to somebody about something for somebody, I don't see why I always qualify for that kind of thing. What's more, I wasn't able to head Evadne off from that flat in Bayswater either. She and Hermione are firmly established there until January, when the Adams woman returns to London to reclaim it. After which they still intend to go to Germany for the Winter Games, wearing shining armor, no doubt, and riding white steeds 'midst snow and ice, under a banner with a strange device—*Excelsior!* (Longfellow.) And I shall probably find it my duty to go along and Speak to them some more. . . .

VII.

JEFF IN GARMISCH-PARTENKIRCHEN TO SYLVIA IN NEW YORK

February, 1936

Dear Sylvie—

Well, it's a great show, I'll say that for it. Snowy Alps— illuminations—rosy girls in becoming ski costumes—bob-sled races, very risky—Sonja Henie's skating, very beautiful—polite friendly Germans everywhere. The *Jews-Unwanted* signs have all been taken down in Garmisch to spare the feelings of the visitors. All the best accommodations have been reserved for the Nazi officials, and the Press has been relegated to particularly uncomfortable *pensions*. When Johnny commented on this, without exaggeration, he was bitterly denounced by the censorship. One highly intelligent American newspaper man has remarked on the interesting fact that there seems to be no Opposition to the present régime! The Opposition is at Dachau, which is a concentration camp not far away. No visitors at Dachau.

Victor was allowed—perhaps I should say assigned—to be present with our party, and has behaved remarkably well, considering, and of course does himself proud on skis, etc. Evadne is pretty enchanted with him, and has persuaded him to attend several of their meetings in London, though he hasn't Surrendered—yet. Of course the Cause will never get going here, as it recognizes a Power higher than Hitler's, which will never be a popular idea to entertain in Nazi Germany. The main danger is that its earnest and Absolutely Honest sponsors (mostly crusading English, like our Evadne) will be made use of, duped, and played up, merely to drag a red herring across the mounting evidence of Germany's plans for aggression. And if the members ever really did control England's policy, which they won't, but if they *did,* the whole country would sit there, starry-eyed and talkative, while the German army marched in. Moreover, if the Germans are allowed or encouraged to convince themselves (as they would like to) that all England thinks the same way, they are much more likely to try something than if they saw England re-arming as though it meant business.

We can't but hope that now with a young King on the English throne and a new Government we may see a general stiffening of policy—though, mind you, there were no flies on George V, whatever his ministers might have to answer for, and which is going to be quite a lot, if the present trend continues. Here I go again, at the wailing wall. But I have just heard—unofficially—that Ribbentrop will be the next German ambassador to London, and I'm feeling a little queasy.

The relatively simple family affairs can wait till you get to London now. We will have a long day together and talk them out endwise. Mab has escaped school for another year, anyway, and will go on as she is, with Miss Sim. I would hate to see her wearing a school tunic and hat-band and carrying a hockey-stick, somehow. Hermione's conversion to the Absolute This-and-Thats didn't really take, though her conversation is studded with its maddening idiom. She goes in for all the showy parts—doing elaborate favors for people and making sure they notice it, owning up handsomely to complicated peccadillos no one had thought twice about, etc. But the she-leopard has not changed her spots. She would still like to see me hanging from a lamp-post, especially as she knows I don't consider her any sort of good to Evadne.

What she calls keeping an eye on things is no more than the most cannibalistic interference with Evadne's life in every way.

As their lease on Miss Adams' flat was up in January, before they left England they arranged to take another, on the floor above, and have settled in there for an apparently indefinite period of time. The family disapproved, but Evadne got one of her obstinate streaks and passionately defended Hermione from a hostile world in all directions. She is the only person who has ever been able to stick Hermione at all, and that's mostly because she has this noble idea of loving everybody in spite of themselves and seeing good in everything and the result is that Hermione, who has done nothing to earn such fanatic devotion, has fastened on to it like a leech. It's all very well for her to act as dragon chaperon between Evadne and people like Victor—if there are any more like him—but if she keeps on she will prevent the poor girl from having any jolly little love affairs with ordinary harmless young men, or even any other female companionship. So far Evadne doesn't seem to mind, or to notice that Hermione's possessiveness puts people off. But the time will come, or ought to, when she will realize that she's missing something. Or else someone will have to tell her. *Not me.*

The minute you know your sailing date cable Bracken's office in London. I shall fly—probably quite literally—to meet you at Southampton. . . .

VIII.

SYLVIA IN NEW YORK TO
BRACKEN IN LONDON

February, 1936

ARRIVING SOUTHAMPTON AQUITANIA MARCH SEVENTH STOP
STEVIE SAYS PLEASE HAVE INTERPRETER MEET US ON DOCK
STOP MYSELF WOULD PREFER JEFF STOP LOVE

SYLVIA

IX.

London

1936

Not only Jeff, but Bracken himself motored down to South-ampton that grey March day. They went aboard with a pass and found Sylvia and Stephen hanging over the rail gazing sentimentally in entirely the wrong direction. Various other members of the company were also on board, and there was a great deal of excitement all round.

The main item of Sylvia's luggage proved to be an elegant gladstone bag with a zippered closing which contained not jewelry but a small chromium cage with a fitted flannel cover, housing the canary named Midge which had been pre-sented to her by an admirer on the night of the New York opening a year ago. Jeff and Bracken had of course heard about Midge, who was green with a yellow cap and tummy, but had not anticipated that he would accompany the show to London. Sylvia at once assured them that Midge went every-where and was an excellent traveller—the only thing was, he must never be in a draught. The gladstone bag also carried his toiletries and provisions, and his large chromium cage, where he lived when not travelling, had a specially made case of its own which accompanied Sylvia's other luggage wherever it went. He didn't sing loud, she explained, he was an alto Roller, very muted and sweet.

Bracken finally succeeded in detaching his cousins from

their talkative fellow voyagers, expedited them through the customs, and handed them into a big black Daimler, chauffeur-driven, which waited at the end of the dock.

"Golly!" said Sylvia, round-eyed and impressed. "Now I know how it feels to be Royalty! Where's the band?"

"Never satisfied," said Stephen. "Now she wants *God Save the Queen!*"

Jeff sat silent in the folding seat facing Sylvia in her corner. His inner happiness was the cosiest thing he had ever known, and required no expression at present beyond the privilege of gazing at her. When she looked back at him their eyes clung, and hers were always the first to turn away, and a little smile, secret and content, deepened the corners of her mouth—a generous mouth, perfectly made up, with curving lips, the lower one fuller than the upper one, like his mother's. Sylvia was his mother's niece, he recalled, tracing the resemblance anew. It made them first cousins. Another Better-not. But it was good to see her again, serene and cherished and confident, as all the Sprague women were, so different from poor Hermione with her awkward heritage of inferiorities and jealousies and resentments, or from dear, foolish Evadne, youngest of Virginia's vivid brood, still a baby when her father died in the war. Virginia had done all anyone could to bring her up intelligently, he was sure, but she was the child of upheaval and distress, always prone to dramatize, martyrize, and idolize, on the slightest provocation. Sylvia would be good for Evadne, Jeff was thinking. Much better than Hermione and the hectic atmosphere she seemed to engender wherever she went. If Evadne got a crush on Sylvia next, there might be some chance of pulling her together and making something of her. They must get her away from Hermione, that was the first thing. And from Victor, who was often at the flat, Jeff suspected. He decided to speak to Sylvia about Evadne at once. Here I go again, he thought ruefully. Always carrying the world on my shoulders.

But Virginia is treed and admits it. A new interest for Evadne is indicated. She could learn a lot from Sylvia. Maybe we could get her stage-struck, that would be a positive rest from what has been going on. And then, of course, there's Mab, dying to know Sylvia too. Mab's parents are so fascinated at having finally achieved a son, they've almost forgotten her, I'm afraid. That Miss Sim can't be very cheerful company for a child like Mab, for all her worthiness. We must get Mab out more, take her to shows, take her for rides in the car, picnics, and so on—Sylvie will be good at that—it's awkward Mab's people living out at Sunningdale, involves such a lot of travel—perhaps they would ask Sylvia for a week-end at least, after the show settles down—but Virginia says they're very self-absorbed, Irene and Ian—still in love with each other, that sort of thing—want to send Mab to school to get her out of the way, I shouldn't wonder. . . .

On the drive up to town Jeff and Bracken heard all about the new show. A fully rehearsed cast of principals had been brought over, to join a fully rehearsed chorus and a couple of new specialties. The theater was ready, the scenery was built, they could whip into shape and open within a week or two. Bracken said that if nothing Went Wrong he would give them a first-night party. "Oh, Bracken, with *wine?*" cried Sylvia, and Bracken said Certainly wine, what kind of party did she think he meant. "But I'm afraid you will have to do without your tea now or we won't get to Town in time for dinner," he added. "Some of the family are coming tonight—those that are in London."

He had got them rooms adjoining the suite that he and Dinah and Jeff occupied at the Savoy, which as their theater was in the Strand would be handy, especially for late meals, a family weakness. If the show looked like running, he said, and nothing Went Wrong, they might look round for a flat or a small house in London to share during the coming summer.

"That's the second time you've said that," said Stephen. "What is likely to go wrong?"

"Hitler has re-occupied the Rhineland today," said Bracken, and added into a rather blank silence, "His troops are marching into Cologne, and Mainz, and Düsseldorf this very minute."

Sylvia sighed.

"I wish I wasn't so ignorant," she said. "I thought they were German towns."

"The area along the Rhine was demilitarized by the Treaty of Versailles," Bracken told her patiently. "The arrangement was confirmed at Locarno in '25. We moved our troops out a few years ago, sooner than we were required by the treaty to do so—in the interests of good will. So now the German army has moved in. If France gets the wind up they may start shooting."

"What about England?"

"If the British Government has any sense at all, they will back up France. In fact, they will egg her on."

"But that would mean—"

"War. Better a little war now than a big one later. *I* think Hitler would back down. Anyway, I'm flying to Paris tomorrow to see what Johnny knows."

"Jeff too?" asked Sylvia in a small voice.

"I suppose you want me to leave Jeff here," said Bracken with a grin. "All right—he'll stay with Dinah. And I'll try to get back for the first night if I can."

"Thank you," said Sylvia, and squeezed his arm.

Virginia had come up to Town especially to be on hand for their arrival, so she and Dinah were the first to greet them. Stephen saw his luggage into his room, heard Sylvia say there was just time for a bath before dinner, and then vanished. Later, when everyone had changed for dinner and gathered in Bracken's sitting-room for refreshments, Stephen was still missing. Sylvia was not surprised.

"He's gone round to look at the theater," she explained. "He always does that the first thing, in every new town. You never saw such a stage-struck boy."

She was quite right, of course. Having inspected the theater and the advance billing at the front of it from every angle, Stephen loitered back along the Strand, bought an evening paper, and digested the front-page news thoughtfully as he walked—GERMAN TROOPS ENTER RHINELAND—*Hurried Talks in Paris Follow Breaking of Treaties*—and re-entered the Savoy five minutes before the hour Bracken had set for dinner.

He approached the lifts with his leisurely amble, and as there was none waiting he pressed the bell and stepped back, consulting his paper again: *Hitler today smashed the Locarno and Versailles treaties by sending troops into the demilitarized zone. . . . In Berlin Hitler handed to the Ambassadors of Britain, France, Italy and Belgium, the guarantor Powers, a note which said: "The Government declare themselves liberated from the obligations imposed upon them. . . ."*

There was a flurry of footsteps on his left, a waft of fresh perfume, and a very pretty girl in evening dress and something of a hurry pressed the lift bell and stood, the picture of impatience, watching the indicator as the car descended. Stephen surveyed her with interest and amusement. It was such an idiotic thing to do, pressing the bell, as though he would be standing there waiting for the lift, without having rung the bell himself. Women, God bless 'em. She was the prettiest girl he had seen in a long, long time. Carried herself. Knew where she was going. By the time the lift arrived he was sure she was the prettiest girl he would ever see in this life, and that it was essential to his peace of mind to know her name, to see her smile, to hear her speak—

The lift opened, with a clang of doors.

"Fourth floor, please," said the girl, as she preceded Stephen into it.

It was Stephen's floor too, so he said nothing. As the lift car rose she felt his eyes upon her and gave him a direct, cool look, and looked away. 'Scuse me for staring, Stephen thought. Well, I *was*, darnit, but this is special. This only happens once in a lifetime. . . .

The car stopped at the fourth floor and the girl stepped out and turned to the right. Stephen followed and turned to the right, where Bracken's rooms were. The girl stopped before one of the doors and raised her hand to knock.

"Allow me," said Stephen, and laid hold of the knob, trusting that the door would open before him, which it did —it was the door to Bracken's sitting-room. The girl stood staring up at him, uncertain, a little suspicious, making no move to enter. "I'm Stephen. Which one of my cousins are you?" he grinned.

And then he did see her smile. It poured over him like sunshine, her eyes dazzled, her teeth shone, she radiated warmth and friendliness and delight. It left him more or less reeling against the door-post. From that moment Stephen was hopelessly, heedlessly, helplessly in love.

"I'm Evadne," she said. "Welcome to London, Stephen."

"Thank you," he said, and kissed her parted, upturned lips. "London is wonderful," he said.

2

Gradually the universe steadied under him and his presence of mind returned. Bracken gave him a cup of tea, and he heard Evadne saying that Hermione had got a perfectly beastly cold and daren't come out tonight.

"That's a piece of luck," said Jeff, and Evadne cried, "Jeff, how *can* you!" and explained that she would not have left Hermione, who really felt wretched, if Hermione had not urged her to come and find out what Bracken really thought about the news from the Rhineland.

About this time Sylvia suggested to Stephen that he go and put on a dinner jacket like Bracken, and Stephen agreed that it would be a very good idea, and drifted away to his own room, carrying his second cup with him. During his actor's quick change, things really began to come home to him. Evadne was the Problem Child, the pretty nitwit Jeff was always wanting to spank, the one who encouraged the Nazi attaché—Evadne was the girl who wrote those letters, the girl who referred to God on the most intimate terms. There must be some mistake. Not on his part, not on Evadne's, of course. Everybody must be all wrong about her. He would prove that they were wrong, Evadne was the girl he was going to marry.

He sat a moment, holding one slim polished shoe, while it sank in. Marry. It was not a word to use lightly. It was not a word he had ever had occasion to use before. But yes, he meant to marry Evadne, or go maimed and empty all his days. It was like lightning striking. No argument. Not from him, anyway. But from Evadne? He tried hastily to recall the references to her in Jeff's letters to Sylvia—she always read him the bits about family matters and politics aloud.

There had been quite a lot about Evadne, one way and another, he felt, but he hadn't paid attention because he had had no inkling that it would ever matter. He retained an impression, however, that she was always in hot water, and that made him grin, as he briskly tied the shoe. All right, so he'd get her out of it. A pleasure. Anything she wanted from now on, there he was, ready, willing, and able. Anything, that is, that God overlooked, he, Stephen, was prepared to tackle. As for the Nazi, trot him out, let's have a look at him. Could he do this? (The slim, polished shoes tapped a rude tattoo on a bit of bare floor between two rugs.) Or this? (He tossed a shiny collar-button into the air and caught it behind him with the other hand in a flourish.) Olympics, eh. Muscle stuff. Beefy, no doubt. But was he fast? (The fresh black tie jerked neatly into a perfect bow.) Well, here's the new show against the Olympics, Fritzie boy. Nothing quite like a first night, after all. A successful first night. And Pop doesn't write failures, he never learned how. Just give me till the end of the first act, fella, and then watch your skis, you're on a down-hill run with a tree in the way. . . .

Moving with that ambling gait of his which was less a walk than a slouch on springs in time to a rhythmic beat which only Stephen heard, he returned cheerfully to the room where the family had assembled. And Evadne, watch-ing his easy, effortless entrance into a roomful of people who, even if they were family, were mostly strangers to him, and noting the way his eyes found her at once among the others, thought how unlike an actor he was, except for something electric in his mere presence, and how plain he was, long-jawed and bony, until he smiled, and reminded herself that theater people kissed everybody, and after all they were re-lated. . . .

He was coming towards her, alight with his spreading grin.

"Dinah is a honey," he said. "She's given me you at dinner, and it's just what I wanted."

"Well—that's nice, isn't it," said Evadne, who was not ac-customed to quite so direct an approach.

"And what's more—it's down stairs where there's danc-ing."

"I'm afraid I'm not very good at dancing, I—"

"Well, believe it or not, I am," said Stephen modestly. "I gotta be! You'll pick it up from me in no time."

"Well—I—"

"Let's go," said Stephen, and linked his arm in hers and marched her off to the lifts after the others.

Dinah was saying that she thought in view of the day's news they needed to be gay, and that dinner down stairs would discourage brooding. A lot of other people apparently had the same idea, and the Savoy was full of well-dressed, well-bred British, who are inclined, as Kipling pointed out, to take their pleasures as Saint Lawrence took his grid.

As soon as a decent amount of soup had been consumed, Stephen turned to Evadne and said, "Come on," and rose.

"I—don't—" she faltered, rising too, and he kept her hand in his till they reached the edge of the floor, where he drew her into his arms and became the music. A little breathless, a little unyielding, she followed desperately.

"Let yourself go," he murmured, and his cheek brushed her hair. *"Dance!"* His right arm tightened, and they performed a spirited pirouette. "See?" said Stephen. "It's fun. Try this one."

She lost the step, fumbled with her feet, and gasped with embarrassment, looking up at him apologetically.

"I'm s-so sorry—I warned you—"

"My fault," he grinned, and his eyes ran over the sedate, rather formal couples which surrounded them on the floor. "It's a serious business here, I see—dancing."

"They're not—professionals," she got out, and missed another step.

"Was that a crack?" he demanded in complete good humor. "No, I can see it wasn't. Just a fact."

"P-please slow up a little," she begged unhappily.

"I can't slow up, it's *their* darn tempo, not mine," he said. "Unless you want to go all off-beat like the Duke of Suburbia over there." And he suddenly became a tall, blank-faced young man with teeth, moving majestically in superb disregard of the band, with his partner held stiffly at arm's length as though she were dripping wet. Evadne laughed, and their feet got into a hopeless tangle. He drew her back again and resumed his own step, which she was learning to like. "That's better," he said before long. "You're in America now. Relax."

Evadne had never been held so closely in a dance before— she felt his breath on her cheek as they turned a corner, felt the perfect rhythm of his movement, was conscious of his stiff white shirtfront and the spiky collar above it, and the hard masculine authority of the arm which encircled her waist in his strong, clever lead. His left hand, which held her right, was neither hot nor clammy, neither awkwardly respectful nor flirtatious. It was just a warm, kind hand which one could cling to, and she did. For all his intensely personal attitude and open admiration, there was nothing tiresome about the way he held her. He did not encroach or presume. He was dancing. Before long Evadne was dancing too, with an ease and abandon she had never experienced before, so that they moved together as one person.

Then the music stopped and he said, "You catch on, don't you. I suppose we must go back to the table now and then."

"Well, how is she?" Sylvia asked him with family frankness when they sat down, and he answered simply, "A bit British at first, but I broke her down."

Evadne blushed and glanced uncertainly round the table as they laughed, and Stephen thought compassionately, "The girl is shy—all tied up in knots. Who's to blame for this?" And as he had never seen Virginia till tonight, for she had left Williamsburg before he was born, he assumed that it must be her fault that Evadne was a mass of tensions, which was unjust.

They danced together again, just before the sweet was brought, and this time she came more willingly, and was pliant and easy in his arms.

"Things are going to be pretty hectic with me till after the opening," he said as they danced. "But I don't want to lose any time. How about your coming to the theater tomorrow about twelve-thirty so we could have lunch together? I'll take an hour."

"Oh, no, not tomorrow, I'm afraid—on account of Hermione." And though she refused unwillingly, she had still no idea of the magnitude of his offer—the star of a new show, who took his work very seriously, allowing an hour for lunch with a girl, on the first day of rehearsals for a London opening barely a fortnight away.

"Isn't there anyone else to look after her?" he suggested.

"There's Mrs. Spindle from nine to twelve—but Hermione doesn't like her, so I'll have to do the tray and take it in. Mrs. Spindle would be sure to muff it somehow."

"You mean Hermione is right down sick in bed with this thing?"

"Oh, yes, we had a doctor. She's miserable, running a temperature and all. You don't get over it in a day."

"Look out you don't catch it yourself."

"Oh, I'm strong as a horse," Evadne said, and he noted again her fragile throat and narrow waist and the lean, high cheek-bones with a long, sweet curve to the jaw.

"What's the matter with Mrs. Spindle?" he asked patiently.

"Matter with her? Nothing."

"That Hermione doesn't like her, I mean."

"Oh, well, that—I don't know, she talks a lot, bless her, and Hermione says she pries. I get along with her all right, but Hermione says I'm just naturally gregarious."

"Good for you," said Stephen. "Who *is* Hermione? I'm all at sea here, you know, among the cousins. Sylvia used to read me bits of Jeff's letters, but I never got the family sorted out from that."

"I suppose we do seem rather a lot of people to you. Hermione is the girl I live with when I'm not at Farthingale with Mummy. We have a flat in Bayswater."

"Yes, but how am I related to Hermione, for instance?" he asked and Evadne hesitated conscientiously.

"I don't think you are at all, really. She's a Campion, like me, our fathers were brothers. But she is Oliver's daughter by his first wife, so of course she isn't related to Jeff."

"Well, that clears that up. The next thing I want to know—"

But the dance ended then, and they returned to the table. He got her address and telephone number written down on a bit torn off the menu before the party broke up. He insisted on seeing her home in a taxi and made her promise to show him London after the opening night was off his mind. She hedged about this until finally he said, "What's the matter, are you spoken for?"

"S-spoken for?" she repeated with that slight near-stammer of apologetic confusion which seemed to overtake her frequently and which he found entirely charming and a little pathetic—as though she anticipated some sort of reprimand for stupidity.

Stephen reached for her left hand in the dark of the taxi and deliberately felt the naked third finger, as he said, "Not engaged, are you?"

"Oh, *no*—no, of course not!" Her denial was hasty and shocked.

"Well, then, why all this quibbling about a few friendly dates?"

"It's only that I—you see, when I go out like that it leaves Hermione alone in the flat, and—"

"Hasn't she got any boy friends of her own?"

"N-no, you see Hermione doesn't—doesn't have many friends and so—"

"Why not?" said Stephen, reasonably enough.

"Well, it's hard to say, really, she—not everyone understands her—"

"And you do?"

"Oh, yes! Hermione and I are very close."

"Mm-hm," said Stephen, without approval. "But surely you can make her see that being a stranger here myself—"

"Perhaps you would like to come to tea at the flat—some day after she gets over this cold," Evadne interrupted nervously.

"Is that permitted?"

"Yes, of course—we often have a few people in to tea, not *big* parties, you know, Hermione doesn't like them."

"Who pours?" asked Stephen.

"Hermione. Why?"

"I just asked," he said.

"I make very nice cucumber sandwiches, everyone says—it's a speciality at our teas. And there's a little shop nearby that sells oatmeal cakes. Hermione hates fussing about in a kitchen, but I rather enjoy it. We leave the dishes for Mrs. Spindle in the morning. We live very simply," she added on that recurrent note of apology.

"Do you like it?"

"Do I—?"

"Like living simply with Hermione."

"Yes, of course! Mummy didn't think it was a good idea at first, but I talked her into it, just to try, so she lets me pay my share, though Hermione says that wasn't necessary. She has her own money and can do as she likes."

"Mm-hm," said Stephen, without satisfaction.

"Why do you sound like that? Have they been talking to you about Hermione?" she demanded suspiciously.

"Who?"

"The family."

"Not had much chance, have they?"

"Jeff, then. Did Jeff write horrid things about her in his letters?"

"I told you I don't remember much about Jeff's letters. I didn't pay attention to them. I'm beginning to wish now that

I had. Why would he write horrid things about Hermione?"

"Because they have never got along. Her father married Jeff's mother, and Hermione always felt that it wasn't right of him, after her own mother died during the war."

"Lots of people have married again since the war," Stephen pointed out sensibly. "It's the only thing to do, to mend their lives and go on, if they can."

"Yes, b-but you see—Oliver and Phoebe were in love, apparently, *before* Aunt Maia died."

"Well, so what? Did they murder her?"

"Oh, *no*, it was during an air raid, she—"

"So what?" repeated Stephen inflexibly.

"Y-yes, I see what you mean in a way," said Evadne faintly. "But all the same, I can see how Hermione feels too."

"I can't. It's none of her business if her father chooses to marry again. He's old enough to run his own life, I should think, without her opinions."

"Yes, I know," Evadne conceded meekly. "But Hermione is very sensitive. And she adored her mother."

"Mm-hm," said Stephen, without sympathy. "Must make it nice for Phoebe!"

"Well, between you and me, I think that was one reason Oliver let Hermione take the flat. Because of Phoebe. Hermione was rather hurt about that. She said they were only too glad to be rid of her."

"I shouldn't wonder," said Stephen unfeelingly. "But what about you?"

"Oh, I enjoy being with Hermione," she assured him. "She's all right once you get to know her. Most people don't bother to try."

"People who enjoy being hard to know usually aren't worth the trouble," Stephen said sagely.

"I don't think Hermione does enjoy it, it's only that she's very reserved and perhaps expects too much of people. Actually I'm sorry for her. There, I don't say that to everybody!" she added impulsively as the cab stopped before a big block of flats in the Queen's Road. "I daren't ask you to come in, she's probably got to sleep by now." Evadne held out her hand and lifted her face to him with her radiant, all-over smile revealed by a nearby street lamp. "Good night, Stephen, thank you for seeing me home. We'll meet again soon, I hope."

"We certainly will," he agreed, and planted another kiss on her lips.

As Evadne went up in the automatic lift she discovered with a genuinely sinking feeling that she had not learned much after all about what Bracken thought of the situation in the Rhineland, and she began hastily to arrange an account of the evening to give to Hermione. Stephen returned thoughtfully to the Savoy in the taxi, and realized that he had not heard one word from Evadne about God. And Sylvia, putting out her light at the hotel, was reflecting that she had never seen Stephen less preoccupied and jumpy about an opening night.

3

At a quarter past twelve the following day the doorbell of the flat in Bayswater rang. Evadne, who was preparing Hermione's luncheon tray in the kitchen, said, "Oh, hang it all!" and dried her hands and went to see what it was. Then she said, "Oh—hullo," and stood there rather blankly, holding the door.

Stephen stood outside on the threshold, his arms piled high with parcels.

"Mind if I come in?" he suggested after a suitable interval. "Some of this is heavy."

"Oh—yes—do come in." Evadne faded back before him

and he passed her down the narrow passage and into the living-room, where he paused and turned towards her again as she followed him in a stunned silence.

"If you will sort of unload me from the top—" he said, and she began still without a word to lay the parcels he was stacked with on the table. "I don't want you to think I have rushed all over town and collected this stuff myself," he said. "That would be giving a false impression. I am putting on a show, but I have a most efficient secretary, and there is a place called Fortnum and Mason's. They did it all."

"Oh, Stephen, that's so expensive," she murmured. "And what a lot of things— Oh, Stephen, it's a whole meal!"

"That was the general idea. You wouldn't lunch with me, so I have brought lunch to you. There are three of everything," he added gravely, as she sent an involuntary anxious glance towards what he surmised was the door of Hermione's bedroom. "All you have to do is dish it up," he said. "They advised that you warm the meat pies in the oven and put the custards in the fridge until wanted."

"Yes—I will—" said Evadne, and stood staring down at the neatly wrapped parcels on the table as though she didn't know where to begin.

"I thought perhaps I might be allowed to present the flowers to the invalid in person," he remarked, and lifted the large paper cone. "Nothing like roses for the morale, the book says. Would she mind if I just looked in to say hullo?"

"Well—I'll ask her." Evadne backed away from the table, still looking spellbound, and departed for the bedroom.

Stephen waited, glancing about the impersonal furnished flat with some curiosity. No photographs, no sewing, no games, no—feminine clutter. What did they do here, in the evenings? How did they amuse themselves? A radio. Books, a few. He couldn't see the titles without snooping, but they were obviously sober books, on a high plane of thought. Stephen, whose own rooms were strewn with all kinds of books from detective stories to the toughest reading there was, with solitaire cards and jigsaw puzzles and chessmen and sheet music and an open piano and gramophone records and fan mail and press cuttings and ringing telephones and stacks of portrait proofs and stills, in the midst of which he existed tidily and happily and always knew where everything was, could not imagine life in surroundings so bleak and bare and uninteresting. They had lived here—how long?—and left no imprint. He wondered about Evadne's room at home, at Farthingale, the room she had grown up in and occupied outside of Hermione's influence. Surely that would be more human? Surely she had accumulated *something?* This place was as austerely functional as a nun's cell.

He could hear a murmur of voices across the passage, during the delay. Hermione would be powdering her nose, he thought. Then Evadne returned.

"She was just sitting up to have some lunch," she said. "She only wanted a cup of broth and some biscuits, but I've persuaded her to eat a bit of what you've brought. You may come as far as the door, but I shan't allow you to go in for fear you'll catch a germ before the opening."

"I'd chance that," said Stephen, who always avoided people with colds like the plague, and gargled after every contact with a crowd for days before a first night.

"No, you must keep at a distance, the doctor says it's the infectious kind. You can look in from the doorway and I'll take the flowers to her."

She led the way across the passage and he paused at the threshold of the bedroom and said, with his grin, "How do you do? We missed you last night."

"From what I hear you all got on very well without me," said Hermione, and there was somehow an implication in the words, as though already she had sensed the tremendous new thing that had happened to him and Evadne as they danced, and would have prevented it if she had been there.

"Oh, well, the more the merrier," he said lamely, thinking, *Cat.* I knew she would be a cat. This Won't Do. She even looked rather like a cat, he thought, with strange light grey eyes set at a slant, a small neat nose, and a tight mouth. Stephen's very adequate knowledge of the female cosmos warned him that she was not, probably, looking her best.

"Darling, see what he's brought you," said Evadne at the bedside, and laid the big white cone on the coverlet.

"Thank you so much," said Hermione perfunctorily, and opened back the paper to reveal large pink tea roses of a truly royal extravagance. "They *are* lovely. We have nothing fit to put them in, I'm afraid."

But Evadne caught the cool, heavy blooms between her two hands and laid her face against them for a moment before she said, "There's the silver pitcher. I'll fetch that."

"Not deep enough," said Hermione.

"We'll try it." Evadne passed Stephen in the doorway. "It's in the kitchen. I'll fill it there."

There was a pause, while Hermione said nothing to make him welcome.

"You must get better before our opening night," he said. "It's going to be quite a Thing."

"Yes, all the family have got to be there, dead or alive," she answered with a smile which showed her small white teeth. (A cat's smile he thought.) "Bracken seems to have bought out the house, and everyone has got a new dress to wear."

Evadne came back with the silver pitcher full of water, heavy in her hands. She set it down on the glass top of the dressing-table and began to stand the roses in it, one by one.

"You must cut the ends off the stems," said Hermione, watching from the bed.

"Oh—yes, of course—" Evadne snatched up a pair of scissors from the dressing-table.

"No," said Hermione. "You must use a sharp knife, and make a slanting cut."

"Wouldn't it be all right if I did that later? You see, Stephen's brought all those things for lunch and it will take quite a while to get them undone, and he has only an hour till he must be back at the theater."

"You can't mistreat lovely flowers like those," said Hermione from her pillows. "Get a knife and do it properly."

"Yes, darling," said Evadne, and again she passed Stephen in the doorway on her way to the kitchen.

He leaned up against the door-post and there was a silence, till she returned with the knife. Rather clumsily, with hurried, reckless hands, while Hermione watched from the bed and Stephen waited in the doorway, she began to slice the end off each stem before putting it into the pitcher. The mouth of the pitcher was too wide, and the roses slid about in it and went into slanting bunches instead of spraying out at appropriate distances from each other.

"It needs one of those things with holes in it at the bottom of the pitcher, to hold them up straight," Evadne said at last, and Stephen wondered if her hands were really shaking or if he only thought so, and she wondered if he noticed, and hated him for looking.

"Really, darling, you're hopeless with flowers," said Hermione kindly from the bed, and there was a dagger in her voice.

"Yes, I know I am, I— Mummy always does them at home, I—" Evadne scooped at them desperately and they went into a bundle and stayed there.

"I'll have to do them myself, later," said Hermione, noticeably patient. "Never mind. I'll get up and do them presently." She rested her head back against the pillow and closed her eyes, forebearing and ill. "You mustn't keep Stephen waiting for his lunch."

"He's brought dear little meat pies," said Evadne, too lightly. "I'll put them in the oven to warm."

"Not for me, *please*," said Hermione delicately. "You *were* going to give me some broth, weren't you?"

"Well, yes, but—"

"After you and Stephen have your own lunch," said Hermione. "There's no hurry. I'm not hungry."

Again Evadne passed him in the doorway, this time with her head held down because her eyes were full of tears. Stephen followed slowly, thinking hard. He knew now what he had come to find out, and it was worse than he thought.

"I'm afraid I've made you a lot of trouble," he said, stepping back out of the way as she carried some of the parcels across the passage to the kitchen.

"It's all right," she said, not looking at him. "You bring the rest out here, will you, and we'll put it on the plates."

"I didn't mean to cause extra trouble, like this," he insisted, arriving in the kitchen with the custards in their white fluted dishes. "I thought it would be fun, I mean—"

"I'm sorry," she muttered, her head still down, above the pies.

"Would it do any good if I went now?"

"No. Please don't. It's only because she doesn't feel well."

"Because if it would be any easier for you, I—"

She made no answer, putting the meat pies into the oven and lighting the fire. As she straightened he caught her by one shoulder, faced her towards him, and cupped her chin in a quick warm hand. Forced to look up at him, she stood quietly in his hold while her eyes spilled over with tears and her mouth trembled uncontrollably.

"Here," he said gently. "Here, now, it's not as bad as that." He took the clean handkerchief from his breast pocket and dabbed at the tears on her face.

"I'm *so* sorry she was like this today," she said unsteadily.

"She's all on edge because of the fever. I shouldn't have let you go in at all, but she *said* it was all right—"

"Now, look, honey, stop it, my feelings aren't hurt a bit."

"But the very first time you come here, and after you took all this trouble—"

"That doesn't worry me, it's the way she treats you I don't like."

"Oh, I don't mind, it's only—" The tears brimmed up again. "I've had three days of this, and I do *everything* wrong, and have to do it over again—"

"You poor kid." He took her into his arms and she hid her face against his shoulder and shook with suppressed sobbing while he held her close, his cheek pressed against her hair. "It's no fun nursing a job like that, you don't have to tell me," he said.

She straightened, gasping, and took the handkerchief from him and wiped her eyes, returned his property, and lighted the fire under a pan of broth on the stove.

"Please don't say anything about this to anyone," she said, very low. "They're all down on her anyway. I'll just take the broth in to her first, and then we'll have our lunch in the living-room. I don't want to make you late."

"Oh, that's all right, I'm the bride, you know," he said comfortably. "They have to wait for me."

They stood silently watching the broth come to a simmer, their shoulders touching. She poured it into a bowl and took it on a dainty tray to the bedroom.

"Watch the pies," she said over her shoulder as she went.

A minute later she came back with the tray untouched, and set it down on the end of the sink.

"She says she's sleepy now and doesn't want it," she reported without expression. "I'll have to heat it up again later. We'll put our things on trays and you can tell me all about the show while we eat. What did you do this morning?"

He filled the next few minutes with entertaining chat, until they were seated at the living-room table with their food.

"I'm afraid I can't offer you a glass of sherry or anything like that," she said anxiously then. "There's no liquor in the house. It's Guidance."

"What? Oh—I see—"

"Hermione never did take anything to drink, she doesn't care for it. I used to like wine now and then, but it Came To Me that I didn't need it at all, it was only an indulgence."

"Is that bad?" asked Stephen, interested.

"We don't believe in pampering oneself," she said solemnly. "And our friends all feel the same way, so we do without it. I'm sorry if you're accustomed to have it—"

"I'm not a drunkard myself, you know. As a matter of fact, I never take a drink during the day when I'm working. That's not Guidance, though, it's just common sense."

"Well, it's the same thing, isn't it, really," she remarked pleasantly. "Stephen, this is a perfectly delicious lunch, and I do thank you for being so thoughtful and trying to help."

"I meant to cheer things up a bit, but I'm afraid I rather put my foot in it instead. Will she be down on me now for the rest of my life?"

"I hope not. You must try again when she's well."

"Why must I?"

"That's the way Jeff talks. It's not fair, really it isn't."

As her eyes threatened to fill up again he changed the subject hastily.

"I still haven't figured out exactly how you and I are related to each other," he observed.

"Well, let's see—your father is my mother's—wait, now, they did explain it to me." Evadne shut her eyes tight for concentration, and said as though reading it off the resulting blackness, "Your father's father and my mother's mother were double first cousins."

"*Well!*" said Stephen in exaggerated surprise. "Does that mean all our children will be idiots?"

For a moment he faced the dreadful possibility that his future wife might be backward in her sense of humor. It could not affect the way he felt about her if she was, as he was past praying for on that, but it might complicate or retard her progress towards feeling the same way about him. For a moment only, Evadne regarded him with large puzzled eyes, taken utterly by surprise. Then the corners of her mouth deepened, and her face turned rosy under his gaze, as she tipped back her head and laughed—and laughed. More than the joke was really worth, more than anyone accustomed to his brand of absurdity would have accorded it, as though from mere relief that there was a joke to laugh at. It occurred to him that Evadne had not encountered enough foolishness in her life, and he wondered what the family could have been thinking of. Meanwhile he sat grinning happily across the table at the modern miracle of a girl who could *blush.*

"You *are* a fool, Stephen," she said then, and it was praise.

During the pause before they began on the custard, the telephone rang, and he noted as Evadne answered it that it was so situated that Hermione in her bedroom and himself in the living-room *had* to hear every word she said. And it was evident at once that this was embarrassing to her. She spoke briefly, non-committally, a few times, and then said on a rising note of defensiveness, "But I *can't*, Victor, not possibly, I . . . No, she's still in bed. . . . But we had a doctor yesterday, and he said she mustn't get up till the temperature came down. . . . Ninety-nine point four. . . ."

Hermione's voice came distinctly from the bedroom.

"Don't *dare* to let him come here," it said.

"No, not today, Victor, really," said Evadne, with a badgered glance over her shoulder. "No, it's better not, the doctor said it was the infectious kind. . . . Oh, nonsense, I'm strong as a horse, I never get colds. . . . Yes, I know. . . . Yes, I will. . . ." This time the badgered glance was for

Stephen, unavoidably listening from his chair at the living-room table. "No, Victor, I won't . . . Yes, I *know*, but—" Again the defensive note, and at the same time apology and confusion. (As though the fellow had some *right*, thought Stephen, looking out the window, pretending not to hear.) "Yes, Victor. . . . Well, not for a few days, I . . . Yes, Victor. . . . Yes, as soon as I can. . . . Yes, please do. Good-bye."

"What did he want?" said Hermione's voice from the bedroom, peevishly.

"He just rang up to ask how you were."

"It didn't take as long as that to tell him," said Hermione, and Stephen thought, Cat.

"Well, he wanted to bring you some fruit or flowers or something, but I put him off, I didn't think you felt up to it. Would you like your broth now?" She rose and started towards the bedroom.

"There's no hurry, is there? Are you going out?"

"No, of course not."

Their voices dropped. There was some kind of discussion. Stephen rose uneasily, and was still on his feet, his hat in his hand, when Evadne appeared again in the living-room doorway.

"I'd better go now," he said. "You've got your hands full today."

"But you haven't had any of that beautiful custard—" She was drooping and distressed.

"You eat it," he said. "All of it. Do you good." He walked across the room and put an arm round her shoulders, hugging her up to him, laying his lips against her temple where the brilliant hair was brushed back in a shining wave. "They're waiting for me at the theater," he said. "If they weren't, I'd stay and help you do the dishes. Next time I will."

"I didn't know if you'd ever come again," she said forlornly, with a glance at the half-eaten meal on the table.

"Look," said Stephen. "I'm here for keeps, see? No ifs, buts, or ands." Again he set his hand under her chin and turned her face up to his. "Now, get this," he said just above a whisper, serious for once in his life. "It's too soon, but I want you to have it all the same, and don't think I won't bring it up again. From now on, it's you and me, *together*, and the heck with 'em all." He kissed her, gently but not lightly, and this time felt a tremor of response before he let her go. "See what I mean?" he said, and left her standing speechless and incredulous in the middle of the room, and found his own way to the door without a word to Hermione as he went.

4

For Jeff and Sylvia, reunion meant mostly that he sat patiently in the darkened theater watching her at work on the stage, waiting for the intervals in her performance when she could slip through the pass door and sit down beside him. They spoke very little then, but sometimes she would slide a slim, clammy paw into his hand. They ate hurried lunches together, either in her dressing-room or at the nearest quick restaurant, and by dinner time she was limp with nerves and fatigue and had to go to bed early to be ready for another day of the same. All the while Jeff marvelled at her stamina and good temper and matter-of-fact acceptance of the organized hullaballoo which precedes even the best-managed first night. "*I* wouldn't do it," he said more than once, in mixed admiration and pity. "Not for all the tea in China. I wouldn't earn my living in the theater, not if I had to sell papers on a street corner!"

"Stevie loves it," Sylvia replied philosophically. "He drops ten pounds before every opening and picks it up again during the first month of the run. He *thrives* on it. You can't let him down."

"Who can't?" said Jeff.

"Well, *I* can't, for one. I'll be all right in a couple of weeks, myself. He's different this time, too—having a bit more fun than usual. I expect it's the excitement of opening in London, I never saw him so gay."

At that moment Stephen came down the aisle behind them in the dark and laid his hands on their shoulders from behind.

"Come out back a minute," he whispered, and they followed him to the dim carpeted space behind the last row of the pit. "Look," said Stephen, and he wasn't a bit gay. "I've just been talking to Evadne on the telephone. She's got Hermione's cold, and they've put her to bed, and she says she won't be able to come to the first night. Now, Jeff, you've got to do something. Get hold of Bracken's doctor and take him there and turn him loose. God knows what sort of quack Hermione has called in."

"But it's Wednesday night you open," said Jeff reasonably. "If she's in bed now with a feverish cold—"

"*Get a doctor!*" snapped Stephen. "Get somebody who can break down that temperature and put her on her feet!" There was a short, pregnant silence in the dark at the back of the theater, while they tried in mutual astonishment to see his face. "She's *crying* because she can't come on Wednesday," said Stephen. "And while I was talking, Hermione came and took the 'phone put of her hand and ordered her back to bed and told *me* where to head in. I don't know what you're all thinking of," he said accusingly to Jeff, "to let her live like that. You must know how Hermione is!"

"Sure we know," said Jeff, rousing to his own defence, and Virginia's. "But wait till you try to head Evadne off from doing something she's been Guided to do!"

"Guided or not, she wants to come to the opening on Wednesday," said Stephen. "And she's going to, in spite of

Hermione and doctors. Or there won't be an opening on Wednesday. I'll postpone it."

"Because of *Evadne?*" said Jeff. "How would that look in the papers?"

"It won't be in the papers. I can always have a cold myself," said Stephen, and it was then that Sylvia realized with a resounding revelation how things were going.

"Mr. Sprague!" yelled a voice from the stage. "Has anyone seen Mr. Sprague?"

"Coming!" Stephen yelled back. "All right, Jeff, I leave it to you, get going. And I wouldn't be the least bit surprised," he added, "if Hermione was only trying to put something across. If she could keep Evadne in bed and make her miss the fun, she *would.*"

"How right you are," said Jeff. "I begin to see a blinding light."

"Well, blind yourself right along to the flat and find out what's going on up there," said Stephen. "And let it be known out loud that if Evadne isn't allowed to come on Wednesday night I shall go to bed myself with double pneumonia until she can. Come on, Sylvie—second act."

Jeff went straight to Virginia at the Savoy, because, he said, he was *afraid* to go to the flat and face Hermione alone. Besides, he wanted help about the doctor. Virginia heard him with a slow, wondering smile.

"Stephen!" she said. "Stephen and Evadne. Oh, God is good. *That* will stop her nonsense!"

"It's going to be something, when Stephen locks horns with Hermione," said Jeff. "I'm looking forward to this. *He'll* give 'em this Absolute What-have-you stuff!"

"He mustn't be allowed to put Evadne's back up about it," Virginia warned him, starting for the telephone to ring up Harley Street. "If anyone attacks Hermione outright, it only makes Evadne sorry for her and she defends her to the death. Tell Stephen to be diplomatic about Hermione, whatever happens."

"He's better brought up than I was," said Jeff. "I find it very difficult not to dot her one now and then, myself, but Steve is still a Southerner about women, he'll do it painlessly if anyone can. I had thought of getting Evadne stagestruck, to take her mind off things, but if we can get her Stephen-struck it will work the same. Although, if you don't mind my saying so, he might have fallen in love with somebody a lot *easier*, if you know what I mean."

"Stephen can cope," said Virginia. "Much better than Mark, or anyone like that. It will be the making of her. She's not *really* hard to get along with, she just needs an *object* in life."

"You mean objective," said Jeff. "Well, she doesn't deserve any such luck as Stephen, I hope you can bring that home to her as time goes on."

Virginia's suspicion that their own doctor, who had known Evadne since she was small, had not been called to Bayswater as he should have been, was confirmed when she talked to him on the telephone. As they had no idea who was in charge there, if anyone, he was reluctant to interfere, and they left it that Virginia should go to the flat at once and exercise her own judgment. If Evadne was able to be moved in a closed car to Virginia's rooms at the Savoy, he would come and see her there.

The car was sent for, and Virginia and Jeff set out, both looking rather grim.

"I do hope we're not making too much of this," said Virginia as they reached the corner of the Queen's Road. "They may have a perfectly competent man. I should feel an awful fool if we took her away over Hermione's dead body and then she couldn't go on Wednesday night after all, or got worse.

But I haven't raised four children to let Hermione tell me what's what about a feverish cold."

Hermione opened the door to their ring, and stood looking at them in angry surprise.

"Well!" she said uncordially. "This is an honor!"

Virginia brushed past her into the flat, saying sweetly, "I wondered how you were getting along with all these colds," and before the words were out of her mouth there was a cry from Evadne's bedroom—"Mummy! How perfectly marvellous! Hermione said you'd get the germ too if we asked you to come!"

"Since when have I dodged my children's germs?" asked Virginia, sitting down on the edge of the bed and laying a knowing hand on Evadne's ears and forehead. "Not much fever, is there? Is your throat sore?"

"A little bit. But I'm nothing like as bad as Hermione was, really. She's being *much* too careful of me, bless her."

"Have you had anything to eat?"

"Just a cup of tea. I'm not hungry."

"No eggs? No broth?"

"Broth for luncheon."

"Out of a tin?"

"Oh, yes, it's just as good, you know."

Virginia found the thermometer on the bedside table, shook it down, and stuck it in her daughter's mouth. It came out showing a scant ninety-nine.

"Get right up out of there and dress," said Virginia. "The car is downstairs. You're coming back to the hotel with me."

"But Hermione says—"

"Never mind that, *I* say you're to see your own doctor at once, and we'll do as *he* says." Virginia went to the wardrobe and chose a thick wool dress. "Put that on. And you'd better drink a cup of mull-cider before you start, to keep you warm."

"There isn't any, I'm afraid," Hermione said from the doorway, with some satisfaction.

"Well, sherry, then. Whisky. Anything."

"There's no liquor here, Mummy," Evadne explained as she got out of bed. "We don't have it."

"My goodness," said Virginia simply. "Would you run to a cup of tea?"

"I think it's most unwise for her to go out today," said Hermione, standing her ground. "She's been very feverish and coughing."

"I don't know what sort of doctor you may have had," Virginia began, and—

"Oh, I didn't have a doctor," Evadne reassured her. "That was Hermione. We didn't think it was necessary for me."

Virginia looked from one to the other. Hermione met her eyes defiantly, Evadne, bending over her slippers, did not see the glance at all.

"Get your clothes on, Evadne," she said, and started for the kitchen to make the tea herself.

The dirty dishes from luncheon were stacked on the sink, and the meal, whatever it was, appeared to have come entirely out of tins, which stood, unrinsed, among the dishes. Cold, soggy tea leaves were still in the pot, and the kitchen smelled of burnt toast. A saucepan half full of some congealed substance remained on the stove. Virginia set it aside and lighted the fire under the kettle.

"It won't be my fault if she has a relapse now," said Hermione, watching from the doorway.

"Won't it?" said Virginia. "Where do you keep the tea, in the dust-bin?"

Hermione found the tea, in its blue tin behind a drying loaf of bread on a shelf, and handed it to her.

"It's all that interfering man," she complained. "He rang up and got her all upset about missing the first night. Surely he could spare just two of us from his Roman triumph!"

"Don't you want to go on Wednesday yourself?" Virginia asked, rinsing the tea-pot at the sink.

"I suppose I shall have to, if he drags Evadne back into it, sick or well. She's going to sit with me, mind. Bracken said our seats were together."

"Very well," Virginia conceded wearily. "Don't you *ever* clean this place up?"

"Mrs. Spindle comes in every morning. I'm not very handy in a kitchen, I'm afraid," said Hermione as though it was something to be proud of. "I've done the best I could for Evadne, but it's been very inconvenient."

"I suppose it was more convenient for her when you were ill."

"Oh, Evadne *likes* messing about with food," Hermione replied coldly, and wandered away to the living-room where Jeff was waiting, his hat still in his hand.

"Why is it," said Evadne gratefully as she drank the hot, strong tea her mother had brewed, "that *nobody* makes tea the way you do?"

"Never mind the blarney," said Virginia, pleased. "Drink it down, and let's get out of here."

"I oughtn't to go like this, you know. Hermione has been awfully good to me, I don't want her to think I don't appreciate it."

"Good to you how?" said Virginia skeptically.

"Well, making me stay in bed and keep warm, you know— she had to go out herself and buy the food, which she hates to do—and she brought me some flowers—"

"And tried to keep you from going to the theater on Wednesday night!"

"But she was in bed for five days herself, and for me that would be Friday, and—"

"All right, all right, put your hat on," said Virginia, and Evadne obeyed without further argument.

When their doctor called at the Savoy he left a bottle of medicine for a night cough, prescribed a hot lemonade at bedtime, and told her to wear something warm on Wednesday night and not get overheated. That was all.

"I knew it," said Stephen, gratified, when Jeff reported to his room after the rehearsal. "Hermione was just throwing her weight around. But for me, she'd have got away with it!"

"Look, son," said Jeff patiently, sitting down on Stephen's bed while he bathed and changed. "Nobody tossed Evadne to the wolves. She packed up and *went,* of her own free will."

"Well, now there are going to be some changes made," Stephen threatened.

"Yeah," said Jeff without conviction. "Wait till she starts changing you. You'll find yourself Surrendered to the cult leader, acknowledging your essential sinfulness in public, having a Quiet Time every morning, listening in and receiving Guidance, recording your thoughts in a little black book to share at the next meeting—and so on."

"Do they really talk like that?" Stephen asked.

"And what's more," Jeff went on, "the next step is Continuance, which means you'll come round trying to change me, and that's when you get a poke in the nose."

"Honest, she hasn't said a word to me about her leader," said Stephen.

"Wait. She's had a cold."

"Well, anyway, I'm done for," Stephen confessed cheerfully. "She's young, and crazy, and confused. But I'm not a bit confused. I know what I want, and I'm willing to sweat it out till she grows up some."

"I suppose you realize," Jeff remarked gravely, "that the desire for married love can be richly sublimated."

Stephen gaped at him.

"Where did you hear that?"

"At one of their meetings. I snuck in at the back."

"Was Evadne there?"

"She was. But she didn't see me, I snuck out again. I felt the way I did the time I treated myself to a burlesque show. All red around the ears and a little queasy. Spiritual nudity is no more attractive than near-naked showgirls."

"No kidding, she *believes* this stuff?"

"There's a lot in it to believe," Jeff admitted. "It's the way they go about it that won't stay down with me."

"Why can't they just go to church when they feel it coming on?" Stephen inquired sensibly. "I do."

"There seems to be a lot of people who are more self-conscious about going to church than about standing up before a lot of back-slapping well-wishers and Solving Their Personal Problems By Public Discussion," said Jeff.

"Well, the whole thing sounds very screwy to me," Stephen concluded without heat.

"Steve, look. You mean this, don't you. You've got it bad for Evadne."

"I have, so help me. That's official."

"Well, excuse me for butting in, won't you. I mean—it's all new to you here. Look, Steve—don't fall for it, will you. This Cause she has taken up with is no good, not in its international scheme, certainly. They say, 'If you want to stop war in the world, stop war in the home.' They say, 'Changed individuals mean Changed nations.' Stuff like that. It sounds all right. But, Steve—all it means abroad is that we've gone soft in the head—easy pickings. They laugh at us, for trying to sell them that kind of thing. I'm convinced that Victor laughs himself sick at Evadne's crowd, but he pretends to string along with them for what he can get out of it—what he thinks is inside stuff on British public opinion and psychology and so on—what he wants to believe is indicative of our state of mind—what he doubtless reports in Berlin as fatty degeneration of the democracies—*and* because he's gone on Evadne."

"He is?" Stephen was watching him soberly now.

"Mind you, he won't ever want to marry her," said Jeff gently, and watched Stephen curl up inside, like a steel spring. "Now, wait a minute, Evadne is sound, she won't —won't stand any downright nonsense from him if she sees it coming. She *is* honest and pure and—all those words they use out loud. But she's all wound up in the idea of being a Good Influence over Victor, and through him over all Germany and the whole darn world. It's her Joan of Arc complex again. You're right up against it, Steve, and you've got a right to know that."

"Thanks," said Stephen thoughtfully. "Thanks, pal."

"And look out for Hermione," Jeff continued. "You can joke about Hermione. I do myself. But there again—the Cause defeats its own purpose. Hermione is using it to hold on to Evadne—she will use anything to do that. She's got her, and she doesn't mean to let her get away again."

"You don't mean Hermione is *queer!*" Stephen demanded.

"No. Not as bad as that, I think," Jeff answered without quibbling. "But it's not good, Steve. I had to mention it."

"I'm glad you did." All the jester, all the clown and mountebank were gone from Stephen at that moment. "I hadn't got it figured out as far as that."

"You're in time," said Jeff. "But you've not got much time to spare, the way things are. Get on with it."

"I will," said Stephen. "Beginning now."

"There's just one more thing," Jeff added. "Evadne is obstinate as heck. Don't give up."

"Who, me?" Stephen's grin came back. "Never mind the obstinacy, I'll take care of that! And what else am I up against? A muscle-bound fritz and a sour old maid! If I can't lick the pair of them I'd better go back to school!"

5

Bracken returned from Paris with the latest score there—which was that it was too late again to do anything. The Locarno Powers had met and expressed indignation, face to face with the grim fact that the Pact signed ten years ago was now extinct. France also expressed the opinion that there would be war within two years if Berlin was not forced at once to back down, but Britain could not guarantee military aid unless France's borders were first violated. The detrainment points for German invasion of France had been advanced one hundred miles, and the Rhine would now be fortified by Germany. The chance of a short, quick war to hold down the Nazis, if not unseat them, had gone by again in inaction and indecision. And the worst thing about it, said Bracken, was that it made the Western Powers look like jackasses in Russian eyes. The League had failed against Italy in Abyssinia, but France nevertheless appealed to the League against Germany in the Rhineland, and sent troops into the Maginot Line.

The days slid by and still nothing Went Wrong. (Nothing More, Jeff pointed out.) So Sylvia got her first-night party, including champagne, and everybody was there, and the general impression of brilliant success mounted. Even Mab was there, rigid with excitement—Jeff had had rather a battle over that, because her mother had insisted that she could just as well go to the first matinee with Miss Sim. Jeff put his foot down and said that Mab was going with him, in the box, as his particular guest, and what's more, she was coming to the party afterwards and taste wine. "It will be something for her to remember," he said to Irene. "Stephen's first night in London can only happen once, and the way things are, when Mab is what you call old enough there might not be any special parties after first nights. There might not be any first nights." "Oh, Jeff you *don't* think there's going to be another war!" moaned Irene, and gave in at once.

Even Midge was there, singing, in Sylvia's dressing-room, and he went on to the party in his big cage, where he sat in state on the grand piano and sang, unheard, in the cheerful hubbub. "That canary ought to be in bed," somebody said. "Part nightingale, no doubt," somebody else said, and the evening had reached a point where that was considered very funny.

By the time Jeff handed Mab his own glass for her first champagne, she was already aware that Sylvia was The One. Nobody, in Mab's opinion, could hesitate between Sylvia and Evadne. And obviously, with Sylvia in the same world, the right age, and of course willing, Jeff would never wait for an obscure child cousin to grow up and improve her looks. Sylvia was there, a ready-made bride for Jeff, the most beautiful, perfect thing Mab had ever seen. She had manners too. She didn't patronize the young, nor ignore them, nor pillory them with too much notice. She just treated them like human beings—people she was glad to see. And even then, Mab had no idea of the miraculous extent of Sylvia's good manners, that in the midst of a London first night she could manage to focus on a small, sensitive, ecstatic child and greet her with the exact mixture of friendliness and formality to win her everlasting worship. She *shook hands*, Mab remembered over and over again. She didn't ask me how old I was, and if I went to school, and if I had a dog. I might have been as old as she is. Sylvia not only sang and danced in a spotlight that followed her all over the stage, she knew how to behave when the show was over. *Almost,* she was good enough for Jeff.

Other people besides Mab were aware by now that Jeff and Sylvia were in love. It was Phoebe who called Bracken's attention to it, and there was no need to remind him of the complications. There was not only Jeff's health, which was more suspect than he believed, there was the cousinship, not so close as the blood tie that had wrecked Sue's young romance with Sedgwick years ago, but close enough for consideration, much closer than the negligible link between Evadne and Stephen. "People don't seem to make so much of it now as they used to," Phoebe said hopefully. "And of course they might not have children. You don't think we ought to bring it up?" "Heck, no, let 'em be happy if they can," Braken sighed.

It was obvious when the reviews came in that the show was good for a run, and Europe was apparently not going to blow up just yet, so Bracken took a large furnished flat in Upper Brook Street as family headquarters in London for the summer. The Italians were bombing the Red Cross in Abyssinia, and using poison gas on Haile Selassie's native warriors. Addis Ababa fell, and the Emperor escaped capture by getting away to Palestine in a British cruiser. The *Illustrated London News* reprinted a full-page imaginative drawing from a German paper showing the presumable result of a gas attack from the air on a modern city—well-dressed women lying dead in the street, their clothing artistically disarranged, with dead children beside them, hats and hand-bags strewn about, every visible human being prostrate, though the surrounding masonry was only slightly damaged. The same reproduction had appeared in the *News* only a few years ago—when the possibility had seemed much more remote. Now it was accompanied by an article on refuge-rooms, garden dugouts, and gas-masks for civilians—in England itself.

Stephen brought Evadne back to the flat in Upper Brook Street one afternoon at tea time—they had been to a picture gallery—and they found Sylvia gazing at the gas-attack pages in horror. She made them look too, and Evadne said, "But it's all so stupid and useless, if only people would *believe* that it needn't happen!"

"But it's no good half the people in the world believing that when the other half don't," said Stephen patiently. "Until Germans believe it too, we can't afford to."

"Victor says that's just the way they feel about us!" cried Evadne. "They think they must do all this in self-defence *too!*"

"Rats," said Stephen.

A little to his surprise, she did not pursue the argument in Victor's defence, as she might have done a few weeks earlier. She was looking down at the magazine in Sylvia's hands, their two heads bent above it—Sylvia's soft honey-colored hair falling in loose waves on her little neck, Evadne's crisp chestnut curls cut shorter, swept back from a high white brow and childish temples. It struck Stephen forcibly in the little silence that fell how different they were, the two most precious women in his life—his cherished, light-hearted sister, serene and shining and secure in her birthright of peace and confidence, and the ardent, troubled creature beside her, so wrong-headed and provoking and unaware, this vulnerable, loving, pathetic Evadne whom he meant to marry if it took him all the rest of his natural life, and sometimes he thought it might, at the present rate of progress.

He had encountered Victor more than once by now, and they had preserved the amenities, but the enmity between them was high, wide, and handsome. Stephen objected to Victor's slightly bullying air of possessiveness with Evadne, affectionate but belittling, even dictatorial, as though she were some kind of pet, a little lower than a horse and a little higher than a dog. He objected to Evadne's unquestioning acceptance of it, and of Victor's flamboyant presence in her life, and to the effect it had on her own puppyish friendliness—so that one was reminded of the way a puppy will abase itself under a fondling hand, pleased and placating and hopeful, as though the favor might not last. It was not, in Stephen's experience, the way a pretty girl had a right to

behave. It was Victor's place to do the wagging and the wor-
shiping, and darn lucky if she encouraged him at all. It
would do Victor good, Stephen thought, to be one of Sylvia's
beaux for a while. Not that Sylvia took advantage or was
a coquette. She simply knew her place, and if anybody didn't
like it they could lump it. Of course, Sylvia had always gone
a bit out of her way for Jeff, but that was different, Jeff ap-
preciated it and anyway Jeff was—well, special. There was
nothing special about Victor, so far as Stephen could see,
and his manners were almost certainly only skin deep. Un-
derneath their showy façade lay a brutal ingrained incon-
siderateness and a humorless lack of imagination, especially
about women. One wondered why Hermione tolerated Victor
at the flat at all, the way he treated her—or rather, the way he
ignored her, as though she simply wasn't there, or as though
she was a grandmother and cross-eyed.

Stephen didn't like Hermione, he didn't like anything
about her, especially the way she bullied Evadne—(why
did *everyone* bully Evadne?)—but at the same time he was
handicapped by the fact that she was female and he was a
Virginian, and naturally a kind-hearted, easy going man
besides. In spite of pep-talks from Jeff, who was inclined
to be tougher than Stephen with people who needed it,
regardless of their gender, and in spite of Stephen's own
increasing exasperation with Hermione in all her ways, he
still hoped that she was human, and could be won over and
made to listen to reason, and therefore he was still polite to
her, humored her rudeness, and sometimes even included
her in his presents and outings. As a consequence Hermione
somewhat more than tolerated him. In fact, she almost bridled
and preened. "She *likes* you," Evadne reported with some
empressement, as though Hermione were the Queen Dow-
ager. "You've got round her." That was all right with Stephen, he was used to being liked, but he had no idea where
in this case it was leading.

He objected also to Evadne's attitude of anxious compliance with Hermione's wishes and moods. Hermione's likes and dislikes—the latter, it seemed, much more numerous—were constantly alluded to in Evadne's conversation, even when Hermione was not present. "Hermione doesn't like—" was sufficient reason for anything to be dispensed with or not done. "Hermione likes—" was ample excuse for going to any amount of trouble. But why, Stephen would put the question to himself soberly in his ruminations, why shouldn't Evadne ever say "*I* like—" as a good reason for something sometimes?

Because of her inarticulate soft-heartedness and passionate loyalties, both stimulated and played upon by the doctrines of the cause, Stephen had no way of knowing that Hermione was her first experience of living with someone who was not constitutionally kind, who worked up moods and grievances and inflicted them on bystanders, who liked to wound with well-chosen words and to create situations in which the guilt for ensuing unpleasantness somehow came to rest on the innocent instead of on herself where it belonged. And because of Evadne's earnest, fumbling good-will and total lack of the *arrière-pensée,* she was never able to see quite how these things got started or who was responsible, and so was reduced by apprehension to spending her life in a somewhat breathless effort to forestall the next crisis without having any idea which direction it was coming from.

Stephen so far saw only the result of this state of affairs, which was Evadne crawling to Hermione, and it puzzled him, for she had spirit enough about everything else. He was never there to encounter the cold, seething silences in which Hermione could exist for hours when he had left them alone together after making Evadne late getting home, or failing in some way to acknowledge Hermione's equal desirability as a companion—nor to hear the devious ways she took to arrive at the conversational opening she needed to make the jibe she had devised. And anyway, if such a matter had been left to him to deal with, he would have reacted with his characteristic cheerful so-what logic instead of regarding each separate occasion as the end of the world which it always seemed to Evadne. Before she went to live with Hermione she was accustomed to the affectionate tolerance of Virginia's household, where if they had to come reproof and discipline were swift and mercifully brief. Therefore she first encountered Hermione's Spanish Inquisition tactics with a kind of bruised astonishment. She protested innocence of intent, ignorance of fault, anxiety never to offend—she apologized, she offered extravagant amends, she meekly accepted a guilt which was never hers, she placated and appeased.

Believing that Hermione had found in her the first true friend of a lonely, misunderstood lifetime, and that without her now Hermione would be bereft and neglected all over again, Evadne subdued her gregarious impulses and her natural frankness and became Hermione's devoted shadow, She tried to learn always to think and to weigh before she spoke, she tried to be content that their few friends should be all of Hermione's choosing, mostly from the very mixed company encountered at their meetings—and Hermione took care to choose the least interesting ones. Their daily routine at the flat was set by Hermione's inclinations, caprices and tyrannies. Even their food was subject to Hermione's diet fads and fancies, on which Hermione kept her figure and Evadne grew quite thin.

As for Victor, Hermione suspected just as Jeff did that he would never want to marry Evadne. His Nazi training, his diplomatic future, and his national preoccupation with war were against any permanent connection with an English girl. The association with Victor was the way Hermione allowed Evadne enough rope to simulate freedom. And she fostered Evadne's hope of bringing Victor into the Cause as a harmless sort of hobby which would end perforce with his ultimate recall to Berlin.

Then Stephen came.

At first he seemed to Hermione just another cousin from America, less tiresome than Jeff because he paid some attention to her own sacred self, but—Hermione had never had any use for men because they had never taken much notice of her—negligibly male. But Stephen proved to be different. Carelessly, in his natural kindness, he spread round her his easy good-nature, his affectionate banter, his constitutional way with women. Hermione had never seen anything like him. She was still smarting from having had to acknowledge publicly that she had been in love for years with a man who showed nothing but indifference to her, if not outright animosity. Her recent overtures to Jeff were a little overplayed because of her self-conscious conversion to the idea that their relations were strained by her unrequited love for him instead of by a straightforward childhood jealousy, and he was plainly still impervious to her Changed personality. So she suddenly ceased her unsuccessful amateur wooing of Jeff and began to allow herself in secret to imagine what it would have been like to be in love with a man so forthcoming as Stephen. Not, of course, that she intended anything should Come Of It, because of course she and Evadne were doing very well as they were. But it did just occur to her now and then. . . .

And nothing was further from Stephen's mind.

Nevertheless, he had Hermione to thank for Evadne's unexpected loss of impetus in the plans for returning to Germany to attend the summer Olympic Games. Hermione had no interest in sports, and had been mortally bored at Garmisch the previous winter, playing second fiddle to Evadne and Victor. Besides, she understood now that the movement was unpopular in Germany and had no future there under the Hitler régime, and that Victor was only encouraging Evadne because it gave him an opportunity to see her. And above everything else, Hermione was lazy, and hated the occasional discomforts and inconveniences of even luxurious travel. She was very snug in the Bayswater flat with Evadne in conscientious attendance, and London can be delightful in summer. And to settle any last-ditch sense of duty to the Cause in Evadne she bought a small car, and because she was too nervous to drive it herself she put Evadne in charge of it, as though it were her own. This meant also that Evadne had to do chauffeur duty at any given moment. But once in a while as a great treat she was allowed to take the car out herself. And this meant that she must always say where she was going, with whom, and when she expected to return, and to account for any deviation from schedule when she got home.

Both Stephen and Victor drove much bigger and handsomer cars of their own, but it gave Evadne pleasure to take them about in hers when she had the chance. Once on a Sunday she had driven Stephen out to Richmond Park for a picnic lunch—they had spread a cloth on the grass and eaten there, with a bottle of hock (Stephen's idea) and a near-doze in the sun afterwards, and a drive home through late golden light with long shadows.

Evadne had run on after lunch that day about the Cause, its beliefs and its aims and its virtues. Stephen didn't interrupt or change the subject. He found her zeal merely touching, and in his sophisticated, somewhat disillusioned, but secretly and simply religious viewpoint the ideas she attempted to expound had a horrid fascination. Stephen had been brought up to believe in God and to attend Bruton Parish Church in Williamsburg. He had never doubted God, but he would as lief have said so in everyday conversation as he would have embarrassed himself willingly in public. Most of what Evadne said and quoted to him seemed so obvious as to be childish, and the rest really shocked him.

And as for writing those letters, that part nearly gave him the giggles. But he preserved a respectful gravity and silence and let her talk, lying on his back on the grass with his hands locked behind his head, gazing up at the leaves between them and the pale English sky. He wanted to laugh, and play the fool, and be affectionate, and lay plans for their immediate future. But he wisely stayed as he was, not moving, not interrupting, until she said suspiciously, "Stevie—?"

"Mm-hm?"

"You're not paying attention."

She noticed as he turned his head towards her that his eyes were as clear and level and defenceless as a baby's, nothing hidden, nothing shirked. She was not experienced enough to know that she was seeing for the first time the eyes of a completely honest man completely in love, with nothing to hide.

"Why should you think that?" he asked slowly, looking up at her as he lay.

"Well, you—you hadn't said anything—or moved—"

"You had the floor." Except for the turn of his head he had still not moved.

"You were half asleep," she accused, and looked away uneasily from that unwavering gaze.

"I heard every word. You've got a lovely articulation, if you'll allow me to say so, and your voice is placed just right. How did that happen?"

"Mummy, I expect. She used to go on about it." Her eyes came back to his, reluctantly. "What made you say that?"

"We notice such things in my business. Maybe I was wondering why I love you so much."

"Now, Stephen—"

"Well, don't run away, I can say so, can't I?"

"We—haven't known each other very long," she reminded him.

"Long enough. For me, anyway." With one of his quick, fluid movements he turned over and laid his hand on hers in the grass between them. "Don't make any mistake about this,.will you. I'm not fooling. I want you for the rest of my life. New York—Williamsburg—London—Paris—wherever I am, I want you to be there too."

His hand on hers was warm and firm and undemanding. It stayed where it was, and she knew that Victor's would soon have slid up her arm if she had not withdrawn. And Victor had never said anything about the rest of his life. More than a little stirred, with a new bewilderment, she sat looking down at their hands and wondering what to say.

"You don't know what to say, do you," he said, as though reading her mind. "It's not what you want, is that it? What *do* you want, Evadne?"

"I don't know," she said with her devastating candor, and he bent his head and kissed her fingers as they rested in his.

"Good," he said. "That gives us a little leeway."

But Evadne was still thinking. New York—Williamsburg—Paris. It would be fun. It would be very gay and perhaps quite exciting sometimes, but it was a selfish idea surely, for if she went with Stephen what would become of her work for the Cause and what would Hermione do without her? No one else understood Hermione as she did, Hermione said so herself, and it would be very wrong to desert her when she had never been so happy and so well taken care of, she said to herself. At first it had been only an experiment in living, but now that they had taken on the new flat and furnished it themselves, and had laid such wonderful plans for working together for peace and tolerance in the world . . .

"Please tell me what's going on in that crazy head of yours," Stephen said gently. "Can't I help?"

But it was all so complicated to try to tell, and she knew he still did not sympathize with or comprehend the high aims and ideals of her associates in the Cause, so she only said,

"I don't see why you should love me so much. I've never been able to do anything for you."

"Thank goodness for that!" said Stephen fervently. "Don't start, will you!"

After a moment's doubt, Evadne decided to smile.

"What a funny boy you are," she said in an elderly way.

"Oh, yeah, I'm funny, all right," he agreed cheerfully. "*I* think a girl like you should have somebody doing things for her, instead of the other way round. Silly, isn't it."

This time Evadne laughed.

"That's better," he said, and sat up, and somehow without seeming to move at all he was close to her, her shoulder against his chest, his arm round her, warm and firm and kind, so *kind*, and for no reason at all she wanted to bury her face against him and cry. Yet she had nothing to cry about, surely, she was quite happy with Hermione and her work. . . .

"Honey, can't you relax?" he was saying against her hair. "Can't you laugh like that a little oftener, and learn to be young and foolish while you are?" He put his other hand under her chin and turned her face up to his. "I want you to have a good time," he whispered. "I want to make a fuss of you—give you things—take you places—see you laugh. I want you to be happy—like this." He kissed her, and she let him, thoughtful and passive in his arms, thinking, Yes, I do like him, he makes it sound very simple, but what about poor Hermione? "Well?" he queried against her lips. "Say it, darling—you aren't in love with me, are you. Not yet." He kissed her again, experimentally, and felt her yield to it in an inexperienced, rather touching way. "But you could learn," he said, and his arm tightened. "In about ten easy lessons."

"Stevie, please, I—can't think when you do that."

"Good," said Stephen. "That's just what I want to hear." He bent his head again. There was a brief interlude, and he found as he had suspected that she went to his head like strong drink, and that all the warmth and eagerness of her were fundamental and real and could be turned into all the things he had ever dreamed of. "See what I mean?" he murmured with some confidence then. "We're wasting time. When it's like this there's no sense in waiting, we don't want to lose any of it, let's get married, darling, what's to stop us?"

"Oh, Stephen, I couldn't decide—anything, all at once like this—I have to—"

"Have to what?" He looked down at her, and she stayed there in his arms, gazing off across the grass to where deer grazed in a clearing. Her lips were soft and smiling, her bright hair was swept back against his rough sleeve where it clung and shone, but her eyes were hidden and troubled. "Have to what?" he repeated patiently. "Ask Hermione?"

"Well, I do have to think of her, after all."

"Why?"

"Because she and I are engaged in the cause. We depend on each other."

"Is that healthy?"

"I don't know what you mean," she said, and he wondered if she did. "We've taken on this new flat together—she *counts* on me—it's a very beautiful friendship—"

"Bit lopsided, isn't it? All give on one side, all take on the other."

"She's lonely."

"Why?"

"She's very reserved, and—people get down on her for no reason at all."

"Plenty of reason. Everybody won't let her wipe her feet on them the way you do."

"Oh, Stephen, she doesn't! That's just her manner!"

"Well, whatever it is, she has only herself to blame. And anyway, you can't spend all the rest of your life being Hermione's only friend. By and by people will begin to think things."

"Don't be silly, it's not as though I was living with a man!"

"If you were," he said deliberately, "I might be able to deal with it better."

"Would you want me anyhow?" she inquired in some surprise.

"I just want you. Period."

To his incredulous delight, Evadne made a little movement which could only be described as nestling, as though she was comfortable there, and as grateful as a tired child for the clasp of his arms round her.

"It would be nice," she said wistfully with a little sigh.

"All right. When?" he replied promptly.

"Not—not just yet, Stephen. I'll have to—I don't know how to tell her, I—can't—just—" But her fingers closed on a fold of his tweed sleeve and clung.

"Honey, I'm going to put my foot down," he said after a moment. "You can't go on living like this, it's not good for you, and it places too much of a burden on you. Hermione needs to learn to live life on her own."

Evadne sat up, unwillingly pulling herself together as with a weary resuming of her burden, pushing herself back with a hand on his chest, looking indignant and a little rumpled.

"I don't know what you mean," she said again, and "I think you do," he answered levelly, meeting her eyes.

"But our cause! What will the group think? Won't they say we've betrayed them."

"Will they?" said Stephen, and gave way to a small smile, and took both her hands. "Sweetheart—let's put an end to it, that's the best way."

Evadne withdrew her hands.

"If I thought for one moment that you thought—" she began angrily.

"It's not me, I know what to think," he said, with resolute quietness. "But the whole thing is all wrong, don't you see —you don't *belong* like that, you belong with me."

"Are you asking me to give up my Work?" she asked coolly, becoming more distant by the moment.

"Now, honey—"

"You've never even bothered to come to one of our meetings," she accused him. "You've never even been *open-minded* on the subject. I don't think you've got any right—"

"All right, so I haven't any right," he agreed soothingly. "Except that I love you. And I want you to be happy. You are happy like this with me, and I don't believe you're altogether as happy with Hermione. *Or* with Victor, for that matter!"

"My happiness has nothing to do with it," said Evadne unsteadily, and she began to gather up and pack away the things left from their picnic that were scattered on the grass round about. "Victor says that our generation can't afford to do what it likes, it must dedicate itself to the future. Thinking of nothing but my own happiness is a very narrow, selfish way to live. If it happened that through me Victor Surrendered and brought all his friends to God it would be a very powerful influence for peace. I must sacrifice everything to that."

"Even me?" he asked gently, and she paused and looked up at him, mutinous, loving, distressed, and quite distractingly beautiful.

"Even you, if it meant the peace of the world," she said slowly, and Stephen's first impulse was to cry, "Oh, rats, come off it, darling," and reach for her again. Whether rightly or not, he was silent instead, respecting her earnestness, in a dreadful new uncertainty he had never known before with regard to a woman. He had so nearly succeeded this afternoon in convincing her that she needed him as he wanted her. For the first time she had seemed to glimpse with him the possibilities of love between them. Should he press her now, or should he wait, and let the sweetness of the past hour sink in and work for him? He hesitated, for nothing had ever mattered to him so much before, and the time was gone.

When they reached London the cinemas were open and Stephen wanted to go on to Marble Arch, but Evadne said nervously that she must get home. He glanced at her with speculation, and pondered silently as far as Church Street. Then he said, "Are you *afraid* of her?"

"Who?" said Evadne carefully, her eyes fastened on the road.

"You know who. What would happen if you did go to a film with me now instead of going home?"

"Well, I—said I'd be home by seven."

"But suppose you weren't."

"She might think something had gone wrong—an accident, I mean."

"Suppose we telephoned, then."

"N-not tonight, Stevie."

"Look, honey, I don't want to badger you, but—*why* not tonight?"

"I said I'd be back for dinner," she said patiently.

"But suppose you just *weren't*. If we phoned and explained, would she be cross?"

"Well, disappointed, you know, and—" Evadne gave great attention to her driving.

"And what?"

"If you—cared to ask Hermione too, we might—"

"I see." It was rather obvious that he made no offer to ask Hermione too.

"Sh-she's been alone all day," Evadne remarked humbly, as a reason for displeasing him.

"Now, don't for goodness sake, start apologizing to *me!*" he said, his irritation all for Hermione, but Evadne set her lips in a sweet, hurt line and watched the road. Stephen touched her hand briefly, on the wheel. "All right," he said gently. "It's been a beautiful day and I'm grateful."

"Oh, Stevie, I'll never forget it," she said tremulously.

"Next Sunday again?" he suggested, and instantly she was cautious.

"I may not have the car next Sunday."

"I've got a car," he reminded her.

"But Hermione might want me to drive."

"I see," he said again.

"Please don't sound like Victor," she said unhappily. "Sometimes I think he's just *jealous* of Hermione." The car stopped rather jerkily in front of the block of flats where she lived. "I shouldn't have brought you here, I should have put you down at the corner where you could get a taxi."

"Meaning I mustn't come in."

"N-not tonight, Stephen."

"Why not?"

"I—wish you wouldn't—" She sat drooping over the wheel, all the spontaneity gone out of her, and a kind of apprehension in its place, as though she dreaded something ahead of her.

"I'm no better than the rest of them, am I," he remarked kindly. "I badger you too, only perhaps not quite the same way, and as they no doubt tell you too, for your own good." He opened the door on his side and got out, came round and opened her door and waited while she stepped down on the curb. "I'm coming up," he said, and took the picnic basket out of the back of the car. "I want to see what goes on here."

"I'm afraid there's no dinner," said Evadne, watching him helplessly.

"Then what's the rush to get back at seven?"

"We were going out to the Corner House at Marble Arch."

"Good grief." Stephen turned towards the door, carrying the basket.

"Wh-what are you going to do, Stephen, are you coming with us?"

"Not to the Corner House, no. We'll put on her hat and go somewhere."

"Sunday's a bit difficult," she suggested.

"I know half a dozen places."

Evadne put her key in the door and they entered a soundless flat where the air was somehow chilly with tension. There was no welcoming voice, no stir to meet them.

"Anybody home?" Stephen called after a moment, as Evadne seemed incapable of breaking the silence, and after an appreciable pause Hermione said, "Well, good evening," and appeared in the doorway of her bedroom. Stephen realized that she did not smile or offer her hand, and that she did not so much as glance towards Evadne. She merely stood there, waiting. "Get your hat," he said imperviously. "Let's all go out to dinner."

"Haven't you two had dinner?" Hermione asked coldly.

"Of course not, it's only a little after seven." Stephen set the basket down in the kitchen and stood with his hat in his hand. "Ran into some traffic. Let's go."

"I have a headache. You two go on without me."

"Nonsense, do you good to come out. Besides, we came all the way back to collect you."

"I'm not dressed to go out."

"You're dressed," said Stephen. "All but your hat. Don't be all day, now, I'm getting hungry."

"I'd rather not go, really," she said between her small white teeth. "You shouldn't have bothered about me, as late as it is now." She looked from one to the other slowly, emphasizing her apartness from their irresponsible thoughtlessness.

"Please, Hermione, you know what Sunday traffic is," Evadne pleaded. "We got here as soon as we could."

"What time did you leave Richmond?" Hermione inquired, unrelenting, and Evadne began to show signs of complete demoralization.

"I don't know, I—we didn't look—we—got talking—"

But why did it matter so, Stephen wondered, watching them. To either of them. It was easy to perceive that this was not just a question of a half hour's tardiness for dinner. This had roots. This went way beyond what met the eye. Evadne was being called to account for something much more complicated than keeping Hermione waiting for dinner. Wasn't it possible, he wondered, that her real misdemeanor consisted in the first place of having a beau to go picnicking with, in the second place of having found him sufficiently absorbing to delay her return, and in the third place of wearing, however unconsciously, the sheen and shimmer of being desirable and desired which still remained like invisible stardust from those kisses in the park?

Stephen was close, he was getting warmer, but the whole thing had not dawned on him yet. He was smart, but he was also modest, for a man in his position. It still did not occur to him that to Hermione the really unforgivable aspect of Evadne's afternoon was that it had been spent alone in his company to their obvious satisfaction. He still did not realize that Hermione was reading Evadne like an open book, and that she knew now, as surely as though she had seen it happen, that Stephen had kissed Evadne tenderly and was very much in love with her, so that Hermione was full of a truly agonizing anger—with Evadne for attracting Stephen, whose easy magnetism had already wrought on Hermione herself, and with Stephen for being attracted to Evadne, who already had everything. He was still unaware that in her own prickly, dissatisfied, poisonous way Hermione was falling in love with him. And so he went disastrously on being tactful and polite to her, to the further undoing of them all. Jeff would have snubbed her before now and walked out, leaving Evadne to her fate. Stephen set compelling hands on Hermione's shoulders and turned her towards the bedroom.

"Get your hat like a good girl," he said tolerantly. "You're holding up the parade."

Hermione looked up at him as though about to bite his head off, and then unexpectedly complied. While they waited for her Stephen leaned up against the wall where he stood in the little foyer, and Evadne wandered into the living-room and sat down on the arm of a chair just inside the door, rather limply.

She was thinking that Stephen meant well, but it was only postponing the reckoning to take Hermione out to dinner now. It was always like this if she went out without Hermione, whether it was with Stephen or Victor or someone quite uninteresting, and whether she got home on time or not. Almost it was not worth going, except that sometimes one forgot for a while, like this afternoon, what was in store, and it was a relief sometimes to be with someone who didn't always need bolstering up. That was the thing about Stephen, he was happy in himself, he was without misgivings and miseries, he had made life work. It was inspiriting to know people like Stephen and Sylvia, even though it made one's own lot drabber by comparison. Of course, they weren't doing anyone any Good, or were they? Surely even by her friends' high standards, the laughter and delight which Stephen's every performance created in his audiences were worth while. Surely everyone who saw him on the stage was the better and certainly the happier for having seen someone so superlatively good at his job, whatever it might be. Even now, Evadne could not get used to the two Stephens—the brilliant dancing star in the following spotlight, and the casual, ambling man who wanted to make her happy, so that even while he kissed her, even while he stood at a relaxed angle against the wall of her own home, she remembered with a small electric thrill all the dash and skill and authority and excitement contained in that slim, facile presence. And each time things like this happened, each time Hermione turned the screw,

the knowledge stirred at the back of Evadne's unhappiness
—Stephen would take me away. And then, hastily— But that's
selfish and wrong. Hermione needs me. Stephen is happy
anyway. Yet the knowledge persisted, unruly and comforting.

Hermione had had no intention of joining them at dinner.
She had meant to send them away together, feeling guilty
and at outs with each other, while she remained dinnerless
in the flat hugging her grievance. And then, when he seemed
really to want her to come, she could not resist the chance to
watch and listen to him again. She told herself while she put
on her hat that she would be on her dignity anyway, at dinner. She would be distant and indulgent and a little sad, forgiving two heedless children who had hurt her. Later when
they had made it up to her enough, she would unbend. Even
now, after that unforeseen gust of anger which had swept
her at sight of them returning home together, she was not
quite ready to face the fact that while her confessed love
for Jeff was Evadne's idea, wished on her as it were, as part
of her Surrender, this feeling for Stephen was something
of her own, secret and unsuspected and unwelcome. For
Stephen had kissed Evadne today, she was sure. And now
she wouldn't touch him herself with a barge-pole. Or would
she?

Of course there was still Victor, she was thinking, while
she put on her hat. Better if they had gone to the Olympics
in Germany, but it was too late for that now. Nevertheless,
Victor might still be of some use if one could get at him. If
Victor persuaded Evadne to go to Germany again, that
would put Stephen in the cart. He couldn't leave London,
with the show running. He would try to talk Evadne out of
going, especially if Victor were going at the same time they
would be in Germany. Evadne was obstinate, and would
quarrel with Stephen if he persisted. And if they parted on
a quarrel, and were separated a while, the thing would die
a natural death and Evadne would be hers again. Stephen

would not mourn long for any woman, Hermione was confident, no man with his opportunities would. She knew that whatever his intentions, Victor was her ally against Stephen. Tomorrow, while Evadne was out shopping, she would ring Victor up and advise him to start something, or Stephen would cut him out entirely. . . .

6

It was a beautiful week-end in late August and Farthingale had never looked lovelier. Tea was being served on the lawn, and the family circle had been enlarged, if not enlivened, by the arrival of a party from the Hall, consisting of Lord Enstone, his son Mark, and his younger daughter Mona, who was Evadne's age but content merely to exist and enjoy herself and consequently was no trouble to anybody. Bracken and Dinah had brought what Bracken now described as the kids—Jeff, Stephen, and Sylvia—by motor from London, pausing at Sunningdale to collect Mab from her always preoccupied parents, who were more than willing to lend her to Virginia at any time for an indefinite stay. And Rosalind and Charles had driven over from Cleeve.

In deference to the glorious weather and the idyllic scene —good-looking men in country flannels, pretty, cherished women in light flowered frocks, the handsome tea-table with its polished silver, steaming kettle, and delicious food—the conversation studiously avoided the Spanish Civil War, which had turned very nasty, and the arrival in England of the Abyssinian Emperor as a defeated exile. Virginia, who was writing a book about her girlhood and marriage before the war to one of Lord Enstone's younger brothers, had started them off in a reminiscent trend, and Dinah, sister to Enstone and to Virginia's husband, joined her in thinking up stories of the old days—stories, however, which skilfully skirted the tragic circumstances of Rosalind's marriage to Prince Conrad which had also taken place about that time. Then Charles said in his gentle drawl, "And don't forget about the part your dressmakers used to play, Virginia—I distinctly remember being smuggled into that Hanover Square place one time to see Rosalind while she was there for a fitting. It was my only chance to talk to her without being chased off by her mamma."

"Phoebe arranged that," Rosalind said with a smile. "But I think it was done quite a lot then. The girls in the shop stood guard, and passed notes, and took messages—all in the most completely innocent way, you know," she added with an amused glance at the attentive younger generation. "Just tissue-paper intrigue—no one nowadays can believe how utterly helpless we were then even to communicate with a man who wasn't approved of at home."

"A little more of that wouldn't do any harm these days," said Lord Enstone, who always rose to cues of that kind like a trout to a fly.

"Nonsense, Edward, you know very well it wrecked people's lives right and left," said Virginia.

"Not always, it didn't. And people can be wrecked by too much freedom too. Look at Evadne," said Lord Enstone, who could never forgive her for not being in love with Mark.

"Well, on the other hand, look at Sylvia," Virginia pointed out, and Lord Enstone did so with visible pleasure.

"But after all, how do *we* know what Sylvia may be up to?" he inquired then genially. "Pretty enough to commit murder and nothing said about it, eh?"

"Evadne's just unlucky," Mark said, speaking as an old friend. "Everything she does makes a splash, somehow. Born to put her foot in it, I always say. Can't help loving the little darling all the same. *Means* so darn well. Give you the shirt off her back, I mean."

Stephen looked about him carefully, making sure that Oliver, who whether it was his own fault or not was after all

Hermione's father, had not joined their circle, and then said, "That's the shirt, isn't it, that Hermione is now wearing somewhat threadbare. And what does anybody here propose to do about it? And if not, why not?"

All eyes were turned upon him, with an interest entirely friendly. Except for Jeff and Sylvia and Virginia, the family had not yet grasped the fact that Stephen had added himself to the list of Evadne's victims.

"I have tried everything I know to break up that combination," said Stephen into their speculative silence. "Short of shooting Hermione, that is. I'm not quite ready to hang for it if there's an easier way."

"It's not Hermione I mind so much, it's that blasted Nazi," said Mark. "I mean, we'd look silly, wouldn't we, if Evadne up and married him."

"Oh, *no!*" cried Rosalind, sitting up in her chair with a jerk. "Virginia, what are you thinking of, why don't you—"

"Why don't I *what?*" retorted Virginia, cut to the quick. "Did any of *you* ever try to control Evadne when she gets a mission? I'm thoroughly sick about the whole thing, but there's no way to lock her up here at Farthingale."

"Cut off funds," said Lord Enstone, offering his sovereign remedy for recalcitrant children.

"But I can't cut off Hermione's," Virginia reminded him. "Not even Oliver can, since she came into her mother's money."

"Oh, *that* woman!" said Lord Enstone, out of an old feud. "Wish we'd none of us ever set eyes on her. Hermione's just like her. Can't think what Oliver was about, to beget a child like that."

Stephen looked at him with the greatest admiration in the world and said he had often thought the same, only not so well put. This brought Lord Enstone's attention to focus on him in some surprise.

"You in the running for Evadne?" he demanded.

"Yes, sir," said Stephen, without flinching. "And I can't even get to first base."

"Wasting your time," said Lord Enstone. "Ask Mark, here. He's been trying for years." (This was news to Stephen, and he sent a humorous, commiserating glance towards the unexceptional Mark, who responded with an airy salute.) "She only likes freaks and foreigners," Lord Enstone consoled them collectively. "Serve her jolly well right if she got landed with one of them, like Rosalind. Why don't you have a good talk to her, Rosalind? Tell her what's what. You're qualified to speak, if anyone is. Keep forgetting that Nazi fellow is your own son."

"It's something I prefer to forget, myself," Rosalind replied quietly.

"You're the one to deal with it, then," said Lord Enstone, having got the idea well lodged. "Isn't she, Virginia. Get Evadne down here and have Rosalind talk to her, straight from the shoulder."

"It's difficult to make them understand—especially if your own experience happened before they were born," Rosalind murmured, and inwardly shuddered at the thought of discussing with Evadne the interview at Cleeve and its revelations. Not even Charles knew to this day why she had returned to him so badly shaken. *I gave him mine.* Once more she stopped the ears of her memory against the words. *But for me he would not have had the gun. . . . I gave him mine. . . .* She had given birth to a monster. Even Charles must never know that. It was a thing to be borne in decent silence, as best she could.

"It's never any good to try to warn Evadne off with scarecrows, Edward, it only makes her more determined to demonstrate how harmless they are," Virginia was beginning when Jeff, whose chair faced the house, said, "Oh, my, we're in for it now!" and they saw coming towards them across the lawn from the open french windows of the drawing-room Evadne, Hermione, and Victor.

"What blasted cheek!" said Lord Enstone, and Rosalind rose in a single movement as though for flight, and dropped back into her chair again, silently, at the quick touch of her husband's hand on her arm.

Virginia left her place at the tea table and went to meet the newcomers, halting them on the grass well out of earshot, to give her outspoken family time to collect itself.

Victor had been having troubles of his own. Ribbentrop as the new German Ambassador to London was, in the English view, dropping brick after brick and not at all improving Anglo-German relations, except with a small pacifist cell of British society who were determined to get along with Nazi Germany at any cost. Closely questioned by his masters as to his own progress in cementing his connections, Victor had very little to his credit. His attempted explanations that his mother's titled husband chose to live the life of a recluse on his country estates, and that as a consequence she was buried alive there herself, were met with suspicion and incredulity. Victor was accused of incompetence and advised to improve his time—to show results, beyond attendance at some strange religious meetings with a noticeably pretty girl.

It was not, of course, a matter of gaining access to plans and formulas and fortifications—nothing so simple as the operetta form of espionage was in Victor's assignment to England. He was merely to infiltrate, to watch, listen, and whenever possible to undermine—and report back to Berlin in endless detail. Therefore, his masters desired to know, How about his Influence, Where were his Followers, Why had he not acquired more Good Will in the right places,

What about the supposed disaffection among the English, the general sub-rosa willingness to co-operate with Fascism, the —Franco had just coined the phrase in Spain—the British Fifth Column? Victor could point to the Mosley people, and the Anglo-German Fellowship people. Ribbentrop knew about them, and was that *all?* The interviews would end on an implication that at this rate Victor would never amount to anything in the SS.

Hermione's telephone call had caught him when his morale was down. She sensed his depression and, knowing Evadne's weakness for lame dogs, she advised him to come and share his sorrows, whatever they were. No engagement was concluded between them, they merely agreed that he was to ring up later when Evadne was in and ask if he might come to tea, and then work on her sympathies. Anything, Hermione thought recklessly as she hung up, to distract Evadne's mind from that entrancing Stephen on the crest of his own wave. Evadne could never resist trying to help someone. If Victor appealed to her on the grounds of having been snubbed for being German, or of dreading an end to his London post, he would recapture her attention. And Victor had certainly been snubbed right and left by the family. . . . Hermione sat with her hand on the telephone, after their rather hurried conversation. Yes—if Victor could be maneuvered into another cold-shouldering by the family Evadne would fly to his defence and quarrel with them all, including Stephen . . .

It was at Hermione's suggestion, therefore, when Victor came to tea, that they planned a week-end motor trip into the country, the three of them, if the fine weather held—on the grounds that they were all a bit stale and needed a holiday. They could stop overnight in some Cotswold village inn, invite themselves to tea at Farthingale on Sunday, and be back in London Sunday night. Evadne was railroaded into it against her better judgment, for she knew that Stephen and Sylvia were to be at Farthingale too that weekend, and Victor and Stephen did not mix.

She was not prepared to find Rosalind and Charles there as well, to say nothing of people from the Hall, drinking tea with the rest on the lawn. She understood that Rosalind had refused to receive Victor again after that first meeting at Cleeve, and she thought it very heartless indeed, without having the faintest idea what had taken place between them. She decided at once that on the whole it might be a good thing for them to have another opportunity to be friends, and she watched with a certain pride Victor's stolid self-possession as he made the rounds of introductions, bowing, kissing hands, murmuring polite phrases, as though in fact he was an invited guest in good standing—until he came to Rosalind, stony-faced and silent in her chair. They all saw the reluctance with which she gave him her hand, they all saw it slip away from his as he bent to kiss it, saw him stiffen, saw Charles cover up by offering his own hand, and they all hastened to create a pleasant bustle about more cups and chairs, which Evadne had requested from Bascombe as she came through the house.

Hermione, looking like a particularly self-satisfied cat, explained how they had been driving in the neighborhood and found themselves parched for tea. Virginia dispensed it from a fresh pot newly made, Stephen handed round sandwiches, and Sylvia, wrought upon by the general nervous zeal to behave cordially or die, offered Victor a vacant chair at her side, which was accepted with alacrity, and before long he was assuring her in audible tones that she was the perfect Nordic type which the Leader so much admired.

Virginia had no sooner poured out their three cups of tea, with another for herself to keep them company, than Lord Enstone stood up, saying with an overdone casualness that he was just going, and Come along Mark, Come along Mona, people invited to dinner at home and all that. With the Earl's party on its feet, Rosalind and Charles were able to rise also and say that it was high time they pushed off, and this got all the men up, because of the ladies. When order was again restored round the tea table, it was discovered that Mab and Jeff were missing, having made their getaway towards the summer house down by the stream while no one was looking. To resume tea with seven empty chairs staring them in the face was a rather hollow procedure, but Virginia did her experienced and gracious best with it, and Victor, who had reclaimed his place beside Sylvia, seemed totally unaware of being treated, Evadne thought furiously, like a leper.

As Hermione had anticipated, all her fierce protectiveness and militant sense of justice rose up hotly to enfold Victor, solaced though he might be by Sylvia's polite interest in his conversation. And she was especially nice to him during the drive home, which he attributed quite wrongly to the lavish attention he had paid to the little American with the idea of bringing home to Miss Evadne, who was inclined to be elusive, the self-evident fact that she was not the only personable young woman in the world.

Hermione was on the whole well satisfied with her maneuver. Uncle Edward had behaved most usefully, as had also Rosalind and Charles. Victor had made rather a fool of himself over Sylvia. And she herself had made a good impression, she believed, on Stephen, sitting beside him while she drank her tea and asking intelligent questions about the theater, so that he at least had no opportunity to sit and moon at Evadne. And anyway, Mark's goose appeared to be cooked for good.

7

It was along about now that Evadne began to notice, belatedly, a change in Hermione's habits. Hitherto she had moped about the flat, often untidy and without make-up on days when no one was expected to call, and had made rather a point of having nothing to do on the occasions when Evadne had made engagements which did not include her. But now she seemed to have some secret life of her own, so that she would dress carefully and go out by herself for the whole afternoon, and even sometimes in the evening when Evadne went to a theater or a concert in another party, and Hermione might be later coming in than she was sometimes, but always alone, and a little pre-occupied, and very uncommunicative, so that without asking outright there was no knowing where she had been or with whom. On the rare occasions when Evadne did ask a casual question, as much from a wish to show polite interest as from curiosity, the reply was brief and vague—a concert, a film, a bus ride—until gradually the thing began to take on the proportions of a mystery. As though she was *meeting* someone, Evadne thought incredulously. As though she was—well, having a love affair. But I *think* I know everyone she does, and I can't imagine who . . .

Because it had eased the situation in the flat a little, and made her own innocent program simpler to carry out, with less aftermath of injured feelings and unspoken resentments, Evadne wanted to take no notice, and determined not to pry. But she couldn't help wondering. And one day, dressing hurriedly to keep an engagement of her own when Hermione had already left the flat for the afternoon, she caught a ring in her last pair of silk stockings and made an ugly snag. Evadne was fussy about her stockings, and always washed them after each wearing, but had fallen behind with several pairs. There was no time to wash them out now, nor to run out and buy new ones.

If Hermione had been at home, Evadne would have thought nothing of asking to borrow a pair, and her request would have been generously granted. With Hermione gone out, she hesitated only a moment and then went into Hermione's bedroom and pulled open the top drawer of the bureau, where Hermione's stockings were kept in tidy, rolled-up bundles. And at the back of the drawer, although in full view when it was opened, lay the six-penny program of Stephen's show, with his picture on the front of it—not the big souvenir program of the opening night, which they had all had and which was worth keeping, but the ordinary daily program you got now. Evadne had been back to see the show again more than once, with friends, and had also seen it from behind, just for fun, but Hermione had never been one of those parties. Yet Hermione had the program, and had kept it, so that Stephen's face looked up from her top drawer.

Under a sort of unwilling compulsion, Evadne picked up the program and it opened in her hands to reveal what seemed to be dozens of ticket stubs which spilled out between her hands into the drawer and on the floor. Feeling breathlessly guilty now, as though she had been caught eavesdropping, Evadne gathered them up and thrust them back between the pages of the program, laid it in place again, and closed the drawer. Then she opened it and returned the pair of stockings she had borrowed, for it would never do for Hermione to know that she had touched them. Returning, shaken, to her own room, she reluctantly put on a pair which had been worn before and went out, late, to her own appointment.

In the bus she sat blindly contemplating her discovery. That was where Hermione went. That was where she was now, for it was a matinee day. Hermione went and sat in the theater and watched Stephen at work, because of some secret irresistible desire to see him, even at a distance. Hermione—and Evadne's stomach lurched with the knowledge—must be in love with Stephen. Remnants of resistance strove against conviction—it was a gay, tuneful show, perhaps she had got a little stage-struck, perhaps— But it wasn't any good. The program, and the ticket stubs, were all of Stephen that

Hermione had, so she cherished those. The quick tears of her ready compassion stung Evadne's eyes. He didn't like Hermione, and she was driven to this, she *paid* to see him, and each stub stood for a meeting between them, a little hoard of secret delight, as people saved dance programs and wilted corsages. Oh, poor Hermione, what could one *do?*

Characteristically, Evadne at once felt compelled in the circumstances to renounce all thought of Stephen for herself from now on, for how could one allow oneself to appropriate the man one's dearest friend wanted too, no matter how hopeless her position in his regard might be? And could one tell Stephen—? To be Absolutely Honest one must tell Stephen. But this was not just one's own affair. Surely it was Hermione's place to be Absolutely Honest with him first? And could one tell Hermione that? It was the Right thing to do, of course, to confess to Hermione at once that one had—well, not snooped, truly, but only stumbled across the evidence in all innocence. And then one could put it to her Honestly, Out In the Open, that she should let Stephen know how she felt, and—and then what? It made Stephen choose between them—an embarrassing, perhaps in his view unforgivable, situation to place him in.

Evadne was at last confronted by an innate sense of delicacy with regard to something it seemed wiser, perhaps, not to have Out In the Open. It was contrary to all her new beliefs, but somehow it wasn't quite the same as with Jeff and Hermione, where there was restitution to make. What's more, one could not share the problem with an associate behind Hermione's back and get advice, because it was not one's own secret, it must be shared first with Hermione, which automatically involved Stephen. Hermione, she knew with fatal certainty, was not going to like it, and she didn't have to be told that Stephen would hate it. If I had not put the stockings back, thought Evadne in something like panic, I would have to mention it to her and then there would be an

Opening. Now I shall have to begin at the beginning. It's going to be dreadful. But I must do something, it's not fair to Stephen—what *is* fair to Stephen?

But though she and Hermione dined together at Stewart's in Bayswater Road and spent the evening at home listening to the radio and catching up on their washing and darning, Evadne could not find an Opening. It wasn't till the following morning, when she overheard Hermione berating Mrs. Spindle for meddling with her things, that Evadne was forced a step further into the dilemma. Mrs. Spindle's indignant denials that she had touched the bureau, and Hermione's violent assertions that she knew better because something had been moved, brought Evadne to the door of her own room across the passage.

"No, Hermione, please—it was me," she said.

"*You!*" Hermione stood staring at her and Mrs. Spindle retreated discreetly into the kitchen.

"Yes, I'm awfully sorry, I—went to borrow a pair of stockings, I didn't think you'd mind, and I—"

"How *dare* you!" said Hermione, perfectly white and with an odd sort of glitter in her eyes, and Evadne thought in spite of herself what a silly thing it was to say outside of a book.

"Well, I only saw that you had one of Stephen's programs," she began. "No, that's wrong, I saw the stubs too. But why shouldn't you go to the show, if you like it?" And whereas Hermione was white with rage, Evadne felt herself going scarlet with embarrassment.

And then Hermione shut the bedroom door in her face without a word. Evadne stood a moment staring at it from her own doorway, and finally went over and knocked.

"Please let me come in," she said humbly, feeling sick, for she hated scenes. "Please don't take it like that, it doesn't *matter*." She could feel Mrs. Spindle's ears flapping in the kitchen, and desperately she opened the door unbidden and went in, closing it behind her. Hermione was flung down on the bed in spectacular floods of tears. Evadne sat down on the edge of it and laid a conciliatory hand on Hermione's shoulder, which was ignored. "Darling, why do you mind so much? I'll never tell a soul if you'd rather not," she said, trying to sound sensible and calm while every nerve tingled with a sense of Hermione's shame, for surely to love a man who made no return must be the last word in mortification, and it was happening to Hermione for the second time.

Hermione was understood to say that she could never look Stephen in the face again.

"But why, if he doesn't know? I promise he'll never know, from me."

"He's in love with you," Hermione moaned into the pillow.

"Well, what's that got to do with it? I'm not going to marry him," Evadne said firmly, and was conscious of a spreading desolation.

"You will, you know you will," Hermione insisted. *"I'm* nothing to stand in your way. He doesn't know I'm alive."

"Why, of course he does, he always—I'm sure he's very fond of you—" The lie faltered and died for lack of conviction.

"You know very well he can't see anybody but you!"

"Well, I—I'll go away," Evadne offered wildly. "There's the conference at Lausanne—members are coming from everywhere to attend that, and they *asked* me to go. I'll stay on the Continent a while, there's a lot of work to be done there."

"What good will that do?" Hermione asked thickly, with suspicion.

"If he doesn't see me for a while he—maybe he'li get over it. I don't think it means anything really, he just—" But she knew better than that, and it wasn't fair to Stephen. "You stay here and I'll go to Lausanne," she said, to end it.

Hermione sat up and blew her nose.

"Nonsense, if you go to Lausanne I'll go too," she said, as though she was being very brave and self-sacrificing.

Evadne's slim shoulders drooped. It suddenly seemed as though she just couldn't bear things the way they were.

"Oh, well," she said dispiritedly, "we don't have to decide this minute, do we."

"You really aren't engaged to Stephen?" Hermione asked, still suspicious but transparently hopeful.

"Of course not. Whatever gave you that idea?" Evadne rose briskly and smoothed the pillows where Hermione had been lying. "He's fun to know, and he makes a fuss of a girl from force of habit. American men are like that." (God forgive me, she added, to Stephen.)

Hermione blew her nose again.

"You'll *swear* never to tell him," she said.

"If you'd rather not."

"Evadne, if you ever *dare*—"

"All right, all *right,* I promised, didn't I?" Evadne was edging towards the door. "We'll just forget all about it, shall we?"

"And hereafter kindly leave my things alone," said Hermione, and Evadne escaped from the room, feeling that she had betrayed all her new-found faith by half-truths and compromise, and had slandered Stephen as well.

8

Meanwhile the end of the run was coming into sight, and Sylvia found herself up against the necessity of returning to America with Stephen to start a new show for the spring opening in New York. As Jeff was booked to go to Geneva immediately after Christmas it would mean another long separation. They discussed it at some length pro and con, with anguish and with laughter, and got nowhere.

Jeff's heart had given no trouble for a long time, and so he went to his doctor and heard all the same things—plus a considered opinion that he was in better shape to marry than lots of people who never thought twice about it. But he felt that heart or no heart he would be letting Bracken down to ask for time off now to go to America on a honeymoon. Sylvia was linked to Stephen's zooming career and was determined not to do to him what Rhoda had done when she married. At last, for everyone came to it sooner or later, they took their problem to Bracken himself, and laid it all out before him, each of them dismally convinced beforehand what his answer would be, and each of them braced for the inevitable parting.

Bracken heard them to the end, poker-faced, with nothing to say, and minute by minute their hearts sank lower. When they had quite finished explaining themselves there was a long pause, while Bracken wandered away to the window and stood there, his hands jammed into his pockets, staring out into the street. Finally—

"Why don't you kids just get married and the heck with it?" he said without turning.

"But—" said Jeff incredulously, and—

"Oh, Bracken!" cried Sylvia, radiant.

"You've got a year—maybe two," said Bracken, his back to them. "In your place I wouldn't fool around. Heck, you're only young once," he said, coming back to them, and he stood over Sylvia, looking down at her with a wry, kind smile. "Maybe I'm giving all the wrong advice," he said. "But you asked me, and for what it's worth you've got it. Suppose I was to lend Jeff to you for a year, beginning now. Mind you, I'll want him back if the balloon goes up, but suppose he was all yours for three hundred and sixty-five days from this Christmas—what would you do?"

"Oh, *Bracken!*" gasped Sylvia, and cast herself lovingly round Bracken's neck.

"What about Geneva?" Jeff asked, unable to believe his ears.

"*I'll* do Geneva," Bracken told him through Sylvia's strangling hug. "Not but what I hate the place. You go along to New York with Sylvia and forget Geneva, it'll keep—if it doesn't blow up in everybody's face. Something is going to break on you-know-what very soon and you'd better stick around for that. But I think after Christmas I can get along without you better sooner than later."

The not-so-very hush-hush romance between King Edward and Mrs. Simpson which Bracken referred to with his euphemism was first mentioned in the British Press on December third, but it came as no surprise to most of England then. A generation which had a little outgrown Ruritania and Graustark and Elinor Glyn had been awaiting the denouement with very mixed feelings, particularly as the high traditions of the fictitious Balkan royalty in the novels seemed to have been outgrown as well. Instead of the noble sacrifice of love and personal happiness on the altar of duty, this very modern king showed a tendency to temporize and to hold out for the privilege of living his life as less exalted persons had more right to do—a course which meant head-on collision with both the elderly Conservative Court faction, which had doubtless made concessions to traditional duties of its own, and with the hard-headed lower classes who had also seen their bleak duty and done it in such tiresome ways as going into the Flanders trenches during four long years of war. There was a general inclination towards the opinion that it was not too much to ask of their King, whom they loved, that he remain faithful to his heritage and to their expectations of him—to say nothing of being an example to the rest of them when they found the going a bit rough. Discussion was open and free in the busses and pubs where Bracken practiced his newspaper man's art of informal conversation without taking notes— 'E'll get the sack, I shouldn't wonder— What's 'e mean, letting us down this way?— Well, what abart *'is* side, why don't we 'ear more of that?— Because they ain't got nothink to say, that's w'y. . . . And it was argued in the drawing-rooms and clubs where Bracken was known and accepted as one of the company— Well, after all, old boy, if things have come to such a pass that we can all behave like just *anybody*—I hope I'm as broadminded as the next person about divorce when it's absolutely necessary, but at a time like this— Besides, it isn't as if he had been *brought up* to act like a spoilt child— And does he think he's the *only* one who has ever had the same kind of choice to make? . . . On December tenth he made the broadcast which shook the Western world, and was gone across the Channel in the night.

It was the biggest news story since the radio had been used to carry news, and while Bracken deplored some abuse of the new medium his own coverage was thorough and required many hours of hanging about waiting for developments, not to say considerable thought in composition. But it had all simmered down by Christmas time, and Stephen's show finally closed, and the family went to Farthingale, where Jeff and Sylvia were to be married. After a brief honeymoon in the neighborhood they would sail with Stephen for New York, an arrangement which would give him time, they hoped, to bring his own affairs to a satisfactory conclusion.

The announcement of Jeff's impending wedding came to Mab not unexpected, but found her still unprepared for the private agony it imposed. Striving for self-control, she reminded herself stoically how long it would be before she was old enough to compare with Sylvia, and anyway nobody ever could. Sylvia was too beautiful and exciting, anybody, even Jeff, was lucky to get her. Mab was quite sure, in a sober, well-considered way, that she would never see anyone in all her own life to come who could hold a candle to Jeff, for he possessed completely her strange, unchildish heart. But one didn't have to get married. Aunt Sue, who had left her house to Jeff, had never got married, perhaps because she too had seen someone like Jeff, after whom no one else was worth looking at twice.

So long as no one *knew*, Mab told herself, she would be all right. So long as no one sympathized. If she could just manage not to cry and make a fuss and give herself away. . . .

And then they asked her to be bridesmaid.

It was a great honor, she was well aware, and there was no way out of it, short of dropping dead. That meant she would have to stand up during the ceremony where everyone could see her, and not show that for Jeff to marry someone else, even though it was Sylvia, was just about going to kill her. In order not to disgrace him she must do her part with dignity and ease, because he must be happy at all costs, and it would only distress him to know that he had broken her heart. . . .

So Mab went patiently through the fittings for her pink bridesmaid's dress, and spent all her savings on a wedding present—a silver bonbon dish chosen with Miss Sim's assistance—and there went her last chance, she supposed, of getting a ticket to America herself. And Jeff would be gone a whole year. . . .

Her inconspicuous, self-contained misery had not gone unnoticed by the two people most concerned. Jeff wanted Sylvia to talk to her, but Sylvia wisely said no, it must come from him, for she was on sufferance only and couldn't put herself forward. And so, a few days before the wedding, Jeff and Mab went for a walk in the woods on the far side of the stream which bordered the lawn. For a while they talked about the weather and the Abdication, making conversation in a way that was unnatural to them. Then Mab said, with an effort at matter-of-factness, "You must take your note-books with you to New York—the ones about Williamsburg. I'll give them back to you, in case you have time to write the book now."

Jeff had thought of the same thing, but was unwilling to ask her for them, so he considered her suggestion very near to mind-reading, and said uncomfortably, "Would you like me to write the book, if I can?"

"Oh, yes, please do—I have one of Phoebe's books, and she wrote my name in it on the front page. It's an autographed copy," she added with satisfaction. "Like having complimentary tickets to Stephen's show, only more permanent, in a way."

"Yes, I see what you mean," said Jeff. "I can do better than either of them. I'll dedicate my book to you." She glanced up at him, not quite sure what that might entail, and he explained, "On the page following the title page, we'll put *For Mab,* in print."

"In *print?*"

"In every copy. And then in your own presentation copy I'll write *For Mab, with love.* Of course, you're taking a chance, my first book may be a dismal flop, you can't tell."

"I wouldn't mind," she said, looking down at her feet scuffing through the brown leaves. "I mean—I'd still be proud."

"And of course, on the other hand, putting your name in it might bring me luck," he remarked lightly.

"Me too," she answered, with her face turned away.

After a minute Jeff sat down on a log and pulled her down by one hand beside him.

"Honey," he said gently, "I know how you feel about my going away like this. But don't take it too hard. We're going to miss each other, but it won't be forever. Look, honey— this comes from Sylvia too, but she wanted me to say it, because we're old friends, you and I—how about my having a little session with your mother and try to fix it so that you could come with us when we sail next month? We're going down to Williamsburg before rehearsals start, to see Sylvia's people and—you could take Miss Sim along and live in my house there for a little while if you like."

"No, thank you, Jeff."

"Rather not?" he asked sympathetically. "Well, it was just an idea—some other time, maybe."

She nodded, her throat too tight for speech, still not looking at him. A bright drop fell on the fur collar of her coat, and they both ignored it.

"You don't hold this against Sylvia, do you, honey. We grew up together, since the time we were your age I guess we've been in love with each other—"

She shook her head, turned away, so that he could not see her face.

"Some day," he said, "not too many years from now I'll be coming to your wedding. Promise to wait for me to get there, won't you, no matter where I am. Promise to let me look him over first, won't you."

There won't be any wedding, she thought, turned from him, though he knew now that she was crying. But you mustn't say that, you mustn't make a fuss. You must let him go, and not make a fuss. A year isn't long. I can still see him sometimes, all our lives, even if he's Sylvia's husband. He'll always come back to England, unless—

She faced him suddenly, her cheeks wet and shining with tears.

"Jeff—if you should be in America and a war began, don't come back. Don't come back and get killed!"

"What kind of thing is that to say?" he asked, appalled, and got out his handkerchief and wiped her face. "What kind of heel do you take me for, to run out on a war? You wouldn't think much of me, you know you wouldn't, if I stayed in America because there was a war over here."

"But they'll drop bombs on London," said Mab with

quivering lips. "Granny says the children will all be sent to Farthingale, but you—"

"Oh, what a world it is," said Jeff, heartsick. "Honey, if there's a war you're the one who will be in America, I'll see to that."

"Oh, *no!*" cried Mab. "I'm not a coward!"

"Well, neither am I, what do you know about that," said Jeff. "So if there's a war, we'll ride it out somehow, wherever it finds us. And it won't come for a while yet, anyway. Bracken says not for a year or two. By then I'll be back on the job over here, and Stephen will bring over his new show, war or no war. In the meantime, I'll write to you every Sunday afternoon, and you do the same for me, is that a deal?"

He put his arms round the small straight figure and drew her over against his shoulder. Mab caught at his coat with one hand and buried herself against the size and warmth and tenderness of him, shaking with suppressed sobs.

"There," he said, holding her. "There, now, I know—it looks like a long time to me too, to be away from England—but a year goes—look how this last one's gone—first thing you know it's Christmas again—I know, Mab, I know, I wish we could do it some other way—"

And holding her, feeling her smallness and the dignity of her grief, he thought, But she's a *child,* she'll get over this—it's worse than I thought, though, I mind it myself, much worse than I thought—what *is* this, between us, almost as though she wasn't a child at all—if it wasn't for Sylvia—but that's crazy—shall I feel like this when Mab marries—serve me right if I did. . . .

9

Stephen by now was going almost out of his mind over Evadne's behavior, for suddenly with no apparent reason she had become impossible to pin down for any sort of engagement worth having, and when he did catch up with her she was absent-minded, non-committal, and maddeningly remote. One of the most piteous aspects of being in love is the unreasoning fear, when things seem to have gone wrong, that one is oneself unwittingly to blame, and Stephen asked himself all the foolish questions familiar to one in his situation— Have I done anything, Did I say something, What have I *failed* to do or say—the sort of thing that is likely to go on all night. His conscience was clear, and his intentions the most virtuous possible. And yet it could only appear that he had somehow offended Evadne and was being sent to Coventry for his sins. She assured him it was nothing of the kind, but whatever it was did not clear up with time, and he began to wonder if Hermione had contrived to undermine him in a really disastrous way, or if the often malicious haze of rumor which surrounds any stage celebrity had contributed to his undoing.

So sudden a withdrawal on her part was especially confusing to him after the definite progress he had made during the picnic at Richmond. That day she had rested in his arms with confidence and returned his kiss in a way all her own, which left him in no doubt that so far as she understood love it was himself that she loved. Since Richmond he had not regarded Victor as a dangerous rival in that respect, however much time and effort she might devote to his conversion to the cause she so obstinately believed in. And yet, all of a sudden it was as though the day at Richmond had never happened. And while ordinary human jealousy did not now enter in, Stephen did feel a growing uneasiness over some malignant influence which he could not bring to light.

Evadne was, it is true, profoundly unhappy, but she did not for a moment lay any blame at Stephen's door. For one thing, Hermione had abruptly given up sneaking off to the theater and was again hanging about the flat in the old way, aimless and self-centered and bored, so that Evadne's own

engagements were again an embarrassment and she sometimes gave them up and stayed listlessly at home herself in
order to avoid a different kind of unpleasantness if she went
out. This state of affairs was most unhealthy for everyone
concerned, but no one outside the flat was in any position to
stop it. Worse, the companionship which had once existed
between the two girls was now overlaid by remorse and
humiliation respectively, and they enacted an elaborate
pretence that the scene about the theater program had never
taken place, though it had become almost impossible to mention Stephen's name.

During the past autumn Evadne had been wholly caught
up in the glittering social swirl which surrounded the German Embassy in Carlton House Terrace. Lavish entertain-
ments took place there, and were given in return by some
of the wealthiest and most highly placed people in London.
Although she had not succeeded in inveigling her uncle
Lord Enstone either into attending one of the Embassy
functions or lending her the Hall to entertain her own guests
at a week-end, nobody had given up hope—nobody, that is,
unacquainted with Lord Enstone—and anyway Evadne was
welcome for her own sake and had unfortunately even caught
Ribbentrop's eye.

Feeling that Stephen's world was now closed to her forever on account of Hermione, and that she must find salva-
tion somewhere from the pervading sense of loss which
threatened to submerge her, she had thrown herself with
more than her former zeal into her belief in her Cause.
She had not known until he was suddenly set beyond her
reach how large a place Stephen had begun to fill in her private scheme of things. And while Victor rather rattled about
in Stephen's niche, he was the one she chose to place there,
because of her wish to believe that through Victor she could
reach the higher powers in Germany and spread the doctrine which assumed and demanded a frank acceptance by

nations as by individuals of the standards of absolute honesty, absolute purity, absolute unselfishness, and daily obedience to God's specific directions.

In the exalted state of mind she had managed to attain
in self-defence against the wreck Hermione had made of
life at the flat, she could only regard Sylvia's wedding as a
tiresome interlude, and arrived at Farthingale on the day
before the ceremony armored in Guidance, purged of
Individual Sinful Desire, and full of Loving, Solicitous Fellowship—though falling a little short of the Radiant Jollity
recommended by the credo. Stephen would be there too,
which she dreaded beyond words, and Hermione came
along with her and shared a bedroom, which was the cross
she had to bear, having lent her own room to Sylvia and the
trousseau. And because she was overstrung and near the
breaking point with strain and ill-digested rhetoric about
Guilt and Sin, she was over-aggressive and over-sensitive in
every direction and drove everybody almost mad by talking
too much about things no one had any desire to contemplate,
at least out loud.

She went for Lord Enstone the first night before dinner,
before he had even had a drink, in an ill-advised attempt
to persuade him to lend his countenance (and decorations)
to a full-dress affair at the German Embassy early in the
new year. Lord Enstone boiled up at the mere idea, and expressed himself at some length in his usual resounding
style. Evadne in turn lost her temper and called him a nar-
row-minded old frump, to which he retorted that she was a
disgrace to the family name, and there was a general Row,
which Virginia was another fifteen minutes in bringing to
order.

Jeff, accepting gratefully a glass of wine which had
been hastily sent for soon after the fracas began, caught
Stephen's astonished eyes with a rueful smile. Poor Steve.
Evadne was right off the deep end again, and it was bound to

be a shock to anyone who was trying to live his life on the assumption that she could be depended on to behave like a human being. Here was where Stephen got disillusioned at last, Jeff thought, and it was going to be tough.

He raised his eyes from shuddering contemplation of his first glass of wine, resolved to see Stephen through if it killed them, even if it postponed his own wedding, and saw that irrepressible chump approaching a still simmering Evadne with a glass in each hand. Asking for it. Poor Steve. Everything crumbling round his ears tonight. Well, might as well get it over with. That's the way Evadne was. It had to come home to him some time.

"No, thank you," said Evadne coldly to the proffered glass.

"Do you good," said Stephen.

"I never take anything."

"I know. That's a mistake."

"Well, I'll—make my own mistakes."

"Don't you ever get tired of 'em?"

"Yes," said Evadne, as though she had just discovered it, gazing at him with admiration and surprise. "Yes, I'm sick and tired of everything this minute."

"I know. Have some wine."

She wavered, looking from him to the glass and back again, breathing a little fast, on edge, ready to bite and scratch, ready for tears, ready (if only the circumstances had permitted) to be kissed and mastered.

"What is that?" she asked suspiciously of the glass in his hand.

"Port. Some of Bracken's best."

His eyes held hers above the glasses which occupied his hands. He was laughing at her, but his eyes were compassionate. Her own filled with tears even while he looked, and she reached out delicately and took one of the glasses, as she might accept with reckless bravado a dose of fatal poison.

"Evadne, *darling,* you're not going to *drink* it!" said Hermione's voice beside them, and instead of taking her firmly by the throat Stephen extended the remaining glass to her with his best smile.

"It's a party," he said sweetly.

"No, indeed," said Hermione, and removed the glass from Evadne's fingers and held it out to him.

"Give me that w-wine!" said Evadne furiously, and although some of it spilled when she snatched it back from Hermione, she drank the rest in one defiant gulp, choked once, and gave the empty glass to Stephen, who lifted his own to her with a congratulatory grin and drank it down.

And Jeff, watching warily from across the room, said, "Well, I'm blowed!" to nobody in particular, and emptied his own glass with a flourish.

It was only natural that Virginia should have seated Stephen next to Evadne at dinner—if she hadn't she would have heard from him—and Oliver was on her other side. Stephen had not much opportunity for private conversation during the meal, and Evadne seemed to avoid it as usual, talking across him to Mona and encouraging Oliver to talk across her to Stephen. It was as though she had taken fright after the wine episode and retreated again into the troubled vacuum from which she had briefly emerged. She would drink nothing at the table, and rose with visible relief when the ladies left the dining-room at the end of dinner.

The men never remained long over the port at Farthingale, and the gramophone was soon going in the drawing-room where the rugs were rolled back for dancing. Evadne danced first with Mark, with hardly a word exchanged between them the whole time, and then it was Stephen's turn. She was stiff and cool in his arms, and he suddenly backed

her out through the doorway into the hall, which was dimly
lighted and empty.

"I want to talk to you," he said quietly, ignoring her star-
tled upward glance, and led her by one hand towards the
library.

"Stephen, really, we can't just disappear like this—"

"Why can't we? They all know we've got something to
settle between us." He opened the library door and pulled
her through it, and closed it again behind them. A log fire
was burning and the lights were shaded and kind. "Now,"
said Stephen, "come and sit down and let's get to the bottom
of this."

"Please, Stephen, I'd rather not discuss it now—"

"But you can't do this to me, I've got to sail in a fortnight. Until lately I've had some idea I might persuade you
to go with me. As my wife, of course," he added, smiling,
into a rather awkward pause.

"Oh, Stephen, I didn't want you to say it again." She was
still standing just inside the door, looking down at the red
chiffon handkerchief stretched tight between her hands.

"That was plain enough. But I've said it. I don't want you
to have any doubts, Evadne. I want to marry you. Remember?"

"I can't," she said, looking down.

"Why?" said Stephen.

"It doesn't matter why. I just can't."

"Of course it matters why. Because of Mark?"

She shook her head.

"You don't mean to marry Mark either."

She shook her head.

"Well, that's that, anyway. Is it Victor?"

She shook her head.

"Can you swear that you don't mean to marry Victor?
Assuming that he asks you, which he won't."

"I don't think that's fair, Stephen—"

"All right, then, he will ask you. Will you say Yes to him?"

"*No,* I—that is, you've no right to question me like this, Stephen, I—"

"I have the right, honey, because I'm fighting for my life, can't you understand that? Something is wrong between us —something new. Because I love you I have the right to know what it is. If you're in love with some other guy—well, I'll shut up, I suppose, and go away. But I don't think you are. I think you're all muddled up about something, and I want to know if we can't straighten it out and be happy together. Because we could be happy together. Couldn't we."

"N-not as things are, Stephen, I've promised—to go to Lausanne for the conference for one thing, so I can't very well just drop that and start off with you instead, and—"

"Because you haven't promised me anything." He waited. "Who made you promise to go to Lausanne?"

"N-nobody made me, I *offered* to go. I can't back out now."

"Is that the only reason?"

She was silent and wretched, looking down, and he moved to take the handkerchief away from her, and she gave ground before him and found the closed door against her back. Stephen leaned one hand on it over her shoulder and she was trapped.

"How does Hermione come into this?" he asked quietly.

"It's nothing to do with her, I just—"

"Look at me, Evadne." But she would not, and he raised her chin with his hand, so that her eyes, tragic and swimming, were forced to meet his. Very deliberately he bent and kissed her, and he was not quite prepared for her response. Her arms went round his neck in a sort of desperate humility, which asked his pardon for past withholdings even more than it promised future surrender. Stephen reacted as might be expected, and it left them both breathless and astonished. "That's all I wanted to know," he said unsteadily, after a moment. "You can leave the rest to me."

"What are you going to do?" she asked apprehensively, and straightened away from him, still helpless between him and the door.

"Well, first I think I'll have a little talk with Hermione," he remarked with a certain relish, and she took fright at once.

"No, please, you can't do that! *I'll* do it. That is—I'll try."

"Let's do it together, then."

"Please let me handle this, Stephen, you must give me a little more time." Her fingers were on his sleeve, tense and pleading.

"Time? I'm sailing in two weeks, and I'm not going to leave you like this. I'm going to find out what's after you and put a stop to it."

"Stephen." She swallowed, and looked him straight in the eye. "You're quite sure you wouldn't rather just go back to America and forget you ever saw me?"

He gave an incredulous breath of laughter, as though trying to see a joke that wasn't there.

"What do *you* think?" he asked in elaborate understatement.

"All right, then." She seemed to make up her mind. "I'll do the very best I can."

"What does that mean?"

"Well—just give me a few more days on it, will you?"

"Is that a promise?"

"I promise to *try,*" she said, with her straight, honest look. "But you've got to let me do it my way. I can't be happy if it means trampling people under foot. I have to do this my own way. It may take a little time, but—it's the only way I can see."

"Will it take two weeks?"

"I don't know. I can try."

He was not satisfied, but he saw that she was almost beside herself with nerves and tension, and it would be wicked to crowd her further at the moment. He opened his arms.

"One more," he said, and she kissed him again, willingly, but with more reserve, already preoccupied with whatever was before her.

She stood a moment, still in his arms, looking up at him, and he had an odd, uncomfortable premonition—it was the lingering, intimate look which goes with a farewell.

"I'm glad there's somebody like you," she murmured. "Anywhere." She opened the door behind her into the hall. "We danced out here," she added. "We'd better dance back in."

Jeff and Sylvia, waltzing together, saw them return and could make nothing of it. "But it looks to me as though she's still holding out," said Sylvia. "I'm glad I'm not deserting him. I could never have done that now. If he's got to go back without her he'll need a new show to put his mind on."

10

The party did not break up till late, though the wedding was at noon the following day. But the time had to come at last when the door of their room closed behind them and Evadne was alone with Hermione. She undressed wearily while Hermione was in the bathroom, which she always occupied for a young eon, and when Hermione emerged smug and fragrant from her bath Evadne was lying motionless with her head buried in the pillow. Hermione moved about the room being tidy and picking up things, and finally snapped off all but one of the lights, saying, "Aren't you going to clean your teeth?"

Sighing, Evadne rolled out of bed with her hair in her eyes and pattered off to the bathroom without dressing-gown or slippers. When she returned, Hermione was in bed, apparently asleep. Evadne, who so often of late had found herself thinking, What have I done *now?* in Hermione's silences, stood a moment, slim and chilly in her silk pyjamas, and then got into her own bed, sitting up with her hands round her knees.

"Hermione," she said quietly.

"Well?"

"I don't think it's fair to Stephen not to tell him why I— why I've got to go to Lausanne."

"You're going to Lausanne because you promised to go," said Hermione, who always became excessively devoted to the cause when it was to her advantage, "and everyone expects you to."

"Yes, but I only offered to go in the first place because I thought I ought to leave London for a while. I thought everything would sort of blow over, and—"

"And won't it?"

"No. I didn't realize."

"What am I supposed to say now?"

"Hermione, I want you to let me off."

"Let you off? What are you talking about?" Hermione sat up too, and they looked at each other warily across the space that divided the twin beds. "It was your idea to go to Lausanne," said Hermione.

"I know, but—"

"Stephen's been speaking of love again. I can always tell. Any man can wind you round his finger."

"Hermione, that's not true! But Stephen—"

"Stephen—Mark—Victor—that violinist from Andorra, or wherever it was—and the Danish tennis player—and the man from—"

"Really, you make it sound as though I—"

"Yes, doesn't it!" said Hermione unpleasantly. "It just

happens to be Stephen now, because he's here, and he's newer than Mark, and more amusing than Victor!"

"I don't know what you mean by that," cried Evadne, trying to keep her head, for her little conquests were truly innocent enough, and would never have happened at all if she had not tried to put her other associations before her dawning love for Stephen. Hermione's interpretation of her rather lost and feckless behavior shocked and angered her into futile speechlessness—she was never good at rebuttal—and the last vestiges of tolerance and affection between them were wearing away under this constant friction. "If you're trying to imply that Victor and I—"

"I don't have to imply. I know perfectly well that you're having a relationship with Victor at the same time you're leading Stephen on, and if you're not careful I'll tell Stephen that, the first chance I get, if he can't see it for himself."

"But you *can't!* It's not *true!*" Evadne was aghast. "He wouldn't believe you!"

"Oh, wouldn't he!"

"But, Hermione, that's *blackmail!*"

"I'm not asking for hush money," said Hermione.

"Then what do you want me to do?"

Hermione was silent, and Evadne sat there, shaking and cold in the middle of the bed, recognizing once more the beginnings of a Scene. If it went on, before very long she would begin to feel sick. And soon after that she would find herself giving in again, saying anything, promising anything, just to end the Scene. Hermione didn't mind Scenes, sometimes it seemed as though she rather enjoyed them, as though she emerged from them refreshed and strengthened, and of course triumphant because of course she always won.

To anyone who had not Evadne's constitutional horror of seeing anyone beside themselves with anger or grief, her cowardice regarding Hermione's Scenes would have been incomprehensible. But outbursts of any kind were not customary in Virginia's household, and Evadne went in dread of Hermione's violent tears and equally violent rages, which frightened her, and outraged her sense of the decencies, and she endowed them with far more importance than even Hermione realized.

Having learned that Evadne would crumble into acquiescence during the course of these emotional hurricanes, Hermione used them pitilessly whenever she needed to get her way. It was no trouble to her to work them up, and they always paid off in headaches which required massage with cologne and a light meal on a tray in bed, prepared by Evadne who had somewhere along the way been thoroughly sick in the bathroom and couldn't bear the sight of food. Evadne felt now the familiar, inevitable surge of nausea in her shrinking midriff, and bit on panic. She had promised Stephen to try.

"There's no need to hate me so," she said miserably after a moment. "I didn't mean any of this to happen. But I may as well tell you—Stephen wants me to go to America with him." And as she said it the corners of the room wavered and leaned, and she shut her eyes.

Hermione sat very still for a long moment, not looking at her. When she spoke, her voice had gone pinched and small.

"Then he *has* asked you to marry him."

"I didn't mean to tell you. But it's difficult to refuse a man and not be able to give him a reason."

"So you want to tell him, I suppose, that I'm being a fool about him and you haven't got the face to marry a man I—"

"Oh, no, *no*, not like that, I only meant—"

"You solemnly promised me never to tell him."

"I won't, truly, without your permission, but—"

"Well, I don't give my permission," said Hermione, and lay down and turned her back.

Evadne sat there, drooping, in the dim yellow glow of one

lamp. It could end here, if she gave way to cowardice again. She could turn out the light and lie down in the dark, and eventually get some sleep, and in the morning they would dress during one of Hermione's watchful silences, while she waited to see if the subject was going to be reopened, quite prepared to do battle again from a standing start right where they had left off. And if nothing more was said about it in the morning things would just go on as they were. Tomorrow was the wedding, and one didn't want to look a fright at Sylvia's wedding. It could end here. . . . But she had promised Stephen to try.

"Hermione, I—want to go with Stephen," she said, and her voice was nearly steady, although the sickness swayed within her.

"*What?*" Hermione sat up again, with a rustle of bedclothes. "But you swore you didn't care anything about him! You *swore* you wouldn't marry him!"

"I—it's different since then. I didn't realize—I'm awfully sorry—" Her voice died away. She leaned her forehead against her bent knees. Her palms were cold and wet.

"What will all our friends think? What about Lausanne? For that matter, what about *me?* Do you intend to walk out and leave me with an expensive flat on my hands? The flat we chose together, as our headquarters for the most important effort towards world understanding that is being made to-day—the *only* important effort, you've said so yourself!"

"Perhaps I could find someone else to come and share the expense of the flat with you."

"Someone else!" cried Hermione, through her teeth. "*Anyone* else, I suppose, to get out of it yourself! It wouldn't matter whether *I* liked them or not, would it, *I* can live with *anybody,* so long as *you* get away with Stephen!"

"Please, Hermione, I didn't mean—"

"What it amounts to is just that you've fallen in love with him yourself!" Hermione accused, getting husky and beginning to sniffle. "The only man I've ever cared tuppence for, but you can't let any of them alone, you have to go on adding one more scalp to your belt! You haven't even got the decency to *warn* me, till after you've made him propose, you let me go on thinking you'll play fair as you promised, and then all of a sudden you spring it on me in cold blood that you want to go away with him! You never think of anyone but yourself—"

At this point Evadne scrambled out of bed and ran for the bathroom and threw up her dinner, while Hermione's voice went on wildly in the bedroom, mixed now with sobs. Returning shaken and limp and chattering with cold, Evadne said sharply, "Oh, do shut up, Hermione, everyone will hear you!" and got into bed and pulled the covers over her head. Even there she could hear Hermione crying out loud, and tried to remember who had the rooms on either side of them. "All right, all right," she said drearily, defeated once more, and raised herself on one elbow and turned off the last light. "I'll go to Lausanne."

A strangled silence ensued from the other bed.

"When?" said Hermione thickly.

"Whenever you like, I suppose."

"Then we'll leave tomorrow, after the wedding, in case you change your mind again." Hermione was never a generous winner.

"Are you coming too?"

"What else do you expect me to do? Grovel to Stephen for his notice after you've gone?"

"I'd grovel to Stephen any day," said Evadne, "if it would do any good."

"It never does any good to grovel to a man," said Hermione, who knew less than nothing about them, but always affected a disillusioned cynicism. "They only despise you for it. But there's one thing about *you*—by the time we get to

Lausanne there'll be somebody else! And the first time the lights are turned down for an Experience Meeting—"

"Hermione, stop it! You're being horrible tonight, I can't bear any more!"

"Then don't take me for a fool!" said Hermione, and black silence closed on the room.

Evadne lay on her back, gazing dry-eyed into the dark. He will despise me still more for giving in to her like this, she thought. But he hasn't any idea of what it's like to cross her, I suppose there are people who could cope with it quite heartlessly and go their way. But I couldn't be happy with Stephen if I had to remember her like this, bitter and lonely and hating me. You can't build happiness by wrecking somebody else to get it. I can't, anyway. The worst of it is, she's getting so that even if I do what she wants, it's wrong. Maybe it isn't any use to try. Maybe I ought to give up on Hermione—but she was so much better for a while. I must try once more to be friends with her. It won't wreck Stephen to do without me. Nothing wrecks Stephen. He'll marry someone in America by and by and never know what happened here. He'll think I didn't really love him. I *don't* love him enough to go to him over Hermione's dead body. Or perhaps I love him too much. I wouldn't be any good to him that way, I'd be haunted and guilty and ashamed. There are more important things than the way I feel about Stephen, she told herself, striving to recall the doctrines of her beleaguered faith. I must try—to find my way back to them—I must try to find— Guidance for Lausanne. . . .

Empty and exhausted, Evadne slept.

11

The sun shone on Sylvia as a bride, and they drove straight away from the church to the little house near Cheltenham which had been lent them for the honeymoon by a friend of Virginia's. They were to have it for a fortnight, and then meet Stephen at Southampton to sail for New York.

Sylvia had dispensed with white satin and been married in a blue going-away suit with a foolish hat, and carried pink roses. Jeff was driving, and for a little while there was silence in the humming car. Then he said, without taking his eyes from the road, "What's the matter, want to go back and say it's all a mistake?"

"I feel," said Sylvia without any heated denials, "as though I had been climbing a long hill for years with no real hope of ever getting to the top—and then suddenly there isn't any hill any more and the sun is shining and the wind is blowing and—I've *got there!*"

"You mean you really wanted to marry this guy?"

"I really did."

"I've often wondered," Jeff began in an academic sort of way, "and of course I've never had a chance to do any practical research on the subject till now—but it's often seemed to me very unlikely that any woman ever drives away from her wedding ceremony without a sudden what-have-I-done sensation."

"Well, take a look at this one," said Sylvia cheerfully. "It was a tough fight, Mom, but I won. Honestly, Jeff, you thought of more reasons not to marry me!"

"But amongst 'em all, I never said I didn't love you, did I."

"No-no, maybe not—"

"Then what are you kicking about?" he asked softly, and she laughed, and touched his hand on the wheel.

"Poor Stevie," she said after a moment. "I feel very wicked to be so happy."

"I'm afraid poor Stevie is right up against it," Jeff agreed soberly.

"You know what I think?" said Sylvia. "I think Hermione is in love with him herself."

"*What?* That viper? She wouldn't know how to be!"

"She doesn't know how, probably. But she watches him— I've seen women do it before. You see, darling, Stevie is a special case. He can't walk across a room, or mention the time of day, without setting up vibrations all round him. It's partly his stage training, his stepped-up magnetism and his terrific vitality—and it's partly just Stevie, which is why he has the rest of it. Women like Hermione, and women *not* like Hermione, for that matter, come to see the show over and over again. They sit out there in the dark, invisible and anonymous, and become the woman on the stage with him. So long as that curtain is up, all his warmth and gaiety and tenderness are for *them*, not for the woman on the stage. Stevie plays in a very special way with his leading-ladies, have you noticed?"

"Can't say I have, no. Go on."

"He doesn't play long, intense love scenes—he doesn't have to. Every word, every look, is a caress, every move he makes in a dance routine does homage to his partner. He swings her from hand to hand only to show her off better, at a new angle, *her* grace, *her* skill, his pride of *her*—and yet without him she'd be nothing exceptional. I know, I've worked with him. He *makes* you dance, he makes you feel beautiful and adored. Even if you're his sister, *playing* his sister, he builds you up and encourages you to feel terrific —and pretty soon you *are* terrific. And that comes over the footlights to the women in the audience. See what I mean?"

"Mm. He has to have something to work on, up there on the stage, though."

"Stevie is the sweetest, most *heartening* person in the world," said his sister. "It makes for a lot of misunderstandings. People—I mean women—just can't believe that it doesn't mean something special, but it's just that he was born friendly and forgiving, and even after years in the theater he still expects the best of everybody and brings it out of them too, in spite of themselves. By all the cynical rules, Stevie ought to be taken advantage of right and left—he isn't careful about contracts and billing, he doesn't elbow and climb, he doesn't think he's the greatest thing on earth— anybody in show business will tell you that's the way to get no place fast. But look at him. Nobody tops him for sheer drawing power."

"Very encouraging," said Jeff. "Go on."

"Well, getting back to Hermione. We both know he can't bear her. But *she* doesn't know, and never will, from him. Because she can take all his charm and tact and good manners to herself, and it makes her feel good, and so she wants more. Hermione could turn into one of those pathetic women who come and worship him at matinees all through the run, if she couldn't see him any other way. And this closer association, by accident, in the family, could be just about as fatal to her."

"In that case, she's probably jealous of Evadne," said Jeff.

"She could be."

"But even so, I don't see how she could hold Evadne back if Evadne really wanted to marry him."

"We don't know what goes on there, Jeff. It's—sinister," said Sylvia, and drew up her shoulders in something like a shiver. "Hermione really gives me the creeps. I wouldn't live with her if you paid me."

"You're telling *me*," said Jeff grimly. "So why doesn't Evadne get out? Why should she be immune to the effect Stephen has on women?"

"I don't think she is. I think she's desperately unhappy about something. I've dreaded for him to fall really in love like this, because heretofore it's always been so simple for him. Easy come, easy go, and no hard feelings, he never really seemed to care much one way or the other. Evadne's different. He's got everything against him now, and he just doesn't know how to bear it."

"This is all very interesting," said Jeff. "And if you can just explain to me *why* it has to be Evadne out of a whole world full of girls, ready, willing, and able—"

"For one thing, she needs help. You've said so yourself."

"She's past it now, I guess."

"Oh, don't say that, don't give her up, Stevie hasn't!"

"Since when has Stevie gone round rescuing maidens from minotaurs?"

"Never till now. And anyway, that first night he saw her at the Savoy he didn't know she needed rescuing. He *says* he fell in love with her then—before he even knew who she was."

"And tell me, Mrs. Day, do you believe in love at first sight?" Jeff inquired with a slanting look.

"It's not our kind, Jeff. But it's just as real to Stevie."

"Of course I'm prejudiced about Evadne," he admitted. "Trying to look at it impartially, I can see that she is a very pretty girl—not my type, mind you, but in her way very attractive, with a kind of nitwittedness which might appeal to the men in the white jackets who come to take you away to the Home."

"She'd forget all that nonsense if she fell in love and got married."

"I've heard Virginia say the same thing. It seems to me a naive, rather old-fashioned view, but there may be something in it. Would it cure Hermione too?"

"He can't marry them both. So Hermione might try to prevent him from marrying the one he wants."

"Does he know all this?"

"He must. I suppose I must make sure, but he doesn't talk about it. I sometimes think he might do better to leave it for now, and try again next year. Give her a chance to miss him, you know. Sometimes that works."

"Unless Hermione pushed her at Victor, or some of his pals, to get her out of Stephen's way."

Sylvia shook her head.

"I somehow feel that Hermione will try to keep Evadne just where she is, which is what I like least about the whole thing. Hermione will take it out on Evadne."

"We're kind of lucky, aren't we!" Jeff remarked thoughtfully. "The way things ironed out for us, I mean. If anyone had told me the last time I was in Williamsburg that today was coming I'd have said they had a touch of the sun."

"*Who's* lucky?" demanded Sylvia. "I've *worked* for this! You were harder to land than a barracuda!"

"I resent that," said Jeff. "I'll take that up with you later when I have both hands free."

"There's our turning!" cried Sylvia, pointing. "On the left. You've overshot it!"

"That's because you were interfering with the driver." Jeff came to a halt and began to back. "You're not supposed to annoy the driver of this bus. Where? Oh, I see. Clever girl. I could think of a lot of suggestive things to say—it's hardly safe to open your mouth about a honeymoon, for fear of being misunderstood. May I put it merely that I want my tea and a little privacy?"

"Put it how you like," said Sylvia. "I'll double it."

"Have I ever mentioned to you," said Jeff, sailing down the left-hand road, "that I love you to what-they-call distraction?"

12

It was not until a rather exhausted family began to trickle in to tea in the drawing-room at Farthingale that Evadne and Hermione were found to be missing. Inquiries brought forth the information that their car was not in the garage, and that in fact they had not returned from the church after the

ceremony. Further investigations revealed a note, hitherto
undiscovered on Virginia's dressing-table, which read:

Darling Mummy: Please don't feel badly, but as I've got to go
I think it's best for me to leave now, while it's convenient, and
no fuss. I shall be quite all right, we are off to the Continent now,
and I will write you from Paris or somewhere in a few days.

EVADNE

There was an enclosure for Stephen, in which Evadne had
written in a rather hurried-looking way:

Dear Stevie: I suppose you will wash your hands of me now,
but honestly I did try last night, and I promise to go on trying,
but there is nothing else I can do or say just now. I won't be seeing you again before you go to America, I'm afraid, and you'd
better not write to me from there as I wouldn't know what to
answer. When I say that I will go on trying, that doesn't mean
I expect you to wait round indefinitely for me to be able to marry
you, that wouldn't be fair to you. If you can get over it and be
happy with somebody else I honestly think you should go ahead
and not think about me any more. If you should still feel the same
the next time you come to England—but I haven't any right to
expect that and I don't, so if ever we do meet again please let's
just start all over again and please don't have any idea that I will
hold you to anything you've said this time, because that would
be embarrassing to us both. I truly can't see my way to causing
any such holocaust as attempting to do any differently now would
mean. We are crossing the Channel tomorrow and will tour
round a bit before it is time to go to Lausanne. Please forgive
me, and try to understand.

Always,
EVADNE

Stephen took it very quietly, as might be expected, and
pretty soon retired to his own room with his share of Evadne's
message, where he sat down in front of a wood fire and tried
to read between its lines. He was more convinced than ever
that she was under some duress, and because he had never

encountered anything of the kind before his imagination boggled—he thought that was the word—at what sort of entanglement she had got herself into, though it looked very much as though Hermione knew where the body was buried and could dictate her own terms. Hermione was pure poison, of course, but he was firmly convinced that any of the more obvious deductions were too easy and not even to be considered. This was something special, it couldn't be pigeonholed under any of the usual labels. Evadne had dreamed up a new one, doubtless so simple and original that Freud wouldn't have known it if he fell over it. Evadne herself doubtless didn't know Freud from Adam. . . .

Sitting in front of his fire holding her note, Stephen found himself wishing that he could consult Jeff again, and reminded himself that Jeff was busy now. Got to paddle my own canoe on this thing, Stephen thought. Can't go putting ideas into Virginia's head, either. Nor I can't go round and ask Oliver if his daughter is certifiable, because if she was he'd have done it long ago just for peace. Not Oliver's fault, anyway, they say it was her mother. I wonder— Darn, I should have had it out with Hermione long before this happened. Easy enough if she'd been a man. But how do you tell a woman how to get off?

So what do I do now, Stephen thought. Go back to America with my tail between my legs? *If you should still feel the same the next time you come to England.* . . . Does she suppose for one moment that I *won't?* But it will be a year before I can bring the new show to London. Anything can happen before then. Even a war. They'll close the theaters if there's a war, they say, because of air raids. Sylvia mustn't stay here then, but if I could get into the Flying Corps—heck, that's no time to get married, just before you get killed. Time to get married is now, like Jeff. . . .

X.

New York

Christmas, 1937

Although his arms were full of parcels, Jeff paused at the hotel desk to collect the afternoon mail and carried it with him to the elevator. The fact that the mail was still there told him that Sylvia had not yet returned from the matinee.

He got their door unlocked, dumped his parcels on the table, hung up his hat and coat, and went into the kitchenette and put on the kettle for tea, while Midge the canary sang a welcome in his cage by the window. And all the time Bracken's letter lay there beside the parcels where he had left it, waiting for him. He was not accustomed to dread Bracken's letters, but he knew pretty well what had to be in this one, or the next one, or the one after that. Time's up, it would say. Back to the salt mines. The honeymoon is over.

Well, it was more than most people got for a honeymoon, he reflected conscientiously, in spite of losing every evening to the theater except Sundays, and two matinees a week, since the opening in April. But that, as Sylvia pointed out, was no worse than if he had gone to an office all day every day while she stayed at home, the way it was with most people. They spent the days together, and in the evenings, while she did her performance, he worked on his book. They had something besides happiness to show for their year. Another new Sprague show was ready to go to London if it ever finished its New York run, and Jeff's novel was accepted and almost ready to go to the printer, with the dedication—*For Mab*—just as he had promised. A newspaper man seldom has the time or the continuity of thought to write a book, but on leave as Sylvia's husband he had got round that.

And there was something more. He hadn't heard from his heart again. Maybe that was one of the things Bracken had had in mind when he gave them the year. You had to get up very early in the morning to beat Bracken to an idea. Sylvia's serenity and love and laughter had helped Jeff build up his margin on nerves—not to mention the fact that there was also an international lull, if you didn't count the Spanish Civil War, which got nastier all the time, and some new trouble in China, and Mussolini's friendly visit to Berlin. . . . You couldn't call it peace, in the old sense of the word. You couldn't count on it to last. But at least one March had passed without a Nazi "surprise" and Hitler was still contained within the borders of Germany, and the European balloon had not gone up. The coronation of George VI in London had not been marred by any untoward events, the marriage of the Duke of Windsor to Mrs. Simpson in France had passed off quietly. Baldwin had been replaced as Prime Minister by Neville Chamberlain, who was at least a good business man, and the fifth Nuremberg Rally of the Nazi Party had seemed if anything a little slowed up. It was not enough to justify optimism, but in times like these one was grateful for an interlude. Till next March? And why always March? Something to do with Hitler's belief in the stars, no doubt.

Jeff realized that he was wandering round the room avoiding Bracken's letter, as though waiting for Sylvia to come in before he opened it. The kettle boiled, and he warmed the pot and made the tea, and hunted out the box of macaroons from the parcels on the table. Midge went on singing. He knew as well as anybody that it was time for Sylvia. Then her key turned in the lock and there was the first kiss after hours apart—the reassurance of it, the recaptured delight, the security— Sylvia had come home.

"Darling, I've asked Stevie in for a cup of tea, he's a little down today. Somebody stopped him in the lobby on the way in, but he'll be right along."

"That's good, I've just wet the tea," said Jeff, using an old North Countryism that they liked.

Stephen lived in the same hotel and on the same floor, but in a separate suite. He had been very firm about that, when they engaged the rooms. He was always scrupulous about not intruding, until they had almost to beg for his company, and there was a while when they were uncertain whether to leave him alone with his unspoken misery about Evadne or to try to pry him out of his shell. By now they had all shaken down to a less self-conscious basis. He often had tea or dinner with them, especially on matinee days, and they usually planned their Sundays all together. What he did for recreation the rest of the time remained obscure. His rooms were full of books of all kinds—he read a lot, especially at night, sometimes all night, if they had known. And he spent endless hours perfecting gruelling dance routines, building up new tricks, and doing a little composing of his own on the piano—the present show was the first to combine the work of himself and his father as a new partnership which gave Fitz enormous satisfaction and was a howling success with the customers. They knew he wasn't looking for consolation in a bottle or from any of the women who would have been only too pleased to supply it. They were almost sure that he never heard from Evadne direct, because of his undisguised eagerness for news of her in the other letters from England. That he was still in love with her was very plain.

"Ooh, you've been to that French place for macaroons,"

said Sylvia, as Jeff took her hat and coat from her and carried them into the bedroom. "Hullo, Midgie, are you a good boy?"

"*Yike!*" said Midge, who was waiting to be spoken to, and he put up his crest and jumped up into his swing, showing off.

"There's a letter from Bracken," said Jeff, returning from the bedroom. "I haven't opened it yet."

"Nice fat one." Sylvia laid it aside and shuffled through the others without much interest. "Aren't you going to read it?"

"Well, I—thought I'd wait till you came."

"Oh, darling—bad news?"

"It's got to be bad news one of these days. Our year is about up." They went into each other's arms and stood quietly, holding each other.

"My own news isn't too good," she said at last, her cheek against his. "We're selling out ten weeks in advance."

"Oh, heck, that's up till March first! I can't possibly wait here that long!" he cried.

"That's what I mean. But you know how Stevie is, as long as people will buy seats he won't close the show. He says he's got no right to throw the whole cast out of work just because the star, who happens to have a bank-roll, is fed up."

"Is he?"

"I don't know. I wish I did. He keeps to himself so. And he's so thin."

"He's always thin," Jeff reminded her.

"Not late in the run like this, only at the beginning—I mean thin so you can't see his shadow," she sighed. "I've got to work with him tomorrow morning, I'm afraid, he's got a new dance dreamed up—with bells! The trick is to keep them silent when you don't want them to tinkle. *He* can do it now. *I* shall go mad, learning! Bring in the tea, darling, he said not to wait." She cleared a place on the table, set out the china, and filled two cups. "Christmas presents?" she inquired, nodding at his parcels.

"Mostly. No peeking."

"Wish we could have gone to Williamsburg."

"Wish so."

"Hadn't we better see what Bracken says?"

But just then Stephen rang and knocked—he always did both, though they left the door unlocked for him. Having signalled his arrival, he strolled in, wearing his between-shows garb—a turtleneck sweater, slacks, and ancient tweed jacket with one button fastened. The sweater today was canary-colored, the tweed was brown. He had removed all traces of make-up as he always did even on matinee days, and his long, lined, naturally plain face looked too fine-drawn and white, Jeff thought, with the recurrent pang of futile conscience that he and Sylvia could be so content while Stephen's life was still all messed up.

"Mmmm—macaroons," said Stephen, reaching for one, and Sylvia handed him a cup of tea.

Tired as he was, he waited till she had chosen her chair, and then set the macaroons within her reach before he himself collapsed bonelessly into a corner of the sofa. She noticed as they sipped and chatted that his left foot was rotating gently on its ankle.

"Stevie—that foot. Is it all right?"

"Oh, sure, sure." He disappeared behind his cup.

"You don't forget it," she remarked.

"The old man is getting so he can't take it, I guess," he confessed lightly. "It's that jump from the table in the second act. I've got so I dread it all evening—the table gets higher and higher as the time comes—when I'm on it, just before we take off, it might be the Eiffel Tower. Say, why wouldn't that be a good idea?" He sat up. "Start with a sort of low coffee-table thing, and have it on trick legs that raise it another notch each time we come round to it—till finally they just know we can't make it again, and that time we use our fannies—we *sit* our way over it!" He snapped his fingers. "Something new for London! Let's get at it tomorrow."

"Instead of the bells? I'm in favor of it," said Sylvia.

"*Besides* the bells. Ten o'clock on the stage, don't forget. I'll have Al rig up something."

Sylvia looked at him compassionately and nodded. There went her own Christmas shopping for another day, but love for her brother welled up in her as she watched him drinking his tea in a corner of the sofa. He had never been better in his life than he was now, so far as the paying customers were concerned. His little miracles with canes and hats and handkerchiefs and other dancing props caused gasps and applause in the middle of his numbers, and he had even trained a chorus of perspiring young men to do some of his own tricks in a shadow-dance arrangement. (His patience here had made Sylvia's head ache. "No, son, look—watch my eyes—not like that, son, watch my left arm—once more, son, keep your elbows down—*that's* the boy, oops, almost, try it again now, keep your left elbow down—all right, fellas, once more, all together now, poppa's coming too this time, wait for the beat—too *fast,* fellas, *relax,* don't beat the beat —slower, son, you're too anxious, there's no fire—keep your elbow down, son—" And so on, by the hour, easy, smiling, helpful, soft-voiced, with the patience of Job—his only letdown when he would occasionally cut loose himself, a tapping, twisting, leaping whirlwind, to show them how it would look when they got it right.)

While the curtain was up and the house was full his inspired fooling never flagged—his humorous hands, his transfiguring grin, his lightfooted grace of movement, his brief comic Donald Duck rages, his mischief, his *joie de vivre,* his all-enduring devotion to a wrong-headed heroine. Sylvie herself knew and wondered at the perfection of his nightly performances, with no faking, no fumbling, no slacking off.

She knew that his elbow would be exactly there for her hand as she swung round to it, that his fingers would always catch hers at the same split second, that his shoulder was ready for her weight, that his hands on a lift were sure and gentle. She threw herself into their numbers with all she had of skill and timing and apparent abandon, and they achieved a spontaneity that she at least had never experienced before. Stephen himself said that she got better all the time, and she felt that the hours of punishing practice his perfectionism imposed were all worth while.

But when there was no audience—that is, when nobody present had bought tickets to see him—all the bounce went out of him. He was cheerful, even-tempered, and polite —elaborately normal. But he did not make up the weight he always lost before an opening, he did not enjoy his food, and his eyes showed that he was not sleeping well. It was perfectly plain to anyone who knew him that there was something very heavy on his mind, and Sylvia had no doubts about what it was. He had left England without seeing Evadne again—he had had no alternative short of putting detectives on the number of her car before it could get to the Continent. Or he could have hung about for weeks until she chose to return from the conference at Lausanne. Sylvia wondered sometimes if they had been right to advise him to sail with them and let Evadne see how she liked being without him, if that was what she thought she wanted. They had pointed out that when he returned in a year's time with a new show he might find her chastened. "If I don't find her married to somebody else," he had qualified once, and Jeff said grimly, "Over Hermione's dead body!" Anyway, Stephen had little choice but to agree at the time. The new show was waiting for them in New York, and Jeff and Sylvia were counting on a few days in Williamsburg before rehearsals began.

For Stephen the year had been a long drawn-out agony

of just living through it, day by day. He had written to Evadne now and then, not too often, not too intimately, and she had never replied. Of course she had asked him not to write. And of course he could not be positive she had received the letters—but on second thought he had addressed one of them to her at Farthingale, just in case Hermione did try to interfere. . . . It was not answered either.

So Stephen had endured his year, as it were incommunicado, picking up crumbs from Virginia's letters and Bracken's, keeping his fingers crossed so long as there seemed to be no news, while the show looked like running forever in New York, and that table got higher each night, as though it already had the trick legs he was going to set Al to figuring out in the morning. His left ankle was not bearing up. And he found himself rearranging in his mind the steps which led up to the table so that he could land on the other foot for a while—there were difficulties connected with the dress Sylvia wore and the fact that he had hold of her at the time and they made the leap together—nothing that couldn't be ironed out with a few rehearsals on the alterations. . . .

"Stevie, why don't you put up the notice?" she was saying over her cup of tea, and he stopped waggling his left foot—there was an ominous little grinding in the ankle joint—and looked scandalized.

"*Can't!* We're selling out now till March!"

"Yes, I know, but—"

"Are *you* all right?" He focused on her in sudden anxiety.

"Oh, yes, I'm O.K., but—"

"I suppose one of these days you'll spring a baby on me," he said resignedly, and Jeff grinned.

"There's a letter from Bracken which probably has sailing orders for me, if that cheers you up any," he suggested.

"Well, it doesn't," Stephen said perversely. "What's he say?"

"I haven't looked yet. I'm kind of afraid to."

"Well, come on, let's know the worst," said Stephen.

"I forgot Midgie's sponge cake," Sylvia said, and went to the kitchenette to get the crumb which constituted Midge's tea-time treat. She picked up the letter on the way, and carried it with her, kept it in her hand while she bent over the cage, and then tossed it to Jeff. "It's like a time-bomb," she said. "Might as well explode it."

2

Jeff's long, deliberate fingers were a little clumsy, opening the letter. He unfolded it carefully and they could see that it was several pages, closely typed. For a minute his eyes ran down the lines without comment, until Sylvia said, "Oh, read it, darling, out loud, I mean. We've got to know now."

"Well," said Jeff unwillingly. "There's quite a lot of it. And it just shows you how out of touch you can get. All kinds of things coming up.

"Dear Kids—(he read, without expression)

"Merry Christmas and Happy Anti-Comintern Pact. Excuse it, please, but anything for a laugh these days. I tried that one on Dinah and she said it was definitely beneath me, but she laughed first.

"It's a crying shame, isn't it, that Stevie's show is such a success that he hasn't got the face to close it before Christmas so you could all go to Williamsburg or even come back here for the holidays. Too bad about him. Well, anyway, we're going to miss you. We almost made it over to New York to join you, but Dinah hates the winter passage and Virginia is always blue at this time of year because it brings back Archie's death, so I gave up coming and we shall go to Farthingale as usual. Johnny and Camilla have arrived from Berlin with hair-raising stories of increasing German Press censorship and the expulsion of various too outspoken correspondents.

"Something's up, Jeff. I have just done a deal with an American radio network for a weekly broadcast from here, on the general state of the world, as far as I can make out what they want.

I am arranging for a hook-up with Johnny as a sort of roving reporter on the Continent, and when you get back I think we shall send you out on the same kind of job. It's a not impossible idea, in our fifteen allotted minutes of air time, to share the broadcast between me in London, Johnny in, shall we say, Berlin or Vienna, and you in, shall we say, Paris or Madrid or Geneva. Geneva, he says, and the League deader than mutton since this Abyssinian fiasco. There will have to be something to take its place, and that will be one of the big stories of 1938. Or if nothing does take its place, that too is pretty sure to be a story—probably not a funny one. The mechanics of making a sort of weekly news round-up by air will take a lot of engineering, but they tell me it is possible by using pre-arranged signals, etc., and it's going to be quite a thing to work out. How do you like the idea? As one of our roving reporters, you will be more or less on your own, subject to orders from my London headquarters, gathering and arranging your own material where you find it, and talking it, not a typewriter, over the network. I happen to have a good radio pitch to my voice, and yours isn't much different, so I don't think you will have anything to worry about.

"Radio is going to play an increasing part, with very dramatic possibilities, in reporting the world scene from now on. We have already had some Spanish war coverage of that kind, and the BBC's handling of the Geneva proceedings on Abyssinia points the way pretty plainly—people will *hear* what is happening *while* it is happening, instead of reading about it afterwards. (Suppose there had been a microphone in the Salle des Glaces at Versailles in 1919!) And of course the Nazis have learned to prostitute radio to their propaganda with deadly effectiveness. We are 'way behind the dictatorships in recognizing the value of broadcasting in the presentation of doctrine, news, facts, *truth* —or, in their case, lies—to the mass of people who can't or won't read and think for themselves. And if we get a general European war, there is of course no limit to what radio can do. It may require a change in our copy-writing, calling for some experimentation—copy to be *spoken*, not printed. You would do well to give some thought to this.

"Everyone here seems a bit too preoccupied with the news from Asia to suit me. No matter what happens out there, which is plenty, it doesn't do to take your eye off Berlin. Johnny says the French diplomatic there are betting on another Nazi attempt on Austria within a matter of weeks. And this time Mussolini will sit on his hands.

"Just in case Hitler blows another gasket this coming March, I would like you to count on being here well before it's due, so that we can get ourselves planted on this new broadcasting stunt. Somebody will have to go and perch in Vienna if it looks like blowing up, and somebody else will have to snoop round Berlin, though it will probably be impossible to broadcast from either place in a crisis. That would mean flying to Paris or London to get a microphone, and then there will always be the problem of getting back into a Fascist country if you've said something they don't like. And they won't like.

"Before you can start you will have to make some voice tests and trial readings, and see how your usual sort of copy sounds over the air. I have tried for years to teach you simplicity—one word instead of three, a short one instead of a long one, and plenty of periods. When you come to speak your own stuff you will see what I mean. I didn't know the half of it till I dealt my own self a couple of tongue-twisters.

"The *Queen* sails from there the first week in February and I would like you to catch her, even if the others must be a few weeks behind you, and I can see your three long, reproachful faces from where I sit. But things can't go on forever the way they are over here now. It's too quiet. Dictators can't afford a status quo. Something is due in the spring. It might be Austria, it might be the Sudetens in Czechoslovakia, it might be something more to do with Spain. There's no League any more, it has gone the way of the Disarmament Conference, Locarno, Versailles, and the scrap of paper. We're on our own, kids. And it won't be long now.

"England has come out of the holiday spirit brought on by the coronation, and is beginning to take notice of what the bombing of Spanish towns means to civilians. It could happen here. Britons are beginning to face facts. And the facts aren't pleasant. If Hitler starts a war, this whole island will be in the firing line. There won't be any non-combatants in the next war. The enemy invades by air now. Napoleon stood on the shore at Boulogne and gazed across the Channel at inviolate England. He must be envying Hitler's advantages today.

"A thing called *constructive pacifism* has been invented here for the further confusion of woolly thinkers, and while there's too much of it and it's far too vocal, it doesn't really mean any-thing. The very same young men who now publicly shudder at the idea of killing and being killed will be flying British bombers within a few weeks of a declaration of war—and doing it effi-ciently and without any fuss. England will fight, if any one of several things happens. I wish Hitler was as sure of that as I am. Ribbentrop saw all the wrong people here, and got a lot of wrong impressions—partly because they were the impressions he wanted to have and that he knew Hitler wanted to hear.

"And what, will you ask now, about Evadne? She is still bark-ing up the wrong tree, wearing herself to the bone with her meet-ings and committees, and even making brave, nonsensical little speeches of her own. I know what they are because I thought it my duty to go and hear her, little as I wanted to. In the old days when Virginia and Dinah were girls, Evadne would have been sent on a cruise to the Mediterranean or banished to the Riviera to distract her mind, and nine times out of ten she would have had a little flirtation or two and come home cured. The world was larger then. And simpler. Nowadays, short of shipping her right out to America I don't see any way of separating her from all the unfortunate influences which surround her in London, but even that is not a practical idea because (a) she wouldn't budge, (b) she would find the same kind of people there too, and (c) you're all headed this way in a short time, we hope. I think for her sake the sooner the better if Stephen means to go on trying. Evadne is in a rut. And I think too if a war does start, she will regard it as her own personal failure and go almost out of her mind. It's not just Victor now, it's Ribbentrop as well, and even Hitler, whom she has met and talked with in one of his more lucid periods at a party in Berlin, and who, she is con-vinced, is merely misguided and misinformed. As her pal Ribben-trop is his chief source of information on England, I don't know quite how she reconciles her tolerance of him with the other idea, but doubtless she is guiding and informing Ribbentrop too, with Victor as a sort of Greek chorus.

"She has been abroad a great deal of the time during the past year as you have doubtless gathered. Hermione goes everywhere with her, like the Old Man of the Sea. When all's said and done on that, it does preserve the proprieties in what sometimes would seem rather doubtful circumstances otherwise, travelling on the Continent, etc. After all, Hermione does prefer to live in England

and intends to see that Evadne comes back from these European
jaunts, which must be to the good. Virginia says she would rather
have Hermione than no watch-dog at all.

"For the rest, we are as well and cheerful as can be expected
—Going On Nicely, as the bulletins on Notable Invalids put it
—and hope you are the same. I realize that this is no kind of
letter to write at Christmas time. I was Santa Claus last year,
remember?

Love to you all, from all of us,
BRACKEN"

There was a long silence in the hotel room when Jeff finished reading the letter, and no one moved till Stephen rose
casually and went to set down his cup on the table. They
watched him wordlessly, and he looked at each one of them
in turn. Jeff's fate was sealed and dated. Sylvia's—possibly
Evadne's too—waited on him.

"Well, I guess the notice goes up for March first," he said
quietly. "I've never done it in my life before, but we're going
to close to good business and take the show to London. It'll
be a matter of six or eight weeks for you two to wait. What
the heck, I've been waiting a year already. And there's no
guarantee when I get there that she'll listen to me. Maybe
if I rolled my *r*'s and clicked my heels and kissed her hand—"
He did so, graphically, where he stood. "—and leered a bit—"
He leered at Sylvia, who did not laugh. "Or maybe—" He
pulled down a forelock, made a double chin, fixed a fanatical
glare on the middle distance, extended his right arm stiffly
at half-mast, and snarled, *"Heil Hitler!"* And even on the
words the pose crumbled, the hair was brushed back, he gave
a rueful grunt of laughter, and walked round the table aim-
lessly. "Don't mind me," he said apologetically. "Where do
we eat?"

"Let's have it sent up." Sylvia reached for the telephone.

"Like me to push off?" Stephen offered gravely.

"No!" they both said at once, and Jeff laid violent hands

on him so that Stephen folded up in the nearest chair with a sheepish grin. "We've had just about enough of your tact, or whatever it is," Jeff went on, and "Room service," said Sylvia at the telephone. "We're all in this together," Jeff continued. "We've got no secrets from you. I've never tried to conceal from you that I'm in love with Sylvia, that still goes, we don't need all this privacy. Stick around, cheer us up, cry on our shoulders, whatever you like, but let us in on it, for goodness sake!"

"Language," said Stephen, pleased. "Tomato soup, club sandwich, and a glass of milk," he added to Sylvia.

"Steak," said Jeff, who didn't have to dance. "And ice cream."

Sylvia gave the orders with her own and hung up the telephone and sat looking at them with a gleam in her eye.

"Let's hear Jeff his lines," she suggested, and assumed a genteel detachment before an imaginary microphone. " 'This is Jefferson Day, speaking from you-know-where and here is the latest news about you-know-who.' "

"It's a funny thing about mike-fright," Stephen took up the cue solemnly. "I wouldn't know, myself, I'm just lucky that way, but I've listened to people who had it, and according to them it's got stage-fright licked to a frazzle. It comes on all of a sudden, without any warning, they tell me, like a kind of paralysis—a *creeping* paralysis—" He began to build it up, with gestures and mugging. "You can't move your feet, they seem to be made of putty, and your hands go stiff and wet with perspiration, and then your tongue begins to turn cold and to swell, and your Adam's apple comes up into your tonsils and gets stuck there till you can't breathe, and you start to choke—*and choke*—" He appeared to strangle and die.

Jeff was clearing the parcels off the table and putting away the tea-things in the kitchenette and pretended Stephen wasn't there at all.

"Wait till the fan mail starts coming in," said Sylvia. "He'll have to hire a secretary, and have some pictures taken, won't he—for mailing out."

"The left side of his face is better, don't you think?" Stephen surveyed Jeff critically from various angles. "Be sure they don't ever photograph you from the right, Jeff, you don't want to scare people."

"*May* I have your autograph, Mr. Day?" pleaded Sylvia with clasped, ecstatic hands.

It wasn't Noël Coward wit, but it tided them over a bad quarter of an hour, and dinner was quite silly.

XI.

London

1938

"This is Jefferson Day in Paris," said the earphones Bracken
wore in the little studio room at the BBC, and he leaned
forward with a glance at Dinah who sat close beside him.
The broadcast was on—the news period beamed at America
which could not be heard in England except through Brack-
en's earphones, but which would carry his voice, and Jeff's,
and Johnny's, to the network in New York, gauged to split-
second timing, a masterpiece of engineering and enterprise.

"I have just arrived here from Vienna, via Berlin and
Amsterdam," the quiet, unhurried voice went on conver-
sationally, as though Jeff sat in the same room. "I was not
allowed to broadcast from Vienna after the Reichswehr
marched in. The Ravag Building in Johannesgasse, from
where I expected to speak, has been taken over by men in
field-grey uniforms with bayonets. The program director,
who is a friend of mine, is a prisoner. It was obvious that,
from now on, Nazi censorship would prevent me from saying
anything I wanted to.

"The outgoing planes were supposed to be all booked up
for days ahead, but I went to Aspern airport early Saturday
morning to see what could be done. Already the field was full
of German war planes, and the Gestapo was in charge. They
finally cleared the London plane. Its passengers were mostly

Jews who would not have sold their places for any coin ever minted, and quite rightly. For many of them this was the last chance. I stood on the field and watched them go—just a hand- ful of them, safe, by the grace of God. The plane to Berlin was not so popular, and I was able to get a seat in that. At Berlin, while I waited for the Dutch plane which would take me to Amsterdam, I bought newspapers, and read in banner headlines that Austria had been rescued from Com- munist chaos, fighting in the streets, a helpless and demo- ralized Government. Yet I had seen Vienna quiet and tragically composed, until Nazi hoodlums took charge and began breaking the windows of Jewish shops and molesting in the streets anyone they chose to label Jew. It will be recalled that in 1934 the Munich radio announced the death of Chancellor Dollfuss twenty-four hours *before* he was murdered—a murder attributed by Germany at the time to Communist chaos in Vienna. But the men who killed Doll- fuss, we know now, were Nazis wearing Austrian uniforms. The Nazi lies get larger and more careless as the Nazi ma- chine grinds on.

"When I left Vienna Saturday morning nearly every house was already flying the swastika flag—produced somehow out of the air. All night hysterical crowds had surged through the Karlsplatz shouting *Sieg Heil!* and *Hang Schuschnigg!* while indulgent police looked on, wearing swastika armbands. The Austrian police have gone Nazi. Chancellor Schuschnigg himself is said to be under arrest and torture. His friends urged him to escape in a special plane provided for him, but he would not leave his country.

"This is Jefferson Day, speaking from Paris. I return you now to Bracken Murray in London."

And Bracken, smoothly resuming his own microphone, with Dinah beside him wiping her eyes on his handkerchief, wanted very much to cry too, and at the same time to shout and pound people on the back. They had done it. London to

Berlin to Paris and back to London, in fifteen minutes without a hitch. Johnny had come through first, revealing among other things that the population of Berlin had seemed to take the Anschluss with something like apathy—and Jeff in Paris sounded steady as a rock. It *worked*. The hours of effort which had gone into the intricate checking and re-checking of wave-lengths, transmitters, and time-cues, the countless telephone calls and cables to Berlin and Paris and New York —it all worked. Hereafter it would be feasible for foreign correspondents to use the air for a sort of newsreel round-up, instead of waiting on cables and telephones. Censorship was still a problem, of course, but a new technique in world-wide reporting had been established. And Jeff would grow up in it, make it his own medium. His voice was right, his timing was instinctive, he had dignity and pace and color. Hallelujah.

2

The broadcast had taken place at midnight Sunday, London time. Stephen and Sylvia had been in England only two days, and Stephen had not caught up with Evadne yet, and all the exhausting minutiae of the London opening were ahead of him. Nobody had come to meet them at Southampton this time, because of Austria, and if war began they might not open at all.

But there was no war. Hitler entered Vienna in triumph, and made a speech from the balcony of the Hofburg. Within a week Austria was completely Nazified, gripped by sadism, Jew-baiting, arrests and disappearances, servile betrayal, and terror. The thing was done. No shooting, no fireworks, no resistance. Only suicides. Austria was dead.

Chamberlain, speaking in the House of Commons, pointed out that nothing could have prevented the Anschluss unless Britain and France had been prepared to use force. What he

did not say was that, instead, they had yielded more ground
—quite literally—and lost face—just as important—and now
it was too late. Now Czechoslovakia was doomed. Sylvia knew
it would be Czechoslovakia next because Bracken was sending Johnny on to Prague to arrange for a hook-up there with
Geneva, as broadcasts at present had to come out over a
telephone line which ran through Germany.

Evadne took the *coup* in Austria very hard, for she could
not see why Victor, for one, had not seen it coming. It was
said that the news that German troops had crossed the Austrian border came through while Ribbentrop was lunching
with the Prime Minister in London; and took even him by
surprise—or so he wished it to appear. All the satisfaction
she could get from Victor during the next few days was a
hurried telephone conversation now and then, excuses,
postponements, half-truths, until it looked as though he
was deliberately avoiding her, which she resented, for she
wanted to upbraid somebody for causing this increased
tension and hostility just when things were going a little
better, and she wanted to hear the unaccountable move
explained and justified.

In the meantime Jeff had returned to London, sobered and
saddened by what he had seen, and even the delight of his
reunion with Sylvia was overhung with darkening European
skies. She found him preoccupied and remote at times, and
wondered what there was that he had still not told her,
wondered if she should encourage him to talk it all out or try
to help him forget it. Dinah, out of her own experience, said
the best thing was to keep as normal as possible oneself, avoiding both an appearance of indifference and of gruesome
curiosity—an adjustment to the finer points of connubial
diplomacy which could only come with practice. Just be
there when wanted, Dinah said, ready to listen or ready to
divert. He'd let you know which. And finally it would sort
of wear off, till the next time.

Stephen's new show opened early in April, with the usual resounding success. His few meetings with Evadne before that occasion were all casual ones, surrounded by the family, on the basis laid down in her final message before he left England a year ago—they were to start all over again, and she would not be holding him to anything that had already been said between them. At the same time, she had been disappointed, as the year went on, that he had taken her so literally. She had asked him not to write to her, and she had received no letters from him. She had said, in effect, that he was not to presume on the past if they met again, and beyond his first hearty greeting he had not kissed her—there had not been, it was true, much opportunity, and with the first night bearing down on him he had not even tried to make an opportunity. Evadne assured herself that this was exactly what she wanted, and continued fervently to immerse herself in her religious associations, in which she was becoming an outstanding figure both for her personal beauty and her single-minded devotion to the Cause.

She was present with the rest of the family at the first-night party after the show. She danced with Stephen—once—and mentioned that she and Hermione must leave early because of getting some sleep before catching a train in the morning.

"*Train?*" he repeated, horrified. "Where?"

"To Scotland. We're going up to a Conference. It's very exciting, we shall be away a week or two, organizing."

"What's up now?"

"There's to be a big crusade meeting in London the end of May with speeches by important people, to launch a new campaign for international peace. It's a very large-scale program now, to go beyond the personal, face-to-face basis and reach labor and capital and government groups and leaders—to make *all* the classes everywhere realize that civilization rests on individual responsibility—on each human being's sense of truth and justice and moral standards."

Stephen's arm tightened in the dance, and his breath was on her cheek as he laughed indulgently.

"I'm glad I don't have to say anything in the show like *your* lines!" he remarked. "I'd dry up every night!"

"Don't you ever take anything seriously, Stephen?"

"I sure do." He was instantly grave. "Once I even thought I'd give this Quiet Time idea of yours a try—but all I thought about in my Quiet Times was you, it's always that way if I let my mind off the leash, and I don't get anywhere with my sins that way, because the more I think about you—" He spun her till her full skirts wrapped his own nimble legs, and he met the end of the music with a long smooth glide, and his arms were slow to release her.

"It's nice to dance with you again," she said, rather formally.

"Well, thanks for saying it first!" he cried in pleased surprise. "I hope you remember everything else I taught you as well."

"I have to go now," said Evadne, and held out her hand, looking a little pink and breathless, while her dazzling, generous, warm-hearted smile enveloped him. "Good night, Stevie—I'm sure the show is a great success. Wish me luck with mine, won't you!"

While he was still reeling she withdrew her hand again from his lingering clasp and was away to join Hermione for their other good nights.

She did not write to him from Scotland either, and she had left him no address, and her stay there extended itself to something over a month, while the show built up a tremendous business and Stephen was reclaimed by all the enthusiastic friends he had left behind a year ago. Despite the ominous rumblings in Czechoslovakia, he found his life in London very gay, very normal, very much to his taste. It was demonstrated to him daily that Evadne was not the only girl in the world, that he knew several others who were much more cooperative, in fact even just a bit *too* anxious, and none of them made speeches about moral standards. But always with something like a crinkle of his heart, as between whimper and laughter, he would acknowledge once more that it was Evadne he wanted, and no one else. Sometimes he wondered cynically if her very elusiveness was part of her charm for him, the traditional virgin come-on in the face of male pursuit—and he knew in the same breath that he wronged her earnestness, her honesty, her maddening immature idealism. It was no game she played with him, for the fun of conquest. She had no conception of feminine caprice in her ardent, muddled little soul. She truly believed that she put him off because her mission as she saw it was more important to the world than her only partly realized love for him. And he knew that if all that radiant devotion and integrity could be captured from its visionary tangents and channelled into any such down-to-earth purpose as love and marriage and children it would be worth all the tact and endurance it would cost the man who was there when it happened. Some day Evadne was going to grow up. And that, Stephen told himself, he wanted to see.

A couple of days after her return with Hermione to the flat they still kept up together, he rang her up and was cordially invited to tea. Hermione never left the room while he was there. A few days after that Jeff rang up the flat and invited Evadne to have lunch with him at a little place in Soho—alone. "Just us," said Jeff firmly. "Not Sylvia. Not Hermione." And he added as she hesitated from sheer stupefaction, "Else it's *off*." Flattered and curious, with some idea of hearing momentous things about the European situation straight from the horse's mouth as it were, she accepted. And five minutes after they were seated at a table in the corner with their backs to the wall, by obvious prearrangement Stephen walked in and Jeff rose at once to give him his chair. "Now you're on your own," he said with a fatherly smile, and departed.

Evadne was surprised, but not, Stephen noticed, angry.

"Well, you needn't have gone to all this trouble," she said mildly. "I'd have lunched with you without a decoy."

"But not without witnesses," he said, picking up the menu. "Ear-witnesses, I mean. I haven't said one word to you since I got back that couldn't be overheard even if I whispered."

"Well, what are you going to whisper now?"

"Same old thing. Let's order first." He did so, and when the waiter had gone he turned to her, his hands rather tense on the table in front of him. "Hullo," he said gently.

"Hullo, Stephen." Her eyes were steady and troubled. "You look tired. Is your foot still bothering you?"

"Who told you I had a foot?"

"Jeff or somebody, I suppose. Is it being a nuisance?"

"I forget about it most of the time," he said untruthfully. "In fact, it's the least of my worries."

"I know. Isn't the news terrible!"

"I don't mean the news either. Honey, aren't you ever going to stop trying to save the world single-handed? Couldn't you agree to hang up your halo and come down off the pedestal and live your life at my level?"

"Victor says that our generation can't afford to think of themselves."

"And what does Victor think of instead?"

"Much bigger things," she told him patiently. "We are in the midst of a world revolution. We have no right to consider our own mere personal happiness."

"And can I infer from that that if you permitted yourself to do as I suggest—you could be happier?"

"Don't try to trap me, Stephen, and put words into my mouth!"

"Then I'll use my own words. Drop all this and marry me."

She sat looking down at the table in front of her. She was

thin, and her lips were soft and drooping. She looked tired too. Stephen waited, watching her, his hands locked on the white cloth beside the silver he had pushed aside.

"Suppose I asked you again not to make it harder for me," she said at last.

"That's my idea exactly. Everything you do now is too hard. I want you to let it all go. I want to make a new life for you. I want you to try it my way."

"I can't do that. I could never look them in the face if I quit now."

"Who?"

The waiter brought their food, and they were silent till he had gone, and then began to make a pretence of eating.

"Look who in the face?" he persisted.

"All my friends. Everywhere."

"Take my friends, then. They'd be delighted."

"I can't," said Evadne with her gentle, infuriating obstinacy, and Stephen took a grip on himself. "We'd better not talk about it any more," she added, like an elderly nanny.

"Darling—be honest with yourself, if with no one else. Look round you at the world today—listen to the news from the Continent—and then tell me what you expect to accomplish, you and your friends."

"A new world," said Evadne, and her chin came up. "A world of good fellowship and understanding and tolerance, where these dreadful things can't happen."

"That's a lot of nice words. But don't you see—so long as any sizable chunk of the same old world prefers violence and tyranny you only make it easier for them to prosper if you—"

"The light can spread," said Evadne.

"Not fast enough, now."

"Then you give up!" she cried tragically. "You *invite* disaster!"

"*Au contraire.* I never give up. Hadn't you noticed?" Briefly his fingertips brushed her hand that held the fork, in a caress so subtle that it could hardly have been seen at the next table, yet she felt her heartbeat quicken. "I love you. You love me. Why can't we get married?"

"But I—d-don't—" she faltered.

"You can't look me in the eye and say you don't love me."

"Well, of all the conceit!" She tried to smile, met his eyes, and was lost.

"Say it, then. I dare you." And when she only sat looking at him helplessly—"You see?" he said without triumph. "I told you. You can't do it. Darling, what happened last year, when you left Farthingale like that? What made you suddenly decide that this thing of ours was impossible? Haven't I earned an answer to that?"

She dropped the fork against the plate, clasped her hands, almost wrung them, in her lap, as though he had tried to catch and hold them against her will.

"There's no *time!*" she gasped defensively. "There's no *time* now to be in love and be happy, Stephen, things are— mounting up all round us!"

"Scared?" he asked softly, watching her.

"Yes, frightfully." She ducked her head in shame. "You don't know what it's like—you're a man. But I'm the family coward, you may as well know that. Rather than sit here helpless while bombs fall on London I'll do *anything!* I've *got* to! I've got to do *something!*"

"I know one thing you can do."

"What's that?"

"Marry me. They won't bomb Williamsburg."

"*Run away?*" She stared at him in horror, and he laughed.

"Fine coward *you* are!" he said.

"But I am, I—can't sleep for thinking of it, and I get the shivers and the shakes. When I think what's been happening in Spain—"

"Sure, anybody with any imagination feels that way."

"*You?*" she asked incredulously.

"Me."

"You're—scared too?"

"Yeah, and let me tell you something." He pointed a long, bony finger. "So is Victor."

"But he's—"

"And if he says he isn't, he lies in his teeth. They're all scared, that's what makes them act the way they do! They're all whistling past the graveyard, and don't you believe different."

"But Victor's trying to *do* something!"

"Such as?"

"He's trying to *stop* it. He's asked me to help him."

"How?" said Stephen skeptically.

"Well, he—he says—"

"How?" Stephen repeated relentlessly.

"He believes in international co-operation and—understanding. He says if only we all spoke German there wouldn't be so many misapprehensions and—"

"How if they all spoke English, would it work the same way?"

Her lips tightened.

"You always make fun of Victor."

The waiter came, and hesitated at sight of their almost untouched plates, and Stephen waved him away.

"You didn't answer my question, did you," he said compassionately. "There's something you won't tell me, about what happened last year. Did you ever kill anybody?"

Her honest astonishment made him smile.

"No, of course not!" she said.

"Then what are you afraid of?" he asked reasonably. "They don't hang you for anything else. Whatever it is somebody is holding over your head—apart from the Nazis, I mean—let 'em drop it, I'll pick up the pieces."

"It's not—blackmail, if that's what you mean."

"Look, honey, I've told you before, I'm not fooling.

Maybe it's none of my business why you choose to live the way you do, maybe you'll hate the sight of me if I keep on, but I want the answer and I'm going to have it. It would save a lot of trouble if you—"

Evadne sagged against the back of her chair with a little hopeless sigh.

"You say you love me, and then all you do is add one more thing to what there is already."

"I'm sorry," he said humbly.

"Then let it go, Stephen. Don't *hound* me."

"My dear, I wouldn't—I couldn't—" Words failed him.

"But you *are*. You only make it worse like this, I—"

Again the waiter hovered, anxious to bring them something they would eat, and Stephen said, "How about an ice? Or a pastry?"

"Just coffee, please."

"Just coffee," said Stephen, and motioned for the plates to be taken away, and when they were alone again, "Honey," he said without any visible exasperation, "you wrote it down last year in the only letter I've ever had from you that we must start all over again, when I came back to London. So we did. I tried my best to convince myself that I was seeing you for the first time—but it was just the same anyway. I fell in love all over again, and I'd never stopped being in love from last time, you must have known I couldn't just turn it off with a tap."

She looked at him long and levelly.

"I thought at least you were trying," she said.

"Didn't you even read my letters?" he asked.

"What letters?" said Evadne coolly, and now his eyes probed hers in what seemed an endless pause.

"You didn't get any letters from me," he said then, rather flatly, and with no interrogation. "You thought I didn't write any."

"Naturally."

"But I did."

"Did you remember to post them?" she smiled.

"With my own hand. There was no room for accidents at my end."

"Then what became of them?" And as she asked it she saw the answer which had already occurred to him, and her eyes widened. "You don't think somebody *took* them!" she gasped.

"What do *you* think?" said Stephen.

"*Hermione?*"

"Who else?"

The waiter brought the coffee. In the silence which came with him, Stephen moved the sugar nearer her cup, but she did not see.

"But we—you can't prove that she did," Evadne said, when the waiter was gone.

"I can't even prove that I wrote them, I suppose. But I sent one to Farthingale, on a sort of hunch, and we may be able to find out something about that one."

"But *Mummy* would never—"

"No. But she may just have forwarded it, so it arrived the same way as the others. How does your mail come, at the flat? Think, now. How do you get your mail, as a rule?"

"It's pushed through a slot in the door. Hermione is usually the first one up in the morning, and she—" Evadne fell silent, looking down into her cup.

"She picks it up. You get your letters through her hands."

"Why, yes, I—Of course there's more than one post a day."

"Do you always meet the others yourself?"

"No, I—never take much notice, my letters aren't very important—"

"There were only five of mine altogether," he said. "A reasonable amount of vigilance and luck would have done for them all." He waited. "You don't seem—altogether incredulous," he remarked, and she would not look up from the cup.

"She didn't want me to marry you," she said thoughtfully. "But I *had* asked you not to write, and so when nothing came I thought—"

"You thought I was learning to be happy with somebody else as you advised," he suggested, and she nodded vaguely. "You were wrong," he reminded her gently, and waited.

Finally, with an effort, she raised her eyes to him.

"Do you suppose she read them?"

"Probably. But don't worry, they weren't love letters, exactly. I didn't let myself go, that is, I only wanted to keep in touch with you till I could get back, and I wanted you to know that I meant to come back, even if I had to start all over again. When you didn't write I remembered you had said in your message that you wouldn't know what to answer, and I supposed you were just determined to have it your way. But you didn't really think it was going to be as easy as that to get rid of me."

"I'd asked for it," she said, and he saw that her eyes were full of tears.

"Well, are you going to stand for this from her, or are you going to have a show-down?" he asked. "It might have done a good deal of harm, one way or another."

"I—don't know what to do," she said helplessly. "I can't just—walk in and *accuse* her, out of the blue."

"Why can't you? If I go along with you and say I wrote five letters and where are they, what can she say?"

"We can't do it that way. Are you *sure* you had the right address?"

"There was the one to Farthingale. Your mother has the right address."

"But if I ask Mummy about that one she'll know there's something up. I don't want the family to—"

"Why protect Hermione now? She'd done about the lowest thing anyone could, hasn't she?"

"If I'm sure she's done it," said Evadne slowly. "I must be *sure*. I must have a little time on it."

"The last time you said that it took a year."

"I know. You've been very patient." She gathered up her gloves and purse. "Let's get out of here. I want to think."

He paid the bill and they left the restaurant and paused on the curb looking for a taxi.

"Let me come along with you now and settle this thing," he urged, as one drew up beside them.

"No, please, I—want to think." She was troubled and sad. "If she's really done that, it's very serious. Things can never be the same. I can't—I really can't put up with anything like that. You'd think she'd know we'd find it out sooner or later."

"Not if I just took offence and drifted away. She may have gambled that I wouldn't come back to London at all, if I didn't hear from you. In which case, I wouldn't give much for her peace of mind right now."

"Perhaps. Thank you for the luncheon, Stephen. Please let me go now, I'd rather think this out by myself."

He had no choice, and the cab drove away.

3

Evadne had given the driver the Bayswater address automatically, and found herself already at Lancaster Gate before she had achieved any sort of coherence in her thoughts. She stopped the cab there and walked diagonally into the Gardens towards the Pond.

It had come as an odd relief to know that Stephen had not kept silence for the past year. Inconsistently she had taken his apparent obedience to her request as dismissal or desertion and it had hurt more than she knew. But now instead there was this new, numbing betrayal of her trust by a friend she had stuck to in defiance of everybody, risking even the loss of Stephen forever for the sake of what she felt was a greater need than his, if only because it was noisier, and an older loyalty of her own. She was still hoping as she came to the Broad Walk and paused there that some perfectly simple, decent explanation could be made if only she could keep her head and handle the thing wisely without getting Hermione upset. She stood looking up and down the Broad Walk in the afternoon sunshine. If she turned to the right the Walk led to a gate at the bottom of the Queen's Road five minutes from the flat. If she turned left she would come to the sanctuary of the little sunken garden which lay behind the old brick Palace.

It was a great time-waster, that square hidden garden, bewitching its habitués into day-dreams and loitering. On a sudden weakening Evadne sought it now with a twinge of conscience for putting off a little longer this new embarrassment between herself and Hermione. The pleached walk which bordered the garden was almost deserted and she stood in its deep shade with her elbows on an iron gate and watched a long-legged, paddle-footed bird playing at the edge of the pool, surrounded by the formal blaze of bloom. She had never brought Victor here during their walks in the Park, he did not know it existed, for part of its enchantment was that its devotees felt a strange reluctance to share it with any but the most select companion, and most often liked to approach it alone with a childish selfishness, cherishing a sweet pretence that it belonged exclusively to them, a secret haven from their own besetting realities. But she thought of Stephen as she stood there, and wished that he could see it now, with the sun across it, and the busy bird, and the stillness, and the color. . . . It was one more sign among many that she loved him, if she wanted to bring him to the garden. . . .

Sighing, she walked on, turned a corner, and paused again

at another opening with a gate, basked again in the brief, stolen peace. Finally, having made the square, she came again to the entrance and emerged resolutely into the Broad Walk and set out for the Queen's Road gate. Even as she entered the automatic lift in the lower hall of their building, she told herself that she did not quite believe that things could be the way they looked. And she discovered with a guilty sense of reprieve that some people had come to tea which she had entirely forgotten about.

She watched Hermione as hostess, at her somewhat patronizing best among the slightly sycophantic friends she seemed to prefer, and Stephen's suspicions became more fantastic by the minute, until Hermione said off-handedly, "Some letters came for you—I put them somewhere—one from Italy, I noticed, it must be the Lorings, we were just talking about them."

Evadne found the letters, in a pile on the secretary-desk they both shared—where she had found letters dozens of times before, arrived in her absence, sorted over, commented on. Suppose one time Hermione had said, "One from America, I noticed, it must be Stephen, what does he say?" Evadne opened the letter from Italy and read out to them all that the Lorings were coming home next week, had had a marvellous time, had lots to tell, and hoped to see them soon. The tea party dragged on, with bright laughter and affectionate, shallow talk, merged into dinner all together at a Corner House, and wound up at a French film which was considered worth seeing.

It was nearly midnight when the two girls arrived back at the flat and Hermione was in such an excellent mood that Evadne hated to spoil it—tomorrow would do—tonight they were tired, and things were bound to go wrong—and she had still no idea how to begin. She slept badly and woke with a headache to hear the morning post thump through the letter slot, and closed her eyes again with dread. Hermione moved quietly to pick up the letters and went into the living-room with them. So easy, Evadne thought, and pulled the sheet over her head. I never thought to *watch* for Stephen's letters, I only hoped that one would come. . . .

She dozed again, uneasily, and heard Hermione making tea in the kitchen. On good days she brought a cup to the bedroom for Evadne. This was a good day, and Evadne drank it gratefully to the sound of Hermione's bath water running. Feeling dull-witted and unable to cope, she got out of bed and into a dressing-gown and hunted up the morning paper. Henlein again—agitating. Why did they let him? Hitler was going to visit Mussolini in Rome. Was that a good sign? It couldn't be. Last time Mussolini had saved Austria. The war in Spain had made them partners now. Part-time ARP workers were wanted in London to be trained. She shuddered. Air Raid Precautions. Blast-proof steel shelters were to be provided by the Government, and gas-masks would be issued to the entire civil population. They hadn't used gas in Spain. Not yet. . . .

Hermione came out of the bathroom in a cloud of fragrance and said she had cleaned the tub. The morning proceeded as usual. They were still sitting over a late breakfast and Hermione was saying that all these ARP wardens were nothing but busybodies, when the telephone rang and Evadne jumped guiltily, in case it was Stephen to ask what had happened, which he would never have done, but anyway if he had she would have had nothing to report.

It was Victor, asking her in a low, hurried voice to meet him at one o'clock in Kensington Gardens beside the statue of Physical Energy. They had often taken that walk before, a reasonable distance from the Queen's Road entrance into the Gardens and far enough from the sailboat activity at the Round Pond to be quite secluded.

Reprieved again, Evadne went off to her room to get dressed. There wasn't time to start a discussion with Hermione now, it would have to wait till after she had seen Victor.

She reached the statue first and stood watching him as he came towards her from the opposite direction along the path which started at the Albert Memorial. He walked with a scissors-like military strut, very different from the easy gait of men she was accustomed to see.

Before she could speak he gripped her arm and turned her down the least frequented one of several paths which meet at the statue.

"I haven't much time," he said in the same low tone he had used on the phone. "But I had to see you. I go to Germany tomorrow morning."

He had been to Germany several times before, though not on such short notice, but something made her say, "But you'll be back soon? You always do come back."

"I don't know. Except that I must go." His voice was harsh. His hand on her arm was without tenderness. They had come to an empty bench and he propelled her towards it, and sat down beside her with a quick, furtive glance round about. No one was within hearing. It was a cool, foggy day, and the Gardens were almost deserted by the usual prams and strolling couples.

"Victor, you're not in *trouble?*"

"Of course not!" he said impatiently, covering his own uncertainty. "Ribbentrop has gone—so I go. It is impossible to say for how long."

"But—surely I'll see you again?"

"Perhaps not. Unless—" He was looking at her fixedly, as though watching for something in her face, waiting for her to say something he expected.

"I hoped you would be here for our London meetings the end of this month," she said uncertainly. "We're expanding our program in a very special way, and—"

"Talk—words—*futilities!*" he said suddenly, through his

teeth. "In Germany we *act!* Come with me now, and see for yourself!"

"Now? But I—you don't mean—" She in her turn was searching his face, finding it grim and secretive.

"I don't mean that I can marry you before I go," he said explicitly and with irony. "That can come later, if you wish."

"If I—"

"It is not a time to be childish, Evadne, and think only of yourself. It is difficult for me to explain in a few words, but you have always said you would do anything possible to help make England and Germany friends."

"Yes—yes, I *will*, Victor, you know that!"

"Then come to Germany *now*. Take the eleven o'clock train to Dover tonight, and go by boat from there to Ostend. We cannot travel together and I am flying over tomorrow, but you will be met at Ostend."

"B-by whom?"

"By a man I shall send. Wait for him at the Continental Hotel. He will bring you to Berlin, where I will have rooms engaged for you. Your passport is in order? Have you enough money?" He reached for his inner pocket.

"Yes, of course—please, Victor, we don't need any money from you."

"You will need nothing once you reach Ostend, everything will be provided. Bring only one small bag, or none at all, to make the journey seem unintended. Don't draw any unusual sum from your bank. Don't let anyone know you are coming."

"But Hermione will want to know more about—that is, I don't myself quite understand what you—"

"Surely you can understand that it is now only a question of how much you are willing to do to prove all this noble talk of spiritual armament and self-sacrifice—if it is sacrifice, which it need not be—"

"But Hermione might—"

"Will you stop arguing and do as I tell you?" he cried angrily, and it was a long moment before she answered.

"No, I don't think I will, if you speak like that," she said coolly, and he recognized danger signals which he had encountered before now.

He leaned towards her, his hard fingers biting into her wrist, and she thought his eyes were a little wild.

"You must forgive me. You must—be kind to me now, I am under great strain. Listen to me, Evadne—when first I came to England I was unwilling. I came to hate, and to make trouble, and to do harm where I could. That was a long time ago. I met my mother and saw what she was. I—fell in love with you. And so I tried to make of myself a bridge between my country and yours. You know how well I have tried."

"Yes, Victor."

"I have failed."

"But how can I—"

"I have failed to convince the English that they can condescend to like me a little, and I have failed to show in Germany that the English are different than at first we think. Because of what I have learned here, about things that seem so natural to you that you do not notice them—I know that Ribbentrop is wrong. He says England is finished as a world power. He tells the Leader that. I do not agree with him. It is very dangerous to discount your Navy as he does. Your Army and Air Force—pitiable. But your Navy—no. We dare not bring your Navy against us yet. No one will tell them that in Berlin. Ribbentrop will not. He does not believe it himself. He believes that England will be easy. He is wrong."

"And you're going back to tell them that yourself! That's splendid of you, Victor, I—"

"Do you think I am mad?" he asked roughly. "Stand up in front of the Leader and say that Ribbentrop does not know what he is talking about? The next thing for me would be the firing squad!"

"Then why—"

"In Germany you cannot work in the open. You must think round the corner and burrow underground. There are people in Germany who will listen to me, if there is still time. People it would be harder to liquidate than me." He gave a snort of rueful laughter. "It is what in England you call a joke. I was a long time learning what is a joke, wasn't I. Listen, this is one. I go back now to beg from the men like my father who are still alive in Germany. I must look to them—to the old generals—to comprehend that our Leader is being misled. He does not know the truth about England. He will not listen to me against Ribbentrop to hear the truth—but perhaps he will listen to *them*." His face twisted in a grimace that tried to be a smile, but gave him for a moment the squared, trembling mouth of a crying child. "If my father were alive now, it is to *him* and his friends that I would have to turn for help to save Germany! I would like my mother to know that, but it is too late. For her it would be a *good joke!*" He tried again to laugh, and beat one clenched fist on his knee.

"Victor—darling, I'm so sorry—" Evadne's quick sympathy stood in her eyes, and she laid a comforting hand on his and it was immediately engulfed in a convulsive clasp. "How did your father die? In the war?"

With everything else for the moment erased, he stared at her.

"Did she not tell you that?"

"Rosalind? She's never spoken of him to me. Or of you."

Victor sat back against the bench, looking bewildered. His eyes travelled slowly round the informal, peaceful Gardens, with their fine old trees, and the green turf on which one was permitted to walk, and the faraway rumble of red busses along the Bayswater Road.

"The *English!*" he said, as though to himself. "I shall never understand."

"What is it, Victor?"

"Not now." He pulled himself together with a visible effort. "That is past. I must go now. There is no more time." He leaned to her, one arm along the back of the bench imprisoning her shoulders, the other hand in hard possession of hers in her lap. "With you at my side there is nothing that is not possible for us to do. They will listen when I show them you, even the old ones—especially the old ones. *This* is young England, I will say to them. Look at her! Is she the spiritless, degenerate weakling you have been led to expect? See what the women of England are like, I will say to them, that she has come, like this, to save our two countries from lies and stupidity. Behold this Englishwoman, I will say, here of her own free will, alone and unafraid, because she believed me when I told her that she was the hope and symbol of a new world— and then think again about the kind of fighting men Englishwomen can breed! Think again about this war you will bring upon us, I will tell them, while there is still time! You *will* come to Germany, Evadne, and stand beside me there!"

She gazed up motionless into his face, so close above hers— a heavy, brooding, pitiless face, she thought, with eyes that ran possessively from her hair to her throat to where the fast beating of her heart jarred the fold of her unbuttoned coat. His strength held her there, with the arm of the bench cutting into her ribs. For the first time she wondered if they quite understood each other on the terms of her journey to Berlin.

"Must we start tonight?" she objected, purposefully matter-of-fact after so much rhetoric from him. "You know how Hermione is about packing. It takes her hours to get ready to go anywhere, even for a week-end!"

"Good God, must we have Hermione even *now?*" he cried, for a duenna was not included in his plans. "She will never come. She has not your courage."

"She is much braver than I am," Evadne declared loyally.

"You will not let her prevent you? You will come without her if she refuses?"

"But we always go on these jobs together, you know that," she reasoned with him. "It's always a team, lone-wolfing isn't approved of. So you see I'm not sure I—"

"How can you hesitate!" he cried impatiently. "The time is *now!* Armies are marching, the thing will not wait!"

"And besides, I had promised to speak at the meetings here, and it's a little late now to notify them—"

"You can notify no one!" he said harshly. "To advertise our intentions ahead of time is to fail! As for these ridiculous meetings, when will you learn that they accomplish nothing except self-importance!"

"Really, Victor, how can you say such a thing, I thought you—"

"Speeches made in London are not listened to in Berlin! When our Leader speaks the whole world listens! You are wasting your time here, you are no good to us if you are here in London, the great decisions will not be made here, they will be made in Berlin! That is where you belong now if we are to accomplish anything in time!" He leaned towards her again, urgent and more excited than she had ever seen him. "You will not disappoint me in this, Evadne! You will do your part now, as you have always boasted. This *is* your part. You said I had only to tell you, when the time came!"

"Very well, Victor, I—I'll do my best. If Hermione balks I'll—try to come myself."

He eyed her a moment closely, afraid to press her further. With or without Hermione, once she reached Germany the question of marriage was bound to arise, and she would have to realize sooner or later how impossible a marriage between them was, in his position. But then it would be rather late, he hoped, for her to turn back. Hermione was already afraid of a war, and would probably take no risks. If she did allow herself to be persuaded to Germany and made too much of a nuisance of herself, there were ways to deal with that. The first thing was to make sure of Evadne now, of her own free will. Once she was in Berlin and the rest of it was made clear to her she would doubtless be willing enough to stay. Indeed, she would have very little choice. Because the German in me, Victor told himself again with pride, always wins.

"I am sorry I have not bought you anything to eat, but we could not have talked like this otherwise," he said, and raised her hand and kissed it, and rose from the bench. "I rely on you to be discreet between now and the time you leave London."

"Yes, Victor." She looked up at him without rising.

"Stay here until I am out of sight. Then go by the opposite way as you came. We don't want now to be seen together."

He turned and was gone, with his tramping step, back towards the Albert Memorial.

4

Evadne sat still on the bench, trying to think. She felt bludgeoned and dazed. At last she stood up and started limply for Lancaster Gate, meaning to get on a bus and ride round a while, collecting herself. She would get no lunch, but she couldn't tackle Hermione yet. Later she would find a restaurant. Later, when she had decided what she must do.

She crossed Bayswater Road and got on the first bus that came, and gave the man three pennies without looking at the notice board. The bus rocked on, down Oxford and Regent Streets and into the Haymarket. She saw nothing of her surroundings, and had no idea where she was, absorbed in the racing of her own mind.

It was no time now to antagonize Hermione about the lost letters, she was thinking, for this was something far bigger than one's own personal life. She needed Hermione now, as never before, to accompany her to Germany. Hermione would argue—she always did—and she had no true conception of what it was their mission to accomplish. She would say it was too late, she would say they were running their heads into a war, she would say that Victor might be had up for treason and leave them stranded, or worse, involved in his own predicament. Would it be possible to coax her into just an ordinary-seeming trip to Germany, as they had gone several times before, without bringing Victor into it at all? Hardly, with that Ostend business so carefully marked out. Why had she agreed to that? Why had Victor proposed it anyway, she wondered. Why couldn't they just arrive in Germany normally under their own steam, in the usual way? What had Victor got in mind? Was it too late now to ask him? He would doubtless be furious if she rang him up now at the Embassy . . .

It's not a nice thing to do to Mummy, bunging off like that without a word, she thought, gazing blankly out the window. But some day if we are successful she will realize that there was no other way. I can send back a telegram from Ostend. If Victor and I bring something off, they will all forgive me. What happens if I run into Johnny and Camilla in Berlin? And what will poor Stevie think now. . . .

The bus lurched to a stop again. I must find something to eat, she thought lucidly, getting out of her seat. That's what makes me feel so funny. I'm hungry. There must be an ABC somewhere near. . . .

She stepped down and drifted away from the bus stop into the Strand, vaguely in search of a restaurant. And suddenly, right in front of her, as though her subconscious had brought her to it, or fate, there was Stephen's theater with the matinee crowd going in. She paused beside a big frame of pictures from the show, and stood gazing at it wistfully. In the center was a portrait of him, with his grin. She wanted it, to take with her to Germany, for company there. If I bought a program, she thought, I would have a picture of Stevie to take with me. And then she thought, I could go in and see the show without his knowing—like Hermione. Just to say good-bye. She joined the queue in front of the ticket-window and got a single at the side. She bought the sixpenny program from the usher and sat staring down at the picture on the front of it till the lights were lowered.

And there was Stephen, all unconscious of her presence, doing his job, getting his laughs, weaving his own particular personal magic. Evadne sat surrounded by laughter, with tears on her cheeks, and watched him. When it was over she put the program into her bag and stumbled up the aisle. She was now quite faint with hunger and had a headache. She knew that she had only to go to the stage-door and send in her name, and Stephen would take charge of everything, she would be fed and fussed over—cosseted, was the word. And if she gave Stephen one hint of what she was going to do he would hit the ceiling and then she wouldn't have to go. . . .

She hadn't reckoned on the doorman's remembering her, so that there was no delay for second thought and flight, before she found herself standing in front of Stephen's dressing-room door, on which the doorman himself had knocked after escorting her there. "Come in!" said Stephen's voice—so light—so gay—oh, Stevie. But she simply stood there, with tears in her eyes, unable to answer or move, and the door was opened from within by his dresser, also with instant recognition in his smile. The lights were very bright in the room. Someone passed her with a murmured apology on his way out. And then Stephen said, "Evadne, *for the love of Mike*—!" as though he hadn't seen her for simply *months*, and his hands were on her shoulders, and she was being put into a low chintz chair beside the dressing-table, and the door closed discreetly behind the dresser, and Stephen was there on one knee beside her, holding both her hands, saying, "I can't believe it, what brought you here, why didn't you *tell* me—were you in front this afternoon?"

"Yes." Dazzled and confused by the blazing happiness in his face, she gave him a rather sidelong smile. "All by myself. I just sort of found myself in front of the theater and bought myself a ticket and went in."

"*Bought* yourself a—!" He was horrified. "You mean you paid good money to see my show? Don't ever do that again! Just let me know, I'll find you a ticket. Where did you sit?"

"On the left, at the side. I had a wonderful time. Oh, Stevie, you're *so* good!"

"Thanks very much," he said, embarrassed and pleased, and he rose from his knee. "It was a nice house today—they got everything. Have something? Oh, no, you don't. Cigarette? No. Can't I give you *anything?*" He turned in the middle of the room, slim and straight in his tightly belted dressing-gown with a clean towel folded inside the neck, the make-up still on his face, both hands flung wide in a generous gesture.

"You couldn't produce a sandwich, could you?" she suggested, still feeling shy and strange in the presence of Stephen the actor, still under the influence of the spotlights and the music and applause, piercingly aware of who and what he was in the eyes of the people out front, unable to accept casually the fantastic knowledge racing through her that he was hers, and that her unexpected arrival in his dressing-room could give him so much pleasure.

"Sandwich? What kind? *Mullins!*" (The dresser, on guard outside, put his head in at the door.) "What kind of sandwich, darling?" Stephen was asking her.

"Anything. Ham, I suppose."

"Tea?"

"Yes, please."

"Ham sandwich and tea, Mullins."

"Yes, sir."

The door closed softly.

"What's the idea of no lunch? Was there a row at home?" Stephen asked, sitting down at the dressing-table and reaching for the cold cream.

"Oh, don't take it off, *please*, Stephen, I—like it."

He paused in mid-air.

"What, *make-up?*"

"It makes you look so—different."

"That *is* an advantage, isn't it," he said genially, and she giggled. He glanced at himself in the mirror, non-committally, and lighted a cigarette, settling comfortably into the hard straight chair under the glare of the lights. She noticed as he crossed his legs that he still wore his dancing shoes and his third-act trousers beneath the dressing-gown. "Why didn't you have lunch?" he asked casually, dropping the match in an ashtray without looking at her.

"I forgot about it. I was on the wrong bus, and wound up here, and there was just time so I came in."

"They serve tea in the interval, don't they, out front? On little lap-trays that somebody always fails to get rid of before the curtain goes up again, so there's a rattle that kills your laugh. Why didn't you have tea?"

"I didn't think about it."

"What on earth *were* you thinking about?"

"The show. It's wonderful, Stevie."

"My stage-struck darling," he said tenderly, touched. "It's just a show."

The dresser knocked and came in with a cup of steaming tea and a ham sandwich on a plate, which he placed with fatherly care on a little table at Evadne's elbow and withdrew himself again.

"Aren't you going to have anything?" she asked, and sank her teeth hungrily into the sandwich with childlike relish.

"Had mine. Early dinner, you know. Care to join us?" he asked carefully.

She shook her head, unable to speak for munching.

"No, I suppose that would be *too* much," he said meekly. "Do you intend to tell me what happened with Hermione or are you going to let me die of it?"

"Nothing, so far. I haven't had a chance."

"Stalling, eh! I might have known."

"Honestly, Stephen, there were people there when I got home yesterday and it went on all evening. This morning there wasn't time before I had to go out."

"Mm-hm," said Stephen wisely.

Revived and sobered by the hot tea and food, after finding her way to him by some sort of blind, befuddled homing instinct, she realized now with awful clarity what she had let herself in for. It was all very well to look at him from the other side of the footlights as a sentimental gesture, but now she was here in his room, seeing him again as a human being with a mutual past and a personal future. Now to say goodbye to him was as it were to wrench herself out of his very hands and leave him trustful and unaware, expecting to see her again tomorrow or next day—for to tell him what she intended would be fatal, just as not to tell him entailed unforgivable deceit. She should never have come through the stage-door. But now that she was here it was good, it was heaven, and she might as well enjoy it as long as she could. When the last drop of tea and the last crumb of sandwich was gone she gave a little sigh and said she would have to go now.

"Aren't you going to say hullo to Sylvia?" he asked, and she said there really wasn't time, and stood up, collecting her bag and gloves.

As she did so her eye fell on a pile of photographs and proofs dumped down on a cabinet in the corner—scenes from the show, portraits of Stephen, action stills of Stephen dancing—dozens of pictures, like the ones in the frame in the lobby. Evadne stood still, hypnotized by the jumbled treasure on the cabinet.

"Oh, Stephen—could I look at those?" she asked, pointing.

"What—*pictures?* Sure, they're mostly from this show—" He picked them up and put them on the dressing-table. "Come over here, the light's better. You've seen most of 'em, I expect." He placed his own vacated chair for her and she began to turn over the photographs one by one.

"C-could I have one of these—to keep?" she asked diffidently, and he looked at her as though he thought she must be joking.

"There are some better ones upstairs in the office if you really—sure, take the lot, anything you like," he said dazedly, for she had never shown any particular interest in the show or in his pictures before.

But she knew she could take only one to Germany without its being conspicuous, so she chose gravely, deciding on a pose similar to the rather blurred half-tone portrait on the front of the program.

"I don't know that it's good for you to come to the theater," he remarked with a grin, slipping the print into a plain envelope for her. "Next thing I know you'll be asking for my autograph. Which reminds me—don't sit around on it, will you. Find out about those letters."

"I will," she nodded solemnly, well aware that she would not be able to bring it up now till after she and Hermione had returned from Germany, dismally conscious of yet another lie. "I'll let you know." She stood a moment looking up at him, the picture and her hand-bag clasped under one arm, and he wondered at the troubled gravity of her gaze. "Good-bye, Stevie," she said, and lifted her face for his kiss, which was prompt and warm and smooth and smelt of grease paint and powder.

"Good night, darling. Luncheon tomorrow?"

She shook her head, backing away from him towards the door.

"The day after?"

Her fingers found the handle of the door behind her back and turned it.

"I love you, Stevie," she said deliberately, and was gone.

To go after her would be only to encounter the dresser and the doorman. He stood a moment, staring rapturously at the closed door. Progress. This was progress.

The dresser knocked and came in, to find his master dancing, dancing, in his dressing-gown, in the middle of the small floor, an intricate, hilarious soft-shoe routine. And while he stood admiring, the gay steps ended in a wincing failure of the left foot, and Stephen dropped into the chair by the dressing-table with a muttered Darn, and reached for the cold cream.

5

I shouldn't have said that, Evadne was telling herself rather lightheadedly as she reached the pavement outside the theater and hailed a passing taxi and gave the Bayswater address. Now he'll count on it, and everything will get still more complicated. It was a mistake to let him know, like that, he'll think it's a promise. How could I ever look Hermione in the face again if I married Stephen? But she had no right to take my letters. Well, it will all have to wait now till we get back from Germany. I can't have her in a foul mood the whole time we're away. . . .

Maybe it was a mistake to promise Victor I'd come to Germany just now, she thought as the taxi turned into Oxford Street. I'm always making mistakes, sometimes it seems as though everything I do turns out to be a mistake, but I can't help it, I only try to do what seems best at the time—you have to do *something*. . . .

It would be no fun, she knew, to return to the flat now, unaccounted for for a whole afternoon which she had presumably spent with Victor. But she could bear that, she was used to that, and the thing was to get Hermione packed for the trip to Germany. She always needed a week's notice for a move, and now she would be in a bad mood to start with.

Evadne was prepared for argument, or procrastination, or endless cross-questioning, when she entered the flat, but she had not anticipated a flat refusal to budge. The discussion raged all through a pick-up dinner and was carried on in slightly raised voices while Evadne cleared away and stacked the dishes in the kitchen.

"It's madness," said Hermione, not for the first time, and her small white teeth snapped shut on the word. "I keep telling you, the evening paper says that German troops are moving towards the border and the Czechs are mobilizing."

"But Bracken's there," said Evadne stupidly. "In Prague, I mean, and he—"

"In the first place, Bracken is an American," Hermione reminded her tartly. "And in the second place, I don't think his presence will influence the Sudetens one way or another."

"Well, Johnny's still in Berlin and if anything did happen—"

"Can't you get it into your head that we travel on English passports?" said Hermione. "We don't want to be caught in Germany if war is declared, we'd be interned for the duration. We might even be killed by our own bombers!"

"I refuse to believe it will go as far as that," Evadne said firmly. "Now is the time to do what we can, while there's still a chance. I'm going to pack."

"Then you'll go alone," said Hermione, and Evadne whirled in the doorway to stare at her.

"You wouldn't let me down like that," she gasped. "It's only for a week or two—just to meet these people of Victor's and stand shoulder to shoulder with him while he—"

"In front of a firing squad?" inquired Hermione. "No, thank you. If Victor is really in some sort of underground movement in Germany, which I doubt, it would be very dangerous to be seen with him there."

"Oh, nonsense, the Gestapo wouldn't touch *us*," said Evadne sensibly.

"Anything can happen there now, you know that perfectly well."

"Victor *said* you'd be afraid to come!" Evadne challenged her. "And I said you were braver than I am."

"It's not a question of being brave or afraid," Hermione replied with dignity. "The German underground, if it exists, is Germany's affair. You know what happened a few years ago in the Purge. We would be perfectly helpless to save Victor and possibly ourselves too."

"But Victor *said*—"

"Victor is simply trying to get you to come to Germany, for his own good reasons, no doubt."

"Now, there you go again, implying that Victor and I—"

"Well, if you want to take a chance on Victor's morals and integrity you can, for all I care. I wouldn't put myself in his power for anything on earth!"

Evadne gazed at her in exasperation. As though Victor had time now to bother about— But that was part of Hermione's trouble, she had a complex about men. According to Hermione, whose experience, Evadne felt, was considerably less than her own, there wasn't a man alive who could be trusted if you were in his power. It was an old-fashioned novelette sort of notion which did her no credit.

"But I couldn't reach Victor now to say we aren't coming," Evadne objected, determined to be reasonable.

"He'll find that out when we don't turn up. If you ask me, it was only a try-on anyway. He doesn't really expect us to come."

"That's a very limited view," cried Evadne. "I don't want him to think *I'm* afraid!" And she flounced off into her bedroom and got out a small suitcase and began to throw overnight things into it.

Hermione followed to the doorway and stood there, watching her.

"You aren't seriously going to take off alone on this wild-goose chase," she said.

"If you won't come with me, I've got to go alone," said Evadne angrily. "Else the sort of thing they like to say about the English will be true. *Some* of us have got to make an effort somehow!"

"And what possible good do you think you can do?" Hermione asked.

"I can stand by Victor as he asked me to! As a sort of—symbol!"

"Rubbish!" said Hermione crushingly. "He's only making a fool of you, why can't you see that? The family would never allow it if they knew," she added, using all the worst arguments with an air of malicious triumph at her own cleverness.

"The family isn't going to know," said Evadne sullenly.

"I can tell them."

Evadne straightened above the suitcase, which was nearly full now, and she was suddenly ablaze with overwrought nerves and righteous anger.

"If you interfere *once more* with my life I shall leave here forever and you can jolly well find someone else to share the beastly flat!" she thundered. "You took Stephen's letters as fast as they came, all five of them, hoping I'd never see him again! You thought I'd never find out, but I did! And if I hadn't stopped him yesterday he'd have walked in this door with me and had it out to your face! I tried to do the right thing last year, I tried to give him up because of you, and that's what I got for it! *Sneak-thieving!* Well, now I'm through trying! I'm all through, do you hear? I shall do exactly as I please from now on!"

Hermione had turned perfectly white in the face, and faded from the doorway back into the living-room. Evadne banged the suitcase shut and fastened it, snatched it up, slammed on a soft hat with one hand and remembered that her bag was on the living-room table. She had more than enough money in it to get to Ostend, which Victor had said was all she would need. She had not enough for a round-trip ticket to Berlin, but once there she could borrow from Johnny, or even Victor, sooner than ask Hermione for a loan now. She went into the living-room and picked up the bag. Hermione lay face down on the sofa, motionless.

"Well, good-bye," said Evadne rather lamely from the middle of the room. "I'm sorry I— Well, I don't expect to be away more than a week or two, but I think when I come back I had better live somewhere else. For a while, anyway. You —can make whatever arrangements you see fit—"

Hermione did not move or reply, and Evadne left the flat, carrying her suitcase.

Before she had got down to the street her inevitable compunctions had set in. I shouldn't have said that, she was thinking as she got into a taxi for Victoria Station. I shouldn't have thrown it at her like that about the letters and then walked out, it's never fair to walk out on a row. The only decent thing to do is give the other person a chance to have his say too. I shouldn't have brought it up about not living there any more unless I could wait to hear her side of it. It's another mistake. I just *keep on* making mistakes. . . .

6

When the door had closed behind Evadne and she did not relent and come back to apologize, Hermione began to cry. But there was no one to hear, and she soon left off and sat up, red-eyed and resentful. She knew that she ought not to allow Evadne to start out alone like that, but she was too muddled with her own unbridled emotions to have any clear idea what to do about it. Evadne would get a train to Dover or Folkestone and cross the Channel tonight, and take any one of several routes to Berlin. Once through that door, she was beyond reach, unless one went to the police. . . . If Bracken was here, Hermione thought. But Bracken was in Prague. Perhaps if she cabled to Johnny in Berlin. . . .

She wandered moodily about the flat, made herself a pot of tea, heard the late BBC news, which was not comforting, thought of ringing up one or two people, and then as a gesture of defiance to her own fears, went to bed. She did not, of course, go to sleep, and lying awake in the dark she began to imagine the things that could happen to Evadne alone in Germany. . . . After an hour or so of that, her anger had cooled and she was thoroughly frightened. She put on the light again and got into a dressing-gown and walked the floor, fighting a growing conviction that she would have to throw herself on Stephen's mercy and ask him what was to be done. Even now, she preferred Stephen to Jeff, convinced that he would be less rude about her part in the affair than Jeff would. And perhaps he need not know, at least not yet, that she knew that he knew about the letters. . . . After a little more of this, she decided that it didn't matter what he knew, she would have to confess everything to him on Evadne's account.

It was now well into the small hours, and she was aware as she called the Upper Brook Street number that she would probably wake them all from their first sleep and have them all down on her in no time. To her relief, it was Stephen's voice which answered, speaking low, as though the others had not roused, and she remembered that the telephone was on a small table in the hall of the flat, with a long flex, so that it could be carried into any one of several rooms and the door closed behind the speaker.

"Stephen—it's Hermione—I've got to talk to you—can anyone else hear?"

"No. The phone was left in my room tonight. What's the matter?"

"It's Evadne—she's gone."

"Gone where?" he demanded sharply.

"To Germany. We—there was a sort of row—I refused to go with her and she was furious and went off alone."

"When?"

"Hours ago."

"What have you been doing ever since? Why didn't you—"

"Don't take my head off, Stephen, I didn't know what to do, I'm frightened, I—must see you—"

"Just one thing. Can we stop her now?"

"She must be on the boat by now. I don't know which route she took."

There was a second's pause while he took it in. Then he said, "I'll be with you in about fifteen minutes if I can find a cab. If I can't I'll walk."

"Thank you—" But he had hung up.

Waiting for him, she tidied her hair, brushed a powder puff across her face, drew her dressing-gown about her, and made another pot of tea. It was brewing on the table in the living-room when his ring came at the door.

"Well, what happened?" he asked grimly, and passed her into the living-room and threw down his hat there and stood facing her as she followed.

"Would you like—a cup of tea?" she asked faintly, her hand on the pot.

"No, thanks. What happened here tonight?"

Hermione poured herself a cup of tea and sat down with it. Her knees were trembling, but he was here, and it would be easier to tell him than anyone else.

"She came in at dinner time," she began. "She'd been with Victor all afternoon—"

"How do you know that?"

"He telephoned before lunch and asked her to meet him in the Park, down by the statue. He told her he was flying to Germany tomorrow—that's today—and somehow got her to promise to meet him there—"

"How do you know that?"

"She *told* me, when she came in. They couldn't travel together, he's flying. I gather he's trying to stop the war from inside Germany—he made her believe that she ought to join him over there as a sort of symbol—to prove to the Germans that Englishwomen weren't afraid to do their part towards creating a new understanding between the nations. Of course I don't believe for a moment that there is anything she can do now—he simply wanted to get her back to Germany—"

"And yet you didn't go with her."

Her eyes fell to the cup in her hand, and she sipped the hot tea nervously.

"I couldn't see any point in either of us going, the Czechs are mobilizing and the war may start any minute. When I tried to make her see that, she flared out at me and packed her own bag and went. To prove she wasn't afraid, I gather."

"Didn't you even try to stop her?"

"Yes, I did. When I threatened to tell the family she called it interfering and got very angry."

"You've never hesitated to interfere before now, that I can see. What became of my letters to Evadne?"

She was silent, looking down.

"You were bound to be found out on that, you know, sooner or later," he added, and she sighed.

"Yes, she told me. That was part of the row."

"You're jealous of her, aren't you," said Stephen incredulously, standing still to stare at her. "You envy her so much that you hate her. Perhaps you wanted Victor to be in love with you instead?"

"Not *Victor*, no!" she cried savagely, and then was silent, paralyzed, for she had not meant to give herself away to him but only to protest the implied insult that she herself was fool enough to care for any Nazi, whatever less enlightened women might do.

For a moment their eyes held, while Stephen felt the hot blood rising, rising, towards his white face till he was enveloped to the hair in a colossal blush. At last with a sort of wrenching movement he turned from her and walked away down the room. Hermione set down the empty cup blindly and hid her face in her hands.

"That's what it was," he said, stunned with revelation, his back to her. "She knew that—last year, when she suddenly balked on me."

"She found out!" cried Hermione, instantly defensive. "I didn't tell her, truly I didn't! She found out, snooping in my bureau drawer!"

He swung round on one foot to face her then, looking puzzled and battered and unable to believe.

"But what did you—how could she—"

"I used to come to the theater over and over again—just to see you in the show. She found that out. I was—humiliated and angry."

"Sure you were," he agreed with a kind of automatic compassion, even now. "She said you didn't want her to marry me, but I—what good would that do? Dog-in-the-manger stuff?" With a few quick steps he had her by the shoulder in a hard grip, his fingers biting in. "Was *that* why you let her go tonight? So that she—"

"No, no, please Stephen, it's not as bad as that," she said, muffled. "I don't—want anything to *happen* to her!"

"Then why didn't you give us a chance to stop her? Why didn't you tell us sooner? What in the name of goodness have you done ever since she left the house? *Slept?*"

She shook her head, her face hidden.

"We could cable Johnny—or Bracken—" she offered hopelessly.

"They're not *bloodhounds*," said Stephen. "If Victor chooses to hide her in Berlin, what can they do? Has she got plenty of money with her?"

"I don't know," said Hermione and began to cry again.

Stephen took a turn round the room, fighting his own panic. Evadne must have known when she came to the dressing-room that she was going to Germany that night. Those last words of hers at the door, which had kept him floating all through the evening performance—that was her good-bye. And the picture—she wanted the picture to take with her on what even she must have known was a perilous venture. If people had not come in after the show—if he had not gone on with them for supper—he would have rung her up before going to bed himself. Even then, she would have been gone, but he might have got it out of Hermione a bit sooner. . . . Now what? he asked himself, to the sound of Hermione's sobbing. What was the most they could do to get to her? Telephone Bracken in Prague—what good was that? Call Johnny in Berlin—Jeff would have to take charge now, Jeff knew the ropes. Jeff had been around. . . .

"Get dressed and come back to the flat with me," he said curtly. "We'll have to get Jeff going on this right away. He may think of something."

"Jeff will only rave at me for letting her go—" she began defensively.

"Get dressed—hurry up—he may want to ask questions that you can answer. I don't even know where to start. Either put something on or come as you are, we're wasting time."

As she went off to the bedroom he grabbed the telephone and rang the flat till Jeff, a light sleeper, answered. Stephen told him the facts, to give him time to digest them, said he was bringing Hermione back with him, and hung up as she appeared in the doorway with a hat and coat on.

The first pinkish grey light of dawn lay over London as they reached the street, and Stephen took her elbow in a firm grasp and set off along Bayswater Road for Marble Arch.

"There's a cab rank at Lancaster Gate," she gasped, unable to hold his pace, and without slackening he said grimly, "All right. Keep moving."

They found Jeff and Sylvia dressed and having coffee and rolls in the living-room in Upper Brook Street, while Dinah still slept behind her closed door further down the hall. Stephen's telephone call saved a lot of conversation to begin with, and Jeff, ignoring Hermione's guilt, plunged at once into essentials. Before long he put in a call for Johnny in Berlin, and when it came through he began to speak slowly and without visible excitement, in a sort of code, to which the rest of them listened spellbound. Virginia's youngest had made a mistake and started for Berlin alone last night, he said—it was a misunderstanding—and would be joining Rosalind's son there at once, but the address had been mislaid —would Johnny please take steps to find the boy and keep track of him—and meanwhile Phoebe's son would be flying over to act as escort back to England, and would Johnny have him met on arrival—passports were doubtless in order as the travellers were experienced, but owing to the misunderstanding there might be a shortage of money which would hamper independent movement—and would Johnny please notify the Embassy at once on Virginia's behalf and get what aid he could in tracing the address. When Jeff finished they realized that the sex and nationality of the fugitive had not been mentioned, and yet Johnny was now in possession of all the facts he needed.

Sylvia was the first to break the silence which ensued when Jeff hung up the receiver.

"You're going after her," she said quietly, and he nodded.

"That talk with Johnny will give him a head start," he said. "Every good newspaper man in Europe has his own private intelligence system, and he can put his to work for what it's worth, till I get there, besides whatever the Embassy can do. They can probably pick up Victor's trail without much trouble, and find out where he lives. But Johnny is too well known there after all these years to be able to move— they watch him all the time and if he started towards Victor now they would know we're after them and anything might happen. I'm a comparative stranger in Berlin and I stand a better chance of getting to her and walking her out of any mess she has got into."

"Will they try to prevent her from leaving?" asked Sylvia in some surprise.

"Depends on just what Victor is up to. If he's really gone underground it's going to be tough. If he's playing both ends against the middle as I think he is, we can get at him. It depends too on how much Evadne has been allowed to know about his activities by the time I try to move her. If she has put herself into his hands and knows too much—she may not be free to go."

"I wouldn't trust him an inch," said Hermione vindictively. "He doesn't *intend* for her to come back, you can count on that!"

"I'd go with you," said Stephen miserably, ignoring her, "if you think I'd be any good. I don't know my way around, and I can't speak the language, but—"

"You stay right here," said Jeff firmly, "and no nonsense about that. You'll be wanted when we get back." His eyes found Sylvia's. "We'll have to pack a bag for me," he said. "Everything all in order—no sign of emergency—I just happen to fly to Berlin, in case anyone is looking."

She nodded and went into the bedroom, and Jeff rose to follow her.

"But, Jeff, what can you *do* when you get there?" said Hermione, beginning to realize the enormity of the thing they were up against.

"I haven't much idea yet," he admitted. "If Johnny has got Victor's headquarters spotted I shall just go there, I suppose, first of all, and ask embarrassing questions in a friendly sort of way. Johnny will cover me from behind, of course. There's no risk—for *me*." He walked to the door and turned there. "If—when I find her, I shall get her to the Embassy as fast as I can. They can deal with it from there if there's any argument. Unless Johnny has some better idea, of course."

He found Sylvia bending over his bureau drawers, and laid his arms around her from behind.

"Please don't worry," he said. "I'll be all right, Johnny can keep track of me. But that girl is really out on a limb this time."

Sylvia leaned against him for a moment, and then went on to lay things into the suitcase which waited open on the bed.

"Take that bottle of stuff in the bathroom," she said steadily.

"Oh, that. Yes, I'll sure load up with that," he agreed easily. "We'll see how much good it does. Sort of a dress rehearsal, maybe." He went into the bathroom and came back with the bottle, which he wrapped casually in a pyjama jacket and tucked into the suitcase. "I think the best thing for me to do is go right down to Croydon and sit there till I can get a seat in a plane going in the right direction," he said.

"But Johnny won't know when to meet you."

"He'll do the same. Somebody will go and sit at the Berlin airfield till I come. We get used to that kind of thing in our business. You know, I wouldn't be at all surprised to find Bracken back in Berlin."

"It's really serious, then—" she said uncertainly, and Jeff

glanced towards the door beyond which was Stephen, trying to behave sanely and leave things to somebody who knew how.

"It's about as bad as it can be," he said. "Nobody but Evadne would expect anything else."

"Oh, *Jeff*—!"

"Sh. Stick tight to Stevie, and don't let him start imagining things—you'll have to let Virginia know too. If we can just move fast enough, it may be all right." He closed the suitcase and turned to her. "I'm off now. Try not to fret, won't you. I'll send you word as soon as I can."

She went speechlessly into his arms.

7

Jeff stepped down on the Tempelhof field at Berlin the same afternoon. Johnny was nowhere to be seen, but as the formalities of arrival were completed and he was free to continue his journey into the city, a small nondescript man appeared beside him and walked along with him, murmuring in German, "Mr. Day—please come with me—"

"Who sent you?" Jeff asked suspiciously, and the man said, "It is in the matter of Virginia's youngest—"

Jeff recognized his own code and stepped into a respectable little car which the man drove himself, and they finally stopped before a small, furtive-looking house in an unimportant street.

"I live here," said the man. "Please come inside."

Inside, Jeff was introduced to a mousy woman who was the wife of his guide, and the man, whose name was Kranzer, went straight to the telephone, announced to someone at the other end of the line that their guest had come, and said to Jeff as he hung up, "Herr Malone will be here soon. You will sit down, please? My wife will make coffee—"

Jeff sat down in the rancid little parlor with Herr Kranzer

and his wife, who had brewed some very nasty ersatz coffee. There was little conversation, in spite of Jeff's excellent German. They were all listening. In what seemed after all a remarkably short time Johnny arrived, bringing with him the same impression of competence and unstampedable knowledge of what was what that made Bracken such a tower of strength wherever he went. Even though he looked a bit anxious, and had practically no news so far, Johnny was in the driver's seat. Jeff, as at the moment of taking off from Croydon and again when landing at Tempelhof, felt the breathless upward seethe of his nervous system which brought his heart action into his consciousness and warned against any quick movements or increased tension. The dose he had taken at Croydon had worn off and it was time for another. The coffee too might have been unwise, but he had craved something hot and hoped that since it wasn't real coffee—

"You look a bit done up," said Johnny, with a kindly but searching glance. "Up all night, I suppose."

"Most of it."

"Well, what for Pete's sake is she playing at now?"

Jeff told him as briefly as possible, while the Kranzers, as unblinking as idols, listened. When he had finished, Johnny took out a pencil and pad and made notations.

"Evadne left London Thursday evening, night Channel crossing to unnamed port, bound for rendezvous in Berlin. Might have gone on from the coast by train, by air, or by car for all we know, if she was met by one of Victor's friends. Why didn't Hermione know which route and when and all that?"

"I guess they never got that far," said Jeff. "It ended in a row because she wouldn't come too."

"Mm-hm. I'm not surprised." Johnny wrote again. "Victor was leaving London by air today—"

"Didn't see him at Croydon," said Jeff. "Doesn't mean he wasn't there, before or after I was."

"Flying all the way, he would arrive at Tempelhof this afternoon," said Johnny. "Like you." He glanced at Kranzer, who shook his head. "Not seen," said Johnny.

"Oughtn't we to keep a watch—" Jeff began.

"There's somebody on the job there," said Johnny easily. "Had to put my whole darned staff on this. If Evadne flew from the Channel port this morning she too would have arrived in Berlin by now. Coming by rail, she would still be on the way. By car—sometime still later. If they really want to smuggle her in, of course, they will use a car, at least the last part of the way."

"But if they don't know we're looking—"

"They think of everything," said Johnny, staring at his pad.

"Do you think—" Jeff swallowed. "—they would try anything against her will?"

"From what I hear she was willing enough," said Johnny.

"But if she—smelled a rat somewhere along the way she may have balked. Could she—would that do any good?"

"Not much, I should think. Not if she had crossed the German border." Johnny did not look up. "Not if they really wanted her."

"Well, oughtn't we to—"

"There's a man at the airfield, and Camilla is with the man at the railway station. Myself, I'm afraid they'll bring her in by car. In that case we're helpless till we can catch Victor in one of his usual haunts and begin trailing him. I would like to put you up at my place, and Camilla sent her love. But you will probably be more useful if you're not seen with me. So I have arranged for you to have a room here with the Kranzers for tonight."

"But can't we—"

"My dear boy, we don't want to tip our hand," said Johnny

patiently. "We can't storm the city, we have to wait till we can catch sight of one of them. Evadne knows I'm in Berlin and how to reach me here, and the first indication we have may come from her to me, if she finds herself in trouble."

"Couldn't I go to his apartment—"

"You could when we can find out where that is. But if she's not there—not there *on purpose*—it might be the worst possible thing to do."

"I see what you mean," said Jeff, thinking of Stephen's face as he had seen it last, and of his own reckless promise to let him hear at once.

"The thing is to get her," said Johnny. "In time, if possible, but anyway, *get* her."

"Yes," said Jeff, and avoided his eyes.

"I leave here roundabout, and I probably won't come back," Johnny said matter-of-factly. "You don't always know if you're being watched, but it's safe to bet on it, and of course my phone is tapped." He took a small blunt revolver out of his pocket and handed it to Jeff. "It's loaded," he said. "You know how to use it, I imagine."

"Mm-hm," said Jeff, and swung the cylinder out familiarly to see its nest of six cartridges. "Any more of these?"

"It's not a war—yet," Johnny told him with a grin. "Don't use it at all, I hope!" He turned with a smile to Mrs. Kranzer and asked her to give their guest some dinner and show him to his room. She started obediently towards the kitchen, and her husband picked up Jeff's suitcase and carried it towards an inner door. Johnny and Jeff looked at each other with rueful smiles in the moment's privacy. "I have always been crazy about your family," Johnny said. "Individually and collectively. But to marry into it is a life-work. You'll hear from me tomorrow, one way or another. Bracken is arriving from Prague—no war this week, anyway. But you probably won't see anything of him either—till afterwards."

"How long can this go on?" Jeff asked, conscious of loneliness.

"We're sure to pick up Victor any minute, unless he's gone to earth for good. Of course it's a nuisance dodging the police instead of asking them to co-operate, but there's no Scotland Yard here."

"Are these people reliable?" Jeff nodded towards the kitchen.

"Completely. There are still a few. But if you should get hold of Evadne don't bring her here or to me. Take her straight to the Embassy."

"I see."

"Good night," said Johnny, with a hand briefly on Jeff's shoulder. "Got something to read?"

"Always. In my bag."

"Good. I have a theory," said Johnny in the doorway, "—mind you, I could be sued for it—that it is the people who have never learned to lose themselves in a printed page who fill up the booby hatches."

"Why don't you write an article?"

"Some of my best friends would take offence," admitted Johnny, and was gone.

8

Jeff woke the next morning to the ringing of the telephone, and recognized his unfamiliar surroundings with the good old leap and bubble of the heart which he so dreaded. He lay still on his back and the commotion in his chest subsided when the telephone conversation ended and no one came to tell him of anything requiring his immediate response. He rose cautiously and dressed and shaved, and swallowed another dose from the bottle. Suppose this went on so long that the bottle was empty before it was time for him to act. It didn't do to think about that.

He did his best to get down the breakfast Frau Kranzer had prepared for him, feeling a little faint and queasy. They conversed spasmodically in German, listened to the radio, which revealed nothing new, and Frau Kranzer cleared away, and the long day's waiting began.

Luncheon time came, and he ate another unappetizing meal, and went back to his book. Outside, the streets ran with rain, and darkness came early. However she had travelled, Evadne was now in Berlin, and apparently no one had seen her arrive. He had nothing to tell Stephen, and dared not communicate anyhow.

A cold supper with the hot ersatz coffee came and went. Jeff had stopped shaking and gone into a numb calm, feeling that the summons might never come. When at last there was a knock on the door they all looked at each other tensely for a moment before Herr Kranzer went to see what it was. He admitted another nondescript man, younger, stouter, who acknowledged Jeff's presence with a kind of bow and said in careful English, "I have the honor."

"*Er sprecht Deutsch,*" said Herr Kranzer briefly, and the newcomer made Jeff another bow and began to explain in German that the man they watched for had been seen to enter the Chancellory, where he was a frequent visitor in the normal way, had remained there several hours, and was then followed to a block of flats where he apparently kept an establishment of some kind in addition to his official living-quarters which were in the Kurfürsten Strasse, and he had not yet come out again.

Jeff was by then on his feet.

"Can you take me there?" he said.

Herr Kranzer insisted that they wait till by his own devious ways he could notify Johnny of the address and arrange transportation there for Jeff.

"Can't you telephone the office?" Jeff asked impatiently, and the stout man murmured that Herr Malone's phone was no good, and anyway it would be better later in the evening, and Herr Kranzer vanished through the door.

Frau Kranzer brewed more of the bitter coffee, which was at least hot, and they sat sipping it. Jeff's palms were wet, and he moved very gently, but was still in command of his breathing. The weight of the little gun in his coat pocket seemed to hold him steady.

When Herr Kranzer came back he said that a car was waiting outside to take them to the address, and it proved to be a Press car with an American driver at the wheel. Jeff got in, followed by the stout man, who gave directions to the driver and they passed through ill-lighted streets and stopped in front of a large, well-kept block of flats in a much better part of town. It was still raining. An inconspicuous man strolled out of the doorway and went off down the street, making no sign of recognition to Jeff's companion, who nevertheless said with satisfaction, "Still there." He told Jeff to go up one flight and take the second door on the left. "Make noise," he said. "Ring the bell long. Rap on the door. Like the police."

"We'll wait here," said the American at the wheel. "If I hear anything unusual or if you don't come back in a reasonable time I'll come in after you, of course."

In the excitement of Herr Kranzer's return and his own departure, Jeff had neglected to get another dose from the bottle. Now as he mounted the stairs he felt his heart skipping in his side and paused a moment to steady his breathing. My first real job as Bracken's substitute, he thought, and if I conk out now I'm done for. He'll put me behind a desk somewhere and that will be that. I've got to come through this. This is the dress rehearsal. . . . If I sound like the police they'll hide her, he thought, as he reached the door. But if I sound like an ordinary caller, perhaps at the wrong door. . . . He rang modestly, and waited, and rang again, briefly.

The door was opened a crack and a stout, elderly house-keeper looked out at him.

"No one at home," she said in German. "What do you want?"

Jeff threw his weight against the door, knocking it open, and walked into the first room he came to, his hand on the gun in his coat pocket. The room was well furnished with comfortable modern stuff and a single shaded lamp showed a girl in a print dress flung down in a corner of the sofa crying. She lifted her head and stared at him, with tears shining on her face. It was Evadne.

"I've got a car down stairs," he said. "Come on." And then, conscious of another presence on his left, he found the gun already out in his hand and covering Victor in the doorway of a darkened room beyond, and heard himself saying, "Stay where you are, this thing might go off," just like the movies. With his free hand he reached out to a light switch in the wall beside him, and the overhead chandelier came on. Victor was wearing uniform, but his tunic and necktie were off and his shirt sleeves hung loose at the wrists with the cuff-links unfastened.

"How did you get in here?" he demanded angrily.

"Surprise," said Jeff. "Get going, Evadne. I'll follow."

"She has made her choice," said Victor. "She came here to me. Now she stays."

"You can't keep her here against her will," said Jeff, the gun very steady and a pounding in his ribs.

"She belongs here now," said Victor. "She has chosen."

"Tell the man where you belong, Evadne," said Jeff softly, and she spoke dazedly, her eyes on his face, his eyes on Victor.

"Honestly, Jeff, I thought I knew what I was doing—but it's no good now, I—"

"I'm not going back without you," said Jeff. "We've gone to quite a lot of trouble over you, one way and another—"

"I'm s-sorry—" But she did not move from the sofa, her hands braced against it as though to save herself from falling, her eyes on Jeff, who never looked at her.

Jeff felt time slipping away, and thought of the man in the car—how long would he wait before he decided it was unreasonably long, and come in after them? What would happen if Victor, caught at a disadvantage now with his gun out of reach, managed to put up a fight for her? He decided to take a long chance.

"Well, maybe we all made a mistake," he said, trying to sound casual. "We had a sort of idea that you'd been sold a bill of goods somehow, and might be glad to see someone from home. Of course, if this is the way you really want it, I apologize for butting in. It's a little hard for anybody raised in our family to understand your so-called choice, but I guess you're old enough to decide these things for yourself—" He began to back towards the door.

"*No, Jeff—wait—!*" At the very last moment of his bluff she had hurled herself from the sofa and across the room, landing hard against him with desperate hands clutching his coatsleeve. *"Don't leave me here—"*

Victor made a quick movement, and Jeff said, "*Quiet, you!* You're lucky it's me tonight, I know a man who would let fly with this thing if he were in my place." He motioned to the right with the nose of the gun, imperatively, Evadne held with his other arm out of the way. "Move over, Victor —away from that door—more, so I can see you from the hall —*move*, I said!" And as Victor gave ground to the right, away from his own gun belt, Jeff said to Evadne, who was clinging to him and crying weakly, "There's a car down stairs—driven by an American in a soft hat. Be sure it's the right car before you get into it—tell him I'm right behind you—leave that hall door open as you go—" He pushed her towards it and she fled, weeping. "Maybe a little more to the right, Victor," he suggested, beginning to back towards the hall door. "It would be awful easy now to let you have one for Steve. Still, we don't want to call attention to this, do we." He felt the casing of the outer door against his shoulder, turned quickly and ran down the stairs. Evadne was in the back seat of the car and its engine was humming. The stout man had disappeared. "Jump for it," said the man at the wheel gently, and as Jeff slammed the rear door the car got under way, and he gathered Evadne's shivering body into his arms.

"All right, we made it," he said soothingly.

"He's got my passport!" she chattered hysterically. "I hadn't any money, and he's got my passport!"

"We'll get you another one," he comforted her. "The Embassy will fix it."

"How did you get here so soon?"

"Well, believe it or not, Stevie raised such Cain in London that the rest of us couldn't get any sleep till we found you for him."

"He—he doesn't—" She had no voice, no words, and buried her face against him and began to cry again.

"Take it easy," said Jeff, patting her, and he took out his big white handkerchief and tried to wipe her face. "How did you get into Berlin, anyhow, we were watching for you."

"Victor said a man would meet me at Ostend. We came all the way from there by car—one of the big black ones."

"Without stopping?"

"Almost. It must be five hundred miles. I was nearly dead."

"Then you—must have arrived last night," he said, feeling his way.

"Yes."

"At that flat?"

"Yes. But it was all right then, though I was never left alone and there wasn't any telephone. I wanted to ring up Camilla but they kept putting me off, which seemed very queer, and Victor didn't come till this evening. He talked to the others a few minutes and they went away—he said there had been a hitch, but that I was to attend a meeting with him tomorrow. I said I wanted to let Camilla know I was here, and he said that was impossible, and then it began to dawn on me—"

"Mm-hm," said Jeff tactfully. "There, now—nothing more to cry about, the Marines have landed. Did you see me pull that gun on him, just like Humphrey Bogart? I never knew I had it in me—"He sat holding her, soothing her, while she got quieter, and he felt his own nerves settle back into the groove. They had made it, yes, without a fight. But he had made it in a very special way all his own. His heart had held out. He had stayed on his feet. It was an extra victory that no one else could appreciate—no one but Sylvia. He could go back and tell Sylvia that because of her he had lasted out the scene in Victor's rooms. He couldn't have explained it, even to Sylvia, but he was convinced that she herself had seen him through. Because of her, because they had dared to go ahead and get married and be happy, his heart had not failed him tonight. With Sylvia behind him, he could do what other people did. He could take it. He was getting well. Maybe next time—whatever it might be—there wouldn't even be those sickening moments of doubt. Maybe by the time they got this war he would be in shape for it. Thanks to Sylvia.

The car stopped and looking out he saw that they were in front of the British Embassy. The driver got out and opened the door and they helped Evadne to step down to the pavement and walked her between them towards the building. She recognized the place as they went up the steps and hung back.

"Why are we coming here? Everybody will be in bed."

"They're expecting us," said Jeff, and rang the bell.

"But I want Camilla," she said, and choked.

"All right, we'll have Camilla here in no time," he promised, as the door opened before them and he half carried her over the threshold.

9

Evadne was put to bed at the Embassy, and they sent for an English doctor as well as for Camilla. He spent some time with her and left her under sedatives with Camilla sitting beside the bed. She was still pretty well knocked out the next day, though she roused to catch gratefully at Bracken's hand and mumble that she wanted to go home, and fell asleep again comforted by the enduring family tradition that everything was under control as soon as Bracken showed up. He went back to Prague that night, but it was Thursday again before the doctor was satisfied and Jeff and Evadne boarded a plane for Croydon.

Wearing a hat and coat borrowed from Camilla, who had gone to Prague the same morning with Johnny, Evadne sat drooping in her seat, lost in depression and her sense of failure and betrayal. Jeff had asked no more questions and she was grateful for that. Stephen was the one she would have to find answers for. She was glad that because of the midweek matinee she need not see him till after Jeff had had time to tell him the story of what had happened in Berlin as far as he knew it. But there were things that only she could tell, and she both longed and dreaded to see Stephen now. Everything Jeff said made it plain that Stephen had not washed his hands of her, as she felt he had every right to do. She wondered if by now he had seen Hermione, who finally had grounds for anything she chose to say and would surely make the most of it. She wondered how she could hold her head up at all, now, and where she could start again to live, and what there was to have faith in.

To her great relief, Virginia was waiting at Croydon with a car, into which Evadne was bundled with no delay and carried off to Farthingale, weeping piteously most of the way because it was so good to see the familiar road again, as though she had been away for months. Jeff went on up to London to see Sylvia and Stephen, and would drive down with them to Farthingale after the performance on Saturday night. So it was only two days till she would have to face Stephen and tell him—whatever he wanted to know. Perhaps, when Jeff had finished, Stephen wouldn't come to Farthingale. . . .

Shaking with nerves and crying again for sheer relief, Evadne went to bed in her own room at Farthingale, and slept the clock round. She woke to find Virginia sitting by the window with a book, and as she stirred Virginia came and sat down on the bed and put her arms around her.

"What a sleep," she said. "You must be starved."

Evadne's clasp was convulsive like a child's, her face was hidden.

"I was still full of dope, I think. Mummy, that Embassy doctor—"

"Yes, darling, I know, and you're having a nervous breakdown or something very like it. We'll get our nice Dr. Fielding tomorrow, you won't mind him."

"I thought I'd never stop shaking."

"But you have stopped now. You're home again, remember?"

"Has the war started yet?"

"Not yet, darling."

"But it's coming."

"I'm afraid so. This house is going to be a warden's post—down here in the country, doesn't it seem fantastic?—all we shall have to do here is issue gas-masks to the village people and arrange about feeding and billeting evacuees, and that sort of thing."

"Who's going to be the warden?"

"Well, I am, sort of, I've signed up for the training, that is, over in the Parish Hall at Upper Briarly. We can't count on Nigel being here much of the time, he'll have other things to do. I have to learn first aid, which of course I once knew very well and it all comes back to me, and how to fit the gas-masks, which we didn't have last time, and so on. And I've registered the cars there too for emergency use. It seems pretty silly so far from London, but they're bound to try for Bristol and Cardiff from the air, and that takes them practically over our heads, and will create a refugee problem. We are listed as a reception area, and shall have floods of snotty-nosed children and expectant mothers to feed and clothe and house, once things start, I suppose."

"C-could I help?" Evadne asked with some diffidence.

"Everyone can help. There's a meeting of the billeting committee at Cleeve next week— Rosalind is making up lists of how many evacuees people can take, and they are probably going to open up the big house for a hospital or convalescent home. You could lend her a hand with that as soon as you feel well enough."

"I'm not ill, it's just—I—" Evadne fought off another crying fit. "I want to *try*. I want everybody to know that I've stopped being a fool and will do anything I'm told to from now on."

"Darling, you mustn't feel—"

"It took a long time, didn't it." Evadne sat up and pushed back her hair with a pathetic, dazed gesture, and met her mother's eyes. "I wonder you'll speak to me at all."

"Oh, nonsense, I always—"

"You always expect me to play the fool, don't you! You must be used to it by now. *Why* do I make so many mistakes?"

"You're young yet," said Virginia matter-of-factly, while her heart ached. "Believe it or not, I was the same once."

"But not about Daddy. You didn't make any mistake about him."

"No," Virginia murmured, drooping on the side of the bed—for having once set eyes on Archie Campion she had ceased almost overnight at the age of eighteen to be a flirt and a heart-breaker. "No, that time I was right."

"I wish I could remember him better," Evadne sighed.

"I wish *I* could," Virginia admitted. "I tried so hard—it's been so long—his voice went first—I can't hear it any more, the way I could in the beginning. Sometimes I think Nigel's is very like—Nigel himself is very like—but it's not the same."

"But you had him for a while," said Evadne enviously. "You were lucky."

"Yes, darling. Luckier than most."

"Was there ever anyone else—after he died?"

"Why do you ask that?"

"I've often wondered. You were quite young—and so beautiful. Why wasn't there anyone else?"

"There was—*almost*." Virginia's eyes went slowly round the room and to the window. "But I couldn't quite bear it—to leave this house and all that had happened in it. I let him go instead."

"Were you ever sorry?"

"Not really. Sometimes I've wondered—"

"Don't you ever see him?"

"No. Oh, no."

"Where is he now?"

"I don't even know if he's still alive." The words sounded a little desolate.

"Oh, Mummy, how dreadful."

"He's probably married and has dozens of children by now," said Virginia, and straightened, and smiled, and smoothed the sheet. "Wouldn't you like a meal of some kind? It's nearly dinner time."

"Mummy—what must I do about Stephen?"

"I wondered if you could be leading up to something," said Virginia. "He's rung up twice to ask about you, and he's coming down on Saturday night after the show."

"Still?" said Evadne in a small voice.

"You weren't ever in love with Victor, were you?" Virginia asked gently.

"No! Heavens, no!"

"Then what sort of hold on you did he have? Why on earth—"

"I only wanted to *do* something about this war! I felt I had to leave no stone unturned. I thought Victor felt the same way, though of course he never actually Surrendered—" Evadne paused, and looked uncomfortable. "I myself haven't felt right about things since the Anschluss, when they went into Vienna," she confessed. "Some of them tried to smooth it over, but I could never find out what Victor really thought about it. I suppose he didn't dare say, even to me. Then when he told me about the old Generals that day in the Park and asked me to help him convince them, I thought it was a ray of hope—I thought he realized that things were really getting out of hand, and that anything was worth a try—and I didn't know until I got there that it was just a come-on for me. Oh, not that the Generals don't exist, and Hitler is afraid of them, and there *is* a sort of underground in Germany, Jeff had heard about that. But as for my part in Victor's plans, apparently I was just supposed to perform as his English mistress—" Under Virginia's sympathetic eyes she flushed painfully. "I kept telling myself that night in Berlin that it was all too much like an American film to be real," she said unsteadily. "But Victor hadn't seen the same films, he was just making it up as he went along—" She hid her face suddenly in her hands, bowed and slender in the big bed. "If only I didn't feel such a *fool!*" she cried again.

"Everybody feels more or less like that at some time or other, for some reason or other," Virginia said sensibly. "Feeling foolish is even worse than feeling ashamed, I always think. But people forget. You just live through it."

"But I'll have to tell Stephen—"

"You won't have to tell him anything. Haven't you learned about Stephen yet? He's a Sprague, and he's in love. Just leave the rest to him." Virginia took her daughter's hands away from a tear-wet face and wiped it with her own fragrant handkerchief. "There. And if you really want to do something about the war, you won't have far to go. Farthingale is too small for most emergency use, but Clare has heard of a nursery school with a couple of young mistresses that might fit in. Or of course we could take in a few convalescent officers, or billet a few whole ones if there should be a camp anywhere near. In either case I shall try to arrange something that will let us keep a few rooms to live in. The Hall will go for a hospital, again, like the last time, with Clare in charge. You could do VAD there, if you liked."

"I'll do *anything!*" Evadne promised wildly. "The nastiest, dirtiest jobs that nobody else wants—I'll do them!"

"That's splendid," said Virginia, determinedly unemotional. "But you'll have to stay in bed a little while first and rest. Then we'll see. Now, how about dinner? What would you like?"

When Evadne woke late on Sunday morning and rang the bell for a cup of tea, a folded note was on the tray: *Sweetheart, may I come up with your breakfast and ask you—again—to marry me? S.*

Tears of gratitude and weakness and disbelief welled up, blurring the words. The maid was still in the room, drawing back the curtains, so that bright sunlight streamed along the carpet to the foot of the bed. Evadne sat with the tray across her knees and her face in her hands, tears dripping through her fingers. There was a tap on the half-open door, and Stephen's voice said casually, "Do you want time to powder your nose first, or may I come in now?"

The maid said, "Good morning, sir," approvingly, and tiptoed out.

Stephen crossed the room with his light, quick tread and

removed the tray, which he placed securely on a table. Then
he sat down on the bed and made Evadne comfortable against
his shoulder, his face in her hair, and said, "There, now—"
and "Poor little soul—" and "Let it come, honey, cry all you
want to, I can swim—" And then he said, cradling her as
the sobbing quieted, "Stevie's here, you're all right now—"
Until at last she lay against him, spent and comforted, looking up into his face which bent above her. And because she
saw that he asked nothing of her yet, with an understanding
so profound that she could hardly bear her own gratitude,
she began from that moment to worship him as he had never
even dreamed. She reached up one hand and touched his
cheek as though to make sure he was real, and he turned his
head to catch her fingers with a kiss, and they fled to anchor
possessively on his coat lapel.

"Stevie."

"Right here," he said, and his arms tightened round her.

"It's hard to believe there are people like you."

"Who, me?" said Stephen, embarrassed. "Ten for a cent,
where I come from."

"I only want one." She quivered into a smile.

"One's enough," he said. "If I wrap it up will you take it
with you?"

"Oh, *darling*—!" cried Evadne, and buried her face in his
coat and wept again, because she loved him so.

Again he held her patiently, making no effort to stop her
tears, sure at last that she was his and that there was plenty
of time.

10

Down stairs in the living-room, Jeff and Sylvia sat alone together with the Sunday papers. Sylvia threw down the *Ob-
server* and said into their companionable silence, "Will you
have to go to Prague if this keeps up?"

"Not till after the wedding, I hope," he grinned, with a glance towards the stairway, and Sylvia smiled tenderly in the same direction.

"You know, it makes me feel quite young again," she observed, and went to sit on the arm of his chair, so that he turned his face quickly into her breast and they remained with their arms around each other, not speaking. Finally Sylvia said, "Jeff, how are we going to work this thing?"

"How do you mean, work what?"

"If Evadne does marry Stephen now he can get along, can't he, and find a new dancing partner, so I can stay with you?"

"In *Prague?* Hunh-unh."

"We'll ask Bracken to let you off Prague. Johnny can do it."

"Camilla might have something to say about that."

"Oh, Jeff, they're *used* to it!" she wailed. "We've had such a little time together!"

"Can't take that away from us, can they," he said comfortably, and there were voices in the hall, and she had to leave it at that for the time.

Evadne slept all afternoon, exhausted but happy, and Stephen came in behind her dinner tray, which had been held back until he finished his own meal down stairs. There was a good deal of foolishness while she ate, or pretended to, and more than once she was threatened again by tears, but his light touch saw them through without disaster, and after feeding her the pudding a spoonful at a time he removed the tray, drew up a big chair facing her at the bedside, turned on a small radio on the night-table, and began to fill a pipe. Music flowed out into the room and was quickly muted to an undertone for the quiet, unimportant things they said. A long silence fell between them. Their eyes met unself-consciously, and they smiled at each other and she extended a hand on the coverlet. He could reach it from where he sat, and their fingers met and clung.

"Oh, Stephen, you *are* good, I almost missed anything like this," she said unsteadily.

"This," he replied with pardonable satisfaction, "is the sort of thing I had in mind all along."

"I shall be all right soon. Perhaps I can get up tomorrow."

"No hurry. I'll come and sit."

"Does it matter so much to you, really? Just being together like this?"

"Fishing," he said, with a knowing look, and bent forward to kiss her fingers in his on the coverlet.

"Those people who only see you dancing—wouldn't they be surprised if they could see you now?"

"Like something you wind up with a key, and now it's run down," he suggested, and quirked an eyebrow at the radio which was playing nostalgic waltzes. He turned it up a little, laid down his pipe with care, and rose, pushing back the chair. "We'll show 'em who's run down," he said, and even as he stepped backward from the chair he took up the beat and began to dance.

It was all spontaneous fooling set to music, made up as he went along, just for her, just to amuse the sick child, the captive princess. And it resolved itself, in and out among the furniture in the high, spacious room, and even across the foot of the big bed, into a lyrical flirtation in pantomime with a totally invisible dream-girl whose imaginary fingertips were held in his, who was twirled and tossed and wooed in a hilarious waltz-time satire of musical-comedy passion which brought delighted laughter and applause from the audience in the bed. When it ended in a highly acrobatic back-bend for the invisible partner, and the radio announcer's silky tones replaced the music, Evadne cried, "Oh, *Stephen,* it's the best you ever did, and it's *mine,* all *wasted,* can you ever do it the same again?"

He switched off the radio voice, pushed the chair back to

the bedside, and resumed his pipe, breathing as easily as though he had sat there all the time.

"If I ever want to," he said modestly.

"But you *must,* you must do it for Sylvia, and you must put it in a show!"

"It wasn't all that good," he said. "We'll work on it. Might amount to something."

"Oh, darling, you're such *fun!*" she cried, quite carried away. "I shall wake up screaming every night now for fear I've lost you after all!"

"Then the sooner we get married the better," he suggested promptly and she sobered.

"Those meetings next week—I've lost faith in them. I—can't go to them now."

"Good," said Stephen, round the pipe.

"But, Stephen, it *wasn't* just self-importance, as Victor said it was. I did believe in them. I did think there was some hope that we could—"

"Not any more," he told her gently. "Too late for that kind of thing now, it only gives a wrong impression. It's no good converting hundreds more bewildered Britons who don't mean to start a war anyhow. No good teaching them to be Christians in the arena waiting serenely for the lions to come and tear them to bits—not these days. Not unless you can first convert the *lions.* Since you can't do that, you may as well face it—and not turn all four cheeks, as somebody has put it."

"But don't you see—without that to believe in I feel naked and cold and—lost. Suppose I *was* all wrong—what have I got now to go on with? I—one wants to believe in *something.*"

He might have said, "Try believing in *me,*" or something equally silly, and got her laughing again. But instead, he knocked his pipe out very slowly, giving it great attention, and said without looking at her, "Have you been to church lately?"

"Ch-church?"

"One of those stone things with a steeple and a bell and stained-glass windows—and an ordained clergyman to do all the talking. There is a certain decency," said Stephen, busy with his pipe, "about a good Episcopal service. Or have you forgotten?"

"Can it stop the war?"

"No. I'm afraid nothing can stop the war now. The only thing to do is make sure Hitler doesn't win it when he starts it."

"You think he *will* start it?"

"I think he has to learn the hard way that he has to stop somewhere. Don't you?"

She sighed.

"I suppose that's what Mummy meant when she said about the work she was doing here, taking up first aid again and all. She and Camilla and Phoebe were all nurses in the last war, it will all come back to them. As soon as they let me get up I shall start learning it myself. Do you think I would make a good VAD?"

"You'd feel so sorry for your patients you'd promise to marry them all."

"Would you be jealous?" she asked with a sidelong look.

"Not very. Especially not if you married me first."

"I will." Her hand came out to him again, with curved, appealing fingers. "Oh, Stephen, *I will!*"

He took the hand, which was a little cold and moist, in his two warm ones.

"And wilt thou have this woman—" he said quite solemnly. "Yes, please God, *I will!*"

"So now that we're married," said Evadne with a long, dreamy look, "what do you want to do, Stephen? I can't stay here in the country with Mummy, if you're in London with the show. From now on I just want to be where I can see you every day."

"How things have changed," he marvelled. "I never thought I'd live to see it. Well, they tell me you will have to take it quietly for a month or so—I'll come down here every week-end. And then we'll be married and live at the Savoy, if you like, or find a flat of our own."

"Hermione doesn't intend to stay in London if there's a war," she said thoughtfully. "If she should want to give up the flat we could take it for ourselves, and I could join the ARP or something. She says the wardens are busybodies, but if Mummy thinks it's worth doing even down in the country—"

"The theaters will close if there should really be a war," he said. "I suppose I'm too old for combat flying, but I might get into the Air Force by the back door somehow."

"But you're an American."

"So what? Do I sit around acting neutral?" he demanded. "Not me!"

"Come be a warden with me, then."

"Maybe. We'll see. Anyway, we're in it together, understand? You won't go riding off in all directions trying to save everybody but me, will you."

"I promise to save you first."

"We'll save each other," he promised. "Or have we done that already?"

"Stevie—" She held out her arms and he came to sit on the edge of the bed. "Stevie, don't let me make any more mistakes. I promise to *obey*—"

11

The war of nerves was on now. People took Holidays as Usual, people went on getting married at St. Margaret's in white satin, the King and Queen attended the Paris Exhibition and came home safely—but the newspapers were full of talk about sanctuary for civilians, blast-proof shelters, gas-detection and gas-masks for everyone, barrage balloons over London, evacuation of the too young and the too old and the too pregnant.

As soon as Evadne was allowed to get up, still feeling rather weak and wobbly and tearful, as though she had had influenza, which was the only remaining result of the prolonged nervous shock she had undergone, Virginia suggested that she come along to one of the lectures at the Upper Briarly Parish Hall, adding as a further inducement that the man was going to talk about gas-masks. With a slight fastidious shrinking in her midriff, Evadne reminded herself that one must make a beginning somewhere, and was ready in the drawing-room when Rosalind arrived to collect them. Virginia had not yet appeared, and there was a moment that threatened to be awkward as Rosalind entered the room and their separate knowledge of Victor confronted them.

Since Evadne's return from Germany, Rosalind had not ceased to blame herself for not taking Edward's unwelcome suggestion that she talk to Evadne, straight from the shoulder, about Germans and Victor in particular. She was still wondering if Evadne would have reacted to the facts of Conrad's betrayal and death by refusing ever to countenance Victor again—and so been spared the consequences of their continued association. And she was still reminding herself that anyway it was too late *now*, that to tell the story now of that interview at Cleeve would be nothing but hysteria and could serve no purpose whatever, as Victor had finally done for himself without any help from her. Unless—there was, she supposed, the possibility that Evadne still cherished some kind of feeling for him, if only acute disillusionment, and so ought to know how ingrained the beastliness was, not just with women, not just this present madness, but for years past —corruption in the blood and bone and brain, inhuman and deadly. And suppose then Evadne said, "Why didn't you *tell* me?" There was no good answer to that. But perhaps it should be faced, if there was any chance that Evadne was not cured forever of infatuation or illusion. . . .

And Evadne, painfully conscious of Rosalind's relationship to her own private nightmare, was trying to think of some way to make her see that it needn't matter between them, and was wondering if it would help to tell her about what he had called the joke. It was a remark which Evadne had not understood at the time, but Rosalind must have the key to it. Neither of them would ever see Victor again, and both were profoundly thankful. Would it bring any peace of mind to Rosalind, she wondered, to know what he had said about his father that last day in London?

For a moment they stood looking at each other with a mutual compassion, and then Evadne said, "I used to blame you for being hard-hearted—back in the days when I thought I knew it all. You knew much better than I did, of course."

"I'm afraid I did," said Rosalind heavily. "Would you have listened to me then if I—"

"No, probably not. I wouldn't listen to anybody, would I." Evadne was able to smile. "Mummy says it's one of those lessons we don't have to learn twice, and that it need never come up again. But there's one thing I think perhaps I ought to mention, if you don't mind—it might make you think a little better of him, in the end."

"I'm afraid I know pretty well what to think," said Rosalind gently.

"Did you know that he had turned to his father's friends now, for help?" And as Rosalind only stood staring at her, she went on. "He said that he wished you could know, but it was too late. That day in the Park when he asked me to go to Berlin he said, 'I go to beg from the men like my father who are still alive in Germany.' He's trying to make the old Generals understand in time that Hitler is being misled into a war he can't win as easily as he thinks. Victor said he wished you knew that because you would think it was a good joke, and—he tried to laugh at it himself and couldn't. I didn't know quite what he meant, but—I thought you might."

"Yes—" Rosalind's face was very still and white. She walked down the room away from Evadne and stood at a window, looking out across the lawn and seeing nothing. "Yes, I know —what he meant."

"But you can't laugh either," said Evadne, puzzled.

"Conrad is laughing," said Rosalind, motionless at the window. "Wherever he is now, Conrad must find it very funny indeed."

"Victor seemed to think it odd you had never told me about him."

"He would," said Rosalind tonelessly. "But now it's just— one of those things that needn't come up again." She turned from the window and came back slowly to where Evadne stood, and laid her hand—she was not a demonstrative woman —on Evadne's sleeve. "Thank you for telling me that, it clears things up a little for me. I wish we could both forget them— both—but we shan't be allowed, shall we, with a war coming on. Their war."

"You don't think the old Generals will—"

"No. They're too old—and there aren't enough of them left."

Virginia's brisk step crossed the hall and she came in, pulling on her gloves.

"I didn't know you were here," she said to Rosalind, with a quick glance from one to the other.

"Charles won't be here, he's going over the big house with a man from some Ministry or other," said Rosalind. "If the Ministry does take it over, they want to cut up all the rooms into little ones and put in fitted basins, isn't it awful? And all sorts of modern kitchen equipment, and perhaps central heating. It's nice to know *somebody* intends to be comfortable in this war!"

They went out to Rosalind's car and she drove them to

Upper Briarly, where the gas lecture was to take place. As they had all lived in the neighborhood so long they knew almost everybody who had turned up at the Parish Hall, and there was inevitably a social air about the whole thing which rose above its grim purpose. But when the man from London produced the snoutish little black affair with the transparent eyepiece and the buckled straps, and put it on his own head to demonstrate how simple it was, and spoke a few words hollowly through it, everyone got a half-hysterical sense of total unreality. It could not be. Pretty soon they would all wake up in bed at home. This was England, and the war had been over a long time. There couldn't be *another* one. Not *already.* . . .

Stephen's show went on as usual, to good business. People wanted to be taken out of themselves and to forget the news. Americans were besieging the steamship lines for homeward passage, but Stephen and Sylvia had no patience with that. Some of the cast, with anxious families cabling and telephoning from New York, got uneasy and arrangements were being made to replace them.

Arriving at Farthingale for the week-end after Germany had called out reserve divisions for opportune "autumn maneuvers"—in August—Stephen listened to Evadne's account of her first-aid lessons and gas lectures, and the stories, funny and not so funny, about how people reacted when they were asked to list all their spare rooms and to indicate their preference, if any, in evacuees—unattended children, children with pregnant mothers, pregnant mothers with no children yet. He saw with relief that her eyes were shining again, and her boundless, bountiful willingness to take trouble about people and to get along with people was functioning as warmly now for potential war waifs and bomb casualties as it had ever done in the interests of Soul Surgery. And when she paused for breath he said, "Honey, let's get married *now.* This week. And don't say it's so sudden."

"All right," said Evadne simply, as though he had asked her out to dinner. "I'll have to come up to Town, this being Sunday we can't arrange to do it while you're here this time. And I haven't done a thing about a wedding dress yet, I—"

"Wear that one."

"*This?*" It was a flowered silk with a black belt at her narrow waist and short sleeves. "People don't get married in things like this! I've got rather a nice plain blue—it's at the flat. Oh, and that reminds me," she went on, while Stephen gazed at her with admiration and perpetual wonderment, "Hermione is in a funk and wants to get rid of the flat at once. Some friends of hers are taking a house in the Lake Country and have asked her to join them."

"What kind of spiritual rearmament is that?" he asked with a grin.

"Now, Stevie. I thought it might be very convenient. For us, I mean. We could live there. After we're married, I mean."

"Would you like to?" he queried in some surprise, but there was no room in Evadne's practical, home-making mind for such things as morbid associations.

"It's quite nice, don't you think? And handy to everything. The bedroom Hermione has is quite large, and we could use mine as a guest-room, it's got twin beds."

Stephen swallowed and said he didn't see why not.

"Of course, if we can't get her out in time we could go to a hotel for a few days," Evadne added.

Stephen agreed dazedly that they could.

"Then I'd better come up tomorrow and see her and arrange to take over the lease, or whatever it is she signed," said Evadne. "And we could get the licence. What's the matter, you look sort of funny."

Stephen said doubtless he would come to in a minute, and her face fell anxiously.

"D-don't you want to take the flat? I only thought—"

"It's the altitude," said Stephen, and put a hand dizzily to his head. "Don't you realize what you've done? I've been working on this, man and boy, for more than two years, and now here we are, married and living in Hermione's flat, *this week!*"

"Well, I—don't want to rush you," she murmured, looking rather pink, and they fell into each other's arms with laughter.

12

By now the build-up was on for the annual orgy of the Nuremberg Congress. Johnny was in attendance there, and when Bracken's Vienna correspondent contrived to fall down a flight of stone steps and break a leg, it meant that Jeff was suddenly dealt an assignment to cover Prague.

Sylvia took the news of his immediate departure without any fuss, but began to feel very gone in the middle, like before a first night. Jeff, having felt his oats in the Berlin affair and lost a lot of misgivings, responded to his orders like a war horse to the trumpet—printer's ink was in his blood, Johnny was his lifelong hero, and now it was his turn, now he was one of them, *now.* The time before he had to catch a plane was mercifully only a matter of hours and everyone was very brave about saying good-bye to him. When he had gone Stephen carried Sylvia off to have tea at the Queen's Road flat, where he and Evadne had been established for about two weeks, and which had suddenly begun to look as though it was lived in, with the addition of a comfortable Sprague clutter.

Evadne was training to be an air-raid warden, and had not come to tell Jeff good-bye because of an ARP meeting about gas-masks at the parochial school which was the depot for that district. When she came in a few minutes after Sylvia and Stephen had put the kettle on for tea, she was carrying a small cardboard box which she set down on the living-room table as though it might go off, and said, "Well, there it is. I've got to go back tonight and help assemble some more of them. We shall be giving them out soon, I think."

Stephen opened the box, handling it delicately, and lifted out the sinister little black rubber object with its snout and its eyepiece and its dangling straps.

"Pretty, isn't it," he remarked, allowing it to dangle from one finger.

"I'll practice fitting it on you," said Evadne. "That's why I brought it. There are three sizes. This one happened to be right for me, let's see—"

Stephen dodged as she took it from him with purpose.

"Can't I have tea first?" he pleaded.

"Hold still, now, it won't hurt a bit," Evadne said professionally, and closed in on him. "Get your chin well into it—that's right—now spread the straps—wait, while I tighten it—there, is that comfortable?—take a deep breath—" She laid hold of the snout and wobbled it gently, ran a knowing finger along the edge in front of his ear. "You want the next size, this one isn't tight enough. Doesn't it smell funny? Can you breathe? Some people start to suffocate right away, we're going to have some trouble with them, I expect."

Stephen said something hollowly inside the thing, and pointed to the mantelpiece mirror which he happened to be facing, and Evadne said, "What?" and slipped it off him, forwards, mussing his hair.

"I said that strangely enough I still look better without it," he repeated. "Come on, Sylvia, it's really something."

Sylvia stood up and Evadne placed a straight chair and asked her to sit in it as that was the way they had to do it at the depot. Sylvia sat docilely as bidden, her hands rather stiff in her lap like at the dentist, and the thing, held between Evadne's hands, approached her face, with its smell.

"We're supposed to wipe them out between fittings, but this is all in the family," said Evadne comfortably. "Put your chin out—that's it—sorry, it's awfully hard on the hair—I'm loosening the straps—there—can you breathe?"

Sylvia shook her head vigorously.

"Take a deep breath."

"I *can't!*" said Sylvia, muffled, and snatched off the mask.

"There, you see?" said Evadne patiently to Stephen, and began to untangle the buckle, which had caught in Sylvia's hair. "Some people just can't. Even among the wardens. I don't know what we'll do about children, either."

"I'll try again," said Sylvia, with a certain doggedness, holding out her hands as the buckle came free. "Let me do it myself."

"Take it in your right hand—use the left for the straps," Evadne told her kindly. "That's better. *Breathe.* Now wait, while I see—" Again she felt the edges and wobbled the snout, and held a square of paper against the nozzle. "Breathe *in.*" The paper clung to the suction. "That's your size, same as me. Take it off now, we'll have tea."

"Do *you* mind it?" Sylvia gasped, emerging.

"Everybody minds, it's just a question of degree. We all wore them at the depot this afternoon to get used to it," Evadne explained. "You do get used to it a bit, I think. It bothers with glasses—you can't wear them inside it, and some people can't see a thing without them, which is a problem." She went off to the kitchen, where the kettle was now boiling, and made the tea and brought it in on a tray with a fresh cake and the cups. She was naturally a housekeeper and it was already plain that Stephen was going to be very comfortable. "I meant to make toast with anchovy paste if I'd got home first," she said, but without the old note of apology. "Do you want to wait for it now?"

Stephen, who was wearing the mask again in front of the mirror, which gave him a look of ghoulish interest, turned to Sylvia, who shook her head, and Stephen then shook his violently from side to side, the black snout swinging.

"Well, you can't drink through it," said Evadne in her nanny voice. "Take it off now and relax." She sat down to pour their tea. "If you want to come round to the school and fetch me on your way home tonight I'll probably still be there."

"Doing what?" asked Stephen, smoothing his hair at the mirror.

"Assembling more of those things. It's quite simple to do, but we need thousands, and some of us are going to keep on at it till late. We think it will give people a certain sense of security to be able to take them away with them after the fitting."

"Will it?" said Stephen, sitting down, and "Has it really come to that?" Sylvia asked, looking rather appalled.

"I suppose we can tell better in a day or two more," Evadne said sensibly. "I don't think they mean to do anything drastic like blackouts till next week." She glanced at the large sash windows with their chintz drapes. "We'll have to get some black stuff to go inside those, I suppose. So many people just can't afford it, it does seem hard."

"Shall you have to wear a uniform for your wardening?" Sylvia asked, reaching gratefully for her tea.

"I expect so, eventually. We've got arm-bands now, and our tin hats will be along any day."

"But—will you have to be right out in it?"

"Well, yes, if it starts coming down—we have to patrol, and take charge of incidents if there are any. An incident is when a bomb actually lands in your district and blows things to bits. There are men assigned to each post, for the heavy work, but ours are all rather elderly, I'm much the strongest of the lot."

Sylvia and Stephen exchanged glances over their tea-cups, each of them marvelling, not for the first time, at how Evadne, once so nervy and uncertain of herself, was now the most collected of them all—perhaps because she had found something definite to do and was doing it.

"I think I'd better get in on this," said Stephen. "Will they put me down for a tin hat and an arm-band too, or do I have to take out naturalization papers first?"

"I don't think they'll put anything in your way," Evadne said with a serious smile. "At least, we can ask them tonight. You could take some daytime duty, if you like."

"What about me?" Sylvia asked.

"You ought to learn first aid," said Evadne. "Everybody ought to know that now. It might make all the difference."

"All right," said Sylvia meekly, trying not to remember that she always got sick at the sight of blood.

"Hunt up your warden, they'll be glad to see you," Evadne promised.

"Yes," said Sylvia unhappily. "Maybe Dinah will go with me. She was a VAD the last time."

"It all comes back to them, Mummy says," Evadne told her, cutting the cake.

That night at the end of the performance Stephen lost no time about getting out of the theater and took a taxi straight to the school where Evadne was working. Half a dozen tired people, both men and women, were still there, smoking, sitting about on the edges of the furniture, looking rather green under the inadequate, unshaded light. Stephen's first impression was that they had finished work for the day but were apparently unable to pull themselves together enough to go home.

Evadne jumped up and came towards him, saying, "Have you heard? The Prime Minister is flying to Berchtesgaden in the morning. It was on the late news bulletin."

"Is that good?" he asked doubtfully, looking from one to the other.

"Oh, *yes*," said a tweedy woman with spectacles. "He must know *something* or he wouldn't go."

"Fat lot of good it did when Schuschnigg went," remarked a drooping young man on the corner of the table which ran down the center of the room. "They marched into Vienna a few days later."

"Well, they can't march in here," said the tweedy woman, who then proved from Evadne's conscientious introductions to be a Miss Piggott.

"I've put your name down for daytime duty," Evadne told Stephen with visible pride. "We can come in tomorrow and arrange. Let's all go home now, can't we, we're absolutely dead and everything will have to wait till he gets back."

"I'd be happier if he'd taken a regiment with him," said the dour young man, who was Miss Piggott's nephew, though his name was Tilton.

"They wouldn't *dare* let anything happen to him!" cried Miss Piggott, and began closing things and putting out lights. "Let's all get some sleep while we can, then, *if* we can."

In a weary, companionable silence they locked up and separated with brief good-nights to go their several ways. On the short walk back to the flat Evadne hung on Stephen's arm and he saw that in spite of Mr. Chamberlain's effort her spirits were sagging.

"I wonder what would happen," he suggested, "if we suddenly gathered up all the planes we have and loaded them to the gunwales with high explosive and simply bombed the heck out of Berlin without waiting."

"He's got a deep shelter under the Chancellory," she said slowly, "and he'd be in it, never fear. And we might kill Johnny and Camilla instead."

"Yes, they're in a bad spot," he agreed. "They can't be interned or interfered with as long as America is neutral, but American citizenship isn't going to be much good in an air raid."

"Is Sylvia worried about Jeff for the same reason?"

"I'm afraid so. She doesn't say much. They'll plaster

Prague with bombs, of course, as soon as anything starts. What can I do to be useful? I should have taken up flying years ago. I meant to."

"Why isn't it just as useful to dig English people out of bomb damage here as to go and help bomb Berlin?" she asked. "That sounds pacifist, but I don't mean it that way. Honestly, Stephen, if they start plastering London you can have a man-size job right here."

"No doubt," he agreed, and sighed. "Well, we'll see what turns up."

"I was thinking—it will be a few days wait now, till Chamberlain comes back—couldn't we have this Sunday at Farthingale?"

"Drive down after the show on Saturday? Let's," said Stephen, as they reached their own front door.

13

But Chamberlain returned on Friday, much too soon for comfort, and there was a cautious reticence in Government circles—no real reason given for so brief a conference—something about a plebiscite (unlucky word) and a readjustment. . . .

Jeff's first broadcast from Prague said that the city was fantastically calm, cold-bloodedly determined to go down fighting rather than submit to Hitler's threats. But there were no demonstrations. Refugees from the Sudeten area were arriving with their belongings in pitiful bundles, dependent on the Red Cross for food and lodging.

On Saturday Poland and Hungary, both with minority populations arbitrarily included within the Czech boundaries manufactured at Versailles, were demanding to have their own back too. Prague declared a state of emergency, which usually precedes by only a few days an outright state of war, and had eight hundred thousand men under arms.

There were all-day cabinet meetings in London and the French ministers had been summoned from Paris for Sunday. Silent crowds stood in Downing Street watching and waiting, it was hard to say for what. Gas-mask distribution had begun in France. . . .

Evadne, looking rather white, said she might be wanted at the depot by Sunday, and they gave up going to the country.

Sunday was dreary and tense. Mussolini made a speech at Trieste, and said that Italy's place in the coming conflict was chosen, but did not say where it would be. Russia and the United States were obstinately silent. . . .

The week dripped away, a day at a time—rioting in the Sudeten land—increasing resentment in Czechoslovakia towards her wavering allies—knowing optimism in Berlin— a growing sense of humiliation and uncertainty in England —the delayed, futile meeting at Godesberg, where Chamberlain's concessions were met by another ultimatum demanding full capitulation by October first. But Austria had capitulated and they took over Vienna anyway. . . .

Jeff's voice came in each night from Prague, steady, unemotional, but grave. General Syrovy was the Czech hero now— they would fight—they would turn out a government which surrendered and establish a military dictatorship—people who spoke English in the streets were unpopular—Americans had been advised to leave Prague, but were buying gasmasks and staying on. . . .

When Chamberlain returned from Godesberg on Saturday, with six days to go before October first and war, Evadne said, "Let's go to Farthingale tonight. We may not get another chance for a while."

Bracken, of course, could not leave London, could not even find time to sleep, and Dinah would not leave Bracken, but they urged the others to go. Stephen's Rolls made nothing of the midnight drive, but the three of them, with Evadne in the middle, her head drooping towards Stephen's shoul-

der, said very little on the way. Everybody went straight to
bed and met at breakfast looking as though they had not
slept. Even Mab was showing strain, and as they walked
home from the village church she kept close to Sylvia's side.

In Jeff's last phone call he had said, "Look after Mab, if
you get a chance. She'll be sent to Farthingale, no doubt, but
she'll worry. Don't let her worry, Sylvie. About me, I mean."
And how, Sylvia was wondering now, enclosing Mab's hand
in her own firm clasp, did he suppose she was going to do
that when she did nothing but worry about him herself? She
saw to it that they fell a little behind the others, and when
they came to the path that led off through the woods on the
far side of the stream, where Jeff and Mab had walked that
day before the wedding, they turned aside into it by mutual
consent. For a while they spoke of Jeff's book, which had
recently arrived from the American publishers, complete
with dedication as promised. Then Mab said, as though she
could contain the question no longer, "Will they have gas-
masks in Prague?"

"Yes, dear. They have to buy them there, but there are
plenty to be had."

"Has Jeff got one?"

"Oh, yes, I'm sure he has."

They walked on slowly for a moment, then Mab stood still,
transfixed by determination.

"Sylvia—I don't suppose Bracken would listen to me—but
won't *you* ask him to bring Jeff home?"

"I can't do that, darling."

"But—Jeff's not a *soldier!*"

"It's about the same thing, Mab, to be a good newspaper
man. Bracken went to war in Cuba when he was young—his
own father sent him there for the paper, just as he in his day
was nearly killed in the war before that one—as a correspondent with the Yankee army. The Murrays all go to war the
same way soldiers like Oliver do—it's their job. They'd be

angry and humiliated if their womenfolk tried to interfere. Dinah knows all about that. Now it's our turn."

"Are you frightened about him too?"

"Yes, I am."

"So you can't sleep?"

"So I can't sleep."

Mab made a little gesture of despair which wiped away her tears.

"London's going to be bad enough. But somehow if he was in London one could *bear* it."

"I know."

"How do you—how does one manage not to show it?" Mab asked humbly. "I don't want to make a fuss. But I don't know how to go on looking as though everything was all right, the way you do."

Sylvia put her arm around the small shoulders and they began to walk again, slowly, along the path.

"Well, in the first place, I'm supposed to be an actress," she said simply. "And our faces are supposed to be more or less under control. But everybody learns, as time goes on, to hide behind their faces. I think you do very well at it."

"German bombers can get to Prague in twenty-one minutes," said Mab, and her voice cracked. "I read it. And the American Ambassador there has ordered Americans to leave. And they've put out the lights in the streets—"

"I know," said Sylvia.

"I'm sorry, I—shouldn't scare you too," Mab said contritely. "I should think of something conforting to say. It's worse for you. You're married to him."

"You love him very much, don't you," Sylvia said, very low.

"More than anybody in the world." There was no self-consciousness or drama in the quiet statement. "But I know it's the same for you. I've got no right to make a fuss, only—" The words ended in a sort of gasp.

"We'll have to stick together," Sylvia murmured. "We'll have to help each other, Mab—no matter what happens."

"You *don't* think I'm a cry-baby—?"

"We're both cry-babies," said Sylvia, and Mab glanced up in astonishment to see Sylvia's face wet with tears. They stood still in the path, their arms around each other, and wept.

"I keep thinking how it was the last time," Virginia said into a long pause during luncheon. "In 1914, I mean. We were all here for the Bank Holiday—playing tennis—having tea on the lawn—I was waiting for Evadne then, but she hadn't begun to be the nuisance she was later on when I needed to be doing things—she was born that December. Of course in a way we all knew there was going to be a war with Germany *sometime,* but things were so peaceful anyhow, right up to the last minute—it's the radio, I suppose, that makes one so keyed up now—we all know so much more about what is happening—I'm not sure it's a good thing—I sometimes think if it weren't for radio we would never have had Hitler at all—"

A maid came in to say that there was a telephone call from London for Evadne, who rose swiftly, saying, "I knew it! I left this number with Miss Piggott in case I was wanted at the depot!" And what Miss Piggott had rung up to say was that distribution of gas-masks in London had begun and all the trained people were needed. Notices had been thrown on the screen at the Sunday evening cinemas, and were read out at sports gatherings and from pulpits—people were beginning to come in—queues were forming at the distribution centers. . . .

"Do you want to go back this afternoon?" Stephen asked. "Or will tomorrow do?"

"You needn't come, Stevie, you and Sylvia. There's a train I can get—"

"Don't be silly, if you want to start now I'll drive you. Sylvia and I will come along to the depot and help if we can."

"That would be awfully nice, somebody has to write down the names and sizes after the fittings—there has to be a record kept, and we'll be swamped, I expect, by tomorrow. What happens here, Mummy, have you got any—"

"I've got one mask of each size—I'm to fit them and write it down, and they will be sent out to us later. London has first call on the supply. I doubt if we'll ever need them here, but I suppose the village people will be trickling in—" She stood up with a sigh, and looked long at Evadne, who had not resumed her chair. "You've come a long way in twenty-five years, haven't you," she said with a queer little smile, and Evadne took her mother into her arms.

"Now, you're not to worry about me," she said firmly. "I shall be perfectly all right, and Miss Piggott says they've begun to dig trenches in the parks for people caught in the street during a raid, and our building has a wonderful basement."

As though you'll be in it, thought Virginia, and straightened, and wiped her nose on a wisp of handkerchief. "It used to be only the boys," she said apologetically. "Promise always to wear your tin hat, won't you."

"Darling, I promise to *sleep* in it, if you'll be happier!"

"That would be very uncomfortable," Virginia conceded. "Keep in touch with Oliver, and ask him to ring me up if it's allowed. One always feels they must *know* something at the War Office, even if they don't tell. Get the car, Stevie, I've stopped being a mother."

The drive back to London through a grey, misty Sunday afternoon countryside was even more silent than the drive down had been. An early dusk was drawing in as they reached the flat and paused briefly for a restorative cup of tea before going on to the depot.

Trenches and shelters were still being dug in London by the light of headlamps and flares. There was a queue outside the dingy school building where the gas-masks were being distributed, and the thin unshaded lights inside were cruel to the white strained faces they shone on. A double row of wooden chairs had been placed back to back down the middle of the long room, and as people rose from them they were filled again from the queue, like a ghastly sort of game. In front of the chairs, bending over the silent, patient people who sat there were the ARP workers, fitting masks. . . . "That's yours, madam—don't carry it by the straps, mind—thank you, good night—will you sit here, please?—get your chin well in—is that comfortable—take a deep breath. . . ." It had been going on for hours. It looked as though it would never end.

Mrs. Piggott's nephew, his spectacles gleaming on his kind, pasty face, his smile nailed on, greeted them with genuine pleasure, and asked Stephen if he would care to lend a hand. "It's quite simple," he said. "Just watch me. Anyone can get the hang of it in no time." Stephen watched, said he had the rough idea, and rather gingerly picked up his first mask. "It will move them faster," said Tilton gratefully. "The more help we have to fit them, the faster we can empty the chairs. Begin just anywhere. These people have been waiting quite a while."

They were two shabby elderly ladies who had come together, almost hand in hand, to face this ordeal. They looked up questioningly, like well-behaved children, as Stephen approached them, mask in hand.

"I'm afraid you'll have to take off your hat," he said politely, with his priceless easiness, his ingrained charm. "*And* your spectacles."

"I can't see much without them," she quavered, and obeyed him with hands that were not quite steady.

"If it comes to that, you probably won't want to see much,"

he suggested with his grin, and mercifully she thought it was funny.

"Will I have to take this down, or cut it off?" Her gnarled, shaking fingers went up to the small grey bun on the back of her head.

"I guess we can dodge that," he said casually, and she laid one hand on his to detain the mask, gazing up at him in surprise, crying, "You're an American!"

"Mm-hm. But I married one of you English girls, so here I am." He slipped the mask over her face, and heard himself repeating by rote the grim patter of the ARP. . . . "Get your chin well in—is that comfortable?—now, this is how we tell." He laid the square of paper against the nozzle. "Take a deep breath." The paper clung. "That's it. That one fits you." He slipped it off and she clutched at her bun, smoothed the hair at her temples. "Not too bad, was it? Don't carry it by the straps, ever—and keep it dry. Were you two together? Let's do this one next—" He reached for another mask.

"Are you going to *stay* here?" She had her hat on again now and her spectacles, and sat looking up at him, still puzzled and anxious.

"Of course I'm staying," he said to her, aside, busy with the straps over the thin grey hair of her friend. "We'll all be here before long, same as last time."

"Oh, I *do* hope so—you *will* come in—?"

"Sure, sure, we'll be in. We always start from behind, but we get there eventually. That's yours, then—you both take the same size—leave your names at the door on your way out, over there where they're writing it down—no, nothing to pay —compliments of the Government—good night—" He reached for another mask.

"You're doing splendidly," said Tilton's voice beside him. "That's two more. So glad you came!"

The empty chairs in front of Stephen were taken by two young women, one with a frightened child of about seven, and one with a baby in her arms. Stephen said to the first mother, "We'll do yours first, then the little girl will see that it doesn't hurt." She nodded, and as she was hatless with a lank bob the fitting was quickly done. The child drew back from the thing in his hands and her face puckered.

"Now, then, Dorrie, be a brave girl," said her mother sharply. "Mustn't keep the gentleman waiting."

"Come on, Dorrie, let's see if it fits," said Stephen, going on one knee. "I've got three guesses, and I guessed this one for you. I bet you tuppence I got it right the first time. Stick out your chin—" He pretended to fumble the mask without really getting it on. "Wrong," he said. "I have to try another one, and I owe you tuppence." He exchanged the mask, felt in his pocket, and put two pennies in the small moist palm. "Let's try again now. That's better, isn't it." It was on. "Now take a deep breath. Once more—breathe in. That's the girl, it works. This one is yours, take good care of it, won't you."

The second young mother wore spectacles and there was the usual argument. When her mask had been pronounced a success she sat still, looking helpless and ready to cry. "What about '*im?*" she asked, pointing to the baby in her lap.

Stephen looked round him hastily for advice and saw Evadne coming towards him along the row of chairs.

"Sylvia's taking down the names as they go," she told him, smiling. "The girl she relieved hasn't moved for hours."

"What do you do about babies?" he asked in a low tone, and she glanced beyond him.

"It's too small. There isn't anything."

"*What?* How can I tell her that?"

"I'll do it." Evadne bent over the stolid, waiting woman, laid a light hand on the somnolent baby, and said, "He's got good nerves to sleep through all this. I'm afraid children under four can't be fitted with these masks. The best thing to do is to wrap the baby in a blanket with its face covered and take it to the nearest shelter."

The woman stood up with the heavy child.

"It don't seem right," she said stupidly.

"I know. They're working on one that you put the baby right into, with bellows that you pump. They'll be ready, I expect, before we really need them. Leave your names as you go out, won't you—at that table over by the door."

The chairs were full again. Stephen and Evadne worked side by side, their voices blending on the limited lines of the dismal patter. The hard, pale light beat down on the trusting faces of old people, the wry smiles or hollow wisecracks of the young, on the tears or the tense docility of children, on sleeping, defenceless babies. The hours went by without relief or refreshment, and Stephen knew that the girl beside him never faltered in courtesy and patience and confidence —the same girl who had said in the Soho restaurant a year ago that she was scared, the family coward, self-styled, the Problem Child. Hermione had gone to the Lake Country with her delicate friends. Evadne was here in London where the bombs would fall, doing something about it, and he was proud to be there too, doing the same thing as the night wore on in endless repetition without monotony. . . . Get your chin well in—is that comfortable?—please breathe deeply —thank you—once more—I think the next size smaller for you —breathe deeply, please—that's it—never carry it by the straps—keep it dry—be careful of the eyepiece—you register just there, on the way out, where the next queue—no, nothing to pay—Get your chin well in—sorry, let's try again —no hurry, sir—spread the straps—is that comfortable? . . .

14

Sylvia slept in the guest-room at the flat and returned with them to the depot Monday morning, and they kept at it all day. Stephen sent out at noon for sandwiches and soda for all the ARP workers, but there was no real break—just a hasty gulp and munch and back to the row of chairs, which were always full. About five o'clock someone handed round mugs of hot sweet tea. Nobody seemed to know where it came from. Soon after that he and Sylvia made Evadne stop for a quick hot meal at a restaurant nearby, and then they went on to the theater while she returned to the depot.

London had changed, they discovered during the taxi ride to the Strand. The unsensational black and white ARP notices had gone up in the windows of public buildings and were pasted on walls and gate-posts—where to get your gas-masks, information about shelters, blackout, gas-proof rooms, etc. There were trenches in the green lawns under the windows of the Ritz. Sand-bags were being laid round churches and museums and banks. Traffic was complicated by trucks loaded with anti-aircraft guns and searchlights and Air Territorials. The evening papers Stephen had bought gave plans for the evacuation of schoolchildren, and what they were required to bring with them. Hitler was to make another speech that night at the Sportspalast in Berlin, replying to the Czech refusal of the Godesberg terms, expounding his October first ultimatum.

"There'll be nobody in the theater," said Sylvia. "They'll all stay home to listen."

"They already know," said Stephen grimly.

"It's like waiting for a first night," she murmured, and he glanced at her sympathetically.

"We'll be closed if war is declared," he said. "You'd better get out of this. Mother will be having a fit."

"*Just what do you think I am?*" she demanded indignantly. "Jeff in Prague—you and Evadne here—I suppose you think the *Lake Country* is good enough for me!"

"Don't get sore, I only thought if you went down to Farthingale—"

"I will not! I may not be up to Evadne's kind of job, but I could drive a car, or do canteen work, or *something* useful without leaving London!"

"Sure, there's lots you can do here, I just—"

"I'll ask Dinah tonight. She'll find me a job."

"O.K.," he said meekly, for once roused from her habitual good-tempered serenity Sylvia was a handful.

But Sylvia in her dressing-room, putting on her make-up with cold hands that trembled, met her own eyes in the mirror with astonishment and chagrin. What's the *matter* with me, she thought furiously. Am *I* going to be the one who can't take it? I'd be all right if Jeff were here. We'd be all right together, anywhere. But people can't be together in a war. It's the same as if he was a soldier. It's only sheer luck that Stephen can be a warden too and work with Evadne. Dinah and I are on our own. Dinah will tell me what to do, she's got used to it by now. Is it really the end of the world, or shall we be able to look back at today and feel ashamed of being so scared? Can this be the end of Jeff and me, so soon? Why am I *sick* with fright, like this? It won't begin till Saturday. . . .

Oddly enough, people did come to the theater that night and seemed to enjoy themselves. At the end of the performance Stephen took Sylvia back to Dinah in Upper Brook Street and went in to hear about the speech. Dinah was alone and had heard the late news. Hitler's patience was at an end again, she said wearily. He had boasted about Austria and attacked Benes. He said he wanted nothing from England. He said Czechoslovakia was the last territorial claim he would make in Europe. None of it was new. So Parliament was meeting tomorrow, and the American Ambassador had advised Americans to leave England. And Bracken thought there would be war on Saturday.

But on Saturday came the Great Reprieve. Chamberlain was back from Munich, where they had traded a ready army of a million men, fortifications second only to the Maginot Line, and valuable munitions works, for a little time.

In the midst of the general relief, which amounted to rejoicing, Bracken was haggard and unsmiling, as though there had been a death—as indeed there had been. Sylvia watched him surreptitiously, feeling guilty because of the irresponsible way her own heart had lightened. Czechoslovakia had paid the bill, but Prague was not being destroyed, stone by stone, and Jeff was not dodging German bombs at that very minute. It was wicked to acknowledge, however secretly, that that was what mattered most, but no one could expect her to be sorry. Of course they said it wouldn't last. But maybe, by the time it got bad again, Jeff would be back in London. She ventured to mention it on Sunday, when Bracken was at home as he had so seldom been during the past weeks to enjoy a cup of tea in Dinah's company again.

"Will Jeff be coming back now?" Sylvia asked hopefully, and Bracken set down his cup and looked at her, and then at Dinah, and then, a derisive eyebrow quirked, at Sylvia again.

"*Women*," said Bracken, as though he just couldn't believe there were such things.

"Well, I only thought—"

"I know perfectly well what you thought," said Bracken, with a mute request for more tea. "Well, that's Czechoslovakia, you thought, and now can I have Jeff back?"

Sylvia returned his sardonic gaze with large, troubled, steady eyes.

"I know," she said contritely. "I suppose I have no social conscience."

For what seemed like the first time in days, Bracken laughed.

"I didn't know you'd heard of such a thing," he said. "As a matter of fact, I think Jeff's had enough for anybody. He'll be here by the end of the week."

That was the week-end when Virginia urged them all to

come down to Farthingale and collapse—an invitation which was gratefully accepted by everybody. The obvious flaws in the Munich settlement were now becoming quite plain to everyone, and disillusionment had set in. It was not peace with honor, and it would not be peace, they were saying, for even Mr. Chamberlain's time, and he was past seventy. They had a little more time to get ready. That was all.

London was suddenly booming, and the show had many more weeks to run. ARP training would intensify rather than slack off. As was usual in a crisis, the family drew together and took stock. Bracken said he gave it till March, anyway.

"Oh, Bracken, how can you *know* when it will start?" sighed Virginia.

"Well, maybe till harvest time," said Bracken, filling his pipe. "They won't wait longer, I should think. Dictators can't afford to wait. Poland will go next, I expect. Danzig. What fools the Poles are to play his game now!"

Mab, whom they had all forgotten, spoke quietly from her place beside Sylvia. She had developed a diffidence about sitting close to Jeff all the time, but it seemed as though she found some comfort in proximity to Sylvia, who was also Jeff's property.

"Are we going to have a war *anyway?*" she asked with a kind of resignation, and Sylvia put an arm round her swiftly, saying, "It's beastly, isn't it, they've only sort of put it off, I'm afraid. But if things get too bad you can always go home to Williamsburg."

"Oh, I couldn't leave Granny now," said Mab, apparently putting Virginia before her own parents. "We'll be all right here, I should think. It's Jeff I was worrying about, Bracken —next time couldn't you keep him here at the BBC with you?"

"I expect I could. If you feel that would be the safest place."

"Well, it's in England, isn't it," said Mab logically. "One can't be sure what might happen to him anywhere else. In England you sort of know where you are."

"That's very true," said Bracken gravely. "And I imagine that when the time comes we can keep him amused here, one way and another." His pipe was well alight now, and he settled back with it, running his eye over them all in a paternal sort of way, and they all looked back at him attentively, waiting for what might come. "Well, here we go again. Mind if I make a few suggestions?" he asked politely, and they assured him that they didn't, and his gaze came to rest first on Stephen. "Going to run through Christmas?" he asked, and Stephen said it looked like it now. "That would still leave time for Evadne to see Williamsburg," said Bracken.

"And for Williamsburg to see her," said Stephen. "I'd thought of that."

"Don't hurry the new show, then," said Bracken. "You've got a foot you're supposed to favor. Why don't you take a year off, the way Jeff and Sylvia did—do you good."

"Pop would get a kick out of that," said Stephen. "We could write the whole new show together, from the beginning. Take our time to it."

"God knows what's coming," said Bracken. "Have a holiday while you can. Look." He pointed at Evadne's radiant face. "About time you two had a honeymoon."

"It's a plot," said Stephen, looking at her. "Are you in on this?"

"I am now," she said.

Sylvia came and sat on the arm of Stephen's chair, leaning on his shoulder.

"Stevie, I'll never desert you, you know that. But let's rest the foot, h'm? You go to Williamsburg with Evadne, and I'll stay here with Jeff, and—don't let's start the new show for a while, h'm?"

"I guess I'm outnumbered," said Stephen.

"Well," Jeff said when he and Sylvia were alone in their oom that night, "it's nice to know that if they really want this war I'm going to be able to take it." He came and knelt down and put his arms around her where she sat brushing her hair at the dressing-table. "Thanks to you," he whispered.

"Me?"

"It's only because of you I can trust my heart. It stayed right on the job, Sylvie, through everything, and I've heard gunfire now, up where the rioting was. Till now, I was afraid we might be sorry we took a chance and went ahead and got married. But it's going to be all right. I can take anything that comes. Have you any idea what that means to me?"

Sylvia held him quietly, his head nestled against her, feeling as though he had only just now come home. Since his return from Prague two days ago he had been remote and troubled and preoccupied—withdrawn from their usual intimacy, seeming to need nothing from her beyond her presence, which he appeared to welcome, and silence, which he seldom broke. She knew that he was very tired, and that his emotions had been lacerated by the things he had seen and heard during his trips into the border territory and in Prague after the Munich verdict, when people wept hysterically in the streets, and foreigners were besieged by pitiful strangers who begged them for help with visas and escape plans. Remembering Dinah's advice, she had tried to efface herself and make no demands on his attention until he had adjusted himself to whatever was pressing down on him. She had resisted unwise impulses to shake him out of it for his own good or to try to cheer him up. She knew by some sure instinct that when you had come right up against it, as Jeff had, you had no use for people who advised you to brace up, or who pointed out bright spots. She knew that there is nothing so infuriating, when you are bearing all you can, as shallow, unrealistic optimism from someone who has not experienced the same disaster. There was nothing anyone who had stayed in London could say to a man who had witnessed the agony in Prague. It was worse than Vienna, for Vienna had never had a hope, and Prague—for a while—had hoped for a fighting chance.

Jeff stirred in her arms, settled against her with a sigh, and said, "Hullo."

"Hullo, darling, have you come back?"

"Yep, I'm back. Thanks for waiting till I got here. You know, if I'd tried to talk about it any sooner I'd have cried like a baby."

"You don't have to talk about it now."

"Not about—what happened over there. But about us. That I want to get said. Honey—when the bombs start here I want you to go home."

"I know I promised to obey," said Sylvia. "But that is where I draw the line."

"Am I going to have trouble with you?" he asked, not moving.

"About that you are."

"Who's the boss around here?"

"You are. Till you start treating me like women and children."

He sat back on his heels, his arms still round her, his hair a little rumpled, and looked up into her face.

"It's no good gambling that it won't happen, you know. It will. Next year—the year after that—as long as Germany is Nazi it's not going to let up. I know now what it feels like to live in a city which expects to be bombed any minute—to have people you love living there beside you. And I want you out of it."

"Millions of Englishwomen—" she began.

"You weren't born here."

She reached out and smoothed his hair, and he rose away from her hand and walked thoughtfully round the room.

"This is the first time we haven't seen eye to eye about things, isn't it," he said, and she made no answer at all, simply waited quietly where she sat, for him to come back to her. "So you're going to get tough about it," he said, eyeing her from the middle of the room. She smiled at him. "I see," said Jeff, and thought of Bracken's ultimate authority and then thought No, I must settle this thing myself, this is between Sylvia and me. "It's not that I don't think you're brave —" he began.

"I'm not brave, a bit. I found that out last week. I shall be terrified," she remarked, and went back to brushing her hair.

"So was I," said Jeff. "So is everybody. I guess that's not got much to do with it, after all." He stood a moment, watching the rhythmic, unconcerned sweep of the hairbrush through her honey-colored mane. "I'd like to get this settled now, so there won't be any argument at the last minute," he suggested.

"It is settled," said Sylvia. "I'm staying here." She laid down the brush and rose and stood looking at him. "I thought you said you had come back," she said. "So what are you doing way over there?"

They met halfway.

For your reading pleasure ...